STRANDED

STRANDED

BOOK TWO
OF THE SHIFTED SERIES

KRISTALYN A. VETOVICH

atmosphere press

For all the Forgotten Storytellers who remembered...

CHAPTER ONE

I fell out of a truck. It feels like I fell out of a truck, which bothers me beyond the obvious issue of pain and stiffness. Because the dead don't fall out of trucks. We can't feel pain. We don't even have corporeal bodies.

I left the burden of skin and bone behind centuries ago, and I never looked back. As a Firn, my job is to guide living souls along their life Plan through gentle nudges and by mystical example. I don't need a body, don't want a body—shouldn't have a body.

But it seems I have one now, and it's a wreck.

Thanks to Jordin, I slammed into the physical world with a crash and everything hurts. My toes ache with a steady searing pain like I stubbed every one of them on a very sharp corner. Both my legs are weightless with the fatigue of running for hours at full speed without rest. My gut and chest feel like an elephant is sitting on them. My arms are limp as linguine, my back would make a chiropractor cry, and a constant throbbing behind my eyes drags me further out of the fog of sleep.

Yet, somewhere amid the pain there's an emptiness, a gap where something has been torn away from me. Something important that I'm afraid to be without.

Maybe it's just the emptiness of being alive, being stuck in the living world again. Jordin knew this was my worst nightmare. That demon Aropfain knows everything about me: my goals, my fears, my most recent life before deciding to stay dead and serve the Plan. Everything he needed to perform a sacrilegious ritual that forced me to Shift away from all my loyalties to El Olam and land me here, and it's all my fault. I shared all of it with him back when we were partners, both Firn hopefuls eager to play our part in the El Olam's Plan to end the world as it is. I thought I could trust him because our souls are a pair. Soulmates in the deepest, truest sense. Two complementary expressions acting in the spaces between life and death, a place the living only glimpse when they're having a very lucky dream.

I'm awake now, and I should open my eyes, but I'd rather not. First, I let it all come back to me: the attack on the Lost Boys and on Phil's gas station. The argument with Jordin in the truck. Kade—my ward, my Neshome—listened to Jordin. He listened to Jordin and ignored me again. And Jordin. Jordin pulled my soul straight out of Lemayle and into Velt, then almost killed me again for good measure.

But it's the fact that I survived that's depressing. I'm alive again. I wasn't born; I don't have a purpose, yet here I am anyway.

I've Shifted.

I'm not a Firn anymore. I'm not sure what that means for me yet, but I'm sure it will put a strain on my relationship with El Olam. My chest aches as the separation from the higher power that I've served for centuries sinks into my newly malformed bones, and a small whimper claws at my throat. All the work I did to become a Firn, to earn the honor of guiding a soul so pivotal to El Olam's Plan has been stolen away and wasted. I'm a traitor, no matter how unwilling. There's no such thing as un-Shifting. It's designed as an act of free will, a last stand. Shifters want what they get, and they deserve the misery that comes with it.

But I didn't ask for this.

My eyes sting, and I squint against it.

"I know you're awake."

The voice is familiar, but I don't care who it is. It's not Mikael, it's not Jordin. It's a living soul who shouldn't be able to see me, which sears my failure even deeper into my nearly see-through skin, as if this body knows as well as I do that we're not truly alive in this state.

The voice doesn't belong to Kade, which means I've abandoned my Neshome—because I certainly don't know where Kade is. I've spent his entire life at his side. What is he going to do now? He has no Firn, no one to guide him and protect him from unseen Aropfain threats, like Jordin. There's only one soul designed to live that way, and Kade is not that chosen one. He was supposed to save her.

"Open your eyes."

I'm hyperaware of my breath as cool air rushes through my nose and down my throat in quick, irregular bursts. A horrible sensation rises in my chest, and I want to gulp the air just in case there isn't enough of it left in the world for an unexpected, unwelcome extra set of lungs. Something warm and wet runs down my cheeks, dried quickly by the chill of the room. I try to focus on my body, but my mind has only one function, one stream of thought.

Where's Kade? Where's Mikael? Where's Jordin? What will Danica Bree do without Kade to save her? Is the Plan still working? Is it my fault if it isn't? How do I get back to Lemayle before Kade sees me?

A hand grips my arm and my whole body jerks. "Open your eyes. You're panicking."

I'm panicking? I don't panic.

I open my eyes to glare at whoever accuses me of something

so stupid and there he is: the one who saw me all along.

"How—" I choke on the thick vibration of sound. Wow, talking with vocal cords is hard. Coughs rack my chest as foreign arms slide under my shoulders to prop me up against a wall behind me. That helps. I cough until I get a grip and take a deep breath to try again. "Enoch, how... did you know it was me?" I wither against the wall and catch my breath. Talking isn't supposed to take that much effort.

There was a time, several lives ago, when I got very sick. I spent several weeks in my bed, weak and exhausted. And then I died.

This reminds me of that, which might not be a bad thing. If I die, I'll be back in Lemayle, back to work. I open my eyes, unaware that I'd shut them again during my coughing fit, and stare at Enoch. His blue eyes search deep into mine, seeing a real person in front of him now instead of sensing my ethereal presence, but he's unfazed.

"You have the same energy as before," Enoch explains. A mischievous smile spreads across his face. "And you just told me. But you do look different. I wasn't sure it was you until one of your people came and confirmed it for me."

One of my people. Someone from Lemayle. Enoch is lucky. As an Avoyde, he can see spirits and feel what they want him to feel. Only the good spirits, though, like Firns and our superiors, the Malekh. Not the Aropfain, so I'm safe from Jordin as long as I'm within Enoch's evil-free zone.

Aropfain can't come near an Avoyde unless the Avoyde wills it–and why on earth would they? The presence of an Aropfain must make their skin crawl like hearing nails dragging along glass. Aropfain are too dense an energy to be tolerated. Emotions are our language of choice because their energy is strong enough to pass through the veil between Lemayle and Velt: where the living souls are. Where I am now. I wonder who in Lemayle has been keeping Enoch updated. I wonder how long I've been sleeping.

"What did they tell you?" I cringe at how dejected my voice sounds. My eyes sting again. I blink against the bothersome itch, and everything goes blurry. I try to lift my hand to rub my eyes, but nothing moves. That can't be good.

"Not much..." Enoch eyes my twitching arm. "Just that you are who I thought you were and that someone would come when you wake up."

My stomach sinks. I should be excited to hear from someone, but I dread it. Even if they bring the best news possible, I'll still be in trouble for Shifting during such a pivotal time in the Plan. The best I can do is get back to Lemayle. I can talk my way out of just about anything. Hopefully, this won't be different. I'll explain how the blame can all be traced back to Jordin. I'll beg for amnesty, and I'll return quietly to Kade's side.

Enoch pokes my arm. "Do you feel that?"

I feel irritated by that, but... "Yes. I can feel that."

He nods, processing. "Good. Not paralyzed. I'll let Asa do the rest."

"Wait—who?" My heart races again. I don't want to meet anyone else. I shouldn't be in Velt for long and it's best that no one speaks to me while I'm here. Enoch is fine because he's an Avoyde. We already know each other. He's been helping me with Kade since we ran into this rag-tag rebel team Enoch runs with.

Enoch senses my objections and sighs his disapproval. "Anaya, you need medical attention, and Asa is the best we have."

Asa is a twelve-year-old boy who was the son of a doctor before he lost his family and joined a band that Kade appropriately dubbed the Lost Boys. Somehow, I think Asa will be a little out of his depth with this one.

"Just let me die. I've done it before. It's not scary. I need to get back to work."

Enoch pauses for a long moment, tilting his head like he's gauging how I'll react to what he says next. "We don't know what your..." He looks me over. "Situation is. You need to stay alive until someone comes to give us more answers."

"I can't see anyone, Enoch. No one is supposed to know about me."

Enoch shakes his head, pressing his hands against his legs. "Asa's been here before. He wrote your condition off as fatal, but now that you're awake, we have to keep you stable." He pauses. "You're not invisible anymore, Anaya. Everyone has seen you."

That's a punch in the gut. I glance down at myself to see what everyone else has seen, realizing I'm the only one that doesn't know what I look like.

In Lemayle, you see others in a way that reflects your relationship with them. To me, Jordin used to have light hair, but when he Shifted it went dark with silver highlights, probably because I like to imagine the real Jordin is still in there somewhere. I guess you can still lie to yourself even when you're dead. Some things never change.

There's no changing my appearance in Velt, though, and that's a shame. I can only see myself from the shoulders down, but I would not want to run into me in a dark alley. Everyone must be horrified. And—wonderful—I'm a girl, the resident damsel in distress. Did Kade see this?

"Did Kade see this?"

Enoch looks confused for a second before pointing at me with the question in his eyes.

"Yes—me. Did Kade see me?"

Enoch sits back on his heels. "Well, yes. He's the one who saved you."

"Saved me?" How mortifying. That's not how this is supposed to work!

Enoch shrugs. "You were in his truck when you..." He

waves a hand over me and coughs the word, "arrived."

My head thumps against the wall, sending throbbing pain straight to the back of my eyes. Knowing that Kade's seen me like this is more than anything else I've learned.

Stupid Kade. This is all his fault. Thinking about it, I realize how true that is. None of this would have happened if he'd just listened to me. We had an agreement, dang it! He was such a wise soul when we spoke before he was born into Velt. He understood the importance of his role, was honored to play such a vital part in the Plan. We didn't consider Jordin's meddling as a factor, but that was a given! Kade promised he wouldn't let me down. He's lived so many times—this was supposed to be his last before he would stay in Lemayle.

What in the world happened?

"He's very worried about you. He asks about your condition every day," Enoch says, like that makes everything better.

"I don't want to see him."

Enoch blinks at me. "But, Anaya, he—"

"I don't care, Enoch. I have nothing to say to him. If he comes in here, I'll tell him off. I swear to you I will." I don't leave room for Enoch to argue. Whatever he has to say won't change how furious I am, just picturing Kade Buxton's face.

Enoch surrenders. "I'll do my best to keep him away, but I'm not sure what to tell him."

"Tell him I don't want to see anyone at all. Make him think it isn't personal." Oh, it's personal.

"Fine," Enoch concedes with the swipe of a hand. "But you're seeing Asa. I won't let you die without permission from a Malekh or someone else from your—" He catches himself and it stings. "From Lemayle."

As an Avoyde, I'd expect Enoch to understand death enough not to fear it anymore, but the fear of respect for the Malekhs is understandable. Mikael is kind, but all the Malekhs have intimidating presence and power.

"Do it then." I challenge him, staring unblinking, because it's the only gesture I can do. Maybe he'll back down and leave me alone.

Enoch sets his face in determination. He pushes himself to stand and regards me, helpless on the floor. "All right. I'll be right back."

The kid's got gusto. I like it.

He leaves the room and shuts the door behind him, and the walls close in on me with a lonely, judging silence. The floor is hard, cold concrete. The oversized, dusty cotton shirt they gave me cannot keep the chill away. Without my rage to keep me warm, I shiver. I can't do that when Asa gets here. He'll diagnose me up and down with every issue he can think of, and I'll never have the room to myself again.

Of course, I'm not enjoying it so much right now. I still have anger to vent, but there's no one to yell at. Maybe I should let Kade see me. I could yell at him until the Reyn Gayst makes her choice between El Olam and Narn. And if she sides with the enemy because Kade wasn't there to help her, I'll yell at him for the rest of eternity.

That almost sounds appealing.

The door clicks and swings open an inch.

"Anaya, we're coming in," Enoch calls. Does he think I'm changing my clothes or something?

"Yeah, I figured. You don't need to announce it."

The door opens and there stands Asa Gastrell, one of the rebel boys that Ainsley and Phil look after. He looks terrified. He's small and timid, nervously wringing his hands close to his chest, and his eyes can't get any wider as he fixes them on me. I might be the first girl he's seen since he fled from his development city. My nose scrunches because I don't want to deal with this, but a motion from Enoch catches my attention.

"Be nice," he mouths from behind Asa.

I roll my eyes, but fine. I want this over anyhow.

Asa takes small steps toward me like I'm a caged animal, snarling and growling at him. I might glower, but I don't have the strength to posture, let alone attack.

When he reaches my side, he gives his most professional nod before settling on the floor. Then his eyes trace over me and his fear vanishes. His mind is at work.

"At first glance, there is certainly some muscle dystrophy," he dictates his observations to Enoch, who nods in interest, chin resting in his hand as he frowns at me. "It's a miracle she's lived this long with such a disease."

Should I tell him I haven't been alive all that long at all?

"I'd also say she's malnourished, dehydrated..." He peers down his nose as if a pair of glasses rests on it, something I guess he saw his father do when he was still with his family. "No other obvious issues." His eyes flick back up to mine. "Are you able to move? Wiggle your fingers and toes?"

I'm about to tell him yes, but Enoch beats me to it.

"She's weak, Asa. Don't let her tell you otherwise."

Asa glances over his shoulder at Enoch. Enoch nods and Asa turns back, tipping his head toward my arms. "Show me."

How embarrassing. My brain screams at my fingers to move. My chest tightens and sweat gathers on my forehead, but all I have to show for my hard work is a single twitch of my fingers.

Asa appears satisfied. "Not paralyzed."

Enoch rubs his chin. "So, what can we do for her?"

Asa raises his eyebrows. "Not much," he confesses. "This type of dystrophy is a disease. It's not something that comes and goes, it's something that was and will always be, and—I hope I'm not the first to tell you, miss—but it's fatal."

Good! Best news I've heard all day!

Enoch shoots me a disapproving glare when he sees the triumph on my face. He rubs his forehead for a moment. He's got a lot of pressure on him, I realize. With me out of commission, the Plan must be scrambling to correct itself and he's probably inundated with visits and assignments to make up for my absence.

He, a living soul, now knows more about the Plan than I do.

That annoying sting rises in the corner of my eyes again and my nose itches like I might sneeze.

"Are you in pain?" Asa looks concerned, clapping a steady hand on my shoulder.

I want to throw his hand off me. I don't want pity or concern. I want action. I want my world back.

"Asa," Enoch interrupts before I get hysterical and tell Asa what I really think of his medical assessment, "assuming she might make a miraculous recovery, for the sake of our group, if we have to move quickly, is there anything we can do to help her build strength?"

Asa studies me again. His face says it's a lost cause, but he humors Enoch. "Physical therapy, I suppose. Low-impact exercises to restore some mobility and strength. And nutrition. She needs as much fuel as possible to keep her going, if she moves at all."

"Oh, she's going to move," I say.

"Anaya, please." Enoch waves me off. He scratches his head and begins pacing. "Do we know if there are any wheelchairs left from when this place was open to visitors?"

Wheelchairs? Visitors? Where are we, anyway?

Asa smiles. "You know, I think there may be. I'll look into it."

Enoch closes Asa's hand in a firm grip. "Thank you, Asa. If you could suggest a few exercises and round up some rations, I would deeply appreciate it."

Asa beams and nods. He seems proud to have Enoch commend him. "I'll see what I can do."

He exits the room on light feet, leaving Enoch alone with me.

Enoch catches my expression and sulks, knowing he's about to hear what I've been dying to say.

"I don't know what you think is going to happen, but I am not leaving this room unless it's with my own two legs."

"You will rest until we get you strong enough to walk, and until then, you will use a wheelchair if you need to, and that's final."

Whoa. It's been a long time since someone has had the gall to speak to me that way. Okay.

My silence has given Enoch a chance to realize he lost his temper, and he drops his head. "I'm sorry. It's just—have you even considered what your being here means? What if you have to go to the bathroom or something?"

"Oh, gross. No. I'm not doing that."

The tension disperses with Enoch's laugh. "Anaya, it's not exactly voluntary."

Kill me now. I forgot how high maintenance a body can be. Someone had better visit Enoch with answers soon. I don't understand what's taking them so long.

My heart rate speeds up again, and every time it happens, it makes breathing even harder. I concentrate on slowing my breath so I can focus. The heart, the soreness, the weakness all make sense with the condition I'm in, but one thing I still can't justify is the emptiness I have in my chest. My chest isn't empty. There are organs and all kinds of things in there now, but it still feels so hollow. What have I lost?

Then I understand. "Where is Kade anyway?" I'm used to being around my Neshome, ever-present in his life. His purpose was my purpose and now I can't even feel him. I'm not at his side and it isn't right.

Enoch watches my reaction as he responds, like he's testing something. "He's been focusing on training with

Ramiro. He's trying to earn Ramiro's trust back, and he wants to get stronger with his weapon." Enoch looks to the side for a moment, then turns sheepish. "Can't you feel him anymore?"

I sigh. "Enoch, all I feel is sore. Everything aches. I can barely think straight." I don't want to consider that I might have lost my link to Kade, too.

"Hm." There's so much going on in his head that he isn't saying. What does he know that he can't tell me? Why can't I know?

I'm so tired of being kept in the dark. Mikael doesn't tell me things unless I need to know them. Jordin keeps me on edge with whatever he's tampering in, and now Enoch? I work so hard—follow orders without question—and for what?

I gasp, and Enoch jumps. He asks me if I'm okay, if the pain is worse, if I can feel my legs, but I ignore him, staring into an abyss as I realize what I just thought.

That was Aropfain thinking. I can't allow that. I can't slip down that slope. That's exactly what Jordin wants—that's why he Shifted me. So I would join him in Narn's Aropfain cult, but I'm not about to let him win. I'm going to get things back to Plan, if I have to go persuade the Reyn Gayst myself. I'm not a Firn anymore, so what's the harm in replacing Kade as the person who helps Danica Bree make the right choice?

"Anaya, answer me. Are you all right?"

"I'm fine."

I'm not as fine as I'd like to be, but I'll make it work.

Enoch doesn't seem convinced either. He looks disappointed. "Maybe you should get some sleep. I'll wake you when Asa brings something for you to eat and we'll see what we can do to get you moving again."

As soon as he says sleep, my eyes accept the invitation, and it's almost impossible to keep them open. Did Enoch do that or did his suggestion give me permission to acknowledge how tired I am?

You know what? I don't care.

CHAPTER TWO

The next time I open my eyes, Enoch is there, sitting in the corner, reading. My head turns without twinging in pain now, so that's progress, and I can see how sparse this room is. The walls and floor are cement, with only a few chips of green paint on the walls. This place is old. It's dusty. The only piece of furniture is the metal folding chair Enoch is sitting on. If I didn't know any better, I'd say the Lost Boys just tossed me into a random room and left me to die. Something tells me only Kade and Enoch have any genuine interest in my survival. The rest only fixate on disrupting the Beta Siberian Organization in whatever schemes they can think of. Little do they know the Organization feels their wrath the way an elephant feels a fly on its back.

If it hadn't been for Enoch, they would have abandoned me. If it weren't for Enoch, Jordin would have won back at the gas station in Albazin.

Next to Enoch's feet is a glass of water and a bowl of what looks like dried cereal topped with beef jerky. *Tres gourmet.* My stomach shutters with an embarrassing noise loud enough to draw Enoch away from his reading.

He smiles and covers his laughter with the book when he

notices my challenging glare. "Hungry?" he asks.

"Sounds like it," I grumble as my stomach growls again.

Enoch grabs the bowl and moves to my side. As he crosses the room, my mind works to figure out how I will eat on my own. Pride won't let me eat out of someone else's hand. I'd sooner turn to dust.

My eyes must tell the story because when Enoch kneels next to me, he looks embarrassed too. In a panicked effort, I focus on my fingers. If I can move my fingers, I can hold a piece of jerky. I'll let Enoch move my arm, if I have to, but I swear I'm holding the jerky.

Enoch's cheeks flush and his eyebrows pinch together. "Maybe I should get Kade to do this?" he offers what he probably thinks is an escape plan. "You two should bond, anyway. You have a lot to talk about."

I don't waste my ragged breath on a response. My face says enough. If I'm trapped in this awkward situation, then so is he.

"It was just a thought." He picks up a piece of beef jerky and takes a preparatory breath.

"Wait. Down here." I loll my head to indicate my motionless hand. Enoch glances down just as I manage it: My fingers twitch, almost curling into a fist. Close enough!

Enoch looks at me with sarcasm on his face. "That's great—but what about your arm?"

"You really know how to kick me when I'm down, don't you?"

He pleads with the ceiling for a moment, then faces me again and gives in. He tucks the strip of jerky between my fingers, and I press them together as tight as I can. It takes all my focus to keep them together as he bends my elbow for me. I eye the piece of jerky and line my face up accordingly to catch it in my teeth as soon as it's in range. I make sure I've got a good enough hold on it and then nod to Enoch that he can let my arm fall.

"Shouldn't you hold it until—?"

"No, I've got this," I assure him, talking around the jerky, and begin the tedious task of nibbling like a rabbit, nearly dropping it several times before finally finishing. When I do, I release the breath I didn't realize I was holding and relax.

That's when Enoch holds up the second of three more pieces. Staring at the jerky, already exhausted, I accept I can't do this. "Fine. Give it here." I catch the strip between my teeth, and we make quick, mechanical work of what's left in the bowl. We agree to skip the cereal and Enoch helps me gulp the water until it's gone, patting my back when I choke and cough on the last sips.

"Feel better?" He asks when I've caught my breath.

My head hangs near my shoulder, the only place I can balance it while I'm this weak. "Actually, yes." I feel a touch more normal, but it's not the relief it should be. I'm adjusting to Velt, to living.

I close my eyes against the panic rising in my throat and sulk against the cold concrete wall. The soothing chill only adds to my shame, but at least the anxiety subsides.

"Any visitors while I was out?" I try to keep the desperate hope out of my voice. Enoch shakes his head.

"They probably want to wait until you're stronger."

I scoff and shuffle my hands beneath me to prop higher against the wall. "Well, if that's not an incentive, I don't know what is."

Enoch smiles. "We'll keep working from the hands and feet up. Move them as much as you can, and we'll go from there."

I nod at his reasonable strategy. It strikes me how fortunate I am to have Enoch here. If there hadn't been an Avoyde hidden among the Lost Boys who captured Kade and Leo, then I wouldn't have an ally now when I need one most—

and Jordin would be after me.

Avoydes are like Aropfain repellent. If they stay true to what they agreed to do for El Olam, they can become virtually untouchable. Jordin may be nearby, but he can never be too close as long as I've got Enoch. It's reassuring to know that Enoch's presence will give me the time I need to recover.

I turn my head toward him to thank him for being here, but he looks nervous.

"What?"

He chews on his lip, as if worried I'll give him trouble for what he's about to say. "Can you really not feel Kade anymore? Not at all?"

I throw my hands in the air. Well, I try to. They flop at my sides like beached fish, but convey my frustration well enough. "How can I when I'm stuck in this?" I glare at the feeble body I'm stuck with. "I can't even sit up, and you want me to teleport?"

"Not teleport." Enoch shifts closer. "I just want to know if your essential link with him is still intact. You may be more physical now, but your intuition and connection to Kade never were. It might have survived the Shift. The Aropfain that did this to you still communicates just fine with living people. It stands to reason that you kept that ability too, right?"

I give him a sideways glance. He has a point. Jordin's always had freaky talent, wielding more power than souls of our caliber should, but every Aropfain can influence living souls. It's how they lure them away from us. Jordin wants me to be an Aropfain—that's the whole point of Shifting—so perhaps...

My heart pounds too much for me to focus. I close my eyes and try to settle my nerves, letting my head fall back against the wall. Several slow, deep breaths later, the energy that flows between Velt and Lemayle swarms around me like a thick gel. It feels like home, calm and still.

If I just keep my eyes closed and ignore the pain, I can imagine that nothing has changed, that I'm still a Firn; I'm still in Lemayle and I haven't had it all ripped away. And I can find Kade, just as I always have.

It's dark in my mind's eye, but I wade through the energy and stumble upon something achingly familiar.

That's Kade. I can't see him like I used to, but images of his face wisp together in my mind as the familiar energy stirs up my memory. Goosebumps run up my arms and I know he's outside in the cold Beta Siberian winter. The fatigue of exercise weighs on my shoulders and legs, separate from my own exhaustion somehow, proof of Kade's training, like Enoch said. My chest feels tight with his anger. He must be training with Ramiro, probably arguing over whose experience is better: Kade's Security Force special training or Ramiro's lived experience as an Association rebel outcast. I can picture the scene, and I have enough information to deduce where Kade is and how he feels. Even a bit of what he must be thinking.

I sigh, sinking into the comfort of having a bit of control back, enough to lay my fears aside for the moment.

"Thank you." My voice is lighter than before, and Enoch smiles.

"That's fantastic." He sighs in relief. "Now, there is something I wanted to ask you..."

And there goes my bliss.

"What?" My light and airy tone falls flat.

Enoch wrings his hands in his lap, a pained grimace on his face. "I still haven't heard from anyone, and I think it would be best to have some support within the group." He dumps the words on me like a bucket of cold water, but before I can react, he defends himself.

"If no one but me can speak for you, Ramiro will have you thrown out soon. He's not happy about you being here. He's growing paranoid. He thinks you're either an Association plant or an asset we can use against them. Once he decides which it is, we'll have to face the consequences."

A tension headache tugs behind my forehead. "I thought Kade was gaining influence in the group. We worked so hard." I catch myself before I whine.

Enoch shakes his head. "He has their respect, but Ramiro's anger is more compelling than Kade's charm. Without you, he's been... aimless."

Enoch sounds disappointed, but I would punch the air if I could raise my arm. Ha! So Kade is sensitive to losing me. I affected him whether or not he acknowledged me before. Take that, Jordin.

"Are you okay?" Enoch tilts his head in concern at the wild expression on my face.

I cough to adjust myself. "I'm fine. What's your point here, Enoch?"

He wrestles with his response but cringes through it. "Ainsley and Leo."

I wait for him to finish, but he doesn't. "Ainsley and Leo... what?"

He groans at me for making him say it, and I'm making him say it because he must know how I'll respond. So, why ask?

He takes a deep breath, shakes his head, and says, "I think we should tell them. I think we should tell them what you are and why you're really here." He makes it sound so simple, like it's the obvious choice.

I lean as close to him as I can, shoulders curled only an inch from the wall. "You're crazy."

Holding up a contrary finger, he says, "I'm not, though. You know it."

I raise an eyebrow at his tone, and he clears his throat and leans back.

"If this is a long-term thing, we need help. Even if long-term is just a week."

Long-term. I don't want to think about long-term. I want to deny long-term until this useless body shrivels up and long-term becomes eternity again as it should be. That's my long-term plan. Wait for this body to give out. Get back home. Get back to work. If Ramiro decides I'm a liability and kills me, I'll remember to thank him for it somehow.

But that plan doesn't suit Enoch's furrowed brow. He knows more than he's letting on. Why is everyone keeping something from me? I'm tired of being coddled at such a crucial time, especially when I'm the one dealing with a forced Shift!

My heart picks up again, and that's annoying too. So much for control. Sure, I can sense Kade, but I can't get to him. I can't even control my own body, let alone what goes on around me.

Of course, if Enoch does know more than he's saying, then he's asking me to see Ainsley and Leo for a reason. Someone from Lemayle wants this to happen and I need to be in Lemayle's good graces. I need as much good karma as I can get, so the consequences of my Shift aren't as severe as they could be.

My head falls to my chest; it's so heavy I worry I won't be able to lift it back up on my own. "Fine. I'll explain things to Leo and Ainsley. Besides, that will help me get through to Kade once I'm back in Lemayle. Sure. Bring them in. But *not* Kade." I point a finger at Enoch with a warning glare.

Enoch says nothing, but his relieved smile is offensive enough. He stands and leaves the room while I brace myself. Should I bother imagining how this will play out? Should I guess how they'll react and try to work out what to say?

Why bother? I can't make any mistakes worse than what I've already done. What's one more pitch of dirt out of this hole I'm digging, right?

There isn't a single part of me looking forward to this. Dread pools in my chest and I get that sting in the corner of my eyes again, but this time, it comes with blurred vision. Tears. Why so many tears? I need to get a grip before Enoch opens that door. I can't lift my arms well enough to wipe my eyes and I don't want those three walking in and fussing over my fragile emotions.

I did not miss the way hormones mess with human emotions. When emotions are just energy, they flow with you. You're aware of them and you can handle them. The issue with living souls is the body screws everything up. It adds hormones and circulation and basic needs like hunger. It's a drag.

Three knocks on the door alert me I've got visitors to deal with. A quick tap into Kade's energy sends a wintry chill and goosebumps up my arms, so I know he's still outside and not here. I take the deepest breath I can and brace myself as the door opens. Enoch enters like normal, but Leo and Ainsley hesitate at the threshold of the room and stare at me. Ainsley's eyes twinkle with fascination while Leo looks a bit dumb with a slack jaw.

They know. Enoch told them. I guess I'm grateful, but I'm also angry for no real reason.

Hormones! You see what I mean?

Enoch sends me a pleading look. I must be glaring like a feral animal, because the message on his face pleads with me to steady myself.

I pull my face together, focusing on my cheeks, then my mouth, then my eyes. How complicated an expression can be. My smile isn't genuine, but it's there.

"Hi, guys."

The words break whatever invisible barrier is keeping Ainsley and Leo out of the room. Ainsley steps in like an old friend, but Leo creeps through the door like he might wake a sleeping dragon. I appreciate that he fears me. It means he respects where I come from. That's very evolved of him.

Enoch drags the folding chair over for Ainsley and sits on

the floor next to me like a protective older brother. I'm hyperaware of how pathetic I must look, weak and crumpled against the concrete wall. I imagine they see a zombie, which explains the unease on Leo's face.

Leo comes from a lifetime of sadness. His mother's mind fled when his father mysteriously died. He's seen a lot. For him to fear me speaks volumes about how awful I must look.

"I promise I won't bite." I try to sound friendly. Leo fakes a laugh and lowers himself next to Ainsley's chair to keep space between us.

And everyone is silent.

I glance at each of them, but no one meets my eyes except Ainsley. Please, don't make me start this conversation. I didn't want this conversation to happen in the first place.

"So, Enoch tells us you're not the average visitor." Ainsley saves the day and makes me laugh at the same time. He's always had a knack for that, even when Kade and Leo were still with him back home in Yuzhno Sakhalinsk. I spent so many nights listening to that old radio and Ainsley's stories in the back room of his disused antique shop. Ainsley doesn't know it, but he's a keeper of knowledge. He's meant to share history and insight into people like Kade, Leo, and the Lost Boys. He is their true teacher, better than any they had in their Association-regulated schools.

My cheeks stretch into an honest smile for him, and I play along. "I'm not from around here."

Leo shakes his head, staring at us like we've lost our minds. "Where exactly are you from then?"

It pains me to see Leo so anxious. I've known him for most of his life, and I've wished more than once that he was my Neshome instead of Kade. Kade never heard anything I tried to tell him. Sure, a Firn can't speak directly to their Neshome, but we nudge their conscience and instincts like their lives depend on it, which is often the case. Kade has a specific purpose in El Olam's Plan. That's why he got me for a Firn. I'm the best. And even I didn't get through to him.

Leo would've listened. I know it.

"Have you ever wondered where you go when you die?" I ask him. He has. Everyone has. He doesn't have to answer, so I don't wait for it. "I'm from there."

I catch Enoch, from the corner of my eye, nodding his approval. Just as living souls wonder what it's like to be dead, Firns dream of what it would be like to have an actual conversation with their Neshomes, to bypass the fluff of nudging and just talk to them. So, yeah, I've imagined this conversation before, especially with Kade. Maybe when Kade dies, I'll ask his soul what I could've done better. What is his soul doing in that physical form that I'm not able to get through?

Leo doesn't approve of my explanation as much as Enoch does. His face pales and his eyes scan the floor, trying to sort out the flurry of thoughts and contradictions in his head.

"Take your time," I tell him. "I get it."

Ainsley reaches out to rest a comforting hand on Leo's shoulder. Sure enough, the tension in Leo's upper body releases, though his face betrays his panic.

My shoulders hitch in my best effort at a shrug. "So now you know. Questions?"

"Why are you here?" Leo still frowns at the floor.

I can't hold back a dry laugh. "There's been a..." How to put this delicately? "An accident."

Leo's eyes, normally a tranquil green like the sea, are piercing as they shoot up to me. "What were you doing in the truck with Kade?"

I consider lying. I've always appreciated that little perk of being a Firn. While I admire Malekh like Mikael, they're such superior beings, they can't lie. It makes them even more imposing, but I imagine it also makes their job of keeping

Firns safe difficult. They know so much that they can't tell, and they can't just make up answers when we ask. In the end, though, the point is to get Leo and Ainsley to trust me because I'm helpless. I hate it, but I can't make my own rules here either.

"Well observed, Mr. Arthur," Ainsley commends Leo. Ainsley had escaped by the time the gas station blew, and I was pulled into Velt and thrown from Kade's truck as he charged a Security vehicle under Jordin's instruction. My cheeks flush with heat at the memory. Embarrassed or enraged, I can't tell what I am anymore. I guess both.

Leo smiles his appreciation at Ainsley, but he doesn't ignore me for long. When he turns back, his face is serious. There's business on his mind, a list of questions that need satisfactory answers before he'll lower my threat level.

He's a smart kid. Why couldn't I have had a smart kid like him for a Neshome?

"I was with Kade." I could say more, and I will, but I'm reading the situation here. They need to ask the questions. They need to feel empowered when facing me. I'm a supernatural being from another plane of existence. I'm a ghost story in a world that rejected superstition long ago.

"Why?"

I glare at Enoch. I thought he told them! Why else would they be so skittish? Now I have to explain everything anyway. With a long and loud exhale, I close my eyes against an oncoming headache on top of every other ache I've already got. "I'm his Firn. I've always been with him." I catch Leo's gaze. "I've known you since you were four, when you met Kade at your dad's store." Then to Ainsley. "And you since you caught Kade before he broke the window to your shop." I force myself not to drop eye contact. That wasn't a proud moment for me. "Thank you, by the way. I was trying to stop him myself, but he never listened." I shift back to Leo. "That's why I'm here."

Anger fills my chest and suddenly I could rant about Kade all day, like insulting him gives me some sort of rush. "Kade never listened, and he screwed up so badly that I'm here now."

"So, you had to come here to get him to listen?" Leo looks skeptical, and I give him the same face, plus a touch of disgust.

"Of course not. I don't want to be here. I'm not supposed to be here." My anger morphs into fear and my heart thumps in my chest again. Lightheaded and dizzy, I press my palms into the floor just to feel the cold of the concrete and calm myself. The room spins, and Enoch puts out a hand to steady me. Ainsley and Leo can tell something's wrong, but they give me a moment to collect myself.

"Kade messed up," I explain when my head clears. "He messed up big. He gave into the influence of an Aropfain and that's bad news. That particular Aropfain wants me out of the way. That's why I'm here and Kade won't be safe until I get back to where I belong."

Ainsley rests his elbows on his knees. "And how can we help you, Miss..."

He's searching for my last name, but I don't have one. I shouldn't share more than I have anyway, but this is Ainsley. The words come before I think to stop them. "Anaya. And I don't know." I send a sideways glance to Enoch to check if he's got any new information, but his face is blank.

My head dips in disappointment. I should've expected as much. "I need to get back where I belong so I can protect Kade and guide him."

Leo's nose scrunches like he smells something foul. "Guide him with what?"

There's a glint of suspicion in his eyes, and I know where this is going. Leo suspects I'm the real reason Kade dragged him away from Yuzhno. It was Kade's idea to investigate the ashy remains of Ainsley's shop after Security burned it down. If Leo hadn't gone along, he would be with his mother and sister right now. And if I'm the driving force behind Kade, then Leo has a new scapegoat. He tried to blame Ainsley, but no one can stay mad at Ainsley.

"For his purpose." I stop him before he can accuse me, leveling my gaze to assert just a touch of dominance and cool off his attitude. "Everyone has one, and everyone has a Firn. Kade is a big deal to us right now, but he's been a pain to get through to."

"That's true." Enoch nods. Enoch's life Plan placed him with the Lost Boys to help me with Kade, and even Enoch was stumped.

Leo looks at Enoch with wide eyes.

"Enoch's been able to see me this whole time," I inform Leo. "He's an Avoyde. He's cool like that."

"I told you about her before," Enoch reminds them, and I remember that he's right. He recruited them to help me get through to Kade before Security attacked Phil's gas station.

Ainsley smiles. "That you did, Enoch. But accepting an invisible presence and then finding her in our world so soon after is quite the pill to swallow."

My jaw slackens. Not Ainsley too...

Leo pins me with a glare. "What are you trying to get Kade to do?"

I know it's not the appropriate reaction to Leo's accusations, but I smile at him, anyway. "I've always appreciated how protective you are of Kade. You do not know how much that helps."

Leo's guard drops a fraction. Flattery is my greatest ally.

"I need Kade to get to Danica."

Leo groans. "What is up with that Danica girl?"

"She's important," I snap. Whoops. I take a breath. "Long story short, it's about to be the end of the world and Danica decides who wins. Kade needs to protect her from the bad guys."

"You mean Jett?"

I lift my eyebrows to correct him. "I mean the influences behind Jett. Don't assume what you see is what's real. Everything that happens in this world is just a chess game played by our world."

Leo bristles at that. He's so human. "So, we're just pawns?"

I smile, nodding. "Some of you." Hey, I'm being honest. "Some are rooks and some are bishops and some…" I think of Danica, "are queens. Game-changers." Leo's face turns grim. I know what he's thinking. "Don't assume for a second that pawns aren't important. Besides, you don't know what your role is."

Leo raises an eyebrow. "Do you?"

I chew my lip for a second. "I know Kade's, so I can guess yours by association, but I'm not going to tell you."

Leo scoffs at me. He folds his arms and turns his face away.

"What good would it do if I told you?" My eyebrow twitches in a feeble challenge. "I'm not your Firn. I don't know who your Firn is, but they understand your role and they guide you like you're the most important person in the world. That should make you feel special enough to play along. You'll be one of us someday, you know."

He swallows at my reminder that he's going to die. Well, sure he is. That's not new. He just doesn't like to dwell on it. Few people do.

"I think we need to calm down for a moment." Enoch breaks the tension with his most gentle tone. "We're getting off the subject."

Ainsley comes to his aid. "From what I gather, Miss Anaya needs our help to recover, but what else can we do, Enoch? How can we assist in this grand game we're a part of?"

Leo relaxes and turns his attention to Enoch, throwing me a wary glance in case I decide to pounce on him.

"We're waiting for news from Anaya's people about how

to cope with this recent development." He nods toward me. My existence is the recent development. "Until then, Anaya needs protection from Ramiro's temper."

Ainsley and Leo give tight-lipped nods. No one can deny Ramiro has anger issues.

Then Leo turns to me, fidgeting. "What about Kade? He's worried about you. He wants to see you."

"Oh, I bet he does," I grumble. "Not happening."

Ainsley frowns. "I should think you'd look forward to seeing him after all you've said. Isn't this an urgent situation he should know about?"

I try not to belittle Ainsley with the expression my face is trying to pull, but it's tough. "I would not be in this situation if Kade could do his job. This happened because Kade is an idiot." They balk at my harsh words, but I'm not sorry. "Twenty years," I remind them, "twenty years of yelling in his face, throwing out the most obvious hints I could arrange—and for nothing. We had to fake your death just to get him moving!"

It's true. The fire at Ainsley's shop happened because Kade ruined my Plan A. Fortunately, Ainsley survived and reunited with us when Ramiro hijacked us. Sometimes El Olam's Plan surprises even me. That was a welcome surprise.

Ainsley processes what I tell him, and I hope he understands my perspective.

"I see how frustrating that must've been for you," he muses after a moment, rubbing his stubbled chin. "But I wonder if perhaps this can become an opportunity for you. You're keen to return to Kade's side as his... Firn, was it?" I nod, but I don't like where this is going. "Then why not reveal yourself so he can cooperate once you do?"

Why? Because I'm angry, that's why.

I lift my chin in defiance. "That's against the rules." If it isn't, it should be. "A Neshome should never know their Firn exists. It compromises their right to free will." Yeah. That's why.

"What if Kade just chooses not to listen to you? What if he heard you fine but doesn't want to do what you tell him?"

I regard Leo with such intensity the room seems a little darker for it. "Then that's a problem. Because Kade's listening to the Aropfain who did this, and that Aropfain works for Narn—someone you may know as the devil."

Leo's mouth snaps shut, so I continue.

"He's condemning both our worlds to lose their free will. We'll have to do as Narn says, and he'll destroy everything we care about until we're too afraid to deny him. If that happens, you can thank Kade."

Ainsley purses his lips in thought. "I'm not sure keeping Kade away will be a simple task."

"Leo can do it. Kade listens to him."

Leo chokes, and I level a flat stare at him. "He listens to you more than anyone else. Between the three of you, I'm sure you can keep him away until I'm off this floor." I catch each of their eyes, making sure they hear me. "Can I count on you? Please? Especially while I'm like this—I can't take the humiliation."

Enoch leans forward on his knees. "I think we can try until you regain some strength."

The others hesitate, exchanging looks, but agree enough to go along with it.

Relief washes over me and I sag against the wall. "Thank you."

Ainsley offers a good-humored smile. "If the fate of the world depends on this, I'll happily defer to our resident expert." He lifts a hand toward me. I'm the expert.

Leo's mouth quirks with questions, but he keeps them to himself and nods. I'll hold him to it.

"Now, let's see if we can arrange some more food for you." Ainsley stands and slides the chair toward Enoch in offering. Enoch graciously accepts. "You'll need as much strength as you can get while you're with us."

Leo stands too. "I'll go find Kade and try to keep him distracted."

I check the energy. "He's outside. Ramiro is not going easy on him. I think he'll be glad to see you."

I enjoy the baffled look on Leo's face and flash a smug grin.

Leo leaves the room without another word. He's eager to see if I'm right. I can't hold back a laugh.

Ainsley's eyes light up at my mischief and he, too, leaves me alone with Enoch.

"Back to your exercises?" Enoch asks.

I sulk. "Still no word, huh?" It's like the powers that be stood me up for a date.

"No." Enoch doesn't skip a beat, as though I should've expected that answer.

Frustration shivers up my spine, and I clench my hands into fists with ease. "I can't believe Kade was so dense it came to this. How could Jordin block him that much?"

Enoch opens his mouth, but it's several seconds before words come out, which means he's afraid to say something. "I've been meaning to talk to you about that."

I shoot him a mean glare. "What about it?"

He's timid, but he doesn't back down. "I have a theory..."

I shake my head and stare at him, waiting.

"I'm not convinced Kade was Jordin's true target. I actually think Kade may be sensitive to your kind."

My heart pounds and heat flushes from my neck up to my ears. "How can you say that?" I yell. "The Plan put you with this group because Kade is so oblivious I needed backup!"

Enoch pushes a breath out of his nose and his lips fall into a tight line. "Anaya, how long has Jordin been interfering with you and Kade?"

"Practically Kade's whole life!" I'd say I have a right to be upset after Jordin blocked my Neshome from me for twenty years, just as the Plan was about to unfold. It's not like this moment is just another era in history. This isn't just a step or phase in the Plan, this is the Plan, the endgame between good and evil. Pass or fail, win or lose. No do-overs. This world ends now with Kade's help, and the new one encroaches on us with every breath we waste on this conversation. If Kade thought he was disappointed after failing out of the Association's Security exams, he has no idea of the pit that forms in your gut when the culmination of everything is about to crumble through your fingers. When you drop the ball at the final second of the game with all eyes on you and every life in your care. Free will lives or dies with us. And Kade is out playing games with Lost Boys.

"Maybe Kade isn't the one with the issue..."

I eye him suspiciously, knowing he can't possibly mean what I think he's about to say.

He flinches like I might strike him—and I might if I could.

"Maybe you're the one who blocked the connection with Kade."

CHAPTER THREE

"How can you even suggest something so ridiculous?" I shout. My problem? Mine? Is spending two decades trying to save someone's destiny a bad thing? Kade's life has been a battle for me between trying to reach him and trying to protect him from harm and the enemy, since Jordin decided to multi-task as both Kade and Jett Tyrrell's Aropfain. Jordin convinced Jett to forsake his Firn and I guess he had his sights set on doing the same with Kade. That would have made life super easy for Narn, considering Jett and Kade have the same mission, but from opposite sides. Kade will help Danica understand what El Olam wants for the world, and we'll pray she agrees with him, but Jett is trying to force her to choose Narn by betrothing himself to her, which he can do as the son and heir to the Chairman of Beta Siberia, Donovan Tyrrell.

My eyes sting again, my vision swims, and my throat chokes up like I've swallowed cotton. If this is crying, I won't let it make me appear weak. I narrow my eyes at Enoch in a warning not to pity me.

Enoch raises his hands in a gesture for me to settle myself. "I'm not saying you did anything wrong on purpose."

I sniff and blink at him and two rogue tears run down my cheeks.

Now that he has my attention, he gives me a nervous, relieved smile. "I'm saying if Jordin has been interfering from the beginning, it's possible Kade doesn't have any defect keeping him from hearing you... Jordin might have been playing mind games with you from the start and convinced you that your efforts won't work, and so they don't." He avoids eye contact because, to a normal person, that sounds ridiculous. "I don't know a lot about how things work in your world, but I know intention is important."

I sniff again and gape at him. Well, huh. I glance away and reference the movie reel of Kade's life in my mind. In every stage, Jordin is there, mocking me and insulting Kade's incompetence. Even when Kade was a baby. I remember getting so frustrated and, I might as well admit it, embarrassed. So I pushed myself harder and resented Kade.

And had it been any other stupid Aropfain, I would have seen straight through that ploy, but this was Jordin, my old comrade, my former best friend. We did so much good together and he was always the weak or confused one who needed my help. I questioned everything when I heard he'd Shifted because I couldn't fathom how he'd cope without me. But he never left me, I realize. He stuck around, messed with my work, and ruined my most important assignment ever.

"That idiot," I seethe through my teeth. "I think you're right. It makes so much sense. That explains why Kade heard Jordin so well. He wasn't blocked—I was. I never got to set a good moral foundation for him to know Jordin is wrong. Jordin was all he had..."

I close my eyes against the rush of humiliation and hurt. "I'm such a failure."

Enoch shakes his head firmly. "I disagree."

My eyebrow lifts and for a second, I'm lost for words. "How can you disagree after you just made it so obvious?"

Enoch shakes his head again and grips my hand. For the sake of finding courage in this pathetic moment, I close my fingers around his and take pride in the strength I'm regaining.

"You didn't fail. You've always been passionate about your work. The Aropfain took advantage of that and of your friendship."

"How did you know we were friends?" There's something a little freaky about Avoydes. They're intuitive. They pick up on things, so you have to be careful of everything—even your emotions—around them.

Enoch shrugs with a sad smile. "It wouldn't hurt so much if you two weren't close." He tries to be delicate, but it stings all the same.

My chest feels hollow, and I hate it. It's helplessness, and it's not something I can accept.

"When I get back, I'm going to fix things with Kade," I swear to myself. Pain twinges in my lower back from hours of sitting in the same awkward position. "Until then, I just want to get off this floor."

Enoch laughs. "Well, you're doing great so far." He holds up our hands to show that I've been squeezing the circulation out of his fingers.

I stare at his poor hand, a giant smile on my face, but I don't let go. "Oh, yes! Next stop, moving my legs!"

It's a sad situation, but there's nothing to do except laugh. Until someone comes to explain what happens next, I'll distract myself by getting strong.

I spend a few hours working myself to exhaustion with Enoch. By the end, I move my arms and legs, slow and shaky, but I'm thrilled with the victory, and I'll keep it up.

"Anaya," Enoch ponders after a while of watching me try to move different limbs in new ways. "I don't understand the Plan like you do. I just do what I'm told to do to help it along."

I watch him because I know there's a question here somewhere. His eyes flick up to mine. "What's happening with the Plan now? Has it adjusted or has it stayed the same? Maybe we can find a hint about what will happen to you."

I like the way Enoch thinks. My neck flushes with heat and nerves, but I nod and close my eyes, going through the motions that are second nature. I clear my mind and expand my consciousness into the vibrations around me like I did to find Kade. I pick up Enoch's nerves, my body fizzing with energy as it tries to heal itself, Kade taking another beating from Ramiro outside. Somewhere in this thick sea of feelings, I should catch a whisper of orders telling me what I need to know about where I am and how I need to work with it. The Plan has been with me from the moment I went back to Lemayle to stay, my personal reference guide in service to El Olam.

I don't find it at first, but that might be because my situation has changed. I'm more removed from Lemayle, so I may need to search harder. My forehead wrinkles with concentration as I scour the darkness for my old companion. I push and push. I wait, trying to be patient despite the panic rising in my energy and in my stomach.

"There's nothing." My words come out thick with grief. My eyes scan behind my eyelids, but it's useless. "I'm cut off."

When I open my eyes, the world blurs with hot tears.

A hand falls on each of my shoulders and Enoch tries to steady me against the sorrow I can't resist anymore.

The Plan is a gift from El Olam. It confirms me as his and connects me to him, keeps me safe from Narn and all the Aropfain, assures me of the purpose behind what I see and what I'm asked to do. It measures my worth.

And now it's gone.

I'm done being strong. I'm done pretending everything is okay. My head falls to Enoch's shoulder, and I cry. I don't care about looking weak anymore. I'm abandoned and I deserve the misery that comes with it. El Olam has forsaken me because I've failed him. I'm not with Kade anymore and I realize now how replaceable I must be.

"Anaya, it'll be okay." Enoch rubs my back to comfort me.

"No, Enoch." I sniff. There's no way to return once you sever yourself from El Olam. We're supposed to know better. We have all made our choices between El Olam and Narn. "No, it won't."

I cry myself to sleep. I haven't done that in ages. It's pathetic, I know, but I have no remorse. I'm an outcast, with no world or dimension to belong to. No wonder no one has come to explain things to Enoch.

In the night I wake up, but I don't bother opening my eyes. The room is dark, and I don't care to see anything. I lie against the wall and think. There must be something I'm missing. I strain to remember everything I know about Shifting. It's an escape route, our one last opportunity to abandon El Olam if we can't handle the pressure or if the Aropfain get into our heads. El Olam doesn't want us to feel trapped in his service, so souls like Jordin and I still have just enough free will to run away. When we do, we go through a ritual to begin the Shift. Our name is removed from El Olam's list of loyal souls and added by an Aropfain of our choosing to Narn's. The lists are ceremonial. It's not like Narn or El Olam keep actual rosters of who owns whom, but the list is a part of our process, something we can see and interact with that forces us to reflect on the consequences of what we're choosing to do. It's El Olam's quiet way of asking us not to go.

Jordin tricked me into erasing my name when I denounced Kade back in the truck. It wasn't real—I didn't mean it—but Jordin had completed the rest of the ritual for me, so I guess it was enough to trigger the Shift.

But El Olam must know the truth. He has to understand I didn't abandon my purpose. It was a moment of weakness, not a declaration of treason. He'll spare me. He'll get me back and put my name back on his list. This was all a huge mistake. I'm not an Aropfain yet, so someone in Lemayle must be working to save me. Mikael wouldn't abandon me like this. It's too cruel, and El Olam would never order it.

Yes, I decide. I need to wait. Mikael will tell me what I have to do, or my body will fail, and I'll go back naturally. I bet that's all this is: downtime while Lemayle sorts everything out. I only have to wait, and when I get back, we'll all laugh about how scared I was and how I actually thought for a second that I was in trouble.

I smile in the dark. That's what this is. Just a mistake that will fix itself. I'm still taken care of. I know it. It's safe here.

I drift back to sleep, but a sound makes my eyes pop open. Something is in the room with me. I wonder how far away Enoch is. He knows he's functional Aropfain repellent, so I doubt he'd go far enough away for Jordin to pay me a visit. But something is in here with me and I can't see in the darkness.

I can't run, can't fight, can't simply vanish like I used to. I play dead, or, well, asleep and focus on breathing, which I'm still not used to, but I will not let oxygen deprivation be my downfall.

Something shuffles in the corner where Enoch's chair is. Typical Jordin: sitting in a chair and soaking in how pathetic he's made me. I bet he's so amused.

I wonder if Narn has rewarded him for eliminating the competition. Anger surges through me and I use it. This energy can help me give Jordin a rude gesture or shock him with a quick movement. I don't know. I don't have many resources.

Do I let him know I know he's here? Do I ignore him and hope he goes away?

The shuffling draws closer and my heart skips a precious beat. I'll just close my eyes and ignore him. Yeah, that sounds good. He might reveal something in the dark he'd never say to my face, so the bravest thing to do is nothing. Yeah...

As he reaches my side and sits next to me, I realize something crucial: I'm not in Jordin's world anymore. I'm in Velt, he's in Lemayle. He can see me, but I can't see him. He can't make noise here, not without expending a ton of energy.

So, who the heck is sitting next to me right now?

It isn't Enoch. Enoch is polite enough to announce himself and he would let me sleep. So that means it's either one of the Lost Boys or...

"I hope you're feeling better," he says, still assuming I'm unconscious. "I've been worried about you, tried to visit, but they said you're not strong enough yet."

If my eyes were open, I'd roll them. What a sap.

He reaches out to brush the back of my hand with his. I twitch and tense up. Didn't see that coming. Okay, breathe.... It's normal for people to twitch in their sleep. He's too oblivious to notice.

"Whatever the Association did to you," he continues, unaware as expected, "we'll get them back. I promise."

What a stupid thing to say.

He sighs heavily and loudly, a classic sign of frustration for him. "I don't understand why they'd bring an innocent girl into this. It's sick."

It's funny how much credit the Association gets for things beyond its control. I recall my description of life in Velt as being a chess game. The members of the Association are Narn's pawns and little more. Everyone in the Beta Siberian Arrangement, even the wealthy, fears the Association and Security. Life is but a dance on thin ice for everyone outside the Tyrrell family, who have run the show from the beginning—Narn's rooks and knights.

"Either way," Kade goes on, resolute. "You're safe here. I'll make sure of it."

He thinks he's so powerful, but he's nothing without a Firn. I laugh out loud, blowing my cover.

I hear him fall backward. A light dazzles my eyes, and I close them tighter against the intrusion.

"You're awake?" Kade demands. Yes, it's Kade. I'll have to tell off Leo later.

I open my eyes to pin him with a strained glare against the key-chain flashlight he's pointing at my face. "You're not supposed to be here," I tell him. "I mean, what time is it? Shouldn't you be sleeping?"

Kade's eyes are wide and his eyebrows pinched together. He hasn't recovered enough to sit upright yet. I guess he wasn't expecting much of a conversation.

"I was worried about you," he defends himself. "Asa said he doesn't think you'll make it."

A sarcastic noise coughs at the back of my throat. "Well, Asa's probably right." Kade won't understand if I tell him that's a good thing.

Kade closes his eyes and shakes off his shock. When he opens them again, his face is somber. "I'm sorry for what happened to you. Do you remember?"

I quirk an eyebrow at him. "You mean do I remember falling out of the truck? Yeah. I remember."

His jaw stiffens and I can see him fighting not to respond to my snark. "I meant, do you remember how the Association captured you?"

I swallow a groan, stare at the ceiling, praying El Olam will appear and get me out of this. "They didn't bring me here..." The Association has no idea I exist. There's no record of me. I was never born. This–the wretched form and the problems it's already caused–is all Jordin's doing. But I know Kade better than his own mother. He won't believe me.

"Of course they did," Kade argues, and I take a deep breath

to stop myself from tearing into him. "You fell out of one of their trucks when they attacked us." He punches his own leg in frustration. "I can't believe they'd use a sick girl against us."

"Why would they bother?" I cut him off. His eyes squint in confusion. "Think about it, Kade. Why would they bring bait to an ambush? Who does that? Who has ever done that?"

His face goes white when I say his name. "So, they told you about me?"

How self-centered can he be? An angry growl rises in my throat. "Don't tell me you think you're my hero." The word comes out with a sour taste.

Kade hesitates, but he can't help himself. "Well, I am the one who saved you."

That's it. "You're also the one who made all this happen!"

Okay, I haven't forgotten what Enoch and I discussed, and I realize Kade isn't as guilty as I want him to be, but I have a lot of pent-up aggression and Jordin isn't here, so Kade will have to do.

Kade looks like I slapped him. "How do you figure that? I've never seen you before in my life."

"Exactly." I nod my bitter agreement. "You have no clue who I am."

Kade lifts his arms like he doesn't know what to do with them. "Why are you so aggressive?"

Now, I admit, Kade doesn't have much experience with the opposite sex. Still, he's always fancied himself a gentleman. But I don't care what gender I am now. It isn't about chivalry for me. It's about the fact of the matter. And I'll be aggressive if I want to be.

"Because you have no idea how stupid you've been!"

As I shout the words, the door to the room swings open and both Kade and I shrink away from the light spilling in from the hall.

I squint to see three figures framed in the doorway.

"A little late, guys."

"Sorry," is Enoch's hasty apology as he strides into the room followed by Ainsley and Leo.

Leo marches up to Kade and smacks the back of his head.

"Ow!" Kade covers his head and glares at Leo.

"I told you not to wander off," Leo scolds him, counting on his fingers because there's more. "I told you not to come here. I told you to actually listen to me for once!" He adds another smack for good measure.

Kade cringes away from any more attacks and shoots Leo an indignant glare. "Why is everyone so mad at me all of a sudden?"

"To be fair, Mr. Buxton, you were asked not to visit Miss Anaya until she was stronger, and you went against it." Ooh, scolded by Ainsley. No matter how polite Ainsley is, Kade never wants to disappoint him. Kade's anger fades into a frown.

With Ainsley's words, the frazzled energy in the rooms subsides. I can breathe more deeply and I don't feel like lunging for Kade's throat anymore. Ainsley is awesome.

Kade recovers from his shame and points at the four of us. "Wait. Why am I the only one who isn't allowed in here?" His voice is soft, less accusing and a little more hurt.

"It's complicated," Enoch tries to explain, sensing another argument brewing.

Kade's head bobs in a quick, heavy rhythm. "I can see that."

"Mr. Buxton," Ainsley calls his attention with a cheerful tone, "do you recall a certain conversation we had back home regarding the various Old World religions?"

Kade closes one eye, straining to remember. "The... one about... the angels and demons and stuff?" The words come out in a drawl, but I'm impressed he can think back that far.

"Precisely."

Kade bounces in place and smiles at himself.

"You recall we talked about how ancient peoples credited angels for good things and demons for bad?"

Kade looks a bit dumb as he nods, not drawing the connections between then and now.

Ainsley wears a pained expression. Subtlety is one lesson Kade could never grasp.

Leo takes over. "What if those were real?"

Kade balks at the suggestion but says nothing.

Leo rubs his forehead, searching for a better approach. "What if..."

I can't take this anymore. "What if you know absolutely nothing about the world and I'm just one of those things?"

Three of the men in the room look flabbergasted at my blunt approach, but they forget who's known Kade the longest. You can't spare Kade's feelings. He'll have them whether you're delicate or not.

Something behind Kade's eyes clicks. He opens his mouth in awe for just a moment, but he's quick to recover his incredulous sneer. "Hold on a second. Do you mean to tell me you're an angel?"

The corners of my mouth tug down, and I raise my eyebrows. "I'm actually impressed you didn't go straight for devil."

Kade lifts his chin to look superior. "Yeah, you should be. With how snippy you've been, I considered it."

I smile at him. A genuine smile. "Yeah, I deserve that." Then my face falls serious. "But I'm not an angel. I appreciate the analogy, but I'm not that forgiving, and I don't have to be." Kade frowns under my stare. "I am on the good side, though. And things have gotten complicated. That's why I didn't want to see you."

"Why me?" Kade demands, exasperated. "Did I make some cosmic mistake and you've come to punish me or something?"

I grit my teeth. "I wish I were here to punish you, Kade."

Kade sits back on his heels. Resentment and a touch of nervousness swirl around him, enough for me to feel them too. "I feel like you guys have been talking about me behind my back."

I raise my hand—because I can now. "Not my idea."

He turns with a betrayed look on his face. How could I have betrayed him? He only just met me.

"What is your deal? If you're some angel-ish being, what did I ever do to you?"

"Maybe we should all take a breath," Enoch suggests when he sees me pull myself away from the wall with new, rage-fueled strength. He presses a hand to my shoulder and pushes me back.

I glare at him, and his eyes bore into mine, strongly suggesting I listen to him. I calm my breathing and realize how flushed and tired I am. My arms are light and tingly, and my heart beats against my chest. I'm getting carried away again.

"No." Kade shakes his head. "I'm done with this." He eyes each of us with suspicion. "I want answers."

Oh, for the love of—"You screwed up, Kade." I say one word at a time, so he'll understand. "There's a delicate Plan, and you threw it off. Is that what you want to hear? You messed up and dragged me out of heaven because of it."

Kade moves to argue, but no words come to him.

"Kade." Leo pushes Kade's arm to get his attention. "She's supposed to be like your guardian angel, okay? But things have gone wrong."

Kade chokes on a laugh. "That's my guardian angel? Well, I feel cheated. No wonder things got messed up." He turns to me, and I feel broken, defective. I was glorious in my true state, in Lemayle where physical bodies don't have to be grown and nourished. I was pure energy. Sure, I'm not imposing or glowing with heavenly glory right now, quite the opposite, but that doesn't excuse Kade's tone. "If that's how you've been guarding me, it's no wonder nothing's ever worked out for me."

He means his failed career with Security, but that was never going to work. His failing was part of his Plan. The training prepared him for this, not for a life in service to the Association. But he doesn't see it that way. He'd rather find somewhere to unload the shame, and he chooses me.

His lip curls as his eyes skim my poor solution for surviving in Velt without a Plan. "Don't blame me because you're terrible at your job."

My face slackens. He did not just say that to me. When I find words again, they come out low and grim. "If anyone is inept here, Kade, it's you. Do you have any idea how much I've fought for you and how many times you've rejected me? Let me tell you, it's been every single time, and people have suffered for it. The fire at Ainsley's? Your fault."

Kade flinches at the mention of something I shouldn't know.

"Leo's leg?" I point a thumb at Leo, recovered now but who was on crutches for weeks, thanks to an angry moose that Kade agitated at Jordin's suggestion. "Your fault."

My head swims and my vision blurs for a second, but I'm not done. "You've been going against everything I tell you your whole life and I'm thinking Enoch might be right."

Enoch shrinks away from the spotlight I throw on him.

"Maybe you're not as dense as I thought you were," I keep going. It won't stop. "Maybe you've known I was there and just ignored me on purpose." My tongue goes numb, and I need to focus twice as hard on my words. I can't get enough air in my chest. Panic swells there instead. My head is heavy and loopy. "Heck, maybe you're an Avoyde like Enoch, but you and Jordin are just so chummy you led me on so he could get an advantage!"

Just as the words leave my mouth, I fall over.

Enoch catches me a second before my head smacks the floor, and he lays me down. I think he's saying my name, but it sounds far away. The four of them smear into black figures crowding around me. This, I remember, is kind of what it's like to die. A spark of joy mingles with the panic. Perhaps I'm going home.

"That's enough, Anaya."

The voice seems to come from everywhere. My vision returns, and I catch my breath with a thirsty gasp. I blink a few times, wondering what dragged me back when my problems were almost over. I scan the room. Ainsley, Leo, and Kade stare at me with shell-shocked expressions, but Enoch focuses on the far side of the room. I follow his gaze and jerk against the wall when I see him.

"Mikael," I breathe. Everyone looks at me like I'm hallucinating.

Enoch takes control, unable to tear his eyes away from the grand vision of the Malekh. "I think we need the room to ourselves for a moment." The others turn to see what he sees, only to end up confused. Kade moves to say something, but Leo smacks him on the shoulder hard enough to get him to listen.

"We don't get it either, Kade. Just let it go for now."

They stand and file out of the room, sad at being excluded. But I don't want them to understand. I want to pretend none of this happened. A surge of joy floods my chest, sending shivers into my shoulders as I realize this is the moment I've been waiting for.

I smile at Mikael like he just fished me from three days of drifting at sea. Then I remember where I am. I remember the aches all over, the struggle to breathe. I remember Jordin Shifted me and no one warned me enough to stop him.

My face reforms into a crooked grimace. "What the heck, Mikael! Where have you been?"

CHAPTER FOUR

Mikael flinches. He doesn't deserve to be spoken to that way by a subordinate, but he seems to think he does now. Mikael is the head of all things Lemayle, so he knows El Olam better than anyone. He may even get to speak with El Olam sometimes. His knowledge of the Plan is deeper than anyone's, but that doesn't mean he shares it. If he did, I probably wouldn't be here.

"First," he begins, moving closer, "how are you feeling?"

My head tilts with a sappy smile. I knew he still cared. "Oh, I'm fantastic," I assure him facetiously. "Utterly thrilled to be here." I remind myself I shouldn't speak that way to my superiors, but I never catch myself before I do it. Always after. And now, of all times, I'm not concerned about formalities and hierarchies of respect. I'm dying and it's being dragged out to an embarrassing degree.

Then Mikael does something I've never seen him do, and my stomach drops. Mikael sits beside me, right next to Enoch, who topples away from him to make room. Enoch has seen my kind before, but I guess this is his first Malekh encounter. It can be overwhelming.

"Anaya, I must apologize." His face is smooth and pained

all at once. It's impossible for a Melakh to wear an unattractive expression. They've got it all, the looks and the knowledge. "I tried to warn you, but resources were... limited."

My jaw slackens. "You tried?" My voice might be a touch too loud. "You tried?" And a little hysterical. I rack my brain for the times I saw Mikael before I was Shifted. Was he in the truck with me? No. Was he there when Kade got himself and Leo arrested by Security back in Vanino? Was he there when Kade provoked the moose on Jordin's suggestion?

No. Mikael showed up before we left Yuzhno and told me to be careful. Be careful. That's it. Not, "Hey—FYI—someone is trying to Shift you." That would have been helpful.

I have said none of this out loud, but I get the feeling Malekh can read minds because Mikael looks like he heard every word.

"I am sorry, Anaya." His voice is soft, and it makes it hard to be mad at him. But I want to be mad at him.

I push out a long, forced sigh and shove my anger aside. "Don't worry. It'll be fine. I'll fix this and get back to work."

Mikael's face doesn't change.

I tilt my head at him. "Back to work," I insist. "Right?"

Mikael doesn't move. I turn to Enoch for support. He's gone from gobsmacked to the same sad expression as Mikael. What am I not understanding here? Why does everyone know everything but me?

"Mikael, I appreciate that you're trying to be delicate, but it's not helping. Just say it." The truth creeps into the corner of my mind, but I chase it away. That is not what El Olam would do. I've done nothing horrible enough to deserve that. Mikael is just making that face to be dramatic. Enoch is just a pessimist. This will be fine.

My heart doesn't agree with me. It leaps in my chest. Fear prickles along my skin, springing goosebumps up my arms. Nervousness settles in the air. I can almost see the energy buzzing around our heads. Once the tension dies down, I'll celebrate another trait I've kept from Lemayle, but I need everyone to calm down first. I can hardly breathe.

Mikael rests a hand on my arm, and the malfunctions vanish, but the fear remains. He's bracing me. I stare at him with eyes wide and mouth open.

No. No, he can't be preparing me for this. It's not true. I've been so loyal. Played by the rules. Worked for so long without question.

"Anaya, I've looked into your case." His tone is even. No trace of hope or despair. "I've searched every law, looked back to find anything similar to work with. I've appealed to El Olam himself."

Wow. All that for little old me? I relax. After all that, Mikael has to have found something.

"You appealed to El Olam for me?"

That is last resort stuff. We don't bother El Olam. We're assigned to small pieces of his puzzle, and he manages everything else. He trusts us to handle the little things, but he works harder than anyone.

Mikael shakes his head. "Nothing in history matches your situation. The rules of Shifting are clear. It is the escape clause of your contract with El Olam. We did not intend it to be a two-way street."

It's plain logic, but panic and confusion compete for space in my brain, making my head pound.

"I think you're trying not to tell me you can't help me..."

The intensity in Mikael's eyes pins me to the wall. "Shifting allows souls the freedom of choice even after they've sided with us," he explains by way of apology. "It preserves every soul's free will, no matter how long they've served El Olam. Shifting is a gift El Olam should never have given, but I am not in a position to question it."

He glares at the floor, gritting his teeth against what he says next. "There is no protocol for a Shift taken unwillingly."

No protocol. I blink, shake my head. "Pardon?"

His eyes lift to mine, sad this time. "Anaya, I've been searching for a loophole. That's why I didn't come sooner, but there's nothing. The Shifter initiates the process. We did not conceive that one soul would force another to Shift."

"So, conceive it!" I push myself away from the wall with newfound strength, slumping forward but holding Mikael's gaze. "Rewrite the rules! Take me home!"

"I don't have that power."

"Well, what did El Olam say?"

Mikael cradles his head in his hand to avoid me, then sits up straight and says, "He remains silent on the matter."

My eyebrows shoot toward my hairline. "So, you're telling me..."

"You can't come home."

I'm glad he didn't make me say it, but emptiness swells in my chest all the same. "There is no returning from a Shift."

I massage my temples with my fingers, and I can't even revel in the victory of lifting both my arms. "So, I'm doomed to become an Aropfain."

"No." He answers so quickly and fiercely that Enoch scoots away from us, unable to take the pressure of Mikael's intense energy.

Enoch watches me, studying my reactions to better understand the conversation. Questions tug at his eyebrows. Maybe I'll explain later.

"No?" I laugh. What else can I do?

"The Plan hasn't changed, Anaya." Desperation glitters in Mikael's eyes, but this is what we exist for. The Plan is everything.

"How—" I choke on my disbelief. Millennia at this job and it still surprises me. "How hasn't it changed?"

"You're still meant to escort Kade to Danica, and time is running thin."

"So, no pressure." My voice is thick and hot tears threaten

to fall again. I won't cry in front of Mikael. I squeeze my eyes shut until I regain my composure, taking a deep breath.

"Let me see if I'm getting this," I start calmly, spreading my sweaty palms on the oversized pair of jeans one of the boys must've donated. "You want me to keep working as Kade's Firn from Velt and get him to Danica's side even though I can't get myself off the floor..." I glance at Mikael for emphasis, but from the corner of my eye, I see Enoch blanch at my recap. "Mikael, I can't even access the Plan anymore. I can't walk. I can't look at Kade without wanting to punch him in the face. Don't you think you're asking for the impossible?"

He hesitates, but says, "If it's in the Plan, it's possible."

A short, loud, skeptical laugh creeps up my throat and I don't stop it. "I used to think that, too."

Mikael catches my hand in both of his and leans in. "Anaya, I won't stop searching for an answer. We need you."

I throw my head back with a groan. "Why can't I just die and come home?" I ask, almost whining.

Mikael's face falls. He pauses for a moment before explaining. "The Shift is El Olam's final mercy to souls with free will. If they make the choice, after knowing his ways and his Plan, then there is no turning back." He searches my eyes for understanding, but he will not find any. The corners of his eyes pinch with remorse, but he continues. "The Shifting soul is supposed to be sure of their choice. That's why the rituals are involved—for the soul to reflect before committing to the Shift. It is the grace of the process. The chance to turn back before committing to the Shift. Every other soul has had that."

"Well, I haven't!"

He nods. He knows. "But you are the first in history. This phase," he gestures to my wretched condition, "is not supposed to happen. I can only assume your soul pulled you into Velt because it wasn't in agreement with the Shift, so it interpreted it as a birth of sorts. It brought you to Velt without a prepared vessel. No body, just a physical manifestation of your soul. It's weak because it was never nurtured and grown, but this is your soul." He shakes his head. It isn't enough reason for him either. "But there is no going back. If you don't complete the Shift and this body dies, you have nothing to return to."

"Nothing to…"

"You will cease to exist entirely."

Did he just punch me in the gut? I look at his hands, still wrapped around mine. My breathing staggers. Panic surges from the pit of my stomach to the top of my head. My vision blurs. I can't get any air.

He tightens his grip on my fingers and it all goes away. All but the fear.

"You still have a choice, Anaya." I quirk an eyebrow at him, and I see Enoch staring at him over his shoulder, looking for hints of what Mikael's saying to match the vibes he's giving off. If I have a choice, we'd all love to hear it.

"You can complete the Shift, or you can continue working for El Olam and accept your fate when it comes, knowing the Plan is preserved."

I say the first thing on my mind. "How will I know what to do?" Let me be clear. I may be dying. I may be desperate. Jordin may have ripped my freedom from me…

But I won't side with Narn. Nothing can make me that extreme. If I'm going out, I'm taking my pride with me. I'll disappear with a smile on my face, knowing Narn will have a shocked face of his own because of me. I'll pull the rug out from under Jordin and his stupid plans. But I need help.

Mikael smiles, and it lights up the dreary room. "We'll do all we can to protect and assist you, Anaya," he swears, breathless with relief. "I promise, everything will be clear once Kade is at Danica's side."

I yank my hand from his and hold a pinky up in his face. "You will promise," I tell him as he stares at my little finger.

"Don't abandon me, Mikael. I'm doing you a solid here."

Mikael tilts his head at my finger with curiosity. I hook his pinky with mine. Childish, yes, but I need a real guarantee that Mikael will help me. I squeeze his pinky and shoot him an expectant stare.

He looks at me and bobs his head. "I still promise."

I relax against the wall. Worst. Day. Ever. But at least I've got the assurance of a Malekh that my death will mean something. I hold back an ironic scoff. How many times have I been on the other side of this conversation, though not face-to-face?

"I can accept this," I tell myself more than them. "But I'm still fuzzy on how you expect me to make it. Have you even looked at me?" I glance down at myself and wish I hadn't. Frail, sallow, skin white and thin as paper. Ugh. Gross. "Every other minute, my heart threatens to beat straight out of me. I'm not familiar with physical stuff anymore, but I know you don't get far without a heart. Or muscles. Or stamina."

Behind Mikael, Enoch is thinking, a finger hooked around his chin.

"I'm doing everything I can," Mikael explains. "It's been difficult. Without a change in the Plan, the usual assignments remain, but I will have every unassigned soul I find helping you."

"They can't help me walk, Mikael. And will I be able to see them?" Firns can't see each other, as a rule. We don't interfere with another soul's work. The Aropfain are an exception because we need to avoid them. The Malekh don't count because they set us straight and they're something higher than a soul. I think, though, that I deserve special treatment.

Mikael doesn't look as sure. "If that were possible, the Plan would allow for it."

So that's a "no."

Mikael squeezes my arm. I tear my gaze away from my lap

to give him my bravest skepticism.

"I will not let you down."

I blink. That's one of the most direct and decisive things I've ever heard a Malekh say. For good reason, they are very vague. They know more of the Plan than we're allowed to. Not everything—only El Olam knows everything—but they know more than I do, for sure.

Still, I eye him, searching for more. "But you can't tell me how you'll help me?" I draw out the words, hoping one of them will get a telling reaction from him.

Nothing but a jovial laugh.

Mikael shakes his head at me. "Of all the souls I've known, you are the most tenacious, Anaya." The laughter fades from his eyes and he gives my arm another squeeze. "Don't lose that now."

He would turn a compliment into an order.

I inhale slowly and push the breath back out. "I won't."

Mikael smiles. Then he turns to Enoch, and Enoch jolts at the sudden attention.

"Enoch, I have to thank you. You are one of the finest Avoydes I've seen, and you are more important now than ever."

He means now that Enoch has to babysit me.

Enoch opens and shuts his mouth like a fish, but the imposing presence of a Malekh has left him lost for words. They have that effect on living souls.

Mikael leans back so he can see both of us. "Get strong." He points at me. "Get Kade to Danica. I'll send you help along the way." He marks Enoch with a glimmer of humor. "Don't let Anaya argue when you know what's best for her. We are working through you. You can trust your instincts. That's what we need you to do."

Then he glances over Enoch's shoulder and nods to something—or someone—unseen. I want to ask about it, but by the time I open my mouth, Mikael is gone.

I turn on Enoch. "Who were you talking to back there?"

Enoch has a hand to the side of his head, squeezing his eyes against an apparent headache. "I've never dealt with two visits at the same time before."

I give him a second to pull himself together, but it drives me mad.

He shakes it off and focuses on me. "I'm supposed to tell you that you need to practice your exercises more. There isn't much time."

I frown at him. "Much time before what?"

Enoch shrugs and shakes his head.

I throw my hands in the air and they flop to my sides. "Well, great."

CHAPTER FIVE

I take the advice to exercise more to heart. I have nothing else to do anyway, and the sooner I can stand in front of Kade Buxton, the sooner he'll respect me. Why was I brought through as a girl? Kade's only real interaction with women has been with his sweet, quiet mother. His father emphasized chivalry and taking care of women because that's how he had to do it. And girls in Beta Siberia media are usually from Nor'ilsk and dying for a chance to impress the most eligible man of power.

Danica is from Nor'ilsk, but she's the Reyn Gayst. She's different. I saw it in her eyes when we crashed Jett Tyrrell's girlfriend-reveal gala. Danica is the pure soul who will decide between El Olam and Narn and tip the scale one way or the other for the last time. She is what I've been fighting for since before I came to Lemayle to stay. When I meet her, we can grumble together about how annoying gender roles are in this society.

The jarring force of hitting the floor is something I'll never get used to.

"You seem distracted," Enoch observes as he pulls me up by the arm. I reach out to grab the backs of the chairs we've set up to help me build the strength in my legs.

"Yeah, sorry." I keep the frustration out of my voice, so Enoch doesn't take it personally. I grip the back of the seat and hoist myself to stand with Enoch's help. My arms are pathetic.

"Just try to hold yourself up and work your legs. You're getting better."

Praise for learning to stand. How embarrassing.

Enoch notices the look on my face and rests an encouraging hand on my shoulder. "You can stand, Anaya. That's huge." He glances away, seeing something in his mind. "To be dragged into this dimension without the chance to grow here and build the strength to stand in under a week..." He shakes his head in awe. "A normal person couldn't do that."

He's right. They couldn't. I can still draw energy to myself like I used to in Lemayle. I'm thinking living souls could too if they tapped into Velt's energy.

I shift myself upright again and bend my legs in short squats to get my muscles warm. It had been a long morning of falling and shouting while Enoch stood in the corner to give me space. Finally, I got angry enough to unleash an energetic pulse that knocked over the chairs I sat between, and Enoch came out of the corner. That was the turning point. If I can shoot energy out, then I can draw it in. I caught my breath and devised my version of steroids.

I've made myself a deal. When I can walk, I can leave this room. I refuse to go out there and meet the eyes of the Lost Boys and even Phil in a wheelchair. I've picked up the vibe that I'm not wanted here. If everyone avoiding me isn't clear enough, the subtle energy seeping under the door whenever someone gets close confirms it. It's good practice though, learning the differences in energy from person to person. It helps me keep my guard up.

Sweat beads on my forehead and my arms shake. Enoch

steps forward, ready to suggest I take a break. I glare at him.

Then a familiar energy sweeps under the door like a heat wave. "Oh, crap." My arms give out. I crumple to the floor as the door opens.

"Whoa, are you okay?" It's Leo. He moves to help me, but Enoch holds up a hand.

"She can do it." There's joy in his voice. He's so pleased at my progress because he's nervous about the news we received after Mikael left. We don't know what's going to happen, but our stay with the Lost Boys is ending. I've got to get up and running—literally.

I pull myself up one foot at a time, impressing everyone. I can't appear weak right now because Leo isn't the only guest in the room.

"I thought you agreed to leave me alone?" The question is for Kade, but I keep my eyes on the wall. Standing takes more focus than I want to let on.

Kade makes a disgruntled noise. "I was supposed to leave you alone until you could get around better. Looks like I kept my promise to me."

I shoot him a glare over my shoulder. Only Kade could veil a compliment with an insult.

"We didn't come here for you to argue," Leo grumbles at Kade. I'm from the afterlife. A small part of Leo is afraid of me, so he won't scold me yet. Kade will have to take the brunt of it. I'm not upset about that.

"What's going on?" Enoch asks.

"Ramiro's ticked again," Kade supplies before Leo can answer.

Enoch peers at me, head hung low, because of course it's me. Ramiro has lost his patience with my being here.

I turn to Leo. "Can someone please explain what Ramiro thinks happened? I know he's jumped to some crazy conclusion, and if I run into him, I'll need a good story."

"Why not just freak him out with your 'I'm from the dead world' story?" The snark in Kade's voice is impressive.

I'd love to do that, to be honest, but it wouldn't be productive.

Before I can come up with something to match Kade's wit, Leo explains. "He's getting nervous about what the Association wanted with you. There's been more activity across the lake from Irkutsk."

"Across the lake?" I gape at them. "You get attacked by Security and bug out closer to the Beta Siberian capital? Whose brilliant idea was that?"

Everyone falls silent, but Leo and Kade glance over my shoulder and then at the ceiling to avoid staring. I turn my head toward Enoch. He looks guilty.

I don't ask. I keep him pinned under my gaze until he gets the point.

"I was told to bring us here," Enoch confesses. My face softens. So, it was a tactical move, not by the Lost Boys, but on Lemayle's side.

"None of us liked the idea either," Kade grumbles, folding his arms. "But Enoch convinced Ramiro, so here we are." His sour tone tells me Kade had argued and lost.

Leo steps to Enoch's side. "It's actually a great place. It's been deserted forever, so no one would've expected people to be hiding here."

"No one alive," I remind him. I'm not sure how Jordin could know where we went, but I wouldn't put it past him.

Kade snorts in distaste. "What, you think a ghost told them?"

I turn as quickly as I can and ignore the dizzy spell. "Denial much, Kade?"

"Denial a ton!" He takes a daring step forward. "What if Ramiro is right, and the Association planted you with a homing beacon or something?"

"And you think my story sounds ridiculous?"

He saunters a few steps closer, bobbing his head. "Yeah, I do."

Leo rubs his forehead. "Guys, this isn't helpful."

I catch myself. He's right. I inhale through my nose and exhale through my mouth like Enoch taught me. "What I can tell you is I know how my world works, and this sounds like a ticking clock to me. Especially with what Enoch heard."

"What did Enoch hear?" Kade asks, exasperated with his own ignorance.

Enoch considers the best delivery and keeps it simple for Kade. "Your journey with Anaya will move on soon."

Kade rolls his eyes. "What journey? Is this about that destiny stuff you talked about?"

I'm tired of twisting myself in half to look at him, so I swap my hands on the chairs and turn to face Kade and Leo. "I don't care how you feel about this, Kade." My voice sounds tired. My energy is exhausted. "I'd like to, but as long as you're acting like that, I don't care. I'll care when you get your priorities straight and start listening, okay?"

He narrows his eyes at me, accepting my challenge. I love knowing what buttons to push to get on his nerves. He's going to prove himself to me, just as he did with Ramiro. I'm not a frail girl to him anymore. I'm the enemy. That's a step in the right direction. Kade respects his enemies.

"We're leaving soon..." Leo scratches his head. "You think Ramiro will kick us out because of..." He glances at me, afraid to say it.

"Actually, I agree with you." I don't need Leo to be afraid of me. He treats me fine as he is. He raised himself, and he did it well. "It's probably going to be my fault." I grin at the irony. "If this weren't such a disaster, I'd almost think it was always part of the Plan just to drag Kade away from here."

Kade stews near the door. I can feel his resentment sitting

right next to my own in my chest. Then something occurs to me. I scrutinize him and he squirms under the attention. "Because you really wouldn't mind staying here, would you? Especially since you can't go back home without Security finding you."

Kade says nothing. His jaw squares, storms in his eyes.

I squint at him. "But you still want to see Danica." He turns away. "I know you do because you blew your cover at the gala just to get her to notice you." I drop my gaze now, pondering. "So that stuck with you, at least."

"Why are you talking about me like I'm not even here?" Kade fumes.

I gape at him. "I'm talking right at you!"

"You're talking to yourself! None of us has a clue what you're saying!"

"Well, some of you would if you'd been more cooperative before!"

The next thing I know, the world spins and Enoch's got his arms under me. I right myself and shake it off. Not a bad dizzy spell that time, but enough to throw me off my feet. I glance around when my vision clears and see concern on Leo's face, but Kade's stony expression has barely cracked.

"If there is movement soon," Enoch says as he lowers me to sit on the ground, "we need Anaya to be ready to go."

I nod at the floor, still a little disoriented. "I doubt it'll be a leisurely exit."

Leo tips his head. "You mean you think there will be an attack?"

I blink a few times to get rid of the stars in my eyes. "You can see it brewing." I meet his eyes, but I'm not very comforting. "If there's extra activity across the lake and we've noticed it, that's a signal." I turn a flat stare on Kade. "That's how we talk to you. You're supposed to understand."

Kade folds his arms and leans against the wall behind him. "So, if I see a snowflake I'd better start canning food for an avalanche?"

I wag a finger at him. "You know, you and I chose this attitude." I control my tone because some of us can adapt to get through this. "We talked about it before you transitioned back here." I can't help the sadness in my voice. Kade was the most exciting assignment I've ever had. I was so honored to meet him, to work with him. It thrilled him to be a part of it as his last excursion into Velt. We clicked. I expected this to be so much fun, maybe even easier than usual.

Now study him, skepticism on his face and a curl in his lip like I've insulted him by suggesting we've spoken before. He doesn't know me, doesn't remember me. A twinge of pain in my heart reminds me of how much I care about what Kade thinks of me.

Heat flushes across my cheeks, and I duck my head to hide it. Even his energy pushes me away.

The silence stretches into awkwardness, but I've said everything I want to say.

"So, we know we're leaving soon..." I smile at Leo's attempt to cheer me up by accepting my story. "But what do we tell Ramiro until then? And do we warn everyone that there might be an attack?"

"How can we do that without sounding like morons?"

"I've been giving Ramiro advice based on visits from Anaya's people for years," Enoch reminds Kade. "Anaya is the reason we knew to prepare for the attack on Phil's gas station." He looks at me and I smile my thanks.

Kade frowns, glancing between the two of us. I seize the chance to read his energy. Confusion at the bond Enoch and I seem to have. Defensiveness, as usual. And resistance to the idea that I was the one to give the notice of the Security attack that brought me here. He can't accept that I'm not a naturally born soul. But also, I pick up on his fear, the fear that recognizing where I'm from means admitting he is at fault. He doesn't want to feel guilty. He'd rather be angry instead.

He catches me staring at him with a victorious grin. I rearrange my features to give him a blank face. I wonder if he understands that I'm still connected to him. Does he feel it?

A soft knock on the door frame drags me away from Kade's energy. I twist around to find Ainsley with a familiar pair of wooden crutches in his hand.

"I felt these might prove useful." He scans the crutches as if they spoke to him, but I know it was his Firn who arranged this.

I throw my head back to thank Mikael for keeping his word and taking care of me. I would thank Ainsley's Firn if I could see him. For a second, I remember that everyone in this room, minus Kade, has a Firn who knows my shame. Does Kade feel my absence like a cold spot where substance used to be, or like a dizzy spell where he used to feel more grounded? Or, since Jordin kept me from him for so long, does it feel like any other day to him? Did he even feel me enough before to miss me now? And did all of Lemayle see it like Enoch did while I carried on kicking metaphysical stones? I sink my teeth into my lip and make myself forget it.

I stare at the crutches and see my freedom in Ainsley's hands.

"Enoch," I wave an excited hand in his direction, "get me up. Get me up."

Enoch laughs as he moves toward me. Leo comes to my aid as well and Ainsley covers the distance between us to prop the crutches under my arms. Despite the pinching of the wood, this is much more comfortable than using the chairs. My arms get a rest and my legs don't have to support all of my weight. This is a leap of progress and I'm thrilled by it. I shift back and forth, getting used to the balance required to make this work.

"These are Leo's, right?"

I smile at the three stunned faces in the room. Yes, I said

it to emphasize what I am. Yes, I enjoy messing with even my favorite living souls. My being from Lemayle is something that will have to sink in gradually, for Kade at least, but everyone will find it hard to believe for a while, no matter how kind they are.

"They are," Ainsley confirms.

"They were," Leo corrects us. He shivers at the memory of the moose that made them necessary.

I take a daring swing forward. My equilibrium abandons me and I almost let go of the crutches to cover my face in case it hits the floor, but I save myself at the last second.

It's official. I'm mobile.

My cheeks hurt but from smiling. Ainsley indulges me in my moment and beams back.

"Thank you." I bow my head to him. "Thank you so much."

"Not a moment too soon," Enoch adds, a touch of relief wafting off him.

Ainsley raises his palms. "This room seemed too confining for a free spirit such as yourself. To come from such a vast space into this one must be a struggle."

I melt at his words. Ainsley gets me. He trusts me. My eyes sting again, but these unshed tears are not sad. It's just nice to have people on my side.

Ainsley turns from me and glances at Kade. He frowns at the childish scowl on Kade's face.

"Once you adjust, Anaya, perhaps I can show you the marvelous complex we're staying at. It's a shame you're confined to the dullest part of it."

I raise an eyebrow at him. Where in the world have we fled to that it's also some kind of fascinating attraction?

"I promise you, I will be ready to be out of here in no time."

Enoch folds his arms and shakes his head. "Don't get ahead of yourself. Prove to me you can cross this room and then I'll let you leave it."

I stand as tall as I can and lift my chin. "You're on."

CHAPTER SIX

I don't make it across the floor before Enoch tells me it's getting late and I'm overworking myself. He takes the crutches with him when he goes because he knows he can't trust me to sleep with them near enough to practice.

I want to be mad, but it's fair. He's right. Every second I spend stuck here is another moment Jordin is helping Jett Tyrrell woo Danica to a place Kade can't save her from. They're Beta Siberia's royal sweethearts already. We're behind, and just thinking about it and doing nothing makes my heart palpitate and my arms go weak.

Help the Reyn Gayst choose. Give her the freedom to choose without interference. Pray to all that is that she sides with us, with El Olam, and not with Narn and his Aropfain.

But I can't do any of that from this stupid, cold floor.

I lie in the darkness, still excited at my ability to get off the floor and determined that tomorrow I will make it across the room and out the door to see what lies beyond this concrete cave.

And in the night, I dream. I dream of a lost era when Jordin was my friend. When the only surprises he had for me made me laugh at him. When he wasn't trying to cut my soul from existence.

Because he knows I'll never complete the Shift. He has to know that. I don't hide my loyalty to El Olam or my ambitions to be an integral part of the Plan. It took centuries of hard work to earn my place at Kade's side for as much of a punishment as it's turned out to be. Jordin was the friend I told too much to. Our bond surpassed professional camaraderie. We joked and shared stories of who we used to be and how many times we'd lived.

He's such a jerk. How could he abandon us right before the most important period in history?

When Enoch knocks on the door, I jolt awake, drained, as though I haven't slept at all. My eyes don't want to open; the light from the hall is offensive. I yawn and indulge in a long stretch while Enoch leans the crutches against the wall and sets a plate of bread and jerky on one of the folding chairs.

"Put the chair on the other side of the room."

Enoch frowns at me with questions in his eyes.

I've grown to love eating. I want that jerky more than I should as someone who resents my physical limitations. So, I'll make myself work for it.

Enoch pieces my plan together and hums his disapproval. "Don't you think you should eat first? You don't want to exhaust yourself right away. Food is our fuel, you know."

"It's also an excellent motivator. Give me the bread and put the jerky over there."

He shakes his head but accepts my terms. He leaves the bread with me and walks across the room with the plate, dragging the chair behind him. It pains me to watch the food walk away. The bread is stale but finished by the time Enoch comes back to help prop me on the crutches.

The plate seems so far away, but the smell of jerky bolsters my resolve. I calculate my strategy. Balance is what I need most. My legs need strength enough to keep me stable as a move, but that's an angles game as much as anything. My hands have to grip and steady the crutches under me—not a strength game, a tactical one. I draw energy to me, careful not to siphon any from Enoch. It drapes over me like an invisible suit that steadies my legs and core.

A solid start is important, so I move the crutches in front of me. The rubber foot of one crutch drags on the floor and twists me. My stomach surges to my throat as I lose my footing, but Enoch is fast at my side.

With a calming breath, I determine, "We'll try that again."

Enoch chuckles and sweeps an arm toward the jerky. "Whenever you're ready."

I push air out of my cheeks, plant my feet, gather energy, swing the sticks. Both land at the same time. My shoulders relax a little and my fingers loosen their white-knuckle grip. I can do this.

Another swing. Another. And another! Look at me go!

I wonder what the terms are if I don't make it the entire way. I don't want to start over. Then again, if I have only enough strength to cross the room, how will I fare outside for more than a few seconds?

The jarring shock of the floor meeting my tailbone answers my question. I yelp and wince as the pain shoots up my spine, straight to the base of my skull.

I release my frustration with an angry "Ow!"

Enoch squats next to me and waits.

I wave a dismissive hand. "Restart. We're doing this right. I'm getting out of here."

He nods and helps me stand. This time, he stays by me as I hobble back to the start. It's shaky. I make more mistakes because I'm upset and shout some more, but when I turn to face the plate of jerky again, I wear my war face.

A few breaths and I'm on my way again. I only need one step more than I got last time.

And that's all I get before my arms buckle and the crutches

fold in on me.

"Again!"

Enoch doesn't need to be told, but I need to yell something that isn't profane.

By my fifth attempt, hunger consumes my thoughts. Two steps from the plate, my knees quiver beyond function. Forget this. I'm having it. With the last bit of strength, I dive toward the chair. My fingers catch the plate and flip it onto my head, showering my hair with beef jerky.

I blow the long brown strands out of my face and wipe the rest away like a cobweb as I roll onto my back. I pat around the floor for the jerky and shove a piece in my mouth, waiting for Enoch to comment. He doesn't.

The process continues for longer than I care to admit. Every other time I fall, I grab another piece of jerky for spite and because my stomach demands it. When only one piece remains, I set it in the middle of the plate and drag myself to the chair to place my trophy for one last chance at victory. No more jerky until success, I tell myself. This is pathetic and I will not seize my prize before I've earned it. (I've already done that, but I won't do it this last time.)

The journey is smoother as I hobble to the other side of the room. Skill supplements my lack of strength, and it's working. I just need to control myself enough to cross this room to master it. Strength will come later.

I level my gaze at that last piece of jerky. I won't take my eyes off it until I've reached the chair. Two crutches, then a swing, and two feet. Focus on the jerky, repeat one swing after the other. When I get closer than before, I push it from my mind. If I pressure myself too much, I'll fall. My arms shudder, my knees turn to jelly, but I have enough. The crutches support me between swings.

And finally, I stand triumphant before this small metal chair as if to conquer its kingdom. A wicked grin spreads to my cheeks.

The smile fades though when I realize something crucial. "I can't reach that." To sit is to crush my prize. To squat down enough to grab it will find me splayed on the floor again. "Enoch!" I whine, exhausted and discouraged after coming all this way. Sweat sticks my hair to my face and my breath comes out in puffs. I don't want to move anymore.

Enoch snickers behind me. He appears at my shoulder and reaches for the plate to make room for me to sit. I thread an arm through one crutch and hold on as I pivot and lower myself, Enoch's hand hovering close just in case.

I melt into the chair and revel in the dry, tough jerky victory, even if it makes my jaw sore just to chew. This is a terrible chair, but right now it's a throne—and I've been royalty before, so I should know. My head lolls back on the headrest and I sit and breathe, trying not to allow reality to creep into the edges of my mind. I just want to enjoy this small, happy moment.

"That was incredible, Anaya." Enoch sits next to me, looking satisfied. "You're making great progress."

"I won't be able to run with crutches though," I point out.

His silence is agreement enough. "But you'll get there," he assures me. "Mikael said he'd watch over you, didn't he?" He wants an answer to be sure he interpreted Mikael's energy correctly. I guess an Avoyde like Enoch can never be sure with only emotions to work with.

I nod at the ceiling. "He did."

He promised. I know he's been working on it. He's the second busiest being in the universe, but he's making exceptions for me. It's only because somehow I'm still needed for the Plan, but I try to believe it's also because we've built a strong rapport over the years. I admire and respect Mikael. I like to think he respects me too.

I feel a spike in the energy and focus on it. If I've got anything left over from Lemayle, I will use it to my advantage. The vibe is hesitant, nervous, protective, loyal, and I try to remember whom I've met who feels the same.

"Leo's here."

There's a soft knock and Leo cracks the door open to poke his head in.

Enoch turns to me with a bright, impressed face. "Nice."

"What's nice?" Leo frowns as he steps into the room.

Enoch waves a dismissive hand. No need to short-circuit Leo's brain with useless information. "Anaya's making great progress, that's all."

I grin at Enoch. It's nice to have a secret with someone. Privacy is a privilege for living souls and I'm more exposed now than I've ever been. Not that I'll keep it for long, but for now it's a secret I can have as my own.

Leo doesn't complain. He has an urgent tension in his eyes that steals my victorious buzz away.

"What's going on?" I lean forward in my chair. The time for comfort appears to be over.

Leo rubs his forehead, massaging the news out of his brain. "I guess you told Ramiro to prepare for an attack?"

Enoch nods, unfazed. He peeks at me, ready for my bewildered reaction. "It was appropriate. We need to make sure we spare as many lives as possible while we escape."

I recover from my astonished expression. Fair enough.

"Well, he's on a rampage." Leo glances at me from the corner of his eye. He's still uncomfortable with me. To him, I'm an alien with unknown abilities. He might as well be wearing a tinfoil hat.

I nod and keep my movements slow so as not to startle Leo. "Ramiro thinks it's my fault."

Leo ducks his head but doesn't look at me. "He does."

"I won't hurt you, you know."

He blinks, eyes wide. Did he think he was hiding his apprehension well?

A laugh slips out. "I may not have been born the same as

you this time around, but I've lived plenty of times. I remember what life is like. We're not too different. I'm just... undead." That was supposed to sound simple and reassuring, but the pallor of Leo's face tells me I missed the mark. Who cares, though? It's accurate even if it isn't comforting.

"You'll get used to it," I reassure Leo, but he doesn't seem so sure.

"Anyway..." Enoch calls our attention back to the matter at hand. "What is Ramiro's plan?"

Leo pauses. He takes more care than I do in choosing his words. "He thinks Anaya has been feeding the Association information somehow."

My eye twitches at Ramiro's logic. I guess it makes the tiniest bit of sense since Association activity stirred after I came to, but that's not enough to connect me with them unless—oh. "He thinks they implanted me with something?" Clever theory. Darn. I don't want to respect Ramiro. Must be the part of me that still roots for Kade.

Leo confirms my suspicion with a nod. "He thinks they've got a homing beacon on you and that you've been transmitting information since you woke up."

"Where would I have kept a radio to 'transmit information'?" They shrink back at my incredulous volume. Not to be indelicate, but the oversized T-shirt and jeans I'm wearing are definitely borrowed and I couldn't have brought clothes through the veil with me.

Leo cringes. "Please don't make me say it."

My mouth opens to demand an answer, but then it clicks. I slap a hand to my face to hide the burning blush in my cheeks. "Please don't say it."

"Anyway..." Enoch pulls us out of the uncomfortable silence once again. "What does he intend to do about it?"

Leo purses his lips to keep from saying it. His eyes flit between Enoch and me, waiting for a reaction, but so am I.

"Spit it out, Leo." My voice strains with impatience. I can't take not knowing.

"He wants you dead."

"Thank you."

"Um, no thank you, actually," Enoch cuts in. "You told him to reconsider, right?"

Leo weaves his head a bit to find words that will satisfy Enoch. "I asked him to..."

"You can't handle confrontation at all, can you?" Leo balks at my flat tone, but he doesn't argue.

Enoch shakes his head at his worn-out shoes. "He's such a loose cannon," he mutters to himself. He lifts his chin, resolved. "I'll fix this." He unfolds his legs and stands. I'm jealous of how easy he makes it look. "Excuse me."

Without waiting for our response, Enoch strides from the room. Leo and I stare at the door long after it closes behind him. I glance at Leo, but he keeps his eyes on the door, chewing his lip, nervous and abandoned.

"Enoch sure takes his job seriously," I break the silence.

Leo does a double take to be sure I'm talking to him. "Uh... yeah. He does."

I grip the sides of my seat and pump my arms with energy to lower myself next to Leo. "Come down here, would you?"

Leo debates with himself but settles to his knees after a moment. He watches with submissive green eyes, ready for me to order him to do something.

I cast my gaze to the concrete floor and pick at a loose thread in my jeans. "Why do I make you so nervous?"

Leo tries conjuring a careful and calculated response, but he fails. Then I see him give up. He drops his head into his hands and groans in frustration.

I pat him on the back. "Let it out."

Leo's shoulders bounce, and I get to see him smile when he sits up.

"You're freaky," he admits at last. I raise my shoulders in an acquiescent shrug. What can I say? He laughs again. "You're from another world!"

"Not so far away, though."

He points at me, a wild look on his face. "That's another thing. You know me. You've said it before, but it's in your eyes and everything."

I squirm under his accusation. "Well... yeah... Is that bad?"

"No!"

I lean away from him. "That came out too quickly."

He scratches the back of his neck. "Yeah. Yeah, it did. Sorry."

I punch his shoulder the way I've seen Kade do countless times. He grabs where I punched. My feeble arms can't hurt him, but he recognizes the gesture.

He stares toward the wall at nothing, out of breath. "You really were there. The whole time." He narrows his eyes at me. "Weren't you?"

I glance to the side and then back at him. "Not exactly hiding it."

His fingers thread through his hair. "Guess not..."

I watch Leo's mind explode as the revelation settles on him. My nerves relax at acquiring a new ally. That makes three: Ainsley, Enoch, and Leo. Good enough for now.

"So, you and Kade..." Leo drifts off.

I lift a defensive eyebrow. "What about us?"

"What happened?"

I open my mouth, but the answer isn't simple. I shrug, lost for words. "Kade was incredible when we talked before he came here. Best Neshome I'd ever met."

"Neshome?"

"That's what we call you." Anyway. "Kade was confident, had lived plenty, knew the job, and was even excited about it." I tilt my head. "Of course, who wouldn't be with a purpose like his? It was built in that he finds the love of his life if he plays by the rules." Unless an Aropfain like Jordin interferes and breaks all the rules first. After all this, it'll be a miracle if Kade ever lays eyes on the Reyn Gayst again.

"Danica?" Leo guesses in response to my implication of Kade's Velt soul mate. Kade and Danica can't be soul mates like Jordin and I are. Danica's brand new and everything stops after she chooses between El Olam's case for eternal free will and Narn's scheme for predetermination, so there's no time and no point in pairing souls up for multiple life missions anymore.

I nod, pleased with myself. "Danica."

Leo's jaw drops as it clicks. "So that's why he's weird about her."

"The one thing that stuck with him when he came here." Hormones again.

Leo frowns at me. "Why Danica?"

I shift into a more comfortable position and put my hands in front of me to preface my explanation. "You know how every epic story has a hero that is the only one who can save the world?"

Leo nods but leans away with apprehension. "That's not Kade, is it?"

"Oh, heavens no."

"Oh good," he blurts out, gripping his chest.

We both take a breath to recover from the thought.

Then I drop the smile playing at the corner of my mouth to gaze deep into his eyes.

"It's you."

He stops breathing. A hand reaches out to grab the chair for support, and I truly think he may have a heart attack.

"Wow, calm down!" I reach for his arm to ground him. "I'm kidding. It's not you."

Leo chokes for air, and his whole body falls limp. He leans

forward to cough.

"Sheesh," I say. "Good thing, too, if that's how you'd handle it."

He glares at me with bloodshot eyes. "That was mean," he rasps, and I can't help myself.

I burst into laughter, tipping backward and falling to the floor. Tears gather in my eyes, but this time it's from overwhelming images of Leo's petrified face in my mind. I think I hear Leo laugh too, which is a relief. I don't want to lose his trust this early, but I just couldn't help myself. My situation is awful. I'll cling to every speck of humor I can find.

As I recover from my cathartic spell, I prop myself on my elbows to wipe a tear from my eye.

"I'm sorry," I apologize between gasps. "I'm sorry. It was too good to pass up."

"Well, now I believe you've been with Kade his whole life."

Poor Leo. I'm glad he puts up with us so well. "But really..." Our laughter fades and the conversation takes a somber turn. Leo leans in closer to pay attention.

"Danica is the one who's going to 'save the world.'" I quote the words in the air. "She's the Reyn Gayst, a soul born for the first time and without a Firn to guide her. Every choice she makes is unaffected by a Firn or Aropfain. She's our ultimate evaluation."

"Evaluation? So, she just has to judge something for you?"

I shake my head. "She has to judge between something. You've heard stories of good versus evil. They're popular because they are the faintest memories left from what your souls remember of El Olam and Narn. The big guys."

Leo leans back to rest on his hands. "The big guys..." He turns the thought over in his head. "Ultimate good and ultimate evil?"

I pick up the doubt in his voice. "Yes, and no." Now I have his attention. I stare at my hands, trying to decide how to put this. "On one hand," the right hand, "you have El Olam. He's got a theory that souls should make choices for themselves and learn from mistakes. Trial and error. That sort of thing." For the sake of my profession, I keep my tone the same for the rest of my explanation. "On the other hand, you have Narn." My expression turns sour at my left hand. "He thinks free will is a dumb idea because souls constantly make terrible decisions that took them down a very weird path a long time ago, and you haven't quite found your way back since."

Leo holds a finger to his cheek. "So, which one do you side with, then?"

I grin because if he doesn't know, then I did a decent job hiding my bias. "Which do you think?"

Leo rolls his eyes. "Now you sound like Ainsley."

"I like Ainsley. He's an excellent teacher."

Leo smacks the floor because he knows I won't give him any hints, and he doesn't want to be wrong in front of someone who understands better than he does.

But this is what El Olam stands for. He encourages choices. He sends us to illuminate the correct choice, and if you're smart and don't have an Aropfain messing with your head, you listen.

"Not easy, is it?" I ask when Leo's struggle becomes too pitiful.

He stares at the floor like the answers should be there for him to study. "It really isn't. It sounds like it would be foolish to side with El Olam if people consistently disappoint him, but Narn has no right to take away people's freedom, just like the Association." He cocks his head at me. "And you're sent by one of them..."

Oh, good. He's figuring it out.

"It must be El Olam. You wouldn't be so angry at Kade otherwise. You'd have forced his hand long ago."

I point a finger at him and nod. "Correct."

"And you need Kade to get to Danica... She's the chosen one..."

"The choosing one," I supply, but he doesn't laugh at my joke.

"How does Kade get Danica to choose? By making her fall for him? That doesn't sound fair either."

Ah. See, here's the problem: I can't tell him all of Kade's purpose. It isn't for anyone to know. It could ruin everything—and I don't remember the details myself. The memory feels close, but teasingly out of reach, like I lost access when I came through to Velt. There was something all my Neshomes had in common, beyond moving the Plan along in leaps toward its completion. Something I specialize in, but what is it? I press my memory for clues, but nothing comes beyond the wispy curl of a faded memory. So, I keep it simple. "She has a choice, though. She could choose Kade, or she could choose Jett." I spit his name out. "She could even choose neither, but the culture in Nor'ilsk wouldn't approve of that."

Leo nods and his head perks up, eyebrows knit with another epiphany. "Wait, then you're saying the Association is..."

I nod. That's exactly what the Association is. I mean, really, they're not working for El Olam.

Leo slaps a hand to the side of his face, and it slides away. "That makes so much sense."

"Doesn't it though?"

When Leo's eyes return to mine, I see understanding. I've got him on my side. I'm so relieved I could sleep.

"I'm sorry," Leo says out of nowhere.

"It's not your fault," I assure him.

He chews the inside of his cheek. "Is it Kade's?"

I want to say "yes" so badly, but we have an honest thing going here.

"No." I shake my head, accepting what Enoch pointed out

about Jordin ruining my connection with Kade. "No, it's not his fault, either."

A short while later, the door opens again, interrupting Leo's and my mundane conversation about fish bait, his livelihood. I expect Enoch with grave news of my impending murder, but Ainsley steps in instead.

"Good afternoon, Anaya."

My jaw drops. "Afternoon already?"

Ainsley's eyes wrinkle at the corners with a sad smile. "Must be terribly difficult to tell time in here."

Leo looks around the room. "You don't even have a clock," he realizes.

"I have no idea how long I've been here," I sulk. "Conscious or otherwise."

Ainsley nods at his own idea. He crosses the room and gathers my crutches, holding them out. "I think it's time you see the sun, hmm?"

My heart leaps at the mention of daylight. I love the sun. I hate concrete. You can imagine the excitement here.

"You are in too fascinating a place to stay cooped up in a drab room."

I study Ainsley's features, wondering where in Beta Siberia I am that could be so fascinating. Leo helps me to my feet, and I'm not concerned about exhaustion. I'm ready to go.

"Do we have time?"

I spin on Leo for questioning my right to freedom after the talk we had—I thought we were friends now.

He balks at the heat of my glare. "I mean, before the attack," he amends quickly.

I turn and aim my grievance toward Ainsley. He's less stricken.

"I have Enoch's approval. He's consulted with his..."

Ainsley considers his words for my sake, "... contacts." Good choice. "We have the time."

"Then get me out of here." I urge them with a wave of one crutch toward the door.

"Ah, ah, ah," Ainsley wags a contrary finger, "you need something first."

I pull my hair in frustration and grimace at how greasy it is. "You're killing me."

Ainsley chuckles as he reaches into a bag on his shoulder that I hadn't noticed before. With old, shaky hands, he produces a weathered pair of boots and a moth-eaten wool coat. My arms tingle in anticipation of the warmth. There's been a chill in my bones since I first woke up from the concrete, but we're in Siberian winter. I'll take any extra layers I can get.

"I can only imagine Ramiro put up a fight over this," I muse as Leo helps slip the coat over my arms.

"He doesn't want you to feel too comfortable here," Ainsley admits. "But he's a troubled young man. I hope you'll forgive him."

I shrug the coat onto my shoulders. "He's lost a lot. I remember Kade pointing it out."

Leo frowns as he holds the shoes for me to shift into and adjusts the crutches for me. It'll take a while for him to adjust to how much I know.

I test my balance and bounce with excitement. Ainsley extends an arm, offering for me to go ahead of him. I set my sights on the door like it's an entire stack of jerky and remember to pace myself as I toddle forward. My first step over the threshold is a giant leap toward independence—and escape from my prison. I'm sure Leo understands that feeling. I glance down the hall to my left and my right.

"Which way?" I don't care where we go. Just get me there.

Ainsley sweeps an arm to the right, and I'm off. My heart

pounds like a rabbit's, a smile stretched across my face, but in reality, I move slower than Ainsley and I notice Leo take shorter steps to stay at my side. Who cares? I'm moving. I'm walking. I'm out.

"I'm going to check on Enoch and see if there's anything he needs to be ready for the attack," Leo announces. I can tell by the frightened gleam in his eyes that the threat of another ambush has him rattled. But we're destined to survive and so are at least some of the Lost Boys. Why worry? Regardless, he leaves us and takes the left turn.

Ainsley and I shuffle side by side for a while, making our way to the front of the building. If I had to guess, it's some kind of old office building. Rooms and public bathrooms line the halls and a registration desk sits at the front, facing sliding glass doors and windows. I suspect the doors were once automatic, but they are still and shattered now. Everything has a layer of dust, with random papers or office supplies scattered here and there. They did not abandon it in a hurry, but no one took care to pack up when they left, either.

I shiver, but I do my best to hide it for fear they'll rip this opportunity away from me because this body can't tolerate the icy breeze sweeping through the broken glass. I want to be here, moving in open spaces, to feel my surroundings. In a way, the cold is a blessing. The human part of me is trying to connect with the environment. It's an instinct of living souls, so I ignore the sting of being one now. Except, I remember, I spend half my time making fun of them.

A dusting of snow on the floor mixes with shards of glass and now I understand why Ainsley gave me these clunky shoes and the coat. Winter accepted the invitation of broken glass.

It's the doors I'm interested in, though, or rather the sunlight beyond them. It is indeed the afternoon. I want to see it all before the daylight fades. I push myself to reach the door faster. Just let the sun touch my cheeks and then I'll slow down.

It's a trick to step over the metal frame and glass fragments, but Ainsley helps. His fingers curl around my arm so I can focus on the ground, careful not to place my crutch on a piece of glass or anything else that might slip out from under me. One crutch, left foot, the other crutch, right foot, like an uncoordinated giraffe. When I lift my face, I take in a crisp and clear blue sky. Here come the tears again. No matter how abandoned I am, the sky reminds me of how big the world is. I remember the bigger purpose—all the cogs and wheels that keep events according to Plan. I think of the other Firns like me, at their Neshome's side, and I try not to think of the one with Ainsley and how pathetic I must've looked to them just now. As long as the blue sky is above me, I can relax. I'm safe.

With a shake to clear my head of rising anxiety, I check out the complex. My eyes spring open in recognition and I almost lose my footing. "Oh, Taltsy!"

Ainsley grins at my knowledge.

"Hey—Ainsley!"

I'd recognize the voice anywhere. My joy flatlines and I prepare the most sarcastic posture I can while propped up like this.

"Ah, Mr. Buxton. I'm glad you joined us."

"You asked me to," Kade grumbles, eyeing me to make sure I know he doesn't want to be here. I glare back at him.

But then I remember the real culprit. "You played me, Ainsley."

Ainsley raises a finger to specify. "I promised an interesting walk."

My brow furrows, and I glance round, desperate. I want to see this place. I never made a list of places to see between Neshomes, but this would make the cut if I had. Even if my company could be better, I'm not missing this chance.

"So, you understand where we are." Ainsley resumes his tour. "I'm impressed."

Clever diversion.

I survey the log buildings and Lake Baikal just behind them, ignoring what will come across the water any moment now. The structures are impressive. Taltsy is an abandoned village of the Buryat people that Phil is always so fired up about.

"This is the Taltsy open-air ethnic museum." The fact rolls off my tongue, drawn from a library of memories I kept through the Shift. Normally, the Plan would provide information like that, about where I am and what I need to focus on, but this is different. I don't feel the telltale fizz at the top of my skull, the quiet voice threading information to me. I just... remember Taltsy.

"This was a good time to be alive." It comes out sadder than I mean it to. "Not that I was, but the people were good."

Kade's lip curls with contempt. "Teacher's pet."

"If only you would have been," I trill back.

He draws closer and hollers, "Stop blaming me for your terrible guiding skills!"

My posture matches his before I can think, caught up in the frenzy of Kade's aggressive energy, outdoing his volume. "I'm not talking about with me. I'm talking about Ainsley!"

"Children."

"What?" we yell together and swing our heads toward Ainsley. I hate that.

"I brought you both here to show you something. Will you indulge me?"

Kade turns his back to me while I sulk at being so gracefully scolded. But who can argue with Ainsley? We say nothing and that's confirmation enough.

Ainsley nods at our submission. "Follow me." He leads us toward the village structures, and I shove down my excitement. I'm not done being angry yet. I have so many emotions now that I'm back in Velt and I can't seem to handle more than one at a time.

"Do any of these appear familiar to you, Mr. Buxton?"

Kade glares at the surrounding buildings. "No," he spits out. "I don't even know what any of this is."

I sling my eyes to the sky, seeking the strength to deal with him. Ainsley catches me.

"Would you care to explain, Anaya? But kindly, please."

Wow. It does sting to be corrected by Ainsley. My sour attitude flees at his words, and Kade snickers at me. I'll show him.

"They're culturally significant buildings," I begin, "from the Buryat: old mills, houses, places of worship. It used to be a village, but they preserved it as a museum when everyone had to leave. They used to have festivals here for all the different old holidays. Their way of celebrating what they thought they remembered of Lemayle." I shake my head, but it was always fun to watch living souls try to guess what Lemayle is like.

"The angels and the demons." Kade tries to keep up with my intellect. That's a race he will lose.

"Very good, Anaya, though I should expect as much, shouldn't I?"

My victory is still sweet. Kade's jealous pout makes me want to laugh at first, but then a pang of guilt catches in my throat. The connection between a Firn and their Neshome is not to be taken lightly. Kade's mother treasures him because she carried him for nine months, raised him, watched him grow. But I designed Kade's personality with him before he was even conceived. I labored over his fate and his role in the Plan with him, picked which interests would benefit his purpose and help him enjoy what he needed to do. This competitive streak he's showing right now? We agreed to it as a motivator for him to give his best to everything he does.

Things didn't go as we'd hoped. He should have heard me

as his voice of reason to reinforce the inherent personality, but that didn't happen. He's got a fair amount of flaws because of it.

"What does this have to do with anything?" Kade complains. His frustration flows from him in waves and clouds my thoughts.

I weave on my feet for a second. Ainsley moves to steady me, but it's Kade who catches my arm in a rough grip.

"Get a hold of yourself," he grumbles before he lets go.

Though I'm still wobbly, I can't help but note that Kade cares. He doesn't want to, but he was born a gentleman so he'd stand a chance at wooing Danica. Perhaps it's not so bad being a girl now. Instead of a handicap, maybe I can use it to my advantage with Kade's chivalrous nature.

Ainsley watches me until I find solid ground. Once I steady myself, I nod at him. He looks me over and seems satisfied. "Let's move along."

We continue down a path lined with wooden houses and buildings of various functions. It's hard to believe this used to be a village. People walked these paths every day. Now it stands as an empty shell of the ever-vanishing past.

Frigid wind sweeps off the frozen lake to our right, stinging my cheeks and stealing my breath. I stiffen and clutch the coat tighter to my face. Ainsley and Kade bear the cold with a brief shiver, but I haven't needed oxygen until recently. It's unnerving to have it whisked away.

I turn my face into my collar and breathe into it despite the moldy smell. My fingers numb and prickle with a needle-like sensation. The lack of circulation from the crutches pinching underneath my arms isn't helping. I am not a fan of the cold. I concentrate on my breathing, relishing in the heat that rushes across my cheeks whenever I breathe into the wool.

Ainsley stops us in front of the old wooden church. Three

spires line the roof, each a unique design topped with an Orthodox cross. "Shall we go inside?"

Kade shrugs, hands in his leather coat pockets, while I exaggerate a nod so Ainsley doesn't miss it. I don't want to expose my face to the air long enough to speak.

Ainsley places a guiding hand on my back, and we make for the entrance. "Will you get the door, Mr. Buxton? They are rather heavy."

Kade does as he's asked but groans at my weakness. When the door creaks shut, the world falls silent save for a few whistles in the eaves. The wind can't hurt me here. I hustle toward the nearest wall and drop the crutches to rub my arms and compose myself.

"There is no reason for wind to be like that."

Kade's eyes glint with confused curiosity. He doesn't want to accept my ethereal background, but he's right to think that no one in Beta Siberia would be this sensitive to biting air.

"I'm not from here." I draw it out so it sinks in for him.

Ainsley reaches an arm toward me. "Come. You can have a seat over here." I lean on Ainsley, who sends Kade a look. Kade drags his feet but lets me rest an elbow on his shoulder rather than prop myself up on the crutches again. It's a team effort to reach the wooden benches that form two columns in the middle of the room leading to a small, ornate altar, robbed of its finery long ago.

My whole body unwinds when I sit down. Ainsley sits next to me and Kade finds a place on the bench across from us, waiting to get to the point of this walk.

"What do you see here, Mr. Buxton?" Ainsley lifts his hands to the church around us and I try to guess what Kade's answer will be.

I'm voting he'll make up something about this being a church, but I know his history. Kade's never heard, and certainly never read, anything about Old World religions.

"It's a place of worship."

I scoff—not so much at Kade's answer, but more at what his answer means these days. People worship nothing but property and government anymore. It stings for souls like me. I lean back a little and cross my legs. "And what does 'worship' mean?"

He glares at me for calling his bluff.

Ainsley intervenes before the fight breaks out. "It is, in fact, a place of worship, Mr. Buxton. Well observed."

Kade smirks at me. I suppose it was a good guess.

"You're sitting in a place where people came together under a common belief." I'm swept up in awe at the classic teaching tone I've always admired about Ainsley. It should offend me to be on the receiving end of a living soul's teaching, but this isn't just any living soul. Any wisdom worth anything Kade has gleaned in his life has come from this man. In a time when I've never been so powerless, I can't help but recognize that Ainsley hears the signals from his Firn loud and clear. This is another message from Lemayle that I can use to find my way through this mess. So, I lean in and listen up.

"Places such as this gave people common ground, gave them something to share with each other," Ainsley explains. He sets his faded blue eyes on me over the rims of his glasses, and I get the message. I cast my glance down to my hands folded in my lap.

"It doesn't matter how you interpret the ways of the world around you. When you find a truth and a purpose, you must pursue it." He directs that at Kade. I watch Kade's head fall, too.

"Anaya." I startle to attention. "As someone from beyond this world, I imagine you know more of the truth than we've had access to."

I pause, unsure what he's getting at. "Yes..."

"Is there anything you think is important to share with us at this point in time?"

I cock my head and flip through my mental notes of what

I know and what I can share. I may have retained the truth from Lemayle, but I lost my access to the Plan. All I know now is how things end—it would be stupid of me to forget something that important—but Kade's specific next steps, where he needs to go on his way to Danica, are lost on me.

It's for the best though, I realize. If I knew, I could tell Kade outright what to do and compromise his freedom to choose. Once again, free will trumps all. That doesn't help me keep the Plan on course, but those are the rules. Free will first, but do your best to suggest your Neshome stick to their purpose. No one promised it would be easy.

"Not much," is the response I settle on. "I've lost a lot of the details."

"Well, some guardian angel you turned out to be," Kade grouses, folding his arms and looking offended.

I stick a thumb to my collarbone. "Hey, I'm the best," I tell him. "That's why you got me. We can't afford any major screw-ups this late in the game."

Kade's eyes scan me up and down and I realize I walked right into this. "Can't afford major screwups? What would you call this, then?" He untucks one arm just to gesture at my less-than-stellar condition.

I tip my head and look him in the eye. The swirling mix of his and my anger makes me want to snap at him, but I need to keep in mind the truth. It's not Kade's fault.

It's not Kade's fault.

I want it to be Kade's fault, but it's not.

So, I search my brain for the best and least aggressive response, which turns out to be, "Unforeseen complications."

Kade stands abruptly and towers over me. I give him a skeptical look. Does he think he's going to fight me?

"I'm tired of you passing off the blame to me."

I can't get up on my own. My legs are still too jittery from the cold, so I make my voice stand for me, composing my tone with every ounce of control I have in this mess of emotions. Even so, it comes through a stiff jaw. "I'm not passing anything to you, Kade." Least of all, wisdom...

Next to me, Ainsley rubs his temples. Not quite the outcome he was hoping for, I suppose.

"You fell out of a Security truck," Kade shouts, one finger in the air to start his list of grievances. "You wake up and the first thing you do is blame me for some fake Plan to do who-knows-what and tell me you don't want me around and somehow the end of the world is my fault. What kind of psycho are you?"

"Mr. Buxton, try to calm down." Ainsley said. Ever the diplomat. "How about a change of subject?" he offers, voice laced with frustration and disappointment. I want to make it better, but every time Kade opens his mouth, I'm overwhelmed with anger. My fingers curl in my lap, trying to control my own emotions and block out the hostility coming from Kade.

"Anaya." Ainsley turns to me with curiosity. "If you're to escape here and go out into the world with Mr. Buxton, what will you call yourself?"

"Huh?" Fair question, but random.

"You'll need a name. I imagine you'll prefer an alias. At the least, you'll need a surname to give people should they ask."

Oh. He's right. I don't have a surname in Lemayle. We don't need them. Everyone has a unique name and feel about them. Lemayle is expansive and cozy all at once. With so many souls there, working or otherwise, we exist at different levels, even there. Working souls like me rarely see a soul who's enjoying their eternal rest and they don't spare a thought about us.

I'm not the most creative soul, and I've never wondered what I might name myself if I came back to Velt because I never wanted to come back. I sift through the ancient memories of my past lives.

"Agnes."

Kade snorts, but I ignore him.

I recall that life and smile. "Agnes DiRoma."

"What kind of name is that?"

I shoot Kade my most piercing glare. I get that he's upset with me, but that's no reason to insult Agnes. "It's the name of a girl who was a martyr and a saint. Someone who believed in her purpose deep enough to die for it."

"Why would anyone do that?" To my dismay, his confusion sounds genuine. I glance at Ainsley, who dips his head, disappointed. Where did we go wrong? How can Kade be so insensitive? He doesn't seem to care that Agnes was me. That he's insulting my choices, my death.

I clutch at my chest as my heart thumps again. Of all my lives, Agnes was the last. She died for what she believed and finished my efforts in Velt, granting me the right to stay in Lemayle and begin my work for El Olam. She is a precious part of me, and I've always been proud of her. "Because sometimes the truth is undesirable, Kade. Sometimes people don't like to hear it, and they destroy the ones who might spread it. Agnes was only twelve when she died. How can you look down on her for being that brave?"

Kade shuts up but fidgets in his seat, looking away from me. I've stumped him, but in typical Kade fashion, he doesn't handle losing an argument well.

"Sorry, Ainsley. I'm done." He makes a show of lumbering out of the church and Ainsley watches him go. I don't. Turning would tip me over and give Kade the last laugh.

The echo of the door bounces off the walls, and Ainsley slides his disapproving gaze to me. I know that look. I've stood by Kade as he received that look countless times, but Ainsley's eyes were never on me. It's Ainsley's disappointed face.

"Sorry..."

"You know,..." Ainsley faces the altar, rubbing his bristled chin. "I believe you. Your story sounds nothing like the religions I've read about, but I believe you."

"Thank... you...?"

"As I understand it, you need Kade to do something important."

My head falls back, and I choke down a disrespectful groan. I get where this is going. "So, I should probably try to earn his trust a little better than that. I know."

Ainsley lifts his shoulders and looks away. "You know better than I."

I stare at the wooden planks on the floor, trying to smile but failing. "You know, Ainsley... I'm not so sure anymore..."

Behind us, the door opens again, bringing a frosty draft with it. I clutch at Ainsley's sleeve so I can turn to see.

With a taut chest, I catch myself hoping it's Kade so I can apologize. But it's Enoch. He enters the church with purpose, taking in the sanctuary as he strides our way.

"Is everything all right, Enoch?" Ainsley asks as Enoch sinks down on the bench that Kade left.

Enoch's shoulders hunch up to his ears, his face pulls into a heavy frown. Someone from Lemayle must have his ear.

I hold up a hand to Ainsley, signaling that Enoch needs a moment. When Enoch's face relaxes, and he sighs, I ask, "How long do we have?"

His eyes find mine, glazed with appreciation at my understanding. "A day?" He doesn't seem sure. Whoever gave him the news must not have given him more than feelings to go by. "Maybe? It felt soon. Like we need to hurry." His words puff out into the cold. "We certainly won't be here for very much longer. They'll raze this whole place to the ground when they get here." A chill runs through him. He saw what will happen. That's no easy burden to bear. I picture the wooden structures of Taltsy burning in the cold Siberian night. I shiver too.

Ainsley looks surprised. Predictions of chaos aren't easy to take, especially when they haven't been a thing for centuries, even false ones. I face him and place a hand on his arm.

"We'll need an escape plan. Do the Lost Boys have another place to go?"

Ainsley blinks at the name Kade gave to the group led by Phillip, Ainsley, and Ramiro when they first captured us. I smile to acknowledge that I realize what I just said.

"Yes..." he reveals after a moment. "We have several places that have yet to be discovered by Security."

"That only leaves one question." I stare at Enoch and take a steady breath. "How does it have to go? How close do we have to cut it for Security to believe they've wiped us out?"

Enoch curls over his knees like he might be sick. "It has to be very close. I..." he drops his head to his hands, the images still fresh in his mind, "I don't know if everyone will make it."

"Hey."

He looks up at me with glossy eyes.

"We're going to plan this out as much as we can. We'll do whatever we can, but I want you to remember something in case the worst happens." I have their attention now. They lean in and hold their breath in anticipation. I hope what I have to say is as encouraging as I intend for it to be.

"I'm living proof—" I cut myself off with an ironic laugh. "I'm living proof that there is an afterlife. You've seen us your whole life. You know there's more than this." My finger twirls to indicate the room. "And remember, every one of you has a Firn by your side. If you trust your instincts, you'll help them get you out alive." I lean down to catch Enoch's eyes with mine. "None of this is your responsibility. You are saving lives by knowing what's going to happen. Don't think any losses are your fault. Just tell everyone to stay sharp and go with their guts. My people will do the rest. We'll cover you."

Enoch smiles at me but says nothing. I can't stand not knowing things, so I reach out to his energy and determine he took comfort from my words. If he'll remember them, should the worst happen, is out of my hands.

"So, it's time to come up with some solutions." I sit back, realizing that I can't just swoop around at Kade's side like I used to. I will have to run with the rest of them.

But a few days aren't enough for me to learn to run on my own.

Now I'm the one who needs a pep talk.

Back in my empty room, I wrestle with the panic threatening to steal my breath. Just this morning, my progress thrilled me, but I forgot we're on a tight schedule.

Everyone else has a job to do in planning the escape, and I'm alone. I don't know what they're doing, what steps they're taking, what ideas they think will work best. I'm used to being in the thick of things, adding my suggestion to the mix and hoping Kade would subconsciously agree. But now I'm out of commission and a liability. I can't expect Enoch to drag me around with him to keep me involved.

I hate how quiet the room is. I haven't been alone since my last life. And even Agnes didn't get much time to herself in her twelve years of life as a stubborn girl in fourth-century Rome. I don't enjoy being alone. So many times I thought I would love just a little time on my own, but this solitary misery is not what I meant.

As I sit on the floor sulking into my knees, a whoosh of energy brushes my cheek. My head whips up. I know this energy. I've been waiting for this energy to come.

"Mikael, help me out here," I plead the moment I see him standing in the corner. I sound desperate. I guess I am.

Mikael crosses the space between us and lowers himself to sit next to me. Even that seems graceful and poignant. I watch him, waiting. A blizzard of questions and complaints fills my head, but I can't pin one down to start with. Answers and guidance are what I need. I want to hear that this was all a mistake and Mikael will fix it. I'd love for him to tell me I won't vanish once this body gives out, or at least maybe that I'll make it long enough to see Kade to Danica.

"How are you faring?" Mikael asks. He seems uncomfortable, like he shouldn't be here.

"Not so great," I confess. "Only a few days? That's all we get? Have you seen me?"

He nods. "You have every right to be anxious, Anaya."

I shut my eyes against his pity. "Don't do that, Mikael. Please, don't treat me like a living soul. I can't take it."

"I am sorry, Anaya. I truly am."

I give him a pleading look, and I don't hold it back. "Then help me! The Association will destroy this place in a few days, and I can barely crawl across the floor without crutches. How do you expect me to get Kade on his way while I'm in this condition?"

Mikael smiles. "That is why I'm here."

I quirk an eyebrow at him. I dare not guess what he means by that.

Mikael grimaces, but with a joyous glint in his eye that I'll cling to until he gets to the good news.

"Jett Tyrrell is planning a wedding," Mikael reveals. He's far too calm about it. Meanwhile, I've forgotten how to function, jaw slack, breath caught in my throat.

"Since when have we concerned ourselves with someone's wedding plans?" It's a joke, obviously. This is the worst news ever. Jett Tyrrell is the Chairman's son, the functional prince of Beta Siberia. And he's been playing into Jordin's hands to become Kade's competition. He announced a competition to find a wife in Nor'ilsk and—shocker—he picked Danica. Jett is planning a wedding with Danica.

"The attack should push Kade into moving on," Mikael

continues. "We need him in position."

"Yep. No arguments here. Kade's got to get going…" Mikael breaks into an amused grin and waits for me to finish. "And I'm supposed to help how?"

"Kade needs your help to understand his role." Mikael clears his throat, something a Malekh doesn't need to do. "It hasn't been going well so far."

"Ah, you've noticed, have you?"

"Anaya, I understand your anger and confusion, but you need to resolve your issues with Kade and learn to cope with his energy. The Plan depends on it."

"Does it?" I ask sarcastically. "I'm sorry. My priorities have been out of order recently. Maybe once I can pick myself up off the floor, my outlook will improve. Oh, wait, this place is getting roasted tomorrow."

"If I told you I brought something to help with that, would you adjust your attitude?" The irritation in Mikael's voice reminds me to check myself. Ainsley's disappointment is nothing compared to an agitated Malekh. I stare at the concrete in shame. This is still Mikael, the one who fights for me where no one else can.

"It would," I mutter by way of apology.

He nods. "I can help you walk, and even run, but you must be careful with it."

My ears perk up when he says I'll be able to run.

"What is it? Do it! I'm in."

Mikael stops me with a cautionary finger. At first, I worry I'll have to wait and my spirit deflates, but then the finger moves. He touches the center of my chest and a jolt of electricity shocks through me. I bolt against the wall, knocking my head on the concrete, but I don't care because the strength in my arms, legs, core, and back cancels out the pain. I feel sturdy and I realize before even trying that I can stand.

So, I do. I hop to my feet, leap into the air—because I can!

Mikael tugs my arm until I sink to the floor, sitting up with my own power rather than slumping in a weak heap. I can't wipe the satisfied grin from my face.

"Be careful with this gift, Anaya. It doesn't reduce your limits. It gives you more energy. Don't waste it."

I hear him, but it's difficult to listen. I can walk! Oh, wait until Kade sees me. Suddenly, I'm not so afraid of the attack anymore. Like I said, it's destiny for us to survive as long as no one screws anything up.

"So, when is the ambush?"

Mikael pins me with a stern expression. He can't tell me. He knows everything, but I can't. I deserve a few exceptions here, but it hits me that, from Lemayle's perspective, I'm an outlaw.

"Mikael..." My voice is small. I'm afraid of the answer, but I need to ask. "Am I just doomed to wander now? What happens to me if this body doesn't last? Am I forsaken? " I spit it out before the archaic, forbidden words choke me. "Has El Olam—"

Mikael grips my wrist. "We have not written you out of the Plan, Anaya." My vision blurs with more infernal tears. "It pains me to admit that El Olam remains silent on the matter, but you are still necessary, so you are not forsaken. Not while you still stand with us."

"I'm lucky I can stand for anything..."

"You have plenty to stand for, and you have a place to stand."

I smile, tears rolling past my ears from looking up at him.

The door opens and Kade steps in with a plate of bread and jerky. Guess it's dinnertime. He sees the weepy mess I'm in and balks at it. "What's wrong with you?"

I roll my eyes and say nothing because I'm in front of management.

Kade snorts and crosses the room to set the jerky down, leaving his back to Mikael and me, and I get an idea.

"Mikael…" I keep my voice low, but Mikael picks it up fine. He lowers his ear to me. "Can you test something for me? Just see if you can make Kade feel something."

Mikael grins with wicked amusement. He checks his expanded version of the Plan with an upward glance. Where my access outlined Kade's progress and placement, Mikael has a general overview plus a rule book.

After a moment, he's satisfied. He raises his hand toward Kade's back and fizzing energy gathers around his open palm. It zooms across the room, and I keep my eyes glued to Kade.

This is my proof. This will show me how sensitive Kade really is. He's not an Avoyde like Enoch because he has no clue that Mikael—an imposing presence to anyone with even a slight awareness of us—is here. But that doesn't mean he's less than average. I need to know.

Just as the energy reaches the middle of Kade's back, a shudder rushes up his spine. He stands up straight and spins on me with a glare. "Did you just throw something at me?"

I try to appear innocent, but I can't help the shock on my face. I shake my head, both in response to Kade and in disbelief.

Kade mumbles about how weird I am and stalks out of the room in a hurry. I gawk at Mikael.

"He's…" I point to where Kade stood when the energy hit him. "He's…"

"Rather sensitive, it seems," Mikael finishes for me.

And now I'm angry. I push myself to my knees to look Mikael in the eyes and poke an accusing finger at his arm and remind myself to stew about it later because Mikael can touch me, but I go straight through him. "You knew."

Mikael smiles. Not helping.

"You knew Kade was sensitive to us. He's no Enoch, but he's got talent, and you knew! Mikael, I've been killing myself for twenty years!"

"I counseled you," is all he says.

I fall back onto my heels. "None of this makes sense." Everything I knew was wrong. I was wrong.

"Anaya, this isn't over." I squint at him like he's insane, but he doesn't blink. "If the Plan is unchanged, then all is not lost and you can still succeed. You received what you asked for if you think about it. You can communicate with Kade more than any other Firn."

"At the cost of my existence!" I remind him.

He ducks his head. He doesn't want to think about it. Neither do I, but I won't act like I wanted this. I asked for help with Kade, not to perish afterward. When El Olam wins, I want to be there to see it. I want to be here to enjoy watching every soul earn their freedom to choose without intimidation and manipulation from Narn. There's so much I dreamed of seeing. I always imagined guiding a living soul without Aropfain like Jordin getting in the way. I want to know what happens after this event we've spent all of history preparing for.

"Anaya, please don't cry."

"I'm not crying."

Mikael brushes a tear from my cheek and shows it to me. His touch is warm and laced with happiness, the purest energy of Lemayle, a reminder of what we all deserve. But the joy feels fake.

"You have a choice, Anaya." He says it, but I can tell he doesn't want to acknowledge my options.

"I'm not Shifting, Mikael." I wipe my nose on my sleeve—I don't care if it's not polite. It's annoying. "I never would. I'd sooner die, and I'll prove it."

The relief in Mikael's eyes only twists my heart. I got my proof that we could have avoided this. Proof that Kade isn't at fault. Kade could've heard me just fine. Kade is sensitive to what I was trying to tell him. No wonder he was so aimless before I got him out of Yuzhno. His soul was waiting for me and I didn't reach him. No. It isn't Kade's fault. He isn't the one who made me trust him only to flee to the enemy's army. He isn't the one who interfered with the most important mission I've ever had and always worked for, only to make me doubt not just my own abilities as a Firm but also the competency of El Olam's chosen emissary to the Reyn Gayst. Kade isn't the matching pair to my soul's energy that I've walked and fought with for thousands of years both living and in death. No, this isn't Kade's fault.

It's Jordin's.

CHAPTER SEVEN

The next time I hear footsteps, I decide to have some fun. I stand up and move to the center of the room, tucking the crutches under my arm. Now that I'm not so focused on adding energy to my legs, I can send more into the world around me and use it.

There are two people heading toward my room. I focus on their vibe. Enoch, of course, accompanied by Leo. I'm impressed that Leo visits as often as he does, but I'm still eager to see them both.

When the door opens, they are both surprised to see me standing with a goofy smile on my face.

"Hey, guys," I greet them cheerfully. "Look what I can do!" I throw the crutches away from me and laugh as they both stumble into the room, ready to catch me as I fall.

But I don't fall. I stand strong and proud.

Enoch's face lights up. "I see Mikael has visited."

Leo adds confusion to the shock on his face.

"Mikael's my boss," I explain. "He helped me with a bit of a boost. It's not perfect, but it's a lot better than what I had to work with before." I look at Leo. "I won't be holding us back anymore."

"When was he here?" The curiosity in Enoch's voice tells me

he's piecing something together and I know where he's going.

"When Kade was," I confirm for him.

Enoch indulges in a laugh. The relief comes off him in waves at the proof there are other forces at work helping him to move us along. I try not to think about the fact that poor Enoch has been our babysitter since I came here. Later, I will feel bad for him. I won't let the embarrassment kill my buzz.

"So, I guess I owe you an apology," I say to Enoch. "Turns out your theory was right. Kade isn't dense. Jordin got to me somehow." My eyes fall to the floor. So much for avoiding the buzzkill. "I guess I was a little hard on him."

"Well, you're here now. You can make it up to him."

Ha! "You make it sound so simple."

"Kade can hold a serious grudge," Leo agrees. "It'll take a lot to get him to cool off enough to listen."

"He will once the series of events prove Anaya right."

I fold my arms and shift my weight to one side. That's a good point. But enough about Kade and the future. I've got more exciting things to focus on right here and now.

I clap my hands together to get the boys' attention. "So, who wants to go for a walk? I'm up for a tour."

Leo looks unsure. "Why do you need a tour?"

"Why don't you want me to have one?"

Enoch studies Leo's face. "Ramiro."

Leo nods.

I groan. "Who cares about Ramiro? I can't stand this room and I want to see what we're working with here and help get ready for this attack. You know I can be useful."

"She makes a fair point," Leo says into his hand, pondering the pros and cons, no doubt.

I can't take waiting, though, so before they can come up with reasons I shouldn't, I quickly grab the last piece of jerky from the plate Kade had brought and head out the door, laughing at the sounds of them scrambling after me.

I nearly skip down the hall and by the time they catch up, I realize just how much I'll have to budget my energy. The strength is there, but the muscles aren't and they tire quickly. I'll have to pace myself, so I'll have what I need when I need it.

"Where does everyone hang out?" I ask Leo.

"There's a lounge upstairs that everyone stays in."

Upstairs. I almost get dizzy just thinking about stairs.

"Don't worry." Enoch grabs my shoulders and guides me around the next corner. "There's an elevator."

"Yes!" I pump my fist in the air. I am unstoppable now.

I rush ahead of them because I want to push the button first. I've never been alive during the elevator era, but I've watched countless living souls compete for the honor of pushing this button. When I punch the button and the light comes on, I expect more of a rush, but it's something to cross off the post-bucket list, I guess.

The elevator takes its time coming down from the second floor, and I cannot see the allure of this technology. "Sheesh, why wouldn't you just take the stairs if you could?"

When the door finally opens, it surprises everyone. Ainsley is inside, cane in hand. I imagine he and Phil are the ones who use this elevator the most.

"Ah, how convenient." Ainsley fiddles with his pocket, smiling at each of us. "I see we've had a bit of a miracle." He motions to me with his cane. "Well, you've saved an old man a trip. I was just coming to see you. But if you're on a journey of your own, might I join you?"

I spread my arms toward him. "By all means! I was just looking for signs of life in this place."

Ainsley shuffles to the back of the elevator to make room for us and I walk straight to his side. I'm taller without my crutches. Taller than Ainsley now by an inch. I scan Leo from the corner of my eye. I still won't be near Kade's eye level if I only come to Leo's chin. They stand at the same height. That's disappointing, but at least now I can hold myself high in Kade's presence.

"Floor two, please, Enoch," Ainsley says.

There are only three buttons on the panel. A first, a second, and a basement.

The jolt of the elevator sends my stomach flipping and, for a second, I worry that I'm going to be sick, but everything falls back into place when the movement thunks to a stop. I put a hand to my stomach, silently thanking this feeble body for not letting me down.

The doors open and I wouldn't know we even moved had I not felt it. The second floor looks exactly like the first so far, and they'd better not be identical, because if there's a lounge on the first floor like the one on the second, then why in the world was I tossed into a cold and empty room? I suspect Ramiro had something to do with it. If I find the first-floor lounge, I'm moving.

Leo and Enoch take the lead out of the elevator and Ainsley stays at my side. I revel in the thought that it now looks like I'm helping him get around, and not vice versa.

We take a few turns and I hope there will be open chairs in this lounge. I can feel my legs running on the fumes of extra energy, but this is a good workout for them.

Eventually, Enoch stops at a door in the middle of a hall and leans around the frame to check inside. He hurries away.

"We may not want to do this now..."

I eye him, reading his energy, which is only fair since he could easily do the same to me. He's nervous.

"Ramiro's in there." It isn't a question. I can tell by the look on Enoch's face.

He swallows his nerves and nods. "Kade too. Everyone seems to be done for the day."

"Then this is exactly when I want to do this."

Leo and Enoch look at me like I'm crazy.

"Listen, they need to get over my being here. We have an escape to plan and I don't want anyone distracted by the weird girl downstairs and if we should leave her behind. Plus, I want to talk to Ramiro."

"Why?" Leo asks too quickly.

I point at Enoch, who looks like I'm about to zap him with some supernatural death ray. But I have nothing more than accusations. "He said that Ramiro has been giving Kade a hard time since I showed up." My head drops. I can't believe I'm going to say this, but it isn't Kade's fault and I'm still his Firn. "I need to mend that relationship."

"Um... again—why?" Leo's face screws up in confusion. "We're leaving soon, anyway. Can't we just let it go?"

I would love that. "We can't. I don't know what's coming and I'm not burning any bridges that we can cross again later. Know what I mean?"

Ainsley nods, wearing an impressed grin. "It's excellent forward thinking, Anaya." I can see the internal struggle of Ainsley trying to remember that I'm an ancient spirit and not a young person like Kade and Leo. But I don't mind his praise, so I'll let it go. Plus, with his endorsement, Leo will go with my plan.

Leo looks between the three of us and finds no allies. It pays to be me in this world. Few people, aside from maybe Enoch and Kade, will question me if they know what I really am. Leo sweeps an arm to the doorway in surrender. "Be my guest."

I would love to say that I strutted straight through that door, but that would not give the right impression. So I urge Enoch with my eyes to take the lead, and he skips into action. I follow Leo through the door and every person in the room somehow knows it.

Ten sets of eyes shoot up to stare at us. I tell myself they're staring at us to make me feel better, but I'm uncomfortably aware that they're all staring at me. I glance around at the various reactions, some blank, some nervous, some—ahem—Kade, cynical.

I wave at them and smile as much as my cheeks will allow. "Hello."

The room looks a lot like the common area back at Phil's gas station. A few couches, an old radio, a kitchenette. It's warmer in here and there's actual drywall on the walls. Now I'm taking my concrete room personally.

At the far wall, Kade sits across from Ramiro, both leaning over a tourist map of the Taltsy museum. Phil sits within earshot. He likes to think he's the glue of this group, but he's just as much a liability as I am. He and Ainsley have become old men, but only one of them has accepted it.

All three of them look irritated by my presence, but Kade most of all. My stomach sinks. That's my fault and I have to fix it. I remember Kade's life and how well he clings to hurt feelings. It's going to be a long process.

Ainsley gives my shoulder a reassuring squeeze and I remind myself what I am... what I was... what I still function as, dang it, and that's good enough for me.

I straighten and cross the room, smiling at anyone who will meet my eyes and reaching out for the empty chair near Ramiro and Kade. As I sit, Ramiro grimaces at my audacity, but he'll have to get used to it.

"How's the planning going?" I ask, looking at their brightly colored map and trying not to laugh.

Ramiro looks like a rhinoceros ready to charge. "How do you know what we're doing?" He leans forward, using his height to intimidate me. But, sir, I've fought demons.

"Calm down." I brush him off. "You're pouring over a novelty map like it's about to explode on you. What else would you be doing?"

Ramiro turns on Kade. "Did you tell her?"

Kade leans away and raises his palms. "Why would I tell her? I'm not even the one who told you!"

I flap my hands at both of them, fanning the flames of their hot heads. "Simmer down, you two. I know. Get over it." I bend over the map, resting my elbows on my knees. "So, what are you thinking?"

"I'm thinking you need to back off." Ramiro uses his arm to push me back into my seat. The pressure against my sternum revives the soreness that I thought I'd avoided. I rub the spot and send him a hurt look.

"We don't even know if this attack is happening for sure," Ramiro grumbles.

And this is the moment that Enoch crosses the room and turns the radio volume up. I hold a finger up to Ramiro, point at my ear and then at the radio. He wrinkles his nose at me, but a voice from the radio booms loud enough to get his attention.

"In other news tonight," the newsman announces, "the dilapidated Taltsy Open-Air Museum, an early Beta Siberian attraction that has remained abandoned for over a century, is scheduled for demolition to remove the blight and allow nature to reclaim the land."

I lift my eyebrows in my best I-told-you-so look as Ramiro gapes back at me. I silently thank whoever gave Enoch the heads up. What timing. I forgot how cool it is to be on this side of the workings.

"This is one of the first declarations of Chairman Donovan Tyrrell's son, Jett Tyrrell, as he now prepares to inherit his father's position in the coming years," the announcer goes on. "Sources say Jett's environmental preservation team will raze the museum to the ground with controlled explosives in an effort to, quote, 'create the freshest clean slate for nature to rebuild upon and to save cost to my fellow Beta Siberians.' The demolition is scheduled to begin tomorrow afternoon."

"How generous of him," Kade growls. Jett's name is a cuss in Kade's vocabulary, as it should be. He catches me smiling at him and a flare sparks in his eyes and he realizes he's playing right along with his Plan, but he isn't ready to accept that yet. He shakes his head and settles back into his angry face.

"I thought you were sick," Ramiro interrupts. "Asa said you should be dead by now."

"Did he?" I turn in my chair to find a pair of frightened eyes. So that's why he didn't come to check on me. He wrote me off. That's fine. I don't blame him, and I send him a smile to show it. He ducks his head down to avoid me. I turn back to Ramiro. "Well, I'm not dead."

"No, you're not." He doesn't seem happy about it. "How did you recover so fast?" He adopts a conspiracy theorist's tone. His forehead scrunches with the effort of coming up with countless reasons to explain how I can be totally fine now.

"I know what you're going to say—"

"I'll bet you were never sick to begin with and this was all some sort of front."

"There it is." I sink in my chair and look at Kade. He's folded himself into a pout and shows no signs of offering any help.

Okay then. Fine. Time for a change of posture. My face softens and I relax my shoulders, looking up at Ramiro to appeal to his alpha mentality. "I can promise you with absolute certainty that I do not work for, nor am I associated with, Security or the Association. I am on your side and I want to see you get out of here safely. You have less than a day to pull this off. You heard the reporter."

"Which is why it's mighty convenient that you're suddenly up and about," Ramiro points out. Eyes all around the room stare as an argument brews. Ainsley stands and leaves the room, probably weary from the constant bickering between Kade and Ramiro.

I can't argue with that. It is convenient. Mikael knew the

attack was coming and gave me a boost, but Ramiro thinks Security did it and how do I convince him otherwise?

"You only want to help with the plan because you're going to tell Security where to find us before we can escape."

I open my mouth to protest, but that's a perfectly rational assumption.

"Don't be stupid," Kade says to Ramiro. "You saw her when we found her. There was no way she was faking those injuries."

We both look at Kade, wondering why he's defending me.

"I'm not saying they didn't injure her," Ramiro points out. "I'm saying they did it to trick us and probably gave her some miracle drug to get her moving again when the time came."

Kade rolls his eyes at the thought, but I come to his aid this time. It's only fair.

"You make a fair point," I agree, and Kade gawks at my diplomatic response. "I confess I don't have any actual way to convince you. I have nothing but my word and no reason for you to trust it."

Ramiro looks stunned, and a little impressed. He buries it quickly, though.

I press on. "I'll be honest, I came here for someone, but it isn't you. Actually, you'll probably thank me because I'm trying to get Kade out of your hair." I laugh, but Ramiro turns a severe look on Kade.

"So, you were a plant?"

Kade slides his chair away from the small table, ready to run.

"No! No, no, no, no, no. That's not what I meant." I reach out and yank Ramiro's sleeve down to keep him in his seat. "I want you and the other boys to get out of here safely, but I'll be going with Kade in a different direction. You won't have to deal with us anymore, and how about this?" I read his face for signs of anger before I continue. "Let me help you all escape, but don't let me know where you're headed next. I'll get Kade and myself out another way, so I'll be too busy trying to keep us alive to rat on you."

Ramiro looks wildly skeptical. "Why do you need to go somewhere with Kade again?"

I lean in and wave Ramiro towards me. Time to bury this mess. "Jett has a major beef with Kade." Not a lie. "I'm here to take Kade to where Jett can't reach him." Also not a lie. "If you let me take him, I'll make sure your trail stays covered until it's out of my hands." Sort of a lie. It's not in my hands to begin with, but if it's a conspiracy Ramiro needs, then I'll give him one.

He leans away from me, eyes wide like he always knew this day would come. He looks at Kade. Kade glances between us nervously.

"What?" he demands. "What did you tell him?"

Ramiro looks back at me, weighing how this will affect his conscience. He looks at Kade with sympathy in his eyes. He picked the boys over Kade. I don't blame him for it. I was counting on it.

Ramiro gives me a decisive nod. "You've got a deal."

Kade gets frantic now. "What deal?" He leans in toward me. "What did you tell him?" Then back in his seat. "What's going on?"

I hold a hand up to silence him. He scowls at me. "Just relax. It'll all work out according to Plan." I give him a meaningful look and he understands what I really mean. He puffs out a frustrated breath and looks away from me. That's fine. We have work to do.

I move closer to the map on the table and scan over it. "So," I say again. "What's the plan?"

Ramiro frowns at the map. "We didn't exactly expect to come here and have to escape again so quickly. Especially not from bombs." His change in tone is remarkable. I don't think I could've gotten more respect from him if he knew where I came from. I've given him a deal, and he took it. He thinks I work for the enemy and could turn on him at any moment.

He's afraid for the lives of his Lost Boys. The memories of ones he couldn't save still swim in his eyes.

Don't get me wrong, I don't want to scare him or play on his weaknesses, but this is the solution that worked.

"No underground tunnels or escape routes of any kind?" I look over my shoulder at Enoch. "What made you come here to begin with?"

Enoch looks at me, then to Ramiro. Ramiro holds his gaze for a moment before he nods his approval and Enoch approaches our little conference.

"The resistance network that Ainsley and Phil are a part of—"

"And what network is that again?"

"We don't know," Ramiro growls at me. "And we wouldn't tell you if we did."

Right. I'm with the Association. I forgot. I gesture for Enoch to continue.

"They have several locations throughout Beta Siberia, mostly outside of developments, of course. This is one of them. Phil used to talk about it a lot."

My head goes fuzzy trying to piece it together. "Yeah, but why so close to Irkutsk? Did you want Jett literally knocking at your door? It's only a jump across the lake for him."

"He's in Nor'ilsk right now anyway," Kade informs me bitterly.

"Precisely." Enoch nods. "This seemed like the best way to stay far from Jett's place of business, seeing as his issues with us seem to be personal." Enoch sneaks a glance at Kade, because Jett only knew about Phil's crew because Kade flubbed our plan to see Danica. Jett doesn't like competition. He made it abundantly clear by tracking us with Jordin's help and blowing up Phillip Urtenk's Gas & Oil station.

"So this isn't one of the most hi-tech locations," I presume. "It's just conveniently far from Jett."

Nods all around the table.

I rub my chin, staring at the map. "If they're going to blow it up, they will not send men in unless they do a sweep beforehand."

"They seem to prefer to let the fire do the work for them," Enoch tells me.

"Yeah, like they did to Ainsley's place back home."

"You make a fair point," I commend Kade. He looks uncomfortable because I didn't have to ask what happened to Ainsley's place. I was there. "But we can't count on that. We need to make sure that if they come in beforehand, everyone has a place to hide until they can escape." Then I remember. "Hey, where are the trucks? The ones from the Security ambush a while ago. Did you bring them?"

Enoch's eyes fly open and he leans in to shush me. Too much information. Ramiro thinks I've only been here since the gas station went up in flames. The ambush was a solid week before that.

I shove a thumb in Enoch's direction. "He told me about it. I..." I search my mind for a way out of this. I can't get Enoch in trouble with Ramiro. He needs Ramiro's trust to keep the group on track for us. "I made him tell me."

Ramiro sweeps accusing eyes at Enoch.

Enoch stiffens. "She's very persuasive?"

Ramiro lets it go for now. I send the most apologetic energy I can toward Enoch, but he doesn't look amused.

"Anyway," I say, drawing back to the point. "Do you have the trucks?"

"We do," Kade tells me. He still looks creeped out, but he goes with it. "They're parked outside the main building."

"Move them," I tell them. "Get them to the edges of the complex in two different directions. You'll want to split up in case one group gets caught."

"Naturally." Ramiro looks ruffled, shoulders tensed up to

his ears. I'm overstepping his authority. I calm myself down and give him room to speak. "Trucks in the East and the South. If you head for Nor'ilsk I want us to be headed as far away from you as possible."

I nod. "That's fair. And that gives three targets for Security to chase—if they notice us."

"How would they not notice?" Kade asks.

"Because..." an idea forms in Ramiro's mind, "we'll hide them in the buildings."

I point at him because that is a stroke of genius. His Firn must be a skilled one.

"Hide them until the explosives drop?" Enoch clarifies.

"We'll have to." Kade curls his hands around his knees. "We can't let them see us before the smoke gives us cover, right?" It's Ramiro he looks to for approval.

Ramiro eyes him for a moment, not the type to give immediate satisfaction to someone he doesn't respect, but then nods.

"There's a lot that could go wrong with this plan," Enoch points out.

I give him a friendly punch in the arm. "Yeah. But it won't."

Ramiro doesn't look so sure. In fact, he seems suspicious of my optimism, but so what? I know Kade and whoever comes with us will make it, and I trust Lemayle will reward the Lost Boys' hospitality.

Ramiro sighs and stands up slowly. "Better get the boys ready." He steps out from behind the table to project his voice to the room. "We're headed out tomorrow afternoon, everyone. Get your stuff packed and then meet back here for instructions."

I watch the boys stand and move without being told twice. I know each face from Kade's time here. Asa, the close-enough doctor; his rash brother, Gavin; the firecracker triplets, Sasha, Sandy, and Xander; and then Beck, who still weirds me out with those wild, owlish eyes of his... They all have a history and a bond among them.

I really hope they make it.

My eyes fall on Phil. I'm prepared to have bittersweet musings about him too, but his eyes pierce me like an arrow. Pure, uneducated hatred rolls off him and I know I'll have to talk to him. It's all part of tying Kade's loose ends so that maybe we can swing on them again later.

Rather than wait for the inevitable, I stand as tall as I can and walk over to him. He's on a cushioned chair by the radio. I drag a folding chair over to him and sit backward on it.

"Whatever you have to say..." My voice is smooth and even. I've tamed tigers like Phil before. "Say it."

His voice is that of an old crotchety man, not refined like Ainsley's. "You're not with the Association."

Not what I was expecting, but I'm impressed. "Aren't I?"

He shakes his head, wrinkling his nose like I smell foul. I probably do. "I don't know what you are, but you've got a funny feel about you."

I reach my energy out to his. It might as well be leaking from him. Phil's soul is outgrowing his physical body. It's almost fully mature, which means it'll be returning to Lemayle soon enough. I look him up and down. Judging by his attitude and the underlying bitterness of many sad years, he's walked a confused road between his Firn and whatever Aropfain may have messed with him. I hope he chooses well when he goes home.

I just hope he doesn't go tomorrow afternoon. He might take a few of the boys with him and they've got so much left to learn.

CHAPTER EIGHT

"We have them all figured out," I recount to Leo later. I've gone back downstairs and found the lounge there. Couches with cushions. I could have been sleeping on couches with cushions and they dumped me on a cement floor. But there's no use getting upset about it now. We're getting ready to leave.

"What about us?" Leo asks. "We're going another way, aren't we?"

"Well..." I tilt my head, thinking of it. "Technically, only Kade has to go to Nor'ilsk. You can stay with Ramiro, try to go home—please don't though, I like you and I don't want to see you killed." Then I remember Leo's family. The way Kade dragged Leo away from home and his father's old bait-and-tackle shop because I needed to get Kade out of Yuzhno, and how Nyla and their mother have no way of knowing if Leo is even still alive. "Sorry about your mom and sister, by the way. I'm sure they're fine." My shoulders hitch in a timid shrug.

Leo goes through a whirlwind of emotions but settles on a lonely smile. "I'm coming with you. No question." I'm about to thank him, but he says, "Someone needs to keep you and Kade from each other's throats."

"Funny."

He laughs.

"But, thank you."

Enoch sweeps into the room and sits next to me. "You're going to make us use the church, aren't you?" He looks pained over it.

I smile a little wickedly. "Ironic, isn't it?"

"I'd have thought you'd respect religious structures."

"We do!" I protest, speaking for Firns everywhere. "We absolutely pine for the days when people still used them. They heard us so much more clearly when they shut up and listened. But it's toast tomorrow anyway once the bombs drop."

Leo appears to agree with me. Enoch still isn't happy, but we don't have time to be sappy over this.

"We have a third vehicle, right?" I ask Enoch.

"The one that brought Phil and Ainsley here," he tells me. "Isn't as rugged as the others, but it'll drive."

I smile, almost laughing. "Well, that's all we need it to do."

Leo shifts in his seat next to me. "You're enjoying this too much. This is dangerous."

"This is destiny!" I place a hand on his shoulder. "You forget, this is all happening by design. Everyone is making the choices that will get us where we need to be. As long as I can drag Kade out of here and you all stick to your instincts, we'll be just fine. The only losses will be ones that were meant to be, anyway."

Leo stares at his lap. "It just sounds so backward and harsh."

"You'll understand someday." Not in Velt. If he ever comes back to Velt, he'll forget again. But in Lemayle it will all make sense.

Leo looks at Enoch. "You believe that too?"

Enoch chews on the inside of his cheek. For him, I'm sure it's not that simple. "I know that much more happens around us than we realize." He shrugs. That's all he's got.

It's not enough for Leo, but he doesn't have many options.

The attack is coming. We have to get out. What else matters until the dust settles?

"We'll park the truck in the church tonight, and everyone else should do the same. Get everything set up in the dark so we can avoid drawing attention in case they're watching. They already know we're here, but they don't know that we know they know." I count the words to be sure I got that right. I did. "If they see us suddenly parking cars in buildings, they'll kill us for sure."

"But you just said this was all by design. Doesn't that mean they won't be watching?" Leo's mind works in overdrive. "Why do we have to be so careful if it's all predetermined?"

"Uh-uh." I shake my head. "It's pre-outlined. We have to follow the outline to make it work. If we mess it up, then we get messed up."

Leo rubs his forehead.

"Someday, Leo." I pat his back reassuringly. "Obviously not today, but someday."

I look around me and realize that I have no possessions to pack. "Who needs help with their stuff?"

Enoch steps toward me. "No, you need to rest. Your energy won't last if you keep going tonight."

He is correct, but I want to argue. I can't trust my energy to keep me going. I only have a glorified adrenaline rush, no endurance. And tomorrow, I'll need to run. Excitement swells in my chest at the thought of running and being a part of the action again. This is not my ideal situation, by any means, but if I have to go, at least I'll go running. And with Enoch in our truck, we'll be unstoppable. Jordin won't be able to get near us, so we can just focus on our mission—which makes this whole sidetrack with the Lost Boys worthwhile.

I settle in on the couch and smile to myself, feeling taken care of. The efforts of my allies in Lemayle are clear in the unfolding of events around me. I can't wait for tomorrow to see what comes next.

Living is more exciting than I remember.

"We're going to get the truck in position," Enoch tells me as he scans the room for anything important. "I'll come back once it's done." He looks at Leo and gives a nod, and they both leave me.

That's less exciting. I want to help. I want to make sure everything goes right, so it lines up with the Plan to get us out of here.

I guess I should try to sleep or something. I tip myself over onto the couch and stare at the old fluorescent lights in the ceiling. Not much renovation went into this place even before it was part of Beta Siberia. I'm surprised any of these bulbs still work. I imagine most rooms are dark.

I sigh. No way I'll fall asleep like this. As important as my energy is, my mind won't have it. I stare at the ceiling, wishing for a distraction.

And I get one when the door opens again. I throw my legs over the front of the couch to sit myself up as Kade steps in. I'm surprised to see him, and he can tell. He scowls at me, so I don't make a big deal of it. He glances around to find a cheap wooden coffee table and drags it over so he can sit across from me, eye to eye.

"What did you tell Ramiro?" he asks without preamble.

I rub my forehead. "I told him I'm an Association spy who's come to take you away." Might as well be completely honest if I'm trying to get Kade to like me.

He doesn't seem to like what I've said, though. "Why would you say something like that?" His pitch rises with each word, and I can feel his defenses pushing against me in his energy.

I almost lift my hands to push back. "He needed to hear something to get him to listen. That's what he wanted to hear, so it did the trick."

"And he went along with it? You tell him you're with the

Association and suddenly he trusts you?"

"He doesn't trust me," I tell him like he's being silly. "He just cares more for the Lost Boys than he does about you." I cringe. "That came out wrong."

"No, it didn't." Kade seems to have resigned himself to Ramiro's unrelenting opinion of him.

I fold my hands between my knees. "For what it's worth, I'm sorry he's giving you a hard time." He raises an eyebrow at me. "It was supposed to be part of your growth! Plus, it got you closer to Danica... for however short a time. You wouldn't have been able to do anything if you were still back in Yuzhno."

Kade fidgets like his skin is crawling. "Why do you know all this stuff?" His voice is a mix of frustration and despair. He's still coming to terms with the reality that I've been by his side his whole life. Every moment. Even when he thought he was alone or abandoned. That's a lot to process.

"I'd tell you, but you wouldn't want to hear it." I lean back and give him a challenging look, hoping it'll make him listen just to spite me.

"How do you know?" he snaps back.

"Because I've already told you and you're still asking!" Ugh. Breathe, Anaya. Don't let him get a rise out of you... again...

He glares at me and opens his mouth to say something, but the door opens again, revealing Ramiro this time.

Neither of us was expecting to see him, so we stay silent as he crosses the room and drags over a chair that matches the couch. Despite our eyes on him, he sits stiff chinned. He holds my gaze as he reaches into his pocket and retrieves a black knife. He turns his body to Kade, still watching me from the corner of his eyes.

"I don't like you," Ramiro tells Kade.

Kade looks to the side but nods. No news there.

Ramiro glances at me and then back at Kade. "But no one

deserves to face the Association defenseless." He holds the knife out to Kade and Kade takes it. He turns it over in his hands and his finger brushes on a small button on the handle.

He jumps. "A gas injection knife?" He looks up at Ramiro. "Where did you get this? It's a diving tool."

"It works just as well on land." I can feel the animosity coming at me like tiny darts.

Kade still doesn't get it.

"He wants you to kill me when you get the chance so you can save yourself." My voice comes out in a long drone. Why is my Neshome so dense? Sure, he may be a naive idealist, but he needs to answer the questions in his head with common sense.

Kade draws his eyebrows together at the thought.

"I'm taking you to the Association, remember?" I tell him through clenched teeth. Ramiro looks at me like he can't believe I'll admit it to my prisoner out loud. Now he's sure I'm a monster.

And if I'm going to be open about it, so is he. He reaches out and takes the knife back from Kade. "All you need is one good hit, then you push this." He passes a finger over the injection button and we both recoil in case it goes off. "You're not very skilled with weapons, but with this, you won't have to be."

Is it bad that I'm almost grateful to Ramiro for looking out for Kade?

"Just keep the sheath on until you need it." Ramiro passes the knife back to Kade and folds his fingers around it for him.

Kade looks at the knife, then looks at me. I see the spark of realization that Ramiro is asking him to stab me and press that lethal button. The picture in Kade's head can't be pretty. That button will send a shot of freezing gas into the world, exploding the area around it and taking about a third of me with it.

"I've only got the one gas cartridge for you. There weren't more in the haul from that raid. So use it wisely."

Kade gapes at the knife, looking at Ramiro's serious face and then at my disinterested one.

"I can't take this." He pushes the knife toward Ramiro.

"Yes, you can." Ramiro pushes it back.

I roll my eyes. "Take the knife, Kade."

Kade looks at me in disbelief. Listen, I obviously don't want him to use the knife on me, but knives are great tools to have around. I just have to make sure I gain Kade's trust before he gets the idea to use it on me.

I focus on Ramiro. "Are your people in place to escape?"

Fear glazes Ramiro's eyes. He takes my words like a threat that my people are coming. That's not reality, but okay. He nods. "Everyone is ready to get out of here. And they'd better make it."

I hold his gaze. "I hope they do, Ramiro. Trust me."

Trust me. That's almost funny.

Ramiro doesn't believe me. He breaks eye contact and sighs. "Guess I'll see you on the other side." He stands and I slap a hand over my mouth to stop myself from laughing. I don't know if they'll see each other on the actual other side, but I love that line.

When the door closes behind Ramiro, Kade looks at me. "What's the matter with you?"

I stop chuckling behind my hand and look at him.

"You act like some sort of psychopath," Kade accuses. "He wants me to stab you and blow you up, and you're laughing at him?"

I blink a few times, trying to find the right words. "Kade, it's so different where I come from."

"The afterlife," he says flatly.

"Yes!" I throw my arms in the air. "Why is that so hard to believe?"

"I guess it shouldn't be," Kade's voice drips with sarcasm.

"I mean, you sure look like a zombie, all stringy hair and skin and bones."

I narrow my eyes at him, unconsciously tugging at the hair that drapes over my shoulders like dry, brown grass. "Oh, very clever, Kade. Sharp wit you have there."

"What is your big plan here?"

"You mean I haven't been clear enough?"

"Um, no. You haven't. All you've said is that I have to see Danica. You've never said why that matters. Why I feel this way." He moves his hands over his chest like he can't explain the feelings in there with words. "What the heck is my purpose that you're so upset about? And why are you here now?"

I move to argue, but I realize I've told everyone except Kade. That's technically my bad.

I sigh to calm my aggression. "You're right." He looks surprised. "I'm sorry. I've had it in my head for so long it feels like everyone should just know."

He waits.

"You have to help Danica decide."

"Decide what?"

"Let me get to that, would you?"

"Sorry."

I nod. "There's a big fight going on where I come from over whether living souls like you can make good choices on your own. We're leaving it up to Danica to decide, for many complicated reasons. I'll tell you later if you're nice, and you're the one that agreed to help Danica decide."

Kade frowns. "When did I agree to that?"

"Before you were born," I tell him simply. "When you were still in Lemayle, we met to discuss how your life would go and what kind of person you would be to get the most out of it. You agreed to all of this. You just don't remember."

"Why would I agree to abandoning my family and dragging my best friend away from his?" Kade's eyes are wild at the thought.

I choke back a groan. "Because there's a lot more at stake here. It's important."

"More important than the lives of our families?"

"You don't want me to answer that," I tell him. "It doesn't sound nice if you don't understand the bigger picture."

He shoots an angry gaze at the floor and curls his hands into fists. "Are Leo's mom and sister going to be okay?"

"I don't know."

He slaps his legs in frustration. "How don't you know? I thought you had the bigger picture?"

"I have the biggest picture and your picture. That's it. The rest isn't my business. I don't have control over it."

"Well, can't you ask someone who does?" He's getting loud. He always does this when he gets angry, and he gets angry so easily.

"We can't see each other."

"Why? That's the dumbest thing I've ever heard!"

It sounds dumb when I put it that way, but it's bigger than even me. I rub the back of my neck, trying to think of the best way to put it, but the sound of shouting draws both of our attention to the door.

"Trucks! Get to the trucks!"

"Oh no," I breathe. "It's happening early."

"I thought we had until tomorrow afternoon," Kade protests.

"Guess not."

"How does that make any sense?"

I look at him. "You know what, Kade? You may never get it, but right now, we have to get out." I grab his arm and pull him behind me toward the door. We need to find Enoch and Leo.

CHAPTER NINE

I run. So much for rest. I throw my eyes to the sky as we exit the main building, wondering what cosmic joke in the Plan put me in this position. My legs ache with fatigue, but I've got to ignore it. I just have to make it to the truck. It's not too far. Just the truck. Then I can sit and channel my energy into shouting orders at Kade to get us out of here. He'll hear me this time.

Stepping through the shattered front door side by side with Kade, my knee gives out and I throw an arm out to grab Kade's sleeve before I fall. He spins on me with ferocious eyes, but when he sees me going down, he plucks me up under my arms and sets me straight.

"You good?" he asks in haste.

I nod, wheezing. "I'm good. Go!"

The air thrums with the sound of incoming Security helicopters. I grab Kade's arm on purpose this time, so I don't lose my footing as I scan the skies for the direction the copters are coming from. He glares over his shoulder but says nothing once he realizes what I'm doing.

Yes, I'm weak. My only asset is my mind and the wisdom I kept from my half-Shift. I'm going to use it.

"Coming in from the West so far, like we hoped." I squint

into the dark. "At least three copters." They could easily spread out and overwhelm us. "We need to get to the trucks before their spotlights hit us."

As I look down, I see boys scurrying everywhere, scrambling toward the trucks I hope they parked earlier.

Kade's energy spikes as his instincts kick in. He's at his best when he relies on his gut. That was when we could work together before. I always looked forward to Kade being afraid. It meant he just might listen. Halfway to the truck, Kade's other hand shoots out and grabs one boy running by. It's Leo.

Leo spins around in Kade's grip, relaxing when he sees his best friend. "I was just coming to get you. Enoch's in the truck."

"Perfect." Kade twists his arm in my grip so that he can squeeze my wrist. At least he isn't trying to leave me behind. His hero mode has kicked in.

We reach the church just as the rain starts, adding a bone-piercing chill to the air that I don't handle well. As Kade and Leo throw open the doors, we all stop just inside at the sight of someone we didn't expect. Ainsley at the window of the truck talking to Enoch like bombs aren't about to be raining from the sky. As we approach, Ainsley taps the door twice, wrapping up his conversation, then he turns to us.

"I've made a few arrangements to help you on your way to Nor'ilsk. I hope they prove useful."

"Thank you," I wheeze, out of breath from the run. "But why are you here? You're supposed to bug out with Phil."

Ainsley nods, nonplussed. "I'll be on my way as soon as I see you off."

The ground shakes with the first explosion. We all spin toward the door. Another shudder reveals that one copter is coming our way.

"There's no way he's walking back to Phil's truck," I tell Kade.

Kade knows. He releases my arm, and I push Leo toward the truck.

Kade grips Ainsley by the shoulders and ushers him to the closest truck door. "We'll drop you off." He leaves no room for question, though Ainsley tries.

We surround the vehicle, scrambling for door handles, and just as my fingers curl to tug the back door open, my eyes catch on a reflection so ghastly I nearly shout to the others that some Aropfain has found us. Or a banshee by the haggish, sallow face ready to scream back at me. But when I close my mouth, the hag shuts hers as well. Clouded, otherworldly eyes pinch at the corners and shimmer with tears as I realize the hag is me. Even with some strength regained, I still look like a ghoul that hasn't known the touch of life for ages.

"Hey!" Kade hollers at me, ripping me from falling into the abyss of my own terrified gaze. "Get in!"

I shake myself off and allow Leo to press me into the cab of the truck, trying to breathe away what I just saw, avoiding the rearview mirror to stare instead at the dash.

When the last door closes, I find myself between Ainsley and Leo behind the seats with Enoch at the wheel, as usual, looking like a kid who stole his parents' car for an underage joyride. Enoch doesn't know how old he is or even his own birthday, but there's no way he's of government age to drive. Still, he's the most skilled driver of all the Lost Boys.

"Where to, then?" he asks Kade.

"Phil was going to be in the easternmost building, right? We'll go there. Even if it isn't Phil, they can take Ainsley to safety."

"If I may," Ainsley says as the engine revs to life, "I don't want to be putting you in unnecessary danger. I'd much rather make my own way."

"You're in the safest place in the world right now," I remind Ainsley of the Plan and who he's working with. "We're destined to make it. The least we can do is help you, too."

"What about what you said about not following the outline?" Leo asks. He doesn't want to point it out, I'm sure, but it's a concern.

I stare at him, warning him not to think about it. He looks at his lap. I don't have time to discuss theory with him. I'm a little nervous myself, but I'm going to talk the biggest game I can.

"I suppose I should just..." Enoch's fingers curl around the steering wheel, his eyes set on the wall where the altar of the church stands.

"Keep the headlights off and ram it." Kade jars Enoch's seat. "We don't have time for this."

"Someone hold on to Anaya," Enoch calls back to us and I feel like I must've misheard. "She's going to bruise too easily if she gets knocked around too much and this is going to be a very bumpy ride."

Leo takes one for the team and gives me an apologetic look as he wraps an arm around my shoulders and steadies me with his free hand. My cheeks flare with heat, but Enoch makes a fair point, so I'll just take it.

Enoch throws the truck into gear and swerves so he won't hit the altar head on. Smart, even if his goal is just to spare the religious relics.

As the truck surges through the church, tossing and breaking pews on its way, I can't believe we're about to plow through a wall to escape bombs. Actually, I can believe that. I just can't believe I'm in this form to do it. We drive right over a few pews, jostling the truck and nearly sending me into the roof if Leo didn't have a hold of me.

"Brace!" Kade shouts, and we all coil in on ourselves as Enoch smashes through the ancient wooden wall like a sheet of massive paper. The whole truck jostles and I'm glad Leo's got a hold of me.

If we head straight, we'll be home free under the cover of darkness. But we aren't doing that just yet.

"To the left," Kade tells Enoch. And Enoch turns. Toward the building where Phil waits.

A whistling sound fills our ears and I know we won't make it to that building.

"Head for the woods," I say with a dull voice. Enoch doesn't question me and just as he swerves, the bomb lands on Phil's rendezvous building with a massive flare of light and a loud boom. The wooden structures surrounding it catch like they're eager to burn to ash. Leo lets go of me and turns to look out the back window at the burning building.

"Don't stop." I put as much command as I can muster in my voice. "Ainsley's coming with us."

"Do you think they...?" Leo can't finish his words. He turns and sits back down.

Ainsley's head hangs low. "Phil is a short-tempered man," he says. "He may not have had the patience to wait. Did anyone see if the building's wall had been driven through?"

The truck is silent. No one saw. When Ainsley realizes he will not get an answer, he leans forward on Enoch's seat. "You know where to go, then."

More explosions erupt behind us, and I turn myself to watch out the window, because I don't know how he'd have done it, but I wouldn't doubt that this demolition is because of Jordin influencing Jett. The only question is, how does Jordin know we escaped to Taltsy? Of course, I was unconscious. Jordin could have followed any of the boys who were out of Enoch's range of protection and traced us.

Jordin is irrational, but he is also thorough. We have to get out of here before he has any chance to spot us. For all I know, Jett himself could be in one of those choppers.

The truck cab fills with a despondent energy. It drags my shoulders down and I get overwhelmed with the sadness. But there's a chopper scanning the area around Taltsy while the others continue their demolition. I keep my eyes on that.

"Don't let the spotlight hit us," I command Enoch. "I'll monitor it for you." And I do. I follow the circle of light as it skims the dead grass and through the barren trees that we've driven into. It zigs and zags, moving in our general direction. I look up and wonder how high the chopper is flying. Is it high enough for Enoch's protection to wane? Is Jordin up there? Why else would the copter head our way?

"We're going to need cover." My voice shakes with nervousness and all but Enoch turn in their seats to get a look at the helicopter.

"He's up there," I whisper. Leo looks at me. "He's gotta be."

"The one who did this to you?" Leo asks.

I nod. "Jordin."

Enoch's shoulders tense. He's never seen Jordin, but he's seen what lengths Jordin will go to. Jordin called on a favor from Narn to get to us once before and Phil's gas station. He might do it again.

More flashes of light fill the sky as the rain becomes a storm. Lightning streaks across the sky and I have to wonder who is at work here. Narn has no control over weather. Jordin has been known to stir up a storm or two, but that's just nature reacting to his unstable emotions. Weather is El Olam's territory, and lightning isn't safe for large, metal helicopters. This has divine intervention written all over it, and all I can do is sit back and watch.

The chopper dips dangerously low to the ground, and the searchlight stretches out in front of it. Definitely shady business happening here.

"Get ready to floor it, Enoch."

A surge of energy rushes through the trees and I can almost see it as much as I feel it. "Gas!" I shout. "He's doing it again!"

Enoch knows what I'm talking about and does his best to

outrun the pulse of energy, but that's hopeless. The wave surges through the trees like a wave of sound and as soon as it touches the truck, the engine dies. It passes through us, and everyone shivers.

Ainsley turns to me. "A work of one of yours?"

I wave my hands in front of me. "Not mine."

"One of those other things you mentioned..." Leo scrunches his face, trying to remember.

"An Aropfain," I tell him. I lean forward to curl around Enoch's seat. "Can you get it working again? Just a spark or something should work."

"I can do it." Enoch nods. "I just need time."

"Oh, I don't think that's something we can get you." I almost throw myself against the back window to get my eyes on the chopper again. It lands at the edge of the woods and several dark-clad Security officers jump out carrying large guns. Are they coming for us? Are they going to arrest us?

"Security incoming." I turn to Kade. He's the only one among us with any sort of combat training. "Do you still have your chain?"

He looks at me with angry eyes, but there's embarrassment in his vibe.

My face falls. "You didn't bring it."

"It wasn't going to work out!" Kade argues.

"You still have the knife, right?"

Kade gapes at me. "What do you expect me to do with that? They have guns!"

"I'm just checking!" I raise my voice to match his. "Do you have it or not?"

"Yes, I have it!"

"Get it out in case they try to get in the truck."

He eyes me suspiciously. I can tell he's wondering if I mean for him to waste his shot. It hurts that he's that wary of me, but I don't have time for it right now.

"Just have it ready, for everyone else's sake."

He eyes me a moment longer and reaches into a backpack on the floor.

From the corner of my eye, I see a flare of orange and realize immediately that they're not planning on arresting us. I turn and kneel at the back window.

"They have flamethrowers."

Kade flips around in his seat. "Flamethrowers? What are they thinking?"

"I believe they are thinking they mean to kill us, Mr. Buxton," Ainsley says, jostling in his seat. I can't tell if that's Ainsley's nerves or humor speaking, but I find it a little funny.

"Won't the rain put it out?" Leo presses his face against the glass to look at the sky.

I shake my head. "It's not heavy enough, and the lightning isn't helping." I can't exactly blame El Olam for that one. I just hope he uses it like I think he's going to, for Kade's sake, and ultimately Danica's.

The trees catch. They're damp from a long Siberian winter, but they'll still burn with a flamethrower urging them on.

"How's that ignition coming, Enoch?" I apply pressure with my voice.

Sweat rolls down Enoch's face despite the cold. He squats on the floor with the console broken open to fiddle with the mess of wires inside. "Getting there." He glances at Kade. "Can I see that knife for a second?" Kade hands it over.

"Get there quicker," I urge him. "We can't stay here much longer."

"I'm aware."

The pulsing thrum of chopper blades fills the air again. They must think they've sufficiently broken us down and the trees are lit enough to burn. I can just imagine how they'll explain this away on the radio.

I have no choice but to watch the flames bloom and spread, wondering who will get a bright idea that will save us in the nick of time, or if Enoch will actually get the truck moving. Something has to happen. This can't be where the story ends. Is it because we took Ainsley? Was Leo right? Did we go too far off the Plan?

Heat seeps into the truck. The snow that wasn't melted by the rain vanishes into puddles around us.

"Enoch..."

"Got it!" He mashes wires together and the engine hums. He plops back into the driver's seat, forces the wheel to turn until the steering column breaks, and says, "Everyone hold on."

We do. I grip the seats in front of me, Leo grips one seat with one hand and me with the other, and Ainsley mirrors him on my other side. I feel so pathetic.

Enoch slams the gas pedal, and the truck lurches forward and revs before it speeds into motion.

"There's an abandoned town on the other side of these woods, isn't there?" Leo shouts to the front.

"There is." Enoch nods. "We can find cover there until morning."

"Be aware of our schedule, Enoch," Ainsley warns him. Three of us give him a quizzical look, but Enoch nods his understanding. He weaves through the trees, outrunning the fire with glazed eyes, like he's listening to something.

Leaning forward, I ask, "I take it we've got help?" I glance around. Mikael is nowhere to be seen, but another Firn could be here to instruct Enoch.

Sure enough, Enoch gives a distracted nod, still listening and turning the wheel at the command of our unseen savior.

Soon, the edge of the woods reveals another old, concrete town, and we head for it. I look behind us. The fire still burns, and the trees light up like candles, one by one.

"Any idea what they intend to do about that?" I point my

thumb behind us.

Enoch shakes his head, almost holding his breath. His mind is so overwhelmed with divine instruction, his own thoughts, and my nagging. I decide it's best not to watch and I sit down and try to stay quiet.

We break onto a road in the abandoned town and scan the buildings for our best option.

"There!" I point between the seats at a garage that just happens to have an open door.

Enoch looks at it, tilts his head as if asking a question, then swerves the truck in that direction. We barely slow down enough to avoid a crash. Enoch slams on the brakes and we all sling forward, caught by seat belts, front seats, or each other's arms before falling back into place. We all look at each other for a moment, but this isn't over. Kade is the first to move, throwing his door open and tumbling out of the truck to make way for the rest of us.

Leo helps me out and I jog to Kade's side to watch as the fire continues to spread.

"Concrete buildings, fewer trees, snow, rain, freezing temperatures." I look up at the sky as it rumbles with thunder and the occasional flash of lightning. "No wonder we've got storms. This rain should be snow. Warm air like that shouldn't be here."

Kade furrows his brow at the sky. "You're saying this is supernatural?"

"Explain it," I challenge him. "Try."

Kade is not a meteorologist, but he has lived in Beta Siberia long enough to know that freezing temperatures mean snow, not rain. He notices the plume of frosty breath that appears every time he breathes out and glares at nothing. He has no plausible explanation.

"That still won't put the fire out," Leo points out as he steps next to us. "We need more than a drizzle."

As if in response, the rain picks up, pouring from the sky so fast that we can hardly see across the street anymore. The only sign of the fire is the ever-diminishing blurred glow in the distance.

Enoch and Ainsley approach us.

"Ask and you shall receive," Enoch says, amused.

"Most impressive," Ainsley agrees.

The damp and cold permeate my skin and my teeth chatter. "I'm going to start a safer fire in there if anyone wants to join me." I spin on my heel and make for the door that connects the garage to the main building.

"I should go make sure she doesn't accidentally set the whole place on fire," I hear Kade say behind me, but I get the feeling he's more concerned about the cold out here than he is about me.

The house is sparse. A living room shares floor space with a kitchen and everything has a layer of grunge. There are two wooden chairs at the breakfast bar and a tattered green couch across the room under the front window. A hall next to the fireplace leads back to what I would wager is a bathroom and a bedroom or two. Unfortunately, no one abandoned this place in a rush, so there's no power and no leftover food, but there is a fireplace. I set about finding the driest burnable things I can. I break a chair leg in half and throw it in, continuing the search for some kindling and something to light it with. Kade watches me from a chair that he won't let me break.

"So, you didn't bring your weapon." I shake my head disapprovingly.

He crosses his legs, sinks into the chair, and raises his chin. "I'm not a weapon type of guy." He pauses. "I thought you'd know that."

He steels his face against my withering scowl. "I know you're hesitant with them," I counter. "I also know you're capable of learning things. You've got a slightly higher IQ than a monkey, after all. The physical and mental exams were never your problem." His eyes widen at my knowledge of his triple failures to join the Security force back in Yuzhno. "It was the ethics, Kade." He never understood what made them reject him. Not until now. "It was ethics every time."

His propped-up leg falls to the floor.

The others file in from outside, carrying provisions they had packed in the truck before we left Taltsy. I scour the cabinets of the kitchen, separated from Kade and the living room only by a thin breakfast bar countertop. Clearly, this was a house among many businesses in this town.

"Looking for something to light the fire, Anaya?" Ainsley asks, reaching into a bag and producing dry, yellowed paper.

I move toward him. "Where did you get this?"

"Desks back at the museum were filled with them," he tells me, opening the bag to reveal more where they came from. "I thought they would prove useful to you all."

I hug him. He stiffens for a moment in surprise, but I don't care. Smart, brilliant Ainsley. I'm so glad he's with us.

I grab a fistful of the paper and take it over to squat at the fireplace. The chair leg would burn, but that would take forever, and I simply didn't have the energy. I throw my hand out behind me. "Kade, let me see that knife."

"Why?" I can just picture him curling around it protectively.

"I need to start this with something."

Kade stays silent. Just as I sigh and turn to yell at him, Leo produces a lighter from one bag and strides my way.

"Here," he says to placate the situation. He slaps the lighter in my palm. "Use this."

I give him a grateful nod and stare at the lighter in my palm. I've never lived in an era that used lighters, but I've seen how this works plenty of times. Just spin the little wheel and poof, you have flame. I press my thumb to the metal wheel and flick.

"Ouch!" What the heck? Why would they make the wheel all spikey like that? I brace myself for the savagery and try again, biting my lip against the sting this time, but no flame appears. I shake it, listening for the swish of fluid. It's not empty.

"What's the deal with this thing?"

"You can't use a lighter?" Kade calls skeptically from his chair.

I half-turn. "I haven't exactly had fingers for a few millennia, Kade."

He grins wickedly and pushes himself up from the chair. He crouches next to me and swipes the lighter from my palm.

"Who's the monkey now?"

CHAPTER TEN

It isn't the sun that wakes me in the morning. It's Enoch, wide-eyed and persistent. I groan, my eyes heavy and scratchy with sleep dust. I rub them, but it doesn't help as much as it should.

I got to take the ripped green couch under the window last night. The perks of being ill, but it wasn't as great as I'd hoped. The seal on the window is busted, and a draft covered me rather than a blanket, but it seemed more sanitary than the beds in the back rooms. Everyone else agreed. They slept on the floor.

Enoch pulls me to sit up and shoves a baggy of beef jerky into my hands before my vision even clears. As I blink away the sleep, I reach into the bag and shove a piece of jerky into my mouth, sighing at the flavor.

"What's the deal?" I hear Kade protest across the floor.

"It's time to get moving, Mr. Buxton. You've got a train to catch."

"A train?" Leo asks quietly, sitting up himself.

"We're short on time. The station is still a few hours from here," Enoch explains, picking things off the floor around the room and stashing them in a duffel bag. "You can sleep in the truck on the way."

I don't know how he gets around so quickly after so little sleep. I bite into another piece of jerky, hoping the chewing will help wake me up.

"Use the bathroom if you need it," Ainsley urges us. "We don't have time to make stops."

I gape at him. I saw the bathroom last night. For a male, maybe it's acceptable, but my soul was dragged into this world female and I'm not feeling so confident. I consider the pros and cons of simply going outside like the good ol' days.

It takes longer than Ainsley and Enoch like to get us moving, but soon we're sitting in the truck, groggy, on our way out of town. Ainsley consults a map next to me and gives Enoch the occasional directions.

"So, where are we going?" I ask once the sun crests the horizon and forces my eyes to accept the new day.

"I took the liberty of making arrangements to start you on your way to Nor'ilsk," Ainsley explains as he reaches into his bag again. He produces three folders and hands one each to Leo, Kade, and me. They seem as confused as I am, so at least there's that.

"A dear friend from back home assisted me," Ainsley explains as we all flip the folders open. Kade and Leo glance up at him at the mention of their home in Yuzhno Shakha-linsk, nostalgia on their faces and relief at the memory of Bentley, who worked in the archives and who we'd assumed perished while helping them escape the city. "They are only temporary, of course, but you'll be in Nor'ilsk long before they expire."

I thumb through the small stack of papers with the name Agnes DiRoma written in specific boxes. I look up at Ainsley. "You arranged our travel forms?" That makes things so much easier!

Ainsley nods. "I also have a friend coming to escort you as far as he can. He'll help you slip under Security's radar a bit."

"What friend?" Kade asks. He looks suspicious whenever Ainsley reveals something new about the double life he's been leading as an antiquities seller and rebel activist.

"There is quite the network of old men seeking to oppose the Association's ideals, Mr. Buxton," Ainsley explains freely. "We are at each other's service whenever one of us requires assistance. This situation most certainly qualifies."

I turn to him with narrow eyes. "How much have you told them?"

His wizened eyes meet mine without hesitation, not caring that I'm from another world. "I've told them enough to convince them to cooperate."

I slap my palm to my forehead, but I feel his hand fall on my shoulder. "Not quite that much. Not about your unique situation." I relax. "I told them Enoch saw the importance of it."

Enoch accidentally hits the brakes for a second. His head flicks up to the rearview mirror to find Ainsley. "You told them about me?"

Ainsley shrugs. "This is a very skeptical contact. I had to give him something to convince him."

"Sorry, Enoch." I lean up to pat his arm sympathetically, though I'm more relieved than anything. "Someone had to take the bullet."

"What's his name?" Leo asks over me. I peek at the folder in Leo's lap. His paperwork is all in the name of Leonard Archer. Brilliant. I wonder what liberties Ainsley's accomplice took with Kade's name.

"You'll learn soon enough, Mr. Arthur," Ainsley assures him.

I lean forward and whack Kade with the back of my hand. "Hey, what name is your paperwork under?"

He looks at me like I've lost my mind. He flips the folder open to prove it, but frowns. "Ken Buxley?"

I press my hand to my mouth to contain the burst of laughter threatening to come out. Kade does not look like a Ken. Kade glares at me.

"Okay, Agnes. Like you have room to talk."

"Agnes was a saint!" I remind him.

"Knock it off, you guys." Leo rubs circles around his temples.

I shrink back a little, remembering how annoying it is to be around constant bickering. I always seem to find myself as the bickerer. Jordin, Kade... it's all the same.

"Sorry..." but then I balk and look at Ainsley. "Why only three folders?" I accuse him.

He gives a sheepish smile. "I'm sorry, Anaya. I'm simply too old to accompany you. And, to be fair, I didn't plan on being here."

I look at Enoch in the mirror. "And you?"

He lifts his eyes to my reflection. "It's not supposed to happen."

I sulk and fold my arms. "You could've told me."

"You would've argued."

Fair enough, but... "What about Jordin? You're the only thing that keeps him away from us right now."

"That didn't seem to stop him from the helicopter," Leo points out.

I point at Leo. "He appealed to Narn for that. That's cheating."

Kade's nose curls, but he keeps his face forward. "Why wouldn't he cheat? It's a war or something, right?"

I sink in my seat. "It is."

The sadness in my voice seems to make everyone quiet for a while and soon we're seeing road signs for an Association way station called Ulan Ude. Ainsley shifts in his seat, cringing at the stiffness from sitting in the back of a truck for so long. "Best study your paperwork, you three. There'll be a quiz upon boarding."

Well, crud. I open my folder and skim the details. Dark brown hair. That I've seen. Eye color: gray. Really? I look up into the rearview mirror. Really taking in my new appearance for the first time. Dark, wavy brown hair. Plain enough face. And, yeah, I guess my eyes are gray. I have a resting depressed face with slightly sallow cheeks, but they've been filling out since I first woke up. I'm sure that'll get better with time. I'm pale, though, and I still look sickly. People are likely to avoid me in a real development city. That's a plus.

I look down at the pages. Age: 19. I send a stink eye at Ainsley for making me younger than Kade. Height: five-foot-five. How do they know that? What? Did they measure me in my sleep? It creeps me out to think of it.

Ainsley leans into the front seat. "Pull over just up here, Enoch."

Enoch does, parking us just outside of Ulan Ude near a thicker patch of trees. Leo, Kade, and I turn in our seats to look around for any sign of this contact Ainsley mentioned.

Ainsley smiles at us. "Over there." He gestures to the edge of the trees where a stern-looking man in an expensive wool trench coat is watching us. "Time to get out, everyone. No use in delaying. Time is short."

It hits Kade then that we are about to leave Ainsley. The closest thing he's had to a father for all these weeks that he's been a runaway. His chest clenches, his throat chokes up, his eyes burn with the threat of tears, and I feel all of it as my own. I wipe false tears from my eyes and sniff.

"Come on, Kade." It's hard to speak with Kade's sadness blocking my throat. "You never know, we may see each other again."

"Shut up," he says thickly, dragging a sleeve over his face to remove the evidence.

I look at Ainsley, and he nods in understanding. As we all jump out of the truck, Leo helping me on the hefty step down,

Ainsley steps up to Kade and Leo, pride stretched in a smile across his face.

"You boys have come a very long way since I met you those years ago," he begins. "I'm sorry that I've dragged you away from your home and families, but it appears there is more at work in it than even I knew." He looks at me and I confirm with a subtle nod. A smile spreads on his face. "I hope it is also in the cards for us to meet again." He places one hand on Kade's shoulder and the other on Leo's. "I am proud of you both."

Sweet sentimentality fills the air, but the sound of a man clearing his throat shatters the moment.

"Cripes, Ainsley, what sort of weaklings are you training here? Why is everyone so weepy?"

Ooh. I like this guy. He wears the collar of his trench coat folded up around his face with black glasses that block his eyes, and a fedora hat. Very noir, not that anyone remembers what that is, and he carries a black leather duffel bag on his shoulder.

"Not everyone," I volunteer.

He steps closer to me and scans me with a distasteful look. "The look of you would make anyone cry."

My confident demeanor drops. Yikes. I turn to Ainsley. "You said he's a friend of yours?"

"What a jerk," Kade agrees.

The man ignores us in favor of rooting around in his bag.

"Children," Ainsley draws our attention and a glare from me, "This is Mr. Canaan Sem. He'll be escorting you on your way to Nor'ilsk."

"Canaan Sem?" Leo repeats in shock. "The Canaan Sem?"

"That business guy that the Association hires for basically everything?" Kade turns to Ainsley. "You picked him for your little old men's club?"

"Who are you calling old?" Canaan demands. He throws a plastic bag into Kade's gut hard enough for Kade to cough. He tosses a bag to Leo and me as well.

"What's this?" Leo asks.

I rip through the plastic. "New clothes," I tell him. "I guess we look far too poor to be walking around high-class developments."

"You in particular." Canaan can barely stand to look at me, but it's no wonder coming from a guy with a manicure.

"Pampered much?" I ask him.

He lifts his nose and tips his hat over his eyes. "I earn what I get."

"I'll bet you do," I mutter.

"Just put it on."

I'd like to have the last word on this, but Ainsley reminds me again of our tight schedule. So, Leo gives me a hand into the truck bed, where I change into my new outfit. It's a navy, patterned dress with black fleece-lined tights and fancy leather boots, with a silver buckle. It's not as practical as I'd like, but it works. There's also a red hair ribbon that I use to throw my hair into an unruly ponytail, but my favorite piece is the black, thick wool coat. It's itchy through the long sleeves of the dress, but it keeps the cold out and the faux fur around the hood feels soft on my cheeks when I tug it around my face. I even get thin leather gloves and a small red purse with a silver shoulder chain.

When I crawl out of the truck bed, I see my boys looking more dapper than I've ever seen them. Both wear black wool coats themselves, and they each have a set of slacks—black for Kade, navy for Leo—and black dress shoes.

We gravitate toward each other, taking in the luxury none of us has ever experienced.

"Passable," Canaan assesses. "It'll have to do." He looks at my hair with disgust. "Leave it down or put that hood up."

I put my hood up as he turns away and stick my tongue out at his back.

Leo smiles at me. "You look fine. Ignore him. He's a snob."

Canaan flicks two fingers in a mock salute. "That, I am."

I turn to Enoch. "Do we really have to go with him?"

Enoch gives me a thin, tight smile. "It's what I was told to do."

"And you're sure you can't come with us?"

He shakes his head sadly.

That just makes no sense. Why would Lemayle leave us as open targets for Jordin? Maybe to avoid him appealing to Narn again... Can't blame them for that, but it terrifies me all the same.

I sigh. "Well, goodbye, I guess."

Enoch hugs me then, which is weird because I'm not that used to existing in the physical, let alone being affectionate. I almost forget to hug him back.

"Remember," he tells me with a glint in his eye. "It's destined to work out."

I shrug and tilt my head. "As long as we stick to the Plan." Whatever that is. I try again to find it in my mind, but I come up empty and abandoned. It takes effort to ignore the sting.

"Enough with the sappy adieus," Canaan shouts at us. "We've got a schedule. Let's go. My car is this way." He turns and walks away. He'll catch that train even if we're not with him.

"You have your papers?" Ainsley asks as though he's sending us off to school. I raise my purse, showing that I've got them in safekeeping. Kade and Leo pass theirs to me as well, and I realize the downfall of being the only one with a bag.

"Do you have your knife and your fishing rod?"

Kade frowns at me because I shouldn't know about that, but he produces the pen-sized telescopic fishing rod from his coat pocket. "The knife's in there, too."

Eventually, he'll accept that I know him more than he

wants to believe. Until then, I'll just keep reminding him.

With everything in order, we have nothing left to do but sigh and turn to follow Canaan before he leaves us behind. We walk in the direction he went and find a sleek black limousine waiting next to a rotted picnic table. The space in the car seems uncomfortably small. I don't think it's wise to get in a car with strangers. I've watched countless mothers warn their children against it, but here I am and in I go, taking my Neshome and his best friend with me.

Some guardian I turned out to be.

But we have heated leather seats and a snack bar. That's nice. Leo, Kade, and I pile in the back while Canaan sits next to the driver's window on the phone with someone important. He meets our eyes and waves toward the bar. "Help yourselves. Just stay quiet. I'm working."

I exchange looks with the boys, and it only takes seconds to come to an agreement. Free food is our food. Kade scurries over to the bar and tosses us packs of peanuts, pretzels, and cookies. He grabs a boxed tray of vegetables and tucks a few bottles of water under his arm before crawling back to us. We eat everything in the bar, and for the first time since coming to Velt, I feel full. It's bliss.

After the food is gone, we fall into an awkward silence. Canaan is still on the phone, sending us occasional disgusted glances. Our manners are nowhere near the standards of elite citizens like Canaan Sem. I brush some pretzel crumbs off my dress and avoid his gaze.

"So, a train." Leo breaks the silence. "Never been on the railway before, but I remember Ainsley talking about it."

That's right! We're traveling on the famed Tran-Siberian Railroad. I'm excited about that. The route is centuries old. It's mostly used as an Old World vintage luxury transportation.

Kade smiles, leans back, and folds his arms behind his head. "I can't believe we get to mingle with the big shots." He glances down at his new pressed slacks, realizing that he may just fit right in.

"You're going to have to run a comb through your hair first," Leo points out.

Kade smacks him with the back of his hand. "You should talk," he counters.

Out of nowhere, a black plastic comb careens between the two and smacks against the seat between Kade and Leo. We're all stunned for a moment. We follow the trajectory of the comb back to a glaring Canaan, still on the phone. He points to the comb and then to Kade's hair with a flick of his wrist.

"I guess you're supposed to use it," I wager.

A breathy whistle draws our attention, and Canaan points to my mess of hair as well. I narrow my eyes at him with half a mind to make some noise to interrupt his precious call, but the fewer people suspect him, the better for us. We pass the comb between us, taking turns making ourselves presentable. My hair poses the greatest fight. Eventually, Leo takes over, putting his skills from caring for his mother and sister to use. I protest under my breath every time he tugs too hard. He laughs and shakes his head.

"You're just like my sister when she was little."

I glare at him, but the glare falters when a leather zipped pouch lands in my lap. I look at Canaan and he points to it. He's getting mighty pushy. I unzip the bag.

"Makeup?" I whisper in protest. Canaan waves the top of his hand at me to encourage me to just put it on. I turn to Leo. "I don't know what to do with this..."

Kade scoffs. "Seriously? It's makeup. Every girl knows how to use makeup."

I choke back my insults at his attitude. "I haven't exactly been alive since the first century, Kade. Makeup was different then, and I only made it to twelve years old. So, yeah. I don't know how to use modern cosmetics." I pull out a clear plastic case of many colors and turn it in front of my face. "What is this supposed to be?"

"It's eye shadow," Leo informs me. "I help my mom with it when her nurses come by. Here." He opens his hand and I drop the case in his palm. He drops to the floor in front of the seat and studies my face. He looks down at the pallet of colors.

"Please don't make me look like a clown."

"Good luck," Kade scoffs.

Leo ignores him. "I'll do my best. I'm not a professional, but I can try. Close your eyes for me?"

I don't want to close my eyes. I don't want to cut off any of my senses, but I know Canaan won't let this go, and we need to be as convincing as possible. A rough pad scratches across my eyelids and I hold back the urge to flinch. First one eye, then the next.

"Okay," Leo says, cuing me to open my eyes. "Now you just need some of this and you should be good enough." He pulls out a pink tube and tugs the cap off. He holds it up and mimes wiping it over his lips, then passes it to me.

I raise my eyebrows. That makes no sense to me, but Leo remains patient. He pulls out a round case and pops it open, showing me a mirror.

"Just sort of brush it on your lips a bit. It just adds color."

I grimace at the tube. "What is wrong with the color of normal lips?" But mine is not to question in this weird superficial world. I lift the tube until I can see it with my reflection. My hand bobs up and down with the motion of the car. This is ridiculously nerve-racking. I finally brush my bottom lip and drag the smooth stick across. Then the limo hits a bump. My hand jerks and drags the color up my left cheek.

Kade bends over, clamping a hand over his mouth to stifle his laughter. I check the mirror and drop my hands.

"So much for not looking like a clown," I grumble.

Across the car, I catch Canaan's eyes. They move to my cheek, and he pinches the bridge of his nose. He waves me off to tell me to forget the makeup as Leo reaches into the bag for wet clothes to remove the smear. He finishes the job for me, which puts him uncomfortably close to my face, staring at my lips like my face is a color by numbers page.

I'm relieved when it's over. I lift my hand to rub at an itch in the corner of my eye, but Kade catches my wrist.

"You can't do that," he scolds me. "You'll mess it all up."

I gape at him. So, I can't touch my face? What is the point of that?

"Makeup is stupid," I spit out.

A loud click startles us all to look in Canaan's direction. He's pulled a leather briefcase out of somewhere and finally tucked his phone away.

"We're here," he says, just as the car lurches to a stop. "Get out."

We look at each other again and file out of the car to see a rather bustling train station. It's a grand design with sloping roofs and ornate gates and fences. Still imposing, but nice about it.

We approach a grand set of concrete stairs and follow Canaan up them and into the main building. I miss a step when I see the wall of Security agents and Leo puts a hand to the back of my shoulders and nudges me forward. Kade and Leo wear stone faces, but they don't waver. I never expected to feel so intimidated by the sight of a Security check, but this is insane. Every officer wears the same angry expression, glaring suspiciously at everyone as they pass. I see a line of people moving single file under a set of metal detectors, and my whole body breaks into a sweat. Kade is going to be caught with his knife and fishing pole. They'll detain us for sure.

"Kade, go to the bathroom and ditch the knife," I whisper

from the side of my mouth.

"You'd like that, wouldn't you?"

"Oh, give me a break! You know I'm not trying to kill you. I'm trying to keep you from getting caught by Security right now. Think about it!" He doesn't look at me. "Don't be like Ramiro, Kade. The world has too much of him with just one to deal with."

"I'm not getting rid of this thing," he insists.

"Would you two stop bickering?" Canaan hisses. "You're going to draw attention. Just follow my lead and don't speak unless you're spoken to." He steps up to the line of people and the first Security agent. They greet each other cordially. Then Canaan reaches into his pocket and flashes a card at the agent. The agent takes the card and looks it over. When he's satisfied, he nods and opens an arm to the second, shorter line on his right.

"They're with me," Canaan mutters and joins the second line. We scurry to follow.

"I have a security bypass," Canaan explains, without turning toward us. "We just have to get through a basic interview. No metal detectors, no pat-downs as long as you answer the questions according to your paperwork."

According to our paperwork. Uh oh. I try to remember the color of my eyes, my hair, how tall I am. I've only seen myself in a mirror twice now. I open my purse and pull out our papers, studying my details and hoping to memorize what they say about me. Where was I born? How old am I?

Canaan reaches back and grabs my sleeve, pushing me in front of him. A well-dressed man welcomes us at the front of the line with a thin, fake smile. "Welcome, Mr. Sem. Pleasure to see you again. And you've brought company."

Canaan flips through a leather folio of papers and says, "I agreed to be their escort." He hands the papers to the man. "Charity work, you know?"

"Of course." The man accepts the papers with a small bow

and ushers us through a door to the right and into a room with two Security officers at their desks. "Please, have a seat and the interview will begin."

I swallow my fear. Canaan takes one seat without preamble and Leo and I push Kade toward the other with the same thought: I'm not going first.

Kade trips forward with an undignified grunt, and I overheat under my frilled collar. Will they recognize him as a former Security initiate—or as a fugitive? I scan the wall for wanted posters or anything that lists Kade's name.

"Name?" the officer drones, staring at the papers without looking up at Kade. Please, I pray, please let him be that lazy for both Kade and Leo. Let this be one of Mikael's helping hands.

"Ken Bux... ley."

I stop breathing and squeeze the hem of my coat with sweaty palms, hoping the officer just thinks Kade talks slowly. The officer pushes a piece of chewing gum into his mouth and moves his pen to the next box on the form. Kade knows the rest because it matches who he is. He finishes the interview with no issues. Then it's Leo's turn. Leo, the better student of the two, has no problem remembering his new name and answers the officer's questions with confidence and respect.

By the time my turn comes, Canaan is tapping his foot and checking his shiny watch by the door. I sit. The room feels hot and the collar of my dress feels tight around my neck. I look at the officer. He doesn't acknowledge me.

"Name?" he asks.

"An—" My breath catches in my throat. Not Anaya. What's my name? Oh, right! "Agnes." Phew.

I hear a low rumble of laughter and look to the corner of the room. Oh, no. Not here. Not now.

But, of course, here. Of course, now.

"This is an important interview, Anaya. One slip and

they'll detain you. Not very useful to Kade in prison, are you?"

There he is: the walking smirk. That didn't take long. He steps next to the unwitting Security officer and leans over the desk to scrutinize my face.

"Is that... makeup?" He would know, spending all his time in Nor'ilsk as Jett Tyrrell's personal Aropfain these days. I glare at him. His warm amber eyes contradict his cold nature. They used to fit him perfectly—a testament to how eager he was to help anyone he could, clumsy though he was. He was at my side for so many missions, and now I can't even talk to him. I'm in Velt now. People will think I'm crazy.

"Last name?" the officer prods. Apparently, he's been waiting.

Last name? I know this.

"When was the last time you had to remember a last name?" Jordin wonders. "This must be so frustrating for you."

I ignore him. I try to peek at the form on the desk, but the Security officer looks up. He narrows his eyes and lifts the papers away from my view.

"What's your last name?" he presses.

"Uh..."

Jordin laughs at me.

The officer scans my face. His lips curl into a snarl. His hand trails toward the phone on his desk.

"Her name is Agnes DiRoma," Canaan drones like he doesn't have time for this. He thumbs through his folio and pulls out a small stack of papers. "She's just been discharged from the Koma hospital. She's lost her memory from the treatment."

"Where did you get those?" I ask without thinking.

Canaan ignores me and hands the papers over. "See what I mean? There's nothing in that brain."

The officer takes the papers with an understanding nod. He skims the lines and wrinkles his nose. "Koma? Those witch doctors?"

Canaan flourishes his hand. "I told you." he sweeps the hand toward me. "Charity work."

The officer looks at me, and I don't have to try to give him a dumb look in return. He inspects my face, how pale it is, my hollow cheeks, the tears I've allowed to gather in my eyes, and nods.

"Get her somewhere she can't hurt anybody," the officer says like I'm a danger to people for having been sick.

Canaan's hand clamps around my arm and he drags me out of the chair, accepting my papers from the officer with his other hand. He pushes me toward Kade and Leo. They catch me and keep me close. "I plan to. Believe me." Then he turns and leaves the room without waiting for us to follow.

As Kade and Leo usher me through the door, I throw one more glance over my shoulder to catch Jordin's trademark smirk.

He lifts his hand to give a little wave. "See you on the train, Anaya."

CHAPTER ELEVEN

The train is a grand spectacle, with elaborate and elegant decorations in every detail. It's also an antique, a spray of art déco, carved wood, and steel bolts, like something from the roaring nineteen twenties, but it's more likely a vintage remake from a more current century. We walk down corridors of red, velvety carpet and sliding wood doors with glass windows peering into sleeper compartments. After the stress of the interview, I can't wait to fold down one of those sleeper beds, no matter how uncouth Canaan might think I am. I'm tired and this is going to be a long ride regardless of where we're going.

I frown. Where are we going? We've all been so stiff with nerves until now that none of us have really looked at the tickets white-knuckled in our hands. I put a steadying hand on Kade's back, so I don't trip up trying to read and walk at the same time. He shoots a glare back at me, assuming I'm pushing him forward, but then I look up straight into his eyes.

"Irkutsk?" His eyes go wide. He discreetly smacks Leo at hip level and jerks his head toward me for Leo to listen. "This train is going nonstop to Irkutsk."

"Nonstop makes sense. There aren't many other developments or Security hubs between here and Irkutsk. It's just around the lake..." Leo rubs his chin. "But why would Ainsley put us with someone who's taking us to the capitol?"

"I can hear you all fussing back there," Canaan drones. "You're welcome to get off and stay with the Security agents if you think that's best. I'm going to Irkutsk because I have business there. I'm getting you closer to Nor'ilsk out of the kindness of my heart." He presses a hand to the center of his chest, but his face lacks emotion. "Come, don't come. I don't care. In fact, it's much less of a hassle for me if you don't come." He stops at a door and turns as he pulls the door open. He sweeps a hand in front of him. "Coming?"

We look at each other. As much as I'd love to put up a fight, we'd lose. I lean into Kade and mutter, "You may need that knife after all..." Then I walk inside and take a seat, keeping my eyes on Canaan as Kade and Leo sit on either side of me and Canaan slides the door closed. My chest thuds with the sound of the latch catching on the door. It feels more like I've just been closed in a jail cell. Other people pass by the window on the way to their own swanky accommodations, but none look into our compartment. Manners, I suppose, but that leaves no witnesses. I wonder how soundproof this wood is.

Canaan sits across from us with a tired sigh. He draws a white handkerchief from his coat pocket and pulls off his mirrored sunglasses to reveal crystal blue eyes. He cleans the lenses of his glasses and offhandedly says, "I guess you've got some questions, and I can't head to the bar until we leave the station, so you've got..." He checks his watch. "About seven minutes."

Kade is ready for the opportunity. He angles his head to eye Canaan with as much suspicion as he can muster. "Is Canaan your real name?"

Leo and I gawk at him. That's what he asks? Of all things?

Canaan laughs. "Well spotted," he says. "No, it isn't."

Leo frowns at this. "What's your real name?"

Canaan shakes his head, smiling like a jerk. "You'll never know."

"Do you all have fake names?" Kade's voice is much less accusatory. "All of you in this old gentleman's club you and Ainsley have got going?"

Canaan leans back to rest against the plush green cushions of the seat. "We're all made up." He makes it sound like they're all ghosts. They're not ghosts, and I almost take offense. Ghosting is a serious issue where I come from. It's not a joke. It's what happens when a soul doesn't choose after they come back to Lemayle, and it leaves them as open targets for the Aropfain.

"What, you thought Phil's real name was Phillup Urtenk? Really?" Canaan's voice brings me back to the conversation.

Kade smacks a fist to his palm. "I knew it!"

Leo pouts a little. "So, Ainsley Vanderpool is a made-up name, too?"

Canaan puffs out a sardonic laugh. "Sorry to shatter your childhood, kid."

"Forget the names." I wave a hand, trying to clear the topic from the air. I lean forward, searching for truth in Canaan's eyes. "How did you know to arrange those hospital papers?" I suspect Mikael had something to do with it, but I'm fascinated about how.

Canaan makes a face. "Ainsley said you looked disgusting," he says.

My shoulders fall and Leo leans in. "I'm sure Ainsley didn't say it like that," he assures me.

Canaan only shoots me a blank stare and continues. "I made a generous donation to the Koma hospital in exchange for some medical records and had them altered to the papers Ainsley ordered for your ID."

"Though no one could blame him if he did." Ah, lovely. Jordin's found our compartment. "You look pretty terrible,

Anaya." He folds his arms and leans against the wall, crossing a foot over his ankle. "I could fix that, you know."

I ignore him, but I can't stop the anger from distorting my face.

"Better question," Kade turns to me. "How could you forget your name?"

And now my anger has an outlet. "Because it's not my name, and it hasn't been for almost three thousand years, Kade."

Canaan raises an eyebrow at that, and I nearly smack myself.

I turn to him. "There's nothing in my brain, remember? Don't worry about it."

Canaan lifts his hands. "I'm not saying anything. You're new to the fake name game. I've been there." He lifts his shoulders. "I never slipped up in front of Security, but you live, you learn."

"Right." I stare at the roof of the car, begging El Olam to put an end to this misery. Jordin notices.

"Appealing to a higher power?" he asks, like he's about to pitch his latest product. "I have a solution for you."

"You almost got us all arrested," Kade continues his argument. He's just venting stress, but I still don't think that gives him the right to be this way. He's an adult, he should have better coping methods. I tried to teach him. My heart thuds against my chest. I press a hand over it.

"How does that help your master plan along?" Kade continues. "And now we're headed to Irkutsk. I'm not sure if you've checked a map lately, but that's not anywhere near Nor'ilsk." He crosses his arms, daring me to challenge his logic. "For all we know, you and Canaan could both be working for Security." He turns to Canaan. "I mean, who has a pass to avoid the pat down?"

Canaan's eyes narrow for a moment. Kade prodded a sore spot. "People with money," he counters. "I can't expect you to understand."

Jordin plops down next to Canaan and studies his face too close for comfort, but Canaan doesn't even know he's there. "I like this guy. Where'd you find him?"

I press my hand to my forehead, sighing at the coolness of my palm against the throbbing behind my eyes. I don't want to answer, and Kade makes sure I don't have time to.

"I don't even know why everyone is supporting you so much. So what if you claim to be trying to save the world?" His voice rises in volume and Leo flinches as people passing glance our way. "You claim that you've known me my whole life, that you've actually been there. I haven't seen proof of any of that. I want to hear the truth!"

I smack the seat on either side of me and shout, "You were born at two in the morning on the coldest November day on record! You broke your arm when you were three because you jumped off the shed next to your house." My heart pounds so much I can almost hear my pulse throbbing in my ears. "You've been dying of boredom on your dad's fishing boat since you were nine years old. You met Leo at his dad's shop when you made a snarky comment about their bait, and he told you to shut your mouth." I gasp between points and my blackness creeps into the corner of my vision, but I am not done. "You met Ainsley when he stopped you from throwing a rock through his display window. You failed the Security entrance exam three times and were just about doomed to a life of obscurity before we left, and you nearly got yourself killed by Security when you decided to trust that creepy man and his weirdo wife in–Vanino? Vanino! Is that enough truth—for you—Kade?" I can't get the words out between gasps of air. The blackness narrows my vision and something in my head flicks like a switch. It's lights out for me.

The last thing I hear is a gasp and Jordin shouting my name.

CHAPTER TWELVE

"You're an idiot, Kade." Leo's voice echoes in my head against the clacking sound of a train moving along the tracks. "She's got heart issues. You know she isn't supposed to overexert herself."

"Heart issues?" The shuffling of papers. "I took a dementia patient's records. Oops."

"Anaya... Anaya, can you hear me? What was that?"

My eyes flutter open, and the first thing I see is Jordin's concerned face. I cringe against the light on the ceiling that makes my head feel like shattering glass and bury my face in the seat cushion.

"She's awake," I hear Leo whisper as I groan into the old-smelling fabric.

"Keep talking like that," I beg him. "Don't be loud. Please don't be loud." I clutch my head in my hands as the searing pain throbs above my eyes and sweeps through my head until my whole body feels like I dropped off a cliff.

Someone kneels on the floor behind me. "Kade, get the lights and close the blinds."

"I'm going to the bar." The door opens and slides shut.

I breathe until my stomach stops threatening to remind

me what jerky looks like post-digestion, and push myself to sit up, grateful for the darkness. It takes a second before I open my eyes again, but when I do, Leo has a glass of water waiting for me.

I take the glass and Leo reaches behind him to produce two small pills. "This'll help your head. Canaan had them in his suitcase. Apparently, he gets migraines a lot."

"More like hangovers," Kade comments. He's probably right. "So, what was with the fainting spell? Did your people summon you or something?"

"Yeah." Jordin nods his agreement. "What happened to you? What's going on?"

Even through the headache, I have plenty of energy to glare at them as I throw the pills back and wash them down. "I didn't exactly have the most natural transition from Lemayle to here." The words to Kade, but my eyes are on Jordin. Jordin curls away from my gaze like I threw a pebble at him. "The side effect is that my body is underdeveloped."

"Gross." Kade sounds offended. He would. "So, you're like a really tall baby?"

I give him the most tired face I can muster. "It means my soul ripped from one dimension to another and I didn't get to grow like you did. So, yeah. I guess I'm a zombie, like you said."

"Well, how do you fix it?" Kade asks. Jordin falls into the seat next to him, watching me eagerly for the answer.

I shrug. "I don't. This is what I have to work with, and every time you tick me off, this is what's going to happen."

Kade shifts into a smug position. "Well then, maybe you should learn to control your anger."

My heart revs up and I drop my jaw, ready to lay into him all over again.

"Or..." Leo interrupts. "You both could attempt to stop fighting."

"So, she's just going to short-circuit every time she gets upset?" Kade asks incredulously.

"Something must've gone wrong in the Shift..." Jordin mutters to himself, a finger hooked around his chin.

I nod to both of them. Leo and Kade don't know Jordin's here, and I'm not sure I want them to.

"I think you're making it up for sympathy," Kade decides. "If we feel bad for you, we'll follow your orders."

Even Jordin covers his eyes and shakes his head.

Kade's hand slides down to his pants pocket, where the gas knife rests. I watch it go, wondering what he's planning. He looks at me with clouds of suspicion in his eyes. I squint. Normally, hazy eyes like that are a sure sign of Aropfain interference, but Jordin is the only Aropfain I see, and, for once, he isn't instigating Kade.

"What are you planning to do with that, Kade?" I push myself to sit up properly, trying to have a stronger presence in case Kade tries anything funny in his weird state. His hand doesn't slip into the pocket, but rests on it, just keeping me aware of what's inside.

At my words, Jordin's noticed too. He squints at the pocket like he's got x-ray vision, then glares at Kade. He sits himself close to Kade, shoulders poised and ready to act on a moment's notice.

I take a different approach. "Kade, I'm not lying to you. If we waited around long enough, you'd see for yourself." The thought hits me. "Heck, you still may if we don't move fast enough."

Kade scrunches his face in frustration. "What are you talking about?" he demands. "Spit it out already."

My head falls at the weight of having to explain. I kept it to myself after Mikael explained everything to me. This won't help Kade's theory that I'm looking for sympathy, but here goes...

"I am from another plane of existence. My place is in Lemayle. I'm not supposed to be here. This," I gesture to the wretched form I've taken, "isn't supposed to happen, ever. It's unnatural. It's a hiccup in the workings of the universe and the universe doesn't know how to handle it, but it did its best." I take a deep breath against the rising panic in my chest. "But it can't last."

Jordin jolts and leans toward me, listening like I wish he would have so many centuries ago when we were still just two Firns—the best in Lemayle—saving the world together.

"Because I wasn't born like a normal person, I didn't get to grow and adjust to the world, but I'm pushing myself like a fully grown adult, and I won't be able to handle it for long. I'm going to fade and eventually I'll die."

Kade and Leo's eyes blink open wide, but Jordin doesn't seem too upset.

"Wait," Leo says thoughtfully. "You said you're from the afterlife, though. Won't you just go back?"

Jordin nods with a goofy, pleased grin.

"No."

He startles to attention and finds me looking straight at him. The boys follow my line of sight in confusion.

"Someone ripped me from Lemayle." Jordin wilts like a guilty child. "I have no medium here. I'm just a soul wrapped in skin. This is no vessel. It's a thin covering." I turn my papery-skinned, pale, veiny arms to illustrate and level my gaze at Jordin. "When I die, nothing will remain. I'll cease to exist completely."

Color drains from Jordin's figure. "W-what?"

"What do you mean?" Leo asks, concerned.

My gaze drops to my lap. "My... boss... gave two options when he visited me." Mikael's words still echo vividly in my mind. "Complete the Shift and work against you." I look pointedly at Kade. "Or keep working with you and disappear—hopefully *after* I get you where you need to be."

Jordin looks to the side, eyes searching invisible images, his mind working at top speed with the new information. He looks upset. I want him to be. He should be. He's killed me and now he gets to watch me drown.

"That sounds so bogus," Kade spits out.

"Which part?" I cry, agitated at his persistent belligerence.

"All of it!" he shouts back at me. "You're from another world. Some demon ripped your soul into this one..."

Jordin makes an irritated noise behind his teeth and rolls his eyes. I can't tell if it's because of Kade's refusal to face the facts, or just an outlet for his own guilt over what he's done to me. It should be both, and if it is, I agree with him. Humans can be so thick. And Aropfain so shortsighted.

"You're supposed to guide me to meet some girl." Guilt flares in Kade's eyes at referring to Danica that way. "And you top it off with," he drapes a hand to his forehead like a damsel in distress and says, with a squeaky voice, "'and... if I don't turn evil... I'll vanish.' How dramatic. You're trying way too hard."

Jordin's head swivels toward Kade. He straightens, lifts a hand, and smacks the back of Kade's head.

Kade's head jerks forward. "Ow!" He reaches back to rub the spot and I can't believe my eyes, but Jordin remains expressionless.

"How did you do that?" I ask without thinking.

"What, this?" Jordin smacks Kade again.

"Ow!" Kade looks around for the source of the assault. "Stop it!" he shouts at the air.

"Yeah." I nod, thrilled and terrified. "That."

Jordin smiles. "Anaya, he's never been immune to us." He says like it's a revelation, a surprise he's finally revealing to me after twenty years of torture. "He's actually quite sensitive." He punches Kade's shoulder and Kade knocks into Leo.

"Cut it out, Kade." Leo pushes him away.

"It's not me!"

I stifle a shocked laugh.

Jordin reaches out and touches the tips of his fingers to the side of Kade's head. "She's telling the truth, kid. You'd better get used to it."

Kade's eyes shoot open and he stares at nothing, but he's terrified of it.

"That feeling you have," Jordin tells him. "That constant paranoia and uncertainty you've been wrestling with since the gas station. It's because you lost your Firn, your conscience. You lost her."

Then I realize. The glazed look in Kade's eyes, the suspicion, the confusion. It's because Kade's soul can feel that I'm missing and it's freaking out.

"You're right, of course." Jordin's voice is smooth, like he's calming a frightened animal. "You're in danger, but—and it kills me to say this—not from her."

Kade's eyes dart to me and I blank on how to respond. I smile and give a little wave, trying to look friendly. Okay, I'm impressed and also confused. Firns understand everything about our Neshome's Plans, which sounds impressive to the living, but there's still so much cosmic information beyond our jurisdiction. Yes, I've always known Jordin has an extreme, mysterious, and terrifying amount of power. Still, this is more than I thought was possible for anyone short of a Malekh. It kills me he's no longer on our side. But why is he helping me now at the end of the world?

"You take care of her," Jordin commands Kade. Then he looks at me, determined. "I know you don't want to hear it," he tells me, "but you should complete the Shift."

"I'm not completing the Shift, Jordin. That's never going to happen."

"But you'll die!" he argues, curling his hands into fists.

Kade's eyes dart between the space of Jordin's presence

and me as his mortal mind clamors to put the pieces of our conversation together.

I cross my arms, ignoring the frowns we're getting from Kade and an excluded Leo. "You should've thought about that before you forced me to Shift back at Phil's gas station."

The boys swivel their heads toward the space next to Kade, searching for a sign of someone there, who might have been behind the attack that ripped me from Lemayle and into the seat next to Kade as he barreled a truck headlong toward a Security vehicle during the attack back in Albazin. But they won't find anyone. Jordin is as invisible now as we both were then. And Kade is just as attentive to Jordin and oblivious of me.

"I'm finishing my job," I continue regardless, and Jordin's fury sets in. The amber eyes smoldering as the vanity lights flicker and buzz like the bulbs may burst. "I'm finishing what El Olam trusted me with and I'll disappear knowing we won. I'd sooner die for good than Shift any day. That shouldn't surprise you."

Jordin's eyebrows pull together and a shadow crosses his eyes, giving him an unusually sinister look. Then, just as fast as it came, it vanishes. He relaxes, leans back, looks passive. The lights return to normal. "Fine. Try your best." He smirks. "But I won't be far away."

He bumps Kade in the shoulder one more time, making Kade jump. "You protect her." It's a threat more than a request. Kade's eyes almost appear to shake from the fear of the disembodied voice.

Jordin looks at me, proud of himself. He vanishes.

I sigh, shaking off the anger that Jordin always leaves behind. I can't afford it anymore.

"That was..." Leo searches for the word. "Odd."

"That was Jordin," I correct him.

Kade looks conflicted, frowning at his shoes.

"You okay over there?" I ask him.

"That was…"

"Jordin."

Kade shakes his head, eyes shut tight. "But that was…"

"Jordin," I persist. "That was Jordin. He's been messing with us your whole life."

"He said things… in my head."

"Mm-hmm," I grumble. I cross my legs and look away. "Figures you'd hear him."

"Nope." Kade stands and grabs his head. "No, this can't be real."

I groan and slump against the back of my seat. "He said you're being paranoid, that you've lost your conscience." I swallow, cheeks hot with embarrassment. "He told you to take care of me."

Kade drops his hands and looks at me. "How did you…?"

"Because this isn't a joke, Kade!" I yell, exasperated. My arms fall to my sides. "I won't argue with you anymore. I can't afford it." I curl up on my side against the velvet cushion. "Believe me or don't, but I'm done yelling. I need to stay alive long enough to get you to Danica. After that, I'll be done. You'll be free of me and you can live the rest of your life however you want."

"Anaya," Leo says just as I close my eyes to sleep off the exhaustion.

I look at him over my shoulder. "What?"

Leo holds up what looks like a muffin. "Canaan got it for you after you passed out. You should eat it. You need energy." He holds it out to me, but I wave him off.

"Later."

I wrap my arms around myself and draw my knees in. I'm too tired for anything right now. I can't deal with all of this: Kade, Jordin, Beta Siberia and Security threats, my deteriorating health, and wherever in the world El Olam is in all this mess.

CHAPTER THIRTEEN

I don't sleep long, and when I wake up, I smell food.

"Sure, but remember that time that you fell off the dock next to my house when we were trying to sneak out to Ainsley's?"

I hear Kade laugh. "Yeah. That was cold."

"It wasn't even winter," Leo adds. "But you were blue for hours. Ainsley had to throw all sorts of blankets at you before you stopped shivering."

"And they all smelled like old people."

"But you've secretly liked that smell ever since," I say as I roll over and sit up, rubbing my eyes and letting out a yawn as they look at me. I put my hand out. "Whatever smells like bacon, I want it."

"How did you know that?" Kade asks as Leo wraps bacon in a napkin and passes it to me.

I smile my thanks to Leo and look at Kade, my face still droopy with sleep. "I was there."

"Of course you were."

I shove an entire piece of bacon into my mouth. "You were trying to balance on a post because you thought it made you look cool," I relay from my own memory. "You told Leo that the mist made the dock slippery, but there wasn't even a lot of mist that day." I look at Leo, then back at Kade. "He didn't buy it, by the way."

Leo laughs. "I really didn't. I thought you just tripped over your shoelaces."

"His shoe came untied in the water," I tell Leo around another piece of bacon.

Leo tilts his head in consideration. "So, you were there for the Michelle incident back in school, then?"

I let out a bellowing laugh. "I was." My eyes fix on Kade, boring into his discomfort. "She had dark hair and blue eyes, too. I took that as a sign that Kade would be on track for Danica."

Kade scowls. "So, you knew it would never work out, but you let me make a fool out of myself, anyway? I landed straight on my face."

I nod. "Yes, you did. The chocolates were everywhere. You saved your allowance for months for those."

"And you didn't stop me?"

"I couldn't!" I give him my best innocent look. "Remember, you've ignored me all your life. Plus, it was cute. You were just a kid."

"It scarred me for life," Kade grumbles.

Leo gives him a friendly shove. "No, it didn't. You were fine."

"You charmed your fair share of girls in high school," I remind him.

"Exactly," Leo agrees, and it feels like I've been able to talk to him all their lives. Like I'm part of the group, inside jokes and all. It's nice. "You had a huge ego back then."

"Back then?" I laugh.

Kade glares at me. "What are you trying to say?" There's a pout under the irritation.

Okay, here's where I have a mind to try, like Leo said. We

need to stop fighting, especially now that Jordin is on our tail. I take a preparatory breath. "Just that you have plenty of confidence." I shrug and look away, ears flushing. I really flubbed that one. Better luck next time. Kade looks away from me, deliberately keeping his eyes on Leo. I've earned myself a cold shoulder.

"There's something I've been wondering..." Leo says somberly. He frowns like he's trying to make sense of something in his head, but it's not adding up. His green eyes clear as the ocean he lives next to. "You say there's this big Plan and that it has a role for everyone." He looks at me to confirm.

"Yes..." I draw out, nervous about where this is going.

"Do you—" he cuts off, second-guessing himself. He regroups and finally asks, "Do you know if my family is okay? Do you have any information about what's happening back home? Are Mom and Nyla alive? Are they safe?" He presses a hand over his chest and leans away from me, which I appreciate.

I want to help him. I want to tell him that everything worked out great. I'd love to tell him that his mother's mental health and his sister's coverage of the family store have miraculously improved since he left. But I can't lie to him, even if Firns like me are capable of it. I can't lie to Leo.

I sigh and shake my head. Kade smiles bitterly, like he saw this coming, and Leo already looks disappointed. "It's not that I don't want to tell you," I admit. "I..." I'm ashamed to say this. "I can't remember anything about the Plan anymore. Not even for Kade's parents."

Kade casts his gaze to his shoes at the reminder of his mom and dad. Even though I'm no longer connected to Kade's thoughts as closely as I used to be, I can still see the conflict on his face. Are they even more ashamed of him now that he's a fugitive?

Turning back to Leo, I shrug helplessly. "I only know we

need to get to Danica because she's such an important part of it all and that Kade has to meet her and help her make her choice." My eyes plead with Leo's for forgiveness for what's beyond my control. "I never had access to your story. That's your Firn's job—and your Firn and your mom and sister's Firns are still in action. They're still working, so I can tell you I believe your family is in good hands."

"Like his dad was?" Kade's voice is dark. He doesn't look at either of us. His elbows rest on his knees and he steeples his fingers, looking at the floor. Life has hit Kade pretty hard in recent months and his eyes have opened to the unfairness in the world. He hasn't been handling it gracefully. His eyes move to me. "Where was his dad's Firn?"

That burns me up. How dare he assume a Firn shirked their responsibility for their Neshome? "His Firn was fighting," I say firmly. "There are several factors in what happened with Mr. Arthur." I check Leo's face to make sure this isn't hurting him too much. There's no use in using a departed loved one as ammo for an argument, especially in front of his son. But Leo, sick as he seems about it, also has curiosity glistening in his eyes. He wants to know.

"The Association and Security are not working for us. They are in the firm grip of the Aropfain and Narn." Somehow, Leo and Kade never seem to be afraid enough when I mention the bad guys. "They're working against the Plan, and sometimes they throw it off.

"Or," I continue, "sometimes our messages don't get through properly and the miscommunication spirals out of control. Or..." I pause because they'll like this option the least, even though it's the one I hope is true for Leo's dad. "Maybe it was the time his soul agreed to go back to Lemayle."

Kade stands in outrage. "Why would Leo's dad agree to be killed when his family still needed him? He had a son, a brand-new baby, and a wife who obviously still needed him. What, your people never make mistakes?" Kade looks at me, at the fact that I'm even present here, and seems doubtful.

"We do." I reconsider. "Some of us do." My track record has been sparkling until recently. "He may have agreed for Leo's sake, for all I know. Maybe what Leo went through prepared him for what he would need to do now. It strengthened him." I give Leo an apologetic look. I feel like I'm sinking and soon I won't be able to stop.

"That's what you people do, then?" Kade demands. "You mess with us so your little Plan unfolds the way you want it to? You just use us?"

Now I stand. "Don't you dare assume that we don't care about you. We spend your entire life at your side, protecting your right to make your own choices, discuss your life at length before you come here, and make sure you are comfortable with your purpose and that you'll find fulfillment in it. We agonize over you, worry about your immortal soul even more than your physical self, and you're telling me that all we do is manipulate you?" I shove a finger in his face. "That's what the Aropfain do, Kade Buxton, and don't you dare accuse us of being like them. You're just upset because I'm your Firn and we're in this situation because you never listened."

He steps forward, shocking me into falling back. "Oh my gosh, I already have a mom!" he protests. "I don't need you. I haven't heard from you, and I've done just fine. Whatever your stupid Plan is for me, I don't even want it. I don't need you."

I open my mouth to argue, but a stinging in my nose and the blur of tears in my eyes stops me. My chest tightens. I look at the window from the corner of my eye to stop the tears.

That's when I see Jordin outside the window, moving next to the train like he's standing on an invisible platform just outside. Showoff.

His usual twisted smirk is absent. He looks upset on my

behalf, the way he used to back when we worked side by side. He tips his head toward the back of the train and disappears. I weigh my options. Stay here and cry in front of my Neshome or run.

    I run.

CHAPTER FOURTEEN

The train is long, carrying passengers and commodities, so it takes a while to reach the last car, filled with luggage and packages. When I shove the sliding door open, he's there, eyes on me like he wants to throw his arms out and offer a hug.

I'm not that overwhelmed.

I ignore the sympathy and cross the floor to sit on a leather-bound suitcase. I sniff because some tears made it out on the way here and my nose is a mess. It feels awkward, but I raise my sleeve to handle the problem.

"Wait," Jordin stops me, "here." He kicks a suitcase, and it opens. That's against the rules. He isn't serving anyone by doing that. He should leave everything untouched. But he finds a handkerchief in the stack of men's clothes and passes it to me. I have to say, though, I'd rather not soil the sleeve of the only dress I have. I accept the offer and try to remember how to blow my nose.

Jordin waits patiently until I collect myself.

"He's stupid," Jordin offers. "He's never listened to anything, and now, without you, he's even worse. I know you can't see him when you're not around him anymore, but, let me tell you, it's like watching a lost puppy growl at the world. You were all the brains he had."

I sniff and look up at him, narrowing my eyes because I haven't forgotten the actual cause of this. "No," I stand straighter. "No, Kade is stupid because you messed with me, and *I* was too stupid to notice." I prod a finger at his chest, but it passes right through, adding insult to my already wounded pride.

Jordin bows his head. "I did do that," he admits. "But I did it for the bigger picture, Anaya." His voice is pleading like he needs me to understand why he's such an insufferable jerk. He's always talking about some bigger picture he sees now that he's on Narn's side, begging me to understand, but I don't understand it. I don't understand any of the Aropfain.

"You fight so hard for living souls," Jordin says, and I can't tell if he's impressed or annoyed. "You slave over their lives and their choices and they never even acknowledge you. You're the same now as you were as Agnes. You martyred yourself screaming at a deaf world back then, too. You've been doing it with every Neshome since then, and you're doing it again now." He stares out the window of the train car, at the whole of humanity beyond the glass. "They screw up and you have to shoulder the consequences for them." He shakes his head. "But what about you? What about your dreams and your right to choose?"

I laugh at the audacity. "You are proof that we still have a right to choose! You just made the selfish choice." My arms fall and I tilt my head to the side. "And you're dragging me with you. How can you preach about choice when you've taken that right away from me?"

He raises his hands, stepping closer. "I didn't know it would happen like this. You were supposed to become one of us." He scratches his head. "I did everything the way they did it for me when I Shifted. I got a relic from Agnes." He counts on his fingers, retracing his steps. "I transferred your name from El Olam's book to Narn's."

"Wait, there's an actual book?" I blurt out before I can stop myself. "I thought that was just a metaphor."

Jordin shoots me a flat stare. "It's a ritual, Anaya. Everything's a metaphor. It's the intention behind it that counts. Any book will do." He waves me off, then tangles his fingers in his own thick hair that drifts subtly in the liminal air.

"I didn't know what to do when you ended up in Velt instead. I had to get more information, but you can still make it." He grips my shoulders and shakes me like he's trying to clear my head. The ghost of a breeze chills my shoulders where his fingers curl around them. "I'm not taking anything from you. I'm trying to show you the truth. They lied to us, Anaya."

I frown. "What are you talking about?"

He releases me and steps back, allowing the shadows of the towers of boxes to cover him. "You don't know the real story. You don't know what it is you're really fighting for."

The hair on the back of my neck stands on end as the energy around him crackles. I edge toward the door. "You're insane."

"Finish the Shift, Anaya. Please. You don't deserve to fade."

I shake my head, still moving. His eyes dart to a stack of suitcases and they tremor and fall, tripping me. I topple backward, and he's standing over me in a flash.

I'm afraid.

He crouches beside me, close enough to stop me if I try to get up and run. He's strong. I've never seen his limits. I don't know what he's really capable of, and Narn's influence and favor have only made him worse.

"I won't let you say no," he says. "The only way to move is forward. You can't disappear."

"Why?" I challenge him. "Because then you'll have to carry my death with you for eternity? I think you deserve it."

He smacks his hand down on a suitcase next to my head. "I won't let you go out like that."

I lean up into his personal space. "Like you said," I taunt, "it's my choice. Mine. And I'd rather die than be as weak as you."

He shakes with rage. The lamp above me swings wildly before the bulb shatters, and all the carefully stacked boxes and cases collapse around us, burying me beneath them. I throw my hands over my face with an accidental scream.

My head throbs. I need to get out. I can't pass out here and let Security find me. They'll think I made this mess and arrest me for sure.

I push the suitcases off me and grumble about how high maintenance these rich people must be to have such heavy bags. I get my legs beneath me and stand, looking for Jordin. The room appears dark and empty, but Jordin is still here. He never vanishes before having the last word.

"Make it to Nor'ilsk," he orders from somewhere in the dark. I turn, trying to discern where he is, but I can't place him. "That's where I'll be, and I'll help you finish the Shift from there where you'll be safe."

"Do you have something stuck in your ears?" I shout at the dark. "I will not finish the Shift! Get over it!"

Suddenly, he's back, flashing closer to me with every word like he strung up a strobe light for the effect. "Yes. You. Will!"

I fold my arms and flatten my eyes, quirking my mouth in an unimpressed smirk. "You can't use scare tactics on me, Jordin. That won't work. I know you, remember."

He flicks an angry, dismissive hand at me. "You know nothing. You're in for a real shock when you finally find Danica." His face shifts from rage to amusement. The room stills like the forest just after a heavy rain: peaceful and fresh. The tension in my chest lifts, along with Jordin's spirits. "In fact, I'll let you see for yourself." He faces me, relaxing back into a friendly pose. "I'm going to help you, Anaya. I'll help you get to Danica."

I feel the dumb look on my face. "What? Why?"

He laughs and shakes his head. He won't tell me. "You want choices? I'll give you reasons to choose."

Someone knocks urgently against the door behind me, and I whirl around to see Leo looking terrified through the glass window. I wave my hands in front of me to tell him I'm okay, no matter how bad this looks, and he throws the door open, looking at the chaos around me.

I jut a thumb over my shoulder. "Jordin," I say. "We had a..." I look at the mess of suitcases at my feet and shrug, "disagreement." I look behind me and find exactly what I expect. Jordin is gone. Leo couldn't see him, anyway.

I look like a madwoman.

"The, uh..." Leo scratches the back of his neck. "The train will arrive in a few hours. We got more food and some blankets. I thought you could use the chance to rest."

I take in the room now that the threat has passed. This is a mess. I don't want to be seen here. I check the corners of the room. No cameras. Security has gotten lax in recent centuries, as people have become more compliant and afraid.

My stomach rumbles. I look up at Leo. "Did you get more bacon?"

"How are we paying for all this?" I ask as I inhale another bacon sandwich, which is a genius combination. My frail form will fill out in no time if I have open access to bacon. I'll die of a clogged artery before my body gives out, but it'll be satisfying. I fall back against the cushioned seat with a sigh, ignoring Kade's irritated eyes on me. He's still not over our argument, but I can't afford to cling to rage, so I cling to bacon. Bacon doesn't argue with me. Bacon makes me happy.

"The lady said we could put it on Canaan's tab," Leo explains.

I pause mid-bite and lower my sandwich. "And you feel okay with that?" I look between him and Kade.

Kade gives a tight shrug. "He's one of the richest men in the world. He even gets to leave the BSA sometimes because he can actually afford it."

I think about it. "Don't we need him to like us? He could turn us over like that." I snap my fingers and do an internal happy dance. I've always wanted to try snapping. It sounds so cool.

Kade rolls his eyes. "Well, I'm sure we'll figure something out if he ditches us."

"What if he turns us in?" I challenge. I'm getting a little tired of Kade's attitude. He's just being contradictory for the sake of it, like he just wants to say the opposite of anything I say. How childish.

"Then I guess we die." He opens his arms. "What would you like me to say?"

"You're sorry, for starters..." I mumble, but Kade hears me.

"You first." He raises his eyebrows, waiting.

I purse my lips and nod. "Yeah. You're right. I am sorry."

He smiles.

"Sorry you're so pompous and arrogant." I shake my head, almost laughing. "If I wouldn't have been so distracted protecting you from Jordin, maybe you'd have turned out more humble. You were supposed to be humble."

Tension grips the room and Leo jumps in. "Guys, we don't have time for this. We'll be pulling into the station in a few minutes. We should clean this mess up." He gestures to the wrappers and disposable plates strewn around us. We look like slobs. Not very high-class.

As Kade and I collect the trash, Leo looks out the window where the train bends around a river to reveal a classically styled Russian city. The city of Irkutsk, remastered to its original glory from the sixteen hundreds. An elegant white arch rises above the river, flanked by spired buildings of the same ivory construction. This time of year, mist from the lake shrouds the rest of the more industrialized development, giving the impression of a small, regal city, but it's just a facade. Those buildings are extremely expensive hotels these days, more tourist traps than functional business centers. They're just there to look pretty and cover up the ugly work that happens deeper in the development.

But if I can shove the reality from my mind, it really is a gorgeous sight. I wish things were just what they seemed to be and didn't hide dark secrets behind beautiful lies. But then I suppose I'd be out of a job.

A woman knocks on the door and slides it open, asking for our trash. We hand it over with bright smiles, trying to look like we belong on this train, and we didn't just sneak on from the street.

As the woman bids us goodbye and a safe stay in Irkutsk, Canaan returns, waiting impatiently for her to stop blocking the doorway. When she leaves, he all but shoves her away and rushes into the compartment, sliding the door shut a bit too loudly.

"We're on the radar," he says as he sits down. His face is flushed and there's a healthy amount of alcohol on his breath. He must've really been working the crowd in the luxury car.

"What?" Kade asks for all of us.

Canaan gives him a tired look. "Security is going to be watching us at the station." He looks at me. "Have you been studying your paperwork?"

I choke. I'd love to tell him I have, but I've been busy wrecking the luggage car and arguing with my Neshome about the greater good, so, "No..."

He rubs his temples, and I can tell he's wondering why he's surrounded by idiots. "It's like you want to be arrested."

"But we've established that she has memory issues," Leo

defends me. "Shouldn't she make sure she doesn't know some things?"

"Some things, sure." Canaan nods. "But her own name? Isn't that the one thing a person should be able to remember?" He looks at me. "Why don't you know your name?"

"This coming from the other guy with a pseudonym," I reply defensively.

Canaan dips his head. "Fair enough. But you need to learn it by the time we hit the station." He adopts a mocking pout. "Think you can handle that, princess?"

I glare at him. I am not a child. He may be surrounded by idiots, but I'm surrounded by jerks—except Leo.

The train slows down and my stomach sinks. We're pulling into Irkutsk station. Jett Tyrrell won't be here, but his Aropfain may be, and I'm sure his father, the Chairman of the Association and leader of Beta Siberia, is. This is the Beta Siberian Arrangement seat of government. Mikael had better be working overtime on this one. I can't think of a less safe place to be in this world, except maybe the heart of a volcano.

CHAPTER FIFTEEN

Customs. Why are there customs between developments? Beta Siberia isn't even an officially recognized country. It's just become such a nuisance that the rest of the world has left it alone. Big mistake in hindsight, seeing as it grew and spread throughout the entire Siberian region like a potent fungus. Now, if someone were to challenge it, they'd have a healthy war on their hands.

And here I stand with Canaan, Kade, and Leo, sweating under the pressure as we inch closer and closer to the customs agent's desk. Here, there are cameras. Everyone must present their paperwork to the agent and try to ignore the camera pointed at them, taking their picture to use against them in case Security suddenly hates them. I can imagine several reasons that would happen to us.

I look around, but there's no sign of Jordin yet. I don't know what to make of that, either, since he threatened to help me.

"Next!" The yell is so close it startles me. I've been swaying forward in the line without thinking. Following Canaan's back, we're pressed so close.

Canaan turns around and grabs my arm. "That's us. Remember your name." He looks to Kade and Leo. "You two wait for the next agent. I'm not listed as your guardian."

Wait, what? No, I have to stay with my Neshome. The customs desks form a row about a hundred yards long, or at least it seems like it. Who knows where Kade and Leo will end up? I need to protect them!

"Come on!" Canaan jerks me forward and all I get is a shrug from the boys.

I trip behind Canaan until we stand at the side of the agent's desk, directly in front of the black camera clipped to the glass, protecting the agent from any threats. Honestly, I think it should be the other way around. In the BSA, the government orders the attacks and blames the people. But no one is supposed to let on that they know it, lest they become the next framed terrorist.

Canaan passes our papers to the agent and waits for the questioning to begin.

"Name?"

Canaan places a hand to his collarbone. "Canaan Sem."

The agent looks at me over his silver glasses. After a moment, he quirks an eyebrow and Canaan steps on my foot.

"Oh!" I close my eyes for a second, trying to picture the form. "Agnes. Agnes DiRoma." I still roll the *r* like I did when the name was mine. That was so, so long ago.

The agent frowns at my paperwork, and I stress for a moment that I got the name wrong. He looks up at me.

"You're sick?"

"Recovering," Canaan corrects him respectfully. "I'm funding her rehabilitation for my charity organization. She has no contagion. I wouldn't put myself in that kind of danger." He laughs, and the agent does too. I glance between them. It's probably best if I just look pathetic. I don't need to say anything now that I'm the butt of the joke that's expediting our interview.

The agent catches his breath as he stamps our papers.

"Enjoy your stay, Mr. Sem. Try not to catch anything from this one."

They laugh again like they're friends now and I work to keep my face blank. I'm not in a position to have an opinion, but as we clear the throng of Security, I kick the back of Canaan's knee and he only just catches himself before he drops to the floor.

"I just saved you," he protests, rubbing the back of his leg. He looks around. "Where are those other kids? We need to get out of here as soon as possible."

I scan the room and spot Kade four desks down, then smack Canaan and nod in Kade and Leo's direction. We move in unison, getting as close as possible without being noticed. Kade slings his coat over his arm, the top two buttons of his slightly rumpled white shirt undone, showing a flush of red running up his neck. The stains on his shirt betray his nervous sweat. Something is going wrong.

I tap into his emotions. Shaky nerves and panic flood my head. I feel edgy, like I'm tempted to make a run for it.

I look at the agent. He leans toward Kade and Leo.

"Where have I seen you before?" the voice of the agent echoes in my ears. I didn't know I could do that, but cool.

Kade scratches the back of his head and gives a nervous laugh. "Not sure, sir. I've never visited Irkutsk before."

The agent hums suspiciously. "Wait, I know where I've seen you..." He turns back to his computer and mashes some keys.

That's when Jordin shows up and my heart stops. He stands at Kade's shoulder, smirking at me.

I smack Canaan again. He looks at me like he'll smack me back next time. "They recognized them. What do we do?"

"They what?"

"You heard me!" I smack his arm again because I need an outlet. "What do we do?"

Canaan tangles his fingers in his hair. "I should've made them dye their hair or something."

"When did we have time for that? On the train?"

I look around. What can I do? I'm stuck in Velt and have no influence outside of my reach.

Jordin reads my mind. "You know," he teases, "I could help you."

I shake my head, trying not to respond in front of Canaan. I'll figure this out. Mikael will show up. Something miraculous will happen. I don't know, just anything but accepting Jordin's help.

I look around, my mind blank from stress. I feel so useless. There are too many people, too much noise, too few resources now that I've lost my influence from Lemayle. I can't knock something over from across the room. I can't whisper clever ideas in Kade's ear and hope he hears them. All I can do is stand here next to Canaan and watch as Jordin does all of those things for the wrong reasons.

No. I'm limited, but I haven't lost yet. There are still a few insignificant tricks up my sleeve.

I close my eyes and try to see through Kade's. If I can hear with his ears, then why wouldn't I see with his eyes? It's blurry, and it burns my eyes, but I can make out two pictures on the man's screen. Two figures from the shoulder up. Dangerous person warrants.

We've been made.

Hopelessness floods my chest, and I move toward Kade. I don't know what I'll do, but I'm doing something. I don't know if it's in the Plan to be captured again. Kade and Leo won't make it out of prison a second time, especially without me. I'd forgotten how frustrating it is not to have access to what is correct and what isn't.

Jordin still watches me from Kade's side. His arrogant face falters when he sees how panicked I am. He glances at the computer screen, then flashes to my side, moving with me.

"You know how easily I could fix this," he reminds me, sounding like his friendly old self. "I can short-circuit his panic button, mess with his head while you slip your Neshome out of there. Clean cut. Just hear me out."

My eyes widen in a wild expression. "I'm busy, Jordin. I don't have time to 'hear you out.'"

Why are legs so slow? There might as well be three feet of snow on the ground for how sluggish I am. I can't let myself panic too much. I already have a light head. But then, maybe...

"Just finish the Shift," Jordin negotiates. "You'll have the freedom to be as annoying to the rest of us as you want. You don't even have to take on an actual assignment. Be like a double agent or something."

Because doing nothing is just as bad as doing something. Narn doesn't care if you're useful to him, as long as you're not useful to El Olam. He's a great guy, Narn.

I suck in as much air as my chest can hold. My body needs oxygen. It's running out of steam. "It's not really the same, Jordin."

He drops his arms in frustration. "You'll just die then."

I nod, running out of breath. "I'll just die then." Hm. I'll just die then... I glimpse Leo at the desk, trying to peek around to the screen and bouncing nervously. His mouth is moving like he's trying to stall the agent. Judging by the cynical look on the agent's face, it doesn't appear to be working.

"All you have to do is agree, Anaya!" Jordin's own exhaustion seethes through his teeth. "Just say the word, even feel it enough, and it'll be done."

I stop moving and throw him a glare. "Haven't we played that game before? That's how I got here in the first place. Not again," I assure him. I let my anger fill me until my breath scrapes my throat and my vision blurs. Surely, I can survive one more of these. I look up through the domed skylight at the gray clouds and hope that Mikael's got my back.

"Anaya..." Jordin's picked up that I'm scheming. "Whatever you're planning, don't. You don't have the strength to do this stuff anymore. Remember, everyone can see you."

I smile. "I'm counting on it."

Everything I've been pushing down roils up. How Kade, my own Neshome, hates me and can't stand to be near me. His childhood and how he never acknowledged me. How I watched him grow and shape himself, robbing me of my purpose in his life. All the times Jordin interfered and what it really meant. How this is all my fault for falling for Jordin's little plot.

I remember that El Olam allowed it to happen and hasn't commented on it since, and how somehow I'm still expected to fulfill my purpose as a Firn, like my existence isn't on the line. That it is—that, even if I perform my duties perfectly, my reward will be to vanish—a true and final death like everyone fears most.

My head throbs and my feet stop moving. I can't focus on anything anymore. The world swims and swirls. The bustle of the checkpoint around me fades into dull echoes.

I glance around for the richest-looking person I can find near the fourth desk. A woman wearing furs and a royal purple dress and matching hat. How textbook rich can you get? I stumble her way, hoping Canaan is nearby. He's going to have some explaining to do.

"I—is there a problem, sir?" I hear Kade's voice in my head, louder now that my own senses scramble. The customs agent's hand is sliding under his desk toward the panic button that Jordin offered to disable. I don't want it disabled, though. I need it working.

Scrunching my face against the pain in my head, I stumble forward and throw my arms out to clutch at the woman's fur shawl.

"H-help... me!" I say it loud enough to draw attention, but my voice rasps and the woman gasps in horror. I wish I hadn't had so much bacon. My stomach churns with nausea. That wasn't originally part of the plan, but I'll take it. When my stomach threatens to empty itself, I let it happen. The woman's shriek is a better distraction than I ever could have hoped for. I close my eyes and unhook my wit from my mind to hang it on Kade's, and experience it all through his eyes.

The customs agent jumps at the shrill sound. His hand hits the button as he stands, tripping an alarm and red siren lights. Everyone in the room ducks to the floor and covers their heads.

Kade sees me take the woman down as I collapse to the floor. He sneaks a peek at the guard and reaches discreetly for their papers. After he shoves them into his coat, he elbows Leo.

"Sir!" Leo exclaims at the jab. The agent swings his head toward them, eyes flared in shock and disgust. "I can help that woman. I know how to handle sick people."

Most people in Beta Siberia don't. Sick people are untouchables here. No one likes to get their hands dirty.

The agent reaches over the desk and shoves Leo away, forgetting what he was doing in favor of his own preservation. "Go then! Get that filth out of here."

I let out a relieved sigh, swimming in the screams around me as I lose my grip on reality. Someone grabs me under the arms and lifts me. I hope it's someone I know.

"That was disgusting," I hear Jordin's voice in my ear. "You should've just let me handle it."

I smile, proud of myself.

Jordin doesn't seem happy. "You'd better survive this, Anaya. This isn't over."

CHAPTER SIXTEEN

I survive, as it happens. In fact, I wake up feeling more comfortable than I've ever felt. My whole body relaxes into a soft bed, wrapped in a plush and warm blanket, no draft in the room, warm sunlight on my face, a cool sensation on my forehead. I feel amazing. For a while, I don't open my eyes. I stay still and appreciate what it is to feel so calm and at ease. I can't ignore the world forever, but I've earned these few seconds.

The coolness on my forehead leaves and returns. I guess I should open my eyes and let them know I made it.

But first, I stretch. I didn't plan to, but I'm not complaining. It feels awesome. I grin to myself as I open my eyes and sit up. A damp washcloth slips off my forehead and into my lap, soaking through a silk pair of blue pajama pants. I guess I soiled my dress beyond salvation. I'm not at all upset. These feel amazing against my skin, and they seem to be stitched together with actual gold thread, but that's impossible. Isn't it?

"Don't you look pleased with yourself," Kade observes. I direct my smile at him, but he cringes. "You're gross."

"You weren't saving yourself," I point out. "Someone had

to do something."

"But that?"

Leo laughs next to me. "Well, I'm glad to see you're feeling better."

I nod and look around. I've come a long way from the train station. We're in a luxury hotel, several dozen floors up by the view from the window. The room is gaudy, designed for royalty in the same baroque design of the arch and buildings we saw coming into Irkutsk. Regal white walls and cream accents enclose two king-sized beds, a giant wall-mounted flat screen television, two closets, a desk with tourist pamphlets scattered across it, and a bathroom that looks like I want to take a very long bath right now. Of course, Canaan would stay here.

"Did we get out without any more issues?" I ask.

"They basically escorted us out," Kade tells me. "They couldn't get rid of us fast enough."

I laugh. "You're welcome."

"Canaan isn't happy," Leo informs me. "He had to answer a bunch of questions about your health and why he sponsored your recovery."

"He had the paperwork." I brush it off. "I'm a mental case. He can either talk or buy his way out of it."

Kade folds his arms. "Well, he's no fan of yours right now."

"I don't need him to be. I just needed to get you out of there safely. They recognized you."

Kade's eye twitches. "How did you know that?"

Oh. It strikes me that I should have told Kade about my supernatural levels of stalking sooner. "I can tap into your head sometimes." I try to make it sound like no big deal, but Kade takes it personally.

Before he can argue with me, I say, "And aren't you glad I can? Otherwise, you and Leo would be in prison, and I doubt Ainsley's got any friends here to help you out."

"Wait," Leo holds up a hand, "You mean Bentley was…"

"A plant." I nod, remembering the chaos of Kade's fake interview for the Yuzhno Archives department that led to them fleeing from the city with Bentley's help. "From Ainsley, and, naturally, from us. At least that's what I picked up on."

"Huh," Leo puffs. "That actually makes me feel better."

I grin. At least I'm good for something in my current state. "Where is Canaan?" I ask.

Kade frowns. "He said he had business here. Something about keeping his reputation intact."

"We have until morning," Leo adds. "Apparently, we've got a flight to catch to Nor'ilsk."

"Awesome," I breathe. So, I made the right choice in getting us out of there.

Leo suddenly looks sheepish, like he's about to ruin my mood.

"What?" I ask.

"He also sent us some more clothes. He had the hotel staff burn your old ones. They were a bit," he looks down, trying not to be rude, "ruined."

My head tilts. Not surprising. I vomited all over a wealthy woman.

"What's wrong with that?"

Kade's shoulders bob with laughter. "He also sent up some makeup to fix your face."

"Very classy, Kade." I sulk against the downy pillows. There goes my good mood.

"He says we need to make you presentable before the flight tomorrow." At least Leo looks sympathetic about it.

I groan as I push myself toward the edge of the bed, missing the blankets before I even leave them, and head to the bathroom. The extravagant stained-glass dome light switches on, and I glimpse myself in the full-length mirror. I'm still not used to it. My face looks better than before. My eyes aren't as sunken in and dark, my cheeks have color, and my face has filled out. I'm still gangly, but that may just be how this body is. My eyes are brighter, which is good and bad. Good, because it means I'm still alive. Bad, because it means I'm more physical than I was before, more attached to Velt than Lemayle. I turn around and shut the door without a word. I turn on the shower, stand inside, and pretend that it's only water streaming down my face.

When I'm done, I bury my face in a fresh-scented, fluffy towel and linger for a moment, breathing and keeping myself calm. I throw on an incredibly comfortable bathrobe and crack the door open, reaching my arm into the room. Someone takes the hint and hangs a garment bag on my fingers. I'm disappointed to find another dress inside, but I guess practical clothes would be conspicuous.

This dress is black with black tights, black flats with more than the usual amount of tread on the bottom, and a red wool coat with a sash around the waist. If I ditch the coat, I can actually work well with whatever comes my way. Canaan must know we've got a rocky road ahead of us.

My eyes catch the makeup bag on the counter, and I pull a stool out from under the counter and sigh. What am I supposed to do with all this? I brush out my mess of brown hair before it tangles into a curly mess and open the door.

"Leo, can you help me again?"

Leo looks cornered. "I don't know," he admits. "Canaan said we need to make you fit in and I don't know how they manage all that stuff they do with their faces here."

"I do." Jordin pops into the corner of the room wearing a grin that says he's going to enjoy this more than he should.

"Oh, no." I shake my head, forgetting that Kade and Leo can't see him. They both slowly turn toward the corner, wary, like they're about to see a ghost. "I'm not letting you near my face."

Jordin pushes away from the wall, arms open in a

nonthreatening embrace. "Anaya, you wound me."

"I wish."

"Are we absolutely sure that she's not just hallucinating?" Kade whispers to Leo.

Leo, bless him, shakes his head. "You should've seen that train car, Kade. No way she could've done that on her own with the strength she has." Leo's eyes dart around the room, searching for a sign of Jordin's presence, which draws Jordin's attention.

He catches himself in his strut across the floor and sets a course for Leo. He leans in toward Leo's face, analyzing him, then rests a hand on Leo's head, but Leo doesn't react. Jordin purses his lips in disappointment.

I deflate a little. Leo isn't as perceptive as Kade is. How messed up is that? All this time, I've had an advantage and never once could I use it.

I glare at Jordin. "Why are you here?"

Jordin moves behind Leo to stand next to Kade and gives me a pleased grin. "I'm here to help you, like I promised." His voice is innocent, but I've never felt so nervous.

I fold my arms over my chest and shift my weight to one side. "I don't know why you even care," I tell him. "If we make it to Nor'ilsk, we'll wreck Jett's chances with Danica."

Jordin bobs his head from side to side. "You'll try," he corrects me. "But you're missing the big picture, Anaya."

"I'm missing the...?" How can he say that? This is the culmination of the big picture!

He doesn't care about the outrage on my face. Instead, he points at me and says, "Don't worry, we'll fix that for you."

My face falls flat. "Like you could cover up my hatred for you with a little makeup."

"No," he admits. "Just your sour face." He lifts his hand in what feels like slow motion and sets it on Kade's shoulder. Kade jolts. My chest tightens with both fear and remorse.

"What is...?" Kade's eyes find mine.

I raise my eyebrows at him. "Not a hallucination."

Jordin leans toward Kade's ear. "I can't pick that stuff up. It's too precise. You'll have to do it for me." Kade's eyes go round and his pupils small, like he's got a gun to his head, which, frankly, is less threatening than an Aropfain at his shoulder. Jordin straightens and looks around. "Hang on." He flicks a hand toward the giant television on the wall and it flickers on. Kade and Leo spin toward the noise of a reality television show that they've never seen, unable to pick up more than the free basic channels on their outdated TV sets back home.

"What is all that?" Leo steps toward the screen. High-class girls are giggling all over it, but none of us can see why.

"It's hilarious," Jordin responds only to me. "They're competing for a place in Nor'ilsk. They have to prove that their good genes will translate to any kids they have. There are DNA tests and background investigations and every week one girl gets sent to a low-income development if she doesn't make it to the next phase."

"That's disgusting."

"What is?" Leo asks me.

I consider explaining it, but Leo and Kade come from a low-income development and, unlike Jordin, I'd rather spare their feelings. I nod toward the screen. "It's a petty competition for a place in Nor'ilsk."

"But the girl for this generation already won," Kade points out. "Why are they still trying to get there?"

I look at him with sad eyes. "They're trying to secure themselves based on the promise of the next generation."

Leo takes the news personally, imagining his sister basing her entire life on the promise of finding someone attractive enough to have the right children with. But that's how we got Danica.

Jordin smiles. "And now we're going to make you look like

them." He places his hand back on Kade's shoulder and Kade shrinks away uncomfortably. "Make that," he points to me and then spins Kade toward the TV, "look like that."

"Wow," I drawl. "Very sensitive, Jordin. Thanks."

Kade turns his head to stare at me. I give him a yes-I-heard-it-I-told-you-so face.

Jordin takes Kade by both shoulders and pushes him toward me. I resist the urge to back away. It'll only make things worse. Canaan ordered the makeover, and he was right to. We need to blend in as much as possible until we find Danica, but why did Jordin have to show up?

Kade jolts to a stop in front of me, his eyes fearful and apologetic.

"And this is the difference between Firns and Aropfain," I explain to him quietly. "You see it now?" I never forced Kade to do anything the way Jordin is steering him right now. Except during that one Security raid, but that was to save Kade's life, and I was under stress.

"Oh, stop being so bitter, Anaya." Jordin turns to the sink behind him and knocks over the makeup bag to see what he's working with. "You sit on the toilet. Kade, grab that little stool right there and sit in front of her."

Kade looks at me with the eyes of a hostage. I rub my forehead and weigh my options. To be honest, why not? I know every step with Jordin is a step toward a trap, but unless Security bursts through the door while I'm mid-lipstick, we're not in danger yet. I sigh and sit on the toilet, which has way more buttons than necessary. How many settings does a toilet need?

A moment later, Kade plops down in front of me, makeup bag in his lap and a thick, awkward tension between us. Jordin kneels next to him, hand still firmly on Kade's shoulder.

"Start with the tube stuff. Palest you can find. She's a ghost."

"It's winter!" I protest.

"Your skin might as well be wax paper," Jordin retorts, nose in the air.

I roll my eyes. "You've spent way too much time around royal snobs this go around."

He ignores me and focuses on Kade. "This stuff can go all over. You can't mess it up."

Kade wiggles in his seat. "Shouldn't Leo be doing this?"

"Leo can't hear me like you can. Just do as I say."

Kade cringes. This is a massive breach of personal space—for me, too. I look over Kade's shoulder to see Leo watching everything from the bedroom. To him, it looks like Kade and I are just having an awkward moment with an imaginary friend, but he knows better. That's why he's being so quiet. He's nervous.

I don't enjoy seeing my boys scared, least of all of Jordin. I'm the only one who can actually see him, so I have the advantage.

"You could use some makeup yourself, Jordin," I jibe. "I can practically see through you."

Jordin gives a bitter smile. "You're not as funny as you think you are."

At this, of all things, Kade laughs, but was it at my joke or Jordin's insult? Whose side is he on?

"I'm plenty funny," I argue as Kade wipes the cold, watery cream on my face. "And don't either of you pull the 'funny looking' line. That's archaic."

Both of them pause like they each had it in mind, and I groan.

"Tilt your face up, Anaya. You're making it difficult for him."

"I'm making it difficult? I'm not the one practically possessing him!"

Leo stiffens at that but does nothing, and I cringe, mouthing an apology. Leo's seen what powerful people do in the dark, human or not, and his instincts won't let him make the same mistakes his father made those years ago. Leo won't let himself get taken out of the game before he has a clear exit.

"Practically is better than actually doing it," Jordin goads me.

"Would you drop that already? It was one time in his entire life, and I have already apologized."

"No, you didn't," Kade chimes in.

I gape at him, appalled. "Did so!" I object. "And you're taking his side? Story of your life, Kade. Seriously. You always take his side."

Jordin laughs. "She's right, actually."

I narrow my eyes at him. "But that's only because you were messing with me. If it weren't for you, I'd have been fine and Kade would have been best friends with Danica by now."

"Wow, I really hope she lives up to all the hype you give her," Kade drones. "All this over one girl?"

"Shut up," Jordin and I say together.

"You think she's gorgeous," I accuse him. "That's why you continue to play along, so don't pretend like you're not part of this."

"She's right," Jordin agrees, shocking me by how easily he changes sides, though it shouldn't, given his record. "You were born for this. You have a natural inclination toward it because that's what you came here to do. It's annoying that you keep trying to deny it. We know you're lying, so just stop giving Anaya so much grief over it."

Both Kade and I give him weird faces. Kade lowers the makeup applicator and turns to stare at the space above his shoulder where Jordin's voice comes from. "What the heck are you?"

"My own person," Jordin replies smugly. "I can do and say whatever I want. That's my freedom."

"Oh, please," I cut in. "You're a puppet."

"And you aren't?"

My chest puffs out. "I'm a Firn," I state proudly. "I'm a public servant, if anything."

Kade falls over at the loud burst of laughter that comes from Jordin. "Public servant? Delusional." He grabs Kade's sleeve. "Get back up here. You've got eyeshadow next."

Eyeshadow, eyeliner, mascara, rouge, various other creams and powders that accent things that aren't really there, and finally lipstick, the most awkward.

"I can do this myself."

Kade happily obliges when I reach for it.

I stand and move to the mirror, glimpsing my face and freezing. I hate to admit it, but I don't look like the clown I expected. All that makeup makes me look nothing like I did before. I look like a moving painting, almost imposingly attractive. I frown at my reflection. I don't like it. It feels like a lie. Accenting features is fine, but this is a different face entirely.

I turn to Jordin. "What does Danica really look like?"

Jordin smiles, hand still on Kade's shoulder. "Danica prefers a more natural look," he assures me. He respects her too. After all, she's everyone's Reyn Gayst, not just El Olam's. "She can afford it, though. She's already chosen. If you're going into Nor'ilsk, you need to look as desperate as everyone else."

"What has the world come to?" I ask my reflection with a sigh.

"The party is just getting started, Anaya." Jordin claps a hand on Kade's back. He smiles at me in the mirror. I'm impressed that I can see his reflection. "Get excited. Great things are coming."

Kade glances up at me, worry in his eyes. I think reality is finally settling in on him. I guess I should thank Jordin for that. But I won't.

"What are you doing next, then?" I ask Jordin. I try to hide the interest in my voice, but I don't think it works.

Jordin lowers his head with a close-lipped smile. He lifts his hand from Kade's shoulder, then meets my eyes. Somehow, with Kade excluded from the conversation, I'm nervous. "I'll be around, Anaya." He takes slow steps my way and watches my reflection in the mirror next to his. "I'll see you to Danica. Don't worry."

I squint at him. "Why are you helping me? Isn't that against Narn's rules?"

"I told you," he shrugs, "we can do what we want. You should try it." He levels his eyes at me, but I shoot him down with a shake of my head.

"Not interested."

He doesn't care. "Besides..." He examines his nails for show. It's not like dirt can get under them. "Getting to Danica in no way ensures you victory." He glances at Kade. "He's not impressive enough for her." He looks back at me, sadness and a hint of fear in his eyes. "I'm more concerned about you."

"Maybe you should've been concerned before you Shifted me." Funny, I can accept the interference with my work on Kade's Plan. That's just business. But I can't forgive Jordin for trying to Shift me. That's too low, even for an Aropfain, but especially for one that trained and served with me before he Shifted.

Jordin squeezes the sides of his head and looks up at me. "I did that because I was worried!"

I tilt my head to give him my best combination of condescension and incredulity.

"Everything's gotten messed up, Anaya." He shakes his head at the floor. "Nothing is what we thought it was."

That's the same argument that every Aropfain uses. They dedicate their energies to serving other souls and then they get selfish. Shifting is extreme, but it sounds like freedom.

"Don't you understand that you're being used?" I try not to sound affected by it. "Narn is using you!"

"And El Olam is using you!" he shouts back. "But we have to pick sides, so I chose the one that gives me the most room to work with."

I can almost see the brainwashed glaze in his eyes. No one ever promised this would be easy. We knew we were going to be following orders from the start—that's what the Plan is, our orders. It's the outcome that makes them worth following.

"You'll see when you get to Nor'ilsk." Jordin straightens with resolve. "I'll show you."

I know we're being set up. Jordin thinks Narn let him off the leash, but that's just the illusion of freedom that keeps him compliant. If Narn allows Jordin to play like this, then Narn wants what will come of it. Jordin is just the bait in Narn's trap. And I'm going to take it, for now. It's not like I expected to get to Danica without issues. If life's a dance, this is the salsa. We have to step quickly and carefully, or we'll trip all over ourselves.

I lift my chin at Jordin. "You can show me all you want, Jordin, but I know whose side I'm on. I know what I stand for, and I know what I need to do. I support it and I believe in it. Can you say any of that?"

Jordin steps chest-to-chest with me and it's odd to feel nothing but empty air while staring into his eyes. For a moment, I wonder what Kade sees.

"I can say anything I want." His voice is low and grave. "And I can write my own rules. Narn doesn't care, and that's the way I want it."

"He seemed to care when you were chasing us down back at Taltsy," I interrupt.

Jordin waves me off. "He hands out aid like candy these days, especially to me because I have to deal with you." He leans back a bit, looking intrigued. "Tell me, Anaya. How much support have you received since you Shifted?" He doesn't let me answer. "Oh, that's right, you're untouchable. No one can come near you anymore."

He obviously doesn't know about Mikael's promise to help me, but I'll treasure any secrets I'm able to keep.

"You have no one," he continues. The bathroom light flickers above us. Kade and Leo notice. I pretend not to.

"Everyone has abandoned you. The only one with any concern for you is me, and you still treat me like an enemy." Jordin's eyes pinch in anger. "If you're that eager to disappear, maybe you're not worth my time either." His words sting in the center of my chest and my head falls an inch. "But I guess time will tell." He steps back and turns away from me, facing the bathroom doorway. "You stood up for me once, Anaya..."

He's right. I did. More than once, actually. It didn't pay off.

"I won't give up on you yet. Not until you've heard the whole story." He looks at me over his shoulder, smiling like he used to. "Remember how that makeup works." He nods to the array of cosmetics on the bathroom counter. "You need it."

I swipe a tube of lipstick from the counter and throw it at him. His shoulders tense and he sends out a pulse of energy. The lipstick ricochets and shatters the bathroom light. Kade covers his head as glass rains on us. I forget for a moment that I'm not in Lemayle and a shard scratches my cheek. I clap a hand over the sting. Jordin's laughter echoes off the tile walls.

For a few seconds, everything is still. I drop my head and let my hair fall around my face. Pieces of glass clink to the ground as I force back tears.

Someone pokes the back of my shoulder, and a pair of shoes enters my vision in front of me. "Don't worry," I say through clenched teeth. "He's gone."

Kade and Leo look around like they're emerging from rubble after an earthquake.

"What happened?" Leo asks.

Kade shakes his head. "I only caught some of it. I could only hear him when he was next to me."

Leo shivers. "That's creepy."

They're both quiet for a moment. I know they're watching me. I can feel their eyes on my back and confusion coming from Kade.

"Are you..." Leo hesitates. "Are you okay, Anaya?"

"I'm fine."

"You're not fine." Kade sighs and grabs a tissue from the sink. The faucet runs for a second before Kade is in front of me, lifting my chin and pressing the damp tissue to the cut on my cheek.

"How did that happen?" Leo stares at the mess on the floor. "Canaan is going to kill us when he sees the bill for this." He scratches the back of his head. "This can't be cheap."

"We didn't do anything," Kade insists.

I let out a hollow laugh. "You can't prove it." I catch his eyes for a second. He wants to look angry, but his anger has a different target now. Someone hurt a girl. That doesn't sit well with him.

"Here..." He reaches for the tubes of makeup and touches up around the cut, careful to avoid getting anything in it. "The cut isn't that bad. It should look fine in a few days."

I blow a stray piece of hair away from my face. I don't want to care about how it looks, but I don't want to draw unwanted attention either.

"Come on." Leo takes my hand and leads me to sit in front of the TV. He kneels in front of me and tries to catch my eyes. "Are you okay?" He searches my face, but I've got nothing to give him.

"I'm fine," I say again. The hollow feeling in my chest makes it hard for me to believe myself.

Kade stands behind Leo, looking thoughtful. "You know what we need?" he decides. "We need to get out."

I raise an eyebrow at him. "Excuse me?"

Leo twists to look at him. "Canaan told us to stay put until morning, Kade." There's a warning in his voice, but we both know Kade has never acknowledged it.

Kade shakes his head and moves to the desk. "If we stay here, we'll drive ourselves nuts worrying about invisible crazy guys." He picks up a brochure and waves it at us. "We should go sightseeing. When else are we going to have the chance to see Irkutsk?"

Leo nods his head slowly. "I never thought I'd get to come here."

"It's the most luxurious place in the BSA," Kade persists. "We have to see it for ourselves and not just through a hotel window."

I look out the window. Chilly mist blankets the city. Sightseeing won't be that interesting. Then the colors of one of the brochures catch my eye. I stand and pick it up.

"Hmm..." I look at Kade, wondering if my developing plan is worth trying. I turn to Kade. "You want to know what's so important about Danica and the BSA?"

He looks stunned. "Um... yeah?"

I give Leo an apologetic look, but I can't hide my smile for long. "We're going out."

"Oh, come on," Leo whines. "Not you too."

I tug my coat up around my neck and press myself against the gales that sweep between the buildings of Irkutsk, cold tears streaking from my eyes. What a pain.

Leo tries to restrain the map, which had nearly ripped from his hands as soon as we stepped through the hotel's front doors. He pulls over to lean against a glossy stone building, spreading the map against his leg to get his bearings. He scans the cartoon images on the map and looks up. "Are we sure this is the same city?"

I press myself against the building next to him and scan the map myself. "Yeah, look." I point to a happy cartoon steeple and draw a line up to the pearly white real thing. "We need to go down the street next to that building."

"You mean cross the street?" Kade barely has enough breath to speak. He sounds like he's choking on every word, his nose and cheeks red with cold and his hood squeezed around his face. "We'll never make it."

I laugh, a real one this time. "Stop being so dramatic. We can make it. I didn't bring you this far for you not to make it across a street. This is nothing compared to what you're in for..." The details of Kade's part of the Plan feel fuzzy and far away. Frustratingly, I still only know that he needs to get to Danica. "I think, anyway..." I was a specialist, dang it! I only guided certain special kinds of souls. But who were they? I can't remember any of them now.

We step away from the wall like we're facing down a dragon, pulling our coats closer to our faces and checking for traffic. There aren't many cars on the street, just a few fur-clad citizens keeping to themselves as they walk along the freezing pavement. We exchange looks and nod. We step forward to make a run for it, but that's when the car horns blare from down the street. Our feet fall hard on the pavement as we catch ourselves and stare toward the source of the noise.

As the fanfare draws closer, people spill out of the buildings and onto the pavement, lining the street with their hands on their hearts and solemn faces.

"What the...?" Kade mutters, but the answer interrupts the question. A sleek, black sedan parts the lake mist, flags stuck to the hood.

"No," Leo breathes. "It's the Chairman."

The world muffles as a sublime feeling settles around us like rain freezing in time. This is the last thing we need right now, but there's too much awe surrounding this person, vital to souls both living and not, that I'm not even nervous, just quiet.

A motorcade of five sedans, two flanking Donovan Tyrrell's limousine, passes slowly in front of us, Security officers walking at pace beside them, scanning the crowd for threats.

"Okay, spirit guide," Kade mutters from the side of his mouth. "What do we do?"

I'd laugh if this wasn't so real. Since Kade can see me as well as I can see him now, I have to control my expression. I feel exposed for the first time since coming to Velt. I'm not protected here and, without me, neither is Kade.

"Just stay still." I reach out to feel for Kade and Leo on both sides. Kade would normally protest, but he's as starstruck as I am. "If we don't draw attention, we can just wait it out, right? No big deal."

"Except that Security recognized Kade and me trying to get into the city," Leo points out. "Do you think they raised the alert after we got away?"

"I'm sure we're fine." Kade means to sound nonchalant, but his nerves wreck it.

"As long as the Aropfain keep to themselves."

Leo tears his eyes from the street to gape at me. "Is Jordin here?"

"No, relax." I understand fearing what you can't see, but I don't think Jordin deserves the respect of being feared. "But Jordin isn't the only Aropfain. They're a veritable army, just like Firns. Stay sharp."

Beside me, I feel Kade hold his breath as he skims every Security officer that passes for signs of Aropfain interference. I sulk a little. He'd make such a good Firn. His soul has already expressed an interest in becoming one for as long as we're needed before the dust settles from Danica's choice. This lifetime was our way of giving him as much of a role as we could in the Plan, since he came to us so late.

The limousine passes in front of us, the back window half-down so we can see him. The BSA's lord and master, Narn's coveted puppet, Chairman of the Association, Donovan Tyrrell.

"Whoa," Kade says when he sees him. "He looks terrible. When did that happen?" His eyes flit to Leo and then back to the parade.

Leo frowns. "I don't know. He looks sick, but there's been nothing on the news."

"That anchor did mention Jett is preparing to take over, though..." Kade recalls, looking pensive. "Is that because his father is dying?"

"They're passing the torch," I realize. "They're speeding up their plans to get ahead of us."

Kade curls a lip at me. "What are you talking about? He's just sick. People get sick. Besides, who are you to talk? You look just as bad as he does."

"Unnaturally ill," I agree.

"Yeah." Then Kade's face pales. "Wait..."

"You think he's being killed?" Leo sounds skeptical.

I nod as discreetly as possible. "I think they're siphoning his energy from him to draw his soul out of Velt sooner than Planned. Jett needs to take over, and Donovan is just an obstacle now."

"But killing him?" Leo looks aghast. The hand over his heart falters.

I raise an eyebrow at him, keeping my face still. "What, you thought the Aropfain were nice?"

"Why him?" Kade asks, but I almost second-guess because he barely moves. "Why Jett? What's so great about him that all the Aro... aro—"

"Aropfain."

"Yeah. Why are they all so focused on him?"

I turn my head to face him, a warm smile on my face. I could break into laughter if we weren't in public. "Same reason the Firns are so focused on you, Kade."

Kade's brow scrunches up like the answer makes him uncomfortable. "I still don't get it."

"That's fine," I assure him. "That's what I'm going to show you."

A spike of fear runs up my back. Something isn't right. I tear my eyes back to the street just in time to see an officer lose his step in the procession, as if something pushed him from behind. The officer recovers and looks around to see who might have noticed his slip-up, glaring in challenge to keep everyone from laughing at him.

And his eyes find us.

"Brace yourselves." That trip was no accident. We have company. I clear my head and prepare for battle. I don't know what I'll do. Security isn't tracking my face like they are Kade and Leo, but I'm still too exposed here. But, if ever, this is where Mikael would make good on his promise to send us help. There are so many people here, so many Firns alongside them. I wonder how many Aropfain are among the procession. Jordin isn't there and I won't see the others unless they want me to. Jordin always wants me to see him.

The wind picks up, sweeping past our ears with a breathy roar. Onlookers clutch at their hats and tug their coats closer to themselves. All of them distracted. But that officer wrestles through the wind. He sees a promotion standing in front of him, not people. He sees financial security for his family—in a world that he knows better than most—is never certain. I almost feel sorry for him—to have become this desperate from fear of his superiors...

But that's no excuse to follow the whims of an Aropfain. Whatever his reasons, this officer made the wrong choice, and it's not my place to fix him. It's my place to protect my Neshome and run.

My hands shoot out and grip Kade's hand and Leo's sleeve.

"Before the wind dies down," I shout for them, praying no one else hears me above the wind. "We have to cross the street before everyone recovers."

"Behind the cars," Leo insists, and I will not argue.

"But we've got company." I jut my chin toward the street. "That guy's still coming."

Before I know it, I'm yanked down to the pavement, scraping my palms on all fours next to Kade and Leo, surrounded by leather boots and fancy fur-covered shoes.

It's quieter down here, so Kade can afford to whisper, "This way," as we crawl to the back of the crowd and up the street. I like his quick thinking, but this is too slow going. We can't keep this up long enough to get where we need to be.

"Move!" the order comes from too close to us. "Step aside!"

"He's onto us." I knock my shoulder into Kade. "Get up." I reach out for Leo's sleeve. "Get up!"

My legs aren't happy about the stress and adrenaline in my system right now, and fatigue slows me down and makes me ache like I've been working them for an hour. Leo notices and gently but swiftly lifts me to my feet like I weigh nothing.

I turn to take stock of our position and lose my breath at what I see: He's behind us, almost upon us. He reaches an arm out and grasps for my coat hood.

It all plays out in my head. He'll get my hood and yank me down. Kade and Leo will come to my defense, spectators will gather around us. Security will drag us away. Game over.

"Officer!"

The Security officer pauses as a woman throws herself against his side. "Officer, I've lost my son! Find him! Please!"

The officer turns to shoo her, and that's all we need.

Kade and Leo each grip one of my wrists so the strong gust doesn't knock me over—I'm not proud to need their help, but I might as well be a leaf in this city—and we run, weaving through the huddled crowd as the wind continues, ripping tears from our eyes. I hope that lady's son is all right, but I know deep down that he is. That wasn't a coincidence. That was a Firn. The boy probably wandered off at his Firn's suggestion and will return to his mother soon. He's safe as long as he listens to his Firn. The mother has nothing to fear with a son like that. I glance up at Kade. His mother had every reason to worry over him as a child, but looking at him now, I can't help but feel just a little proud of how he kept a piece of himself despite my absence in his life.

We make it into an alley street between two taller buildings that break the wind and catch our breath. I see the library, but my lungs burn too much to speak. I support my hand on my knee and point with the other one, still panting. The boys follow and see the looming, neglected building before us. Reminiscent of Ainsley's Antiquities, the Association has not kept this building up any time in the last century. Some of the stone facade has crumbled away. I'm surprised they did not board the doors shut, but the large panes of glass cracked or shattered long ago. It won't be much warmer in there, but we'll have cover. We'll be safe.

Without a word, I make my way up the stone steps and through the door, expecting the boys to follow, and they do. We throw ourselves inside and immediately bend over to catch our breath and let our pulses slow.

The library has a cavernous feel to it, like the makers carved it into the side of a mountain. Our breaths echo in the eerie silence. It smells musty, and it pains me to realize that's the smell of damp books. Hopefully, we can find a book intact enough to show what I'm looking for.

I straighten and shake off my nerves. Back to business. "We need the history section."

Kade snorts, brushing the dirt from the pavement off his pants. "So the smallest section."

I nod. It irks me that the BSA doesn't like to acknowledge the rest of the world. The only history we'll find is what they want us to know. But, for my purposes, that's enough. This little tidbit of my past in Lemayle I can remember clearly. In the grand timeline that I've witnessed over several thousand years, this is recent history. It might as well have happened just yesterday, even though it's been a few centuries.

We split up to search. I rub the cold out of my arms as I skim the signs above each section. My heart aches at the sight of empty shelves where knowledge should be. In its place are cheap vases and elegant-looking things, all purchasable at the dilapidated gift shop near the door. It makes my stomach churn to think such an institution of learning could fall so low. I reach for the first proper book I see. It falls open in my hand, the pages nearly flipping out of the worn binding, and several—surprise, surprise—torn out altogether. How did the people allow this to happen?

Oh, right. Money.

"I found it," Kade's voice echoes on the walls. I have to turn in a circle to find out where it came from. He sees me before I see him and laughs at my lost expression. "Over here." I spin one more time to find him waving from across the room, Leo already at his side.

I knock my palm to my forehead. "Duh." They smile at me as I maneuver around the desks and tables in the center of the room to reach them.

"What are we looking for here?" Kade sounds bored and we haven't even started yet.

I poke his shoulder as punishment. "You want to know why Danica is such a big deal, why the BSA is so cosmically important, and what it all has to do with you." He nods, not seeing how that relates to this. "I'm going to show you." I take a deep breath. "Find a book about the Tyrrell family history and the founding of the BSA. I'm not Ainsley, but I'm about to teach you a lesson."

While they search the stacks, I find the faculty rooms. I'm going to make this exactly like Ainsley's. They always listened to him more when they had the radio for background noise.

I get a thrill of rebelliousness as I press my hands to the door that reads Faculty Only and push. The wooden door has fallen apart over the years, so aside from it dragging on the floor as it goes, I open it without issue. It's a dusty mess back here. Papers and cups sitting underneath years of settled dirt remind me of Taltsy. So many places in Beta Siberia have come to this. It's such a shame.

In the kitchenette, I find an old boxy radio, antenna and all. I blow some of the dust away and scratch the dirt from the tuner band, praying the batteries still work. It's heavier than I expect, but that's because I'm weaker than I expect.

I carry it out and set it on the long wooden table closest to Leo and Kade. Leo has an armful of books while Kade only carries one. It's like looking at a chart of their interest in education. Kade is definitely at the bottom of the curve.

At the sound of the radio hitting the table, they turn. A smile tugs at Leo's mouth, but Kade looks confused.

"It's to help you focus," I tell him before he asks. "You've only ever listened to one person who tried to teach you anything, and I need you to understand this. So, we'll do it Ainsley's way."

Nostalgia lights in Kade's eyes like he's having a flashback. He stares at the radio and slowly sits at the table, setting his book to the side. Leo does the same, more consciously. I fiddle with the radio, trying to find the power switch. When I find it, all I get is static. I move the tuner until I find signs of sound. It takes a few attempts to find a voice in the ether, but finally, one AM frequency station makes itself heard. I set the radio aside, satisfied, and fold my hands in front of me. The books on the table are newer than the one I'd flipped through, but no better kept. I reach for one about the BSA and handle the pages delicately until I find pictures, because time is short and Kade is dense.

Once I find what I'm looking for, I turn the book to face them and point at the image of the expansion of Irkutsk. "Do you know why the BSA is called the Beta Siberian Arrangement?"

"It was an experimental community prototype," Leo says mechanically.

"Yeah," Kade chimes in. "Beta testing."

I nod. "So why did the Beta never fall off?"

They exchange uncertain looks.

"Because it blew up too quickly," I supply. "The Beta Siberian Arrangement was supposed to be a placeholder name until they were ready to go more public, but the public took to the concept so quickly that a name change was pointless." I move on. "Do you know why they formed the BSA?"

"It was a prototype community," Kade repeats. He doesn't understand where I'm going with this. I can feel his frustration from across the table.

"It was only supposed to be one development," Leo recalls, memories replaying in his mind from his school days. "But they got more orders than they expected, right?"

"That's right." I nod. "They were only supposed to be luxury housing in case of the polar shift."

Kade laughs at the words. "Yeah, when is that supposed to happen again?"

The planet has been through a lot in the last few centuries, but not a shift of its magnetic poles. Theorists projected Siberia to be the most temperate climate on earth post-shift, and business-minded people saw the opportunity for major profit. It worked almost too well. Thanks to their gloom-and-doom propaganda, people flocked to the safety of Siberia while the rest of the world did their research. Polar shift doesn't work the way the BSA sold it, but no one in the Arrangement hears from the outside world, so they don't know that the rest of the planet moved forward without them. It's a veritable world peace out there, but no one wants to associate with the BSA. The BSA doesn't play well with others.

"Who founded Beta Siberia?" I ask them.

"The Tyrrell family." They say it together, but the tones are completely different. Leo is matter of fact; Kade rolls his eyes.

I nod at Kade's reaction. I relate to his disdain. "They did. And that's when they put a target on their heads."

Both of them frown. "There's never been an assassination attempt on any of them," Leo says.

I hold up a clarifying finger. "I didn't say the target was for living souls."

"You mean your people are out to get the Tyrrell family?" Kade leans back in his chair with a skeptical look. His hand drifts toward the gas knife in his pocket.

I give him a commanding glare. "Calm down."

His hand freezes and Leo looks over to see what's going on.

"My people, as you so kindly put it, have never been out to get anyone. But Narn is just as opportunistic as the Tyrrells were." Both boys relax into their seats. Leo leans forward at the mention of Narn, but Kade does his best to look indifferent. "We've known the Reyn Gayst was coming since the beginning of recorded history," I explain. "Because we've been fighting with each other since long before that. At some point, Narn and El Olam struck a deal that whoever swayed living souls in their direction would win and the other would concede that their opinion is best."

Kade stops himself from shaking his head.

"If El Olam wins," I ignore his attitude, "then free will sticks around and living souls get to make their own choices, mistakes and all. If Narn wins, then he'll do away with free will completely, and Firns and Aropfain will both have to force living souls to stick with what their Plans brought them here to do."

"What are they... um... we sent here to do?" Leo tilts his

head in interest.

"Right now, you're sent here to learn as much as you can and to help other people learn what they're supposed to learn, because El Olam is still in control."

"And what if Narn was in control?" Kade plays devil's advocate for the devil himself. I can't believe this is my Neshome.

I shake my head. "If Narn is in control, it doesn't matter what you learn because you'll have to do whatever he decides regardless of your wishes and needs." I take a breath. "He wants to get rid of the necessity of Velt altogether. It'll just be souls in Lemayle milling around under Narn's rule with no education or consciousness."

"You mean to tell me that our whole lives are just really long school terms?"

I give Kade a flat stare. He's missing the point here. "More or less. It'll make sense later."

Leo's heard that before, and he doesn't like to think about it, so he changes the subject. "How did that make the Tyrrell family a target?"

"Ah, thank you. I got distracted." I grab another book, one about the Tyrrells, and flip to an image of their family tree. "It became clear some time ago that the Reyn Gayst, who gets to make the ultimate decision between Narn and El Olam, would be born in Beta Siberia. We just didn't know when." I point to the top of the tree at the Tyrrell that founded the BSA. "Originally, the Plan didn't involve the Tyrrells becoming a royal family. It was never supposed to get this big. Narn is very good at business himself and the Aropfain can conjure up some tempting offers to greedy people. Who wouldn't want to be king, right?"

Leo and Kade shrug.

"So Narn took the family under his wing. He influenced the shape of Beta Siberian culture, including Nor'ilsk becoming the hot spot for picking spouses. If the Reyn Gayst showed up in the BSA, the Tyrrells could find them, boy or girl."

"Why was the Reyn Gayst a girl?" Kade asks. "Jett's all about women, so why not make her a boy so he wouldn't be interested?"

I rub my forehead. "The Reyn Gayst doesn't get a Firn." They both look at me like I'm stupid. I know. It sounds bad and I shrug. "She's supposed to be impartial, so none of us are allowed to interact with her..." I tilt my head. "Not directly anyway." I level a meaningful gaze at Kade, indicating the loophole he represents for the Firns against the Aropfain the same way Jett Tyrrell functions as an ace to stack the Aropfain's hand against us. "So, no one really knows the Plan for Danica except El Olam. We know absolutely nothing about her purpose before she chooses. We only know that we guide the people who set up the information she'll base her choice on, particularly you, Kade. You're pretty 'about women' yourself."

He folds his arms in disgust. "I am not! Don't compare me to Jett."

"Sorry."

I'm not. He has to have certain similarities to Jett. They have the same purpose. "Anyway, there's a lot that I'm not privy to in my position, and even less now that I'm an outcast, but what I know is that Narn favored the Tyrrells to gain an edge. The BSA developed as it did because his hand was in it, stirring the pot, so to speak."

Kade leans back in his seat. "And every single Tyrrell in history fell for it?"

"No, but the ones who didn't were the ones who didn't last long in power." I point to the tree at the dates of reign for each member of the family. A few only lasted a year or two, and some ended the same year as the family member's death. All are technical failures by Firns like me. It's not something we're proud of. "This isn't a government," I tell them. "It's a chess-board, a match between Narn and El Olam. Our side has lost some players along the way, but so has theirs."

"Lost some players..." Kade's anger shows in the stillness of his voice. "You talk about them like they didn't die for your petty cause."

My hand slams on the table before I can stop it. "It's not petty. I don't know how else to tell you we're fighting for your right to choose how to live your life." I press the same hand to my chest, remembering to control my breathing so I don't get out of hand. "Listen, I know death seems terrible to you, but it's not the end of everything. I mean, sheesh, I've died over a hundred times! So have you! You just won't remember until you get back to Lemayle. Life seems scary to you, but it's nothing compared to what happens when you take physics out of the equation and still have evil people." Memories of my encounters with certain malicious Aropfain steal my breath for a moment. When I look up, they look startled. "Listen," I compose myself, "if you die, it's not the end of the world. If we lose the balance, it is. I know that sounds insensitive, but you'll understand once this whole mess is over."

Voices crackle behind the static on the radio. Another news report. Leo's eyes dart to the radio and he all but lunges for the tuner to adjust the station so we can hear clearly.

"Authorities are still on alert for the possibility of two convicts, thought to be dead until an incident at the Irkutsk customs screening area yesterday."

Leo and Kade balk at the news and stare at each other.

"Citizens are asked to be aware and contact Security if you see one of these men. Photos and descriptions can be found online in the alert section of any website."

"We're alert-worthy?" Leo says incredulously.

"Of course you are," I tell him. "You're Jett's competition

and Jordin is at Jett's side, pulling the strings."

"I guess that explains the officer from the motorcade..." Kade muses.

"Citizens are asked to exercise extreme caution, as these men are considered dangerous. They were first spotted trying to kidnap Danica Bree at Jett Tyrrell's betrothal reveal gala last month. Security pursued them, but they escaped capture. All citizens of Irkutsk are instructed to remain alert and report any possible sightings as part of their civic duty to the Beta Siberian Arrangement."

"He badmouthed you to Danica." My voice isn't angry. I'm actually impressed. "So now, if you meet her, she'll suspect you. Well played..."

"So, that guy from the bathroom..." Kade pieces it together.

"And the woods with the moose, and the gala, and the gas station, and the chopper..."

Kade nods like he gets it, and I can stop now. "Yeah. He's... really the one behind all of this, isn't he?"

I don't know if I should applaud that he finally got it or not. Somehow, I don't think it would help my situation. "Yes," I say instead.

Kade studies the pictures in the book, pieces moving into place in his mind. "So, this isn't about the BSA or the Association setting things on fire..." Which is how the Association has been purging the less sophisticated members of society lately.

"It's not even about the world..." Leo muses.

I nod as it all falls into place. "It's about every soul who ever lived for the rest of eternity and their freedom. Including yours, living and dead."

CHAPTER SEVENTEEN

It's a quiet walk back to the hotel. There are people on the street, the same type as before, so it's not impressive anymore. We don't look at them. We keep our heads down. If the news of Kade and Leo as the BSA's most wanted hit the radio, then the television reports and many news streams will have gone viral by now. It's a blessing that the air is so cold and it's a weekday during business hours: Few people are out to recognize them. But that doesn't keep the reality from eating at their nerves.

The world looks different to Kade and Leo now. I saw it happen just behind their eyes. They know the truth—well, more of it than most people do. Everything they see around them looks different from before, more superficial. Was it appropriate for me to reveal that much to them? I don't know. I don't have a Plan to reference and no one showed up to stop me because, like Jordin said, I'm untouchable, diseased, a convict to my people, just like Kade and Leo. The rules of the world have changed for me too, and I'll play the game however I have to.

When we pass through the automatic glass doors to the hotel, the boys keep their collars flipped up around their faces, protecting themselves from wandering eyes more than the chill of the wind, which none of us complained about on the walk back.

When we finally reach the door to our room, the light is dim as the sun dips in the sky and that makes the silhouette of Canaan even more intimidating. We freeze in the doorway at the sight of him, arms folded in disapproval, foot tapping impatiently, face ready to reject any explanation we come up with. We file into the room, shut the door, and bow our heads in shame.

"I did not agree to Ainsley's request to be your parent," Canaan starts off. "I am not your father. I am not your friend. If anything, I am your courier. Do you three understand that?"

Eyes glued to our shoes, we all nod.

"What is this?" He extends an arm toward the bathroom, glass still shattered on the floor. We meant to clean that up when we got back, I swear. "I'll have to explain that. I'll have to pay for it because I'll bet my life none of you have any money." He pauses for a moment to give us the opportunity to object, but he knows better, and we say nothing. "I thought so."

Movement from the corner of my eye catches my attention. Kade's fingers curling and uncurling as he tempers his rage. He wants to argue that it wasn't our fault, that we didn't break the light. I slide my foot to kick his shoe. He discreetly looks at me. I shake my head. Canaan won't buy it. It's not worth making him angrier. Kade goes back to working his hands as an outlet.

"You're going to clean this up." It isn't a request. "And you two are going to dye your hair and clean that up as well. Don't think I haven't seen the reports." He strides toward me and lifts my face, scanning every inch with scrutinizing eyes. I feel myself blush for real underneath the rouge. His lip curls less than usual. "Passable," he decides. "You'll get by as fresh blood in Nor'ilsk, and you can afford it now that Jett's engaged."

"Engaged?" Kade spits the word out.

Canaan turns on him. "Yes, engaged. Perhaps you haven't been watching the news, but when they're not talking about the two escaped kidnappers," he enunciates in their faces, "Jett's engagement announcement to that Bree girl is the headline."

A pulse of fiery anger hits me from Kade's direction. I'm a little pleased, but I feel for him all the same.

He pushes Kade and me apart to get to the door behind us. "The flight leaves at 4 a.m." He opens the door. "I expect you awake, ready to go, and for this place to be spotless." He turns on us. "You all have updated papers over there." He nods toward the desk.

"All of us?" I ask without thinking.

"I'm not claiming responsibility for you anymore," Canaan says. "You look fine. Healthy enough to blend in with all the other fragile Nor'ilsk girls, at least." He gestures to the desk one more time. "Study them. I don't want any slipups." He slams the door behind him.

We stand in silence for a long moment.

"At least he's still taking us to Nor'ilsk." I shrug. The boys nod and we numbly spread out to clean. The larger shards are easy to pick up, but I soak a towel to wipe up the finer pieces. We toss the remnants of the light in a drawer and tuck them away to forget about them.

Sitting next to the sink are two boxes of hair dye, each with a name written on it in marker. Canaan left nothing to question. Kade's chestnut hair would be black, a complement to his brown eyes. Leo's blond hair would be brown. They won't draw attention, that's for sure, but I'm surprised to realize that I don't like the idea of Kade changing. I've known Kade, protected him, longer than his own parents. He may not remember me, he may not even like me, but I can't help but feel protective of him.

I hear water rushing from the tub and give the boys some privacy as they resign themselves to the hair dye. I turn the television on and sit on the bed. Should I watch the news, or will it only make me angry? My legs pulse with fatigue and I decide to just flop back and listen to the music on the hotel's default channel with the occasional advertisement for things to do in Irkutsk. I close my eyes and feel myself creeping toward the edge of sleep, but I don't want to sleep yet, not here anyway. I hogged the bed last night and I want to give the boys a say in the arrangements tonight.

I sigh and turn my head, noticing a manila envelope on the desk with our names scrawled in the same handwriting as the boxes of dye. Another gift from Canaan. I slide papers out of the envelope to find the new identities for Kade and Leo and a clean bill of health for me. I smile. Since Jordin tricked me, I have come a long way. I've got a longer way to go, but at least now people don't look at me and see a zombie. Like Canaan said, I'm passably fragile. It's still an insult, but a more tolerable one.

I scan the papers. My name and birthday are the same, but now I'm from Nor'ilsk. Easy enough to remember. I'm not in any system, so as long as Security doesn't search their database for me, I'll be fine.

Kade and Leo have a much harder profile to memorize. I skim their papers and can't stifle a laugh. Still reading, I walk over to lean on the bathroom doorframe. "Hey Kade, guess what your new name is?"

Kade, head under the tub faucet, flips his head up, sending an arch of water through the air to look at me. "What?" He blinks as dye gets into his eye.

I freeze. Even before his hair has dried, slicked back from being soaked, Kade looks different. A pang of sadness jabs my throat at not recognizing him as easily as before.

He looks at me like I've got two heads. "What?" he asks again.

"Oh, right." I look at the papers again. "You've both got new names and stuff." They both sulk with an internal groan. "Leo, you're... Blake Amsel."

Leo mouths the name to himself like he's trying it on. He frowns in distaste. I agree. It doesn't suit him.

"What about me?" Kade asks, rubbing his eye as the sting becomes too much.

I purse my lips to hold back the laughter. "Gerald Finley."

"That's not fair!" Kade whines. "Now he's just being a jerk."

I catch Leo turning away to laugh, but I can still see his smile in the mirror's reflection. "Gerald Finley."

"Shut up, Blake." Kade cups his hand under the running faucet and tosses the water at Leo's back, soaking through his shirt. Leo arches his spine against the assault and instinctively grabs a wet towel to throw at Kade's face. We all dissolve into laughter and it feels like a release. For the first time since I came to Velt, I don't feel any animosity from Kade. I try not to notice or to feel it too deeply. I don't want to get my hopes up just yet. Especially because it'll mean I basically have Jordin to thank for convincing Kade of what I am and why he should respect me.

Why does everything always come back to Jordin?

Leo tosses Kade a dry towel and they swap places, Kade drying his hair while Leo dips his head under the water to say goodbye to his blond hair.

"What's your new name?" Kade asks my reflection in the mirror, using the towel to dry out his ear.

"Same," I tell him. "I'm just not a psych patient anymore."

Kade lowers the towel with a pout. "That's not fair."

I lift my hands. "I'm not the one on Security's radar anymore. My fifteen seconds are over. They hate you again." I think about Kade and Leo's arrest back in Vanino. "You should be used to it by now, though, right?"

His eyes narrow in the mirror and I feel like I'm caught in

the crosshairs of his gaze. "You were there, weren't you?" he asks openly. "You were actually there. The whole time."

I notice Leo's hands pausing in his hair. He's listening, anticipating a fight between us.

"Yes, I was." I haven't hidden it, so I don't pretend that I have. For Kade's sake, I try to keep sarcasm out of my voice, hoping to build a bridge between us.

"Hm." Kade looks at the sink and that's all he gives me. No snark, no shock. It's the best I'll get, and I'll gladly take it.

Not wanting to push my luck, I move back into the bedroom and sit on a cushioned chair in the corner near the window. I mindlessly play with the swivel of the chair, spinning in quarter-circles and half-circles, kicking off the wall, and spinning back.

Kade comes out soon after me, squeezing the last bit of damp from his hair and yawning. I can't help but stare. First, he hasn't properly washed his hair in years, if this is how clean hair is supposed to look. Maybe it's the frou-frou shampoo from the hotel, but I've never seen Kade's hair bounce and shine like that when it was brown. He seems to have noticed too. He keeps shaking his head and glancing up at the hair as it swooshes.

"Bet that feels funny," I comment without thinking. "Your hair used to be flatter."

"Used to be shorter too," he agrees, still swooshing.

I nod. "Fair point."

Next, Leo creeps from the bathroom and turns out the light. He hunches his shoulders as water drips down the back of his shirt and takes a chill with it. Leo turns to him.

"Looks good, man."

Leo glances at him, not buying it, but Kade's right. Leo's brown hair and blue eyes look fine together. He doesn't look like himself anymore, but I know more than anyone that outer appearance does not make the man.

"You'll adjust," I tell them both. "It's weird to see an

unfamiliar person in the mirror," I should know, "but it doesn't change a thing."

Understanding dawns on Leo's face and he sits down next to me, placing a friendly hand on my arm, and smiles. They've accepted my history. It's about darn time.

"We should probably get some sleep," Kade says, casting his eyes around the room. "I'll take the floor. I had the chair last night."

I remain awkwardly silent. It would be polite to offer to take the floor myself, but my bones might as well be toothpicks and I deal with an underlying soreness all day as it is. It feels selfish, but if I want to keep up and maybe even be helpful, I need to be at the best that I can be. I'm not proud of it.

"It's fine," Leo whispers as if he's read my mind, but it must be on my face. "We wouldn't let you take anything but the bed, anyway. You're saving us an argument."

I smile at him. Whoever his Firn is, they did a great job with him. I try not to think about it too much or I'll have to accept that there is another person with us at all times: Leo's Firn. It was fine when I was still invisible, but now it creeps me out to know that someone else is watching, judging, nudging everything we do. And they're working twice as hard because of me. I'd hate me if I were them, but Leo is such a forgiving person. I hope that means his Firn is, too, to have partnered with him.

"It's massive, though," I try. I know how this will end, but I have to make myself look a little better.

I don't get to finish the thought before both of them shake their heads at me. "Nope," Kade says. "That would be seriously inappropriate. Besides, you should probably stretch out as much as you can for..." he scratches behind his ear nervously, "your muscles and all that. I know I would if I were overdoing it."

I smile at how red his face is. "That's a really nice thing to say, Kade."

"Yeah, I know." He shrugs it off with ego.

"Okay, everyone," Leo steps in. "We need to rest up. We only have a few hours to sleep."

I hand a pillow to Leo and throw one at Kade. Kade grabs extra blankets from the closet, and we all settle down once Kade flicks the light switch. I bury myself in the blankets and the soft mattress, returning to the state of mind from this morning where nothing can go wrong as long as I'm this warm and comfortable.

Then my eyes pop open in the dark.

"Did anyone remember to clean up the bathroom?"

There are groans from either side of me and the light flicks back on.

CHAPTER EIGHTEEN

The question I forgot to ask was if anyone had set the alarm. None of us had. We all startle awake to the sound of banging on our door and Canaan's impatient shouting. Kade scrambles from the floor to grip the doorknob and open it before he's properly awake and finds himself pinned under Canaan's glare.

"Ugh, what did we do wrong now?" he complains. Canaan steps around him.

"The flight leaves in half an hour and you're all still in bed?" he demands. "Get up!"

I try to hurry, but my legs tangle in the blankets as if they don't want me to leave as much as I don't want to leave them. I stumble from the bed and Kade comes to my rescue.

"You slept in your clothes?" Canaan snarls when he sees my rumpled dress. He presses his fingers to his forehead and closes his eyes. "We'll have them pressed on the plane. Just come on. Grab your things." He turns to leave the room but catches himself. "Don't forget your papers! You'd better have them memorized!"

I hope on one foot trying to slip my shoes on. "I think he means you, Gerald," I whisper in Kade's direction. He glares at me for a second, but then he panics.

"Crap. What's my last name again?"

"Finley," Leo supplies. "You're Gerald Finley, I'm Blake Amsel." He walks by us, rubbing sleep from his eyes. I don't think he went to sleep when Kade and I did. He looks like he only slept for an hour. I hope I'm wrong, but our papers are in his hands, and he didn't grab them from the desk. He had them when he woke. He hands my folder to me. "You were born on Christmas."

"I was?"

"Nineteen years ago," Leo confirms.

I feel sad for Leo. He's taking this seriously, and he's had to deal with Kade and me.

"Come on!" Canaan hisses from the door. "The car is waiting."

"Don't you have, like, a private jet or something? Don't they leave whenever you say they leave?"

"Simpleton..." Canaan says it just loud enough to make sure we hear him. "There are other planes that need to use the runway and they won't wait for us to get there."

We fall silent. It's a good point. We file out of the room, past Canaan's judging gaze and into the elevator, stuck in the thickness of Canaan's disapproval.

The car outside is almost identical to the one from Ulan Ude.

"How many of these do you have?" Kade asks as he slides in.

"You get what you work for," is all Canaan says.

The door shuts, and the car pulls out.

"You're coming to Nor'ilsk too?" Leo asks politely.

Canaan laughs. "It'd look pretty bad if I didn't. All the Beta Siberia snobs are flocking to Nor'ilsk."

"Why?" I ask.

"So, you admit you're a snob." Of course, Kade would pick

that out. He reaches toward the snack bar and tears open a pack of peanuts, tossing one to Leo and me. Breakfast is served.

Canaan ignores him, but he doesn't look offended. Maybe he admits he's a snob. In fact, he looks almost proud of it. "Apparently," Canaan looks out the window as the airport comes into view, "there's going to be a wedding."

Kade chokes on a peanut, and my eyes fly open. "You're kidding," Kade says with disdain.

"Well, what did you think they were going to do?" Leo asks.

I grip Kade's shoulder too tightly, trying to be supportive but not taking the news all that well myself. "We'll figure it out," I promise.

Kade shakes his head like he's trying to clear it. "How long is this flight again?"

Canaan laughs a bellowing laugh. "Fourteen hours."

"Fourteen hours?" My voice is almost too shrill for me to recognize.

"You're not in a small country, darling," Canaan reminds me. "Nothing is close to anything. That's how they want it."

I nod because it makes sense, and I knew that. It's just never directly affected me before. I'm used to being able to travel in the blink of an eye.

"At least we'll have plenty of time to catch up on sleep." Leo rubs his eye.

"If it helps," Canaan says dryly, "we're leaving before most people. We'll get there first."

Kade eyes Canaan suspiciously. "Why haven't you asked us about why it matters?"

Canaan raises his eyebrows at him. "Because I honestly don't care."

Kade opens his mouth, but Canaan cuts him off, waving his hands in front of him. "No, no, no. Don't tell me. Once I drop you guys off, I don't know you. We never met. That's the deal." He crosses his legs and leans back into the leather seat to look out the window at the private jet we're pulling up to.

The car lurches to a stop.

"Get out," Canaan orders. And we do.

He corrals us toward the stairs that lead to the door and we're welcomed by a petite, smiling flight attendant. She bows slightly and spreads a hand toward the cabin where seats and couches are open for the taking. We awkwardly bow back and whisper rushed thank-yous, then quickly settle into an arrangement of seats that face each other.

Canaan breezes past us and drops into a solitary seat near the back window, already on his phone.

"Please find your seats and fasten your seat belts for takeoff," the attendant says over the speakers, even though we're all within earshot. She hangs up the phone she spoke into and steps to our corner. "Can I offer you any fresh beverages when we're in the air?" Her voice is too sweet. I can tell she needs this job and her security is based on her performance.

"Um, water, please?" Leo shifts uncomfortably.

"Do you have soda?" Kade asks.

"I'm fine, thanks." I smile at her.

The attendant nods and writes it all down on a tiny notepad before going to her seat to buckle in.

The plane rolls along the runway, and I relax. Everything is fine until we reach Nor'ilsk. Plenty of time to study our papers and come up with a plan. That makes me nervous. I've never had to create an entire plan before. The ultimate Plan was always curled in the back of my mind as reference, and I only had to get creative with distractions and sidetracks. But now, I don't know the best way to get Kade to Danica. There's a path he's intended to take, and I can't remember it. I know I knew this. It hurts my head to feel that missing information. I don't like it. It makes me feel inadequate where I used to pride myself on my worth.

"You okay over there?" Kade asks.

For a second, my face gets away from me. I feel heat in my eyes and realize I'm on the brink of tears. I rub my eyes with my palms.

"Yeah," I say hastily. "Just holding back a yawn." I give a nervous laugh, but neither Kade nor Leo seem to buy it. Whatever. I'm too tired for this conversation and they seem to respect that.

The plane turns on the runway and picks up speed for takeoff. My eyes burn, still tired from last night's lack of sleep. I try to blink it away, but it's no use. I lean my head against the pad on the side of my seat as we jostle around and find that it doesn't keep me from slipping back to sleep before we even lift off the ground.

When I wake up, it's because the sun is in my eyes. I cringe away from the light and press my palms to my eyes to find more darkness until I'm ready to open them. It's quiet, just the thrum of the plane and the shuffling of kitchenware, and it's warm. I open my eyes and wish I had a camera.

Kade's face presses against the plane wall next to the window, his head tilted back so far that his jaw couldn't keep up. It gapes open with just a single shining line running from the corner of his mouth. Leo's face isn't as visible. He's fallen onto Kade's shoulder and cuddled onto his seat, arms wrapped around his legs.

Twenty-year-old children, I think. There's still so much they don't know.

"They're cute," a voice says next to me.

It startles me, but it's just the flight attendant holding a tray of the drinks Kade and Leo ordered before takeoff and an extra glass of water for me. I smile my gratitude as she places the drinks on the small table between our seats.

"Yeah, they're all right."

"Can I get you anything else?"

I squirm a bit. I don't enjoy being served, even if she is being paid for it. It feels rude to me. "I'm fine," I tell her. "But you can sit, if you want." I look behind my seat at the attendant's special space on the plane. She's the only one and the door to the cockpit is securely closed.

She looks too, then her head swings Canaan's way, and she weighs the consequences. He's asleep, trench coat draped over his head for darkness and privacy.

"Don't worry about him. He won't say anything, even if he notices."

She looks at me with a quiet, excited smile. "Okay, why not?" And she quickly sits down like the seat might move away from her if she isn't quick enough. She looks around once seated.

"New view for you?" I ask.

Laughing softly, she nods. "These are so much more comfortable than mine."

I pull a leg up onto my seat and lean into the corner where the seat meets the wall. "I hope he pays you well. No doubt he can afford it."

Her eyes flare wide and she nods with enthusiasm. "Oh, he does. I'm very well taken care of."

"He pays you to say that, too, doesn't he?" I give her a wry smile, and she doesn't deny it.

"So, you're all dignitaries heading to Nor'ilsk for the official engagement announcement?" she guesses.

I almost shake my head, but that's a great cover story, so I catch myself and nod instead. "Yep. Can't pass up a chance at free food."

She curls her fingers around the tray in her lap and rocks back as she laughs. The volume of the laugh doesn't match her movement, and I realize how well trained she is. She could fit in with any BSA elitist to my untrained eyes, but they'd probably spot her in an instant. What does that say about me?

I'm not wearing enough makeup.

I look at Kade. He should be fine at first glance. I just hope he doesn't open his mouth in front of anyone.

A shoulder nudges mine, and I look back at the flight attendant. "You seem attached to him," she nods in Kade's direction where he's still drooling away, "are you two...?" She doesn't have to say it; the insinuation in her voice is plenty.

"Oh—no." It comes out too quickly. She gives a knowing, teasing nod, like she thinks I'm fooling myself, but Kade's heart beats for someone else. I wasn't even supposed to be here. Romance is certainly not my priority right now. "Really," I stress, "it's not like that. I'm just... protective..."

"A sister?" She says it like it's the most natural assumption.

"No..."

She frowns.

I straighten, offended. "What, we can't be friends and not related?"

She considers it. "I guess so..." She looks at Kade again. "If you two aren't involved, maybe I could..."

"Nope."

She looks at me, off guard, at my sudden and solid disapproval. "Why not?" She looks at Kade and grins. "He's cute."

"You don't even know him!" I try to keep my voice down. The last thing I need is for him to wake up and argue with me in her defense. I set my rage to simmer and keep her pinned with my gaze.

"That's the point, isn't it?" she counters. "I can get to know him." Her shoulders move up and down in a casual shrug. "It's a long flight."

"If you try it, it'll be the longest flight of your life."

She pouts at me and folds her arms, expertly balancing the tray on her knees. "So, there is something between you."

I open my mouth to deny it, but you know what? I sigh instead. "Yes, okay? I have a thing for him. I just haven't made my move yet. I'm..." I bite my lip, hating myself. "I'm too scared to tell him."

Her hands fly to her mouth, and she bounces with excitement. "That's so adorable! Ah! It's a romance playing out right in front of me!"

She uses a hushed voice, but it still squeaks and it's enough to cause Leo to stir. His bleary eyes open and take a second to focus. He sees Kade's shoulder pressed to his face and blinks, pulling away and rubbing at his eyes to wake himself up.

"What's going on?" he asks. When he can finally see straight, he notices my new friend. "Hi..."

The attendant shivers with the thrill and looks at me. An obvious question on her face.

"No," I shut her down. She can't pursue Leo either.

She sulks. "Keeping your options open?" she accuses me.

"No." I flick her nose and she jumps. "I just can't stand you looking so desperate."

She doesn't deny it. I'm not the first to say something. "Sorry," is her sheepish reply.

"You're a Nor'ilsk native, aren't you?"

She nods. I smile and set a forgiving hand on her shoulder. They raised her to think the most important thing in life was to attract a wealthy husband, and now that Jett's off the market, she's probably panicking.

"Sorry," I say. She nods her thanks. I lean in close. She knows a secret is coming her way, and she leans in too. "They'll disappoint you," I explain. "It's not their money, you know? We're a charity case for Canaan. We don't even have bank accounts."

She pulls back, almost aghast. The sparkle of interest in her eyes doused like a bucket of water over a candle to be replaced by disappointment. She recovers and nudges me with her elbow. "I can still help you, though. Build up some good karma for myself, you know?"

I gape like a fish for a moment. I don't want her help with Kade. There's nothing to help! And how does she know what karma is? Of all the spiritual concepts through the ages, that's the one that survived? I guess living souls never completely gave up the idea that something outside of themselves was involved in the unfairness of life.

Oblivious to the exchange between the flight attendant and me, Leo kicks Kade's calf, and he jerks awake, wiping his mouth and frowning like his face has betrayed him.

"Don't worry," I jibe, "at least you don't snore."

Kade doesn't get the joke, mind still riddled from shallow sleep. He points at the drinks on the table. "Is one of those for me?"

"Maybe I should get you some coffee." The attendant excuses herself for a moment and brings back three mugs and a full electric pitcher of coffee. "Let me know if you need anything else," she says, back to business. "I'll be right over here." She winks at me and the boys notice. They give curious looks and my cheeks flush.

"Nothing. Don't ask."

"How long were we out?" Kade looks out the window like the stretches of frozen ground below will be some sort of sign of the time of day.

"Two hours, I think." The sun's up now, so it's a fair guess.

"Only twelve hours to go..." Kade makes it sound like he'll die of boredom in the meantime. He rests his cheek on his fist and stares out the window while Leo pours the coffee.

Leo passes a warm cup to me, and I wrap my hands around it, enjoying how the heat on my palms somehow sends a comfortable shiver through the rest of me. I almost don't want to drink it to avoid losing my hand warmer.

Leo takes a sip. His shoulders sink and he sighs. "That is good coffee."

I tilt my head at my mug. It certainly smells good. I don't know what's happened to coffee in the last few centuries. It was discovered and developed after my time in Velt was over, but I've noticed how popular it is. I lift it to my face, knowing that my tongue is in for a shock of burning liquid, but still not prepared for the experience of boiling, bitter water rushing down my throat. My body reacts. I jerk forward as soon as I swallow and choke, coughing because, for some reason, my body thought gasping and swallowing could happen at the same time.

Leo is in the seat next to me in a flash, rubbing my back and asking if I need help. I can't speak, but I lift a hand to put him at ease until I can finish coughing.

"Wow." Kade laughs. "You really are new. You've never had coffee before?"

I don't feel like explaining this to him. "It's been a while," I say dryly.

Kade nods. "I guess so."

"That's the same reaction you had the first time you tried coffee, though," Leo recalls. "You had tears in your eyes and everything."

I perk up. "Hey, that's right! You have no room to talk!"

Kade folds in on himself. "I got used to it. I drink it just fine now." He takes a long gulp to prove it, sighing once it's down. "It really helps wake you up."

"Yeah, but that was only after about two years of choking it down," I argue. "You used to shiver the minute you took a sip, but Leo had no problem, and you didn't want to be outdone."

"Over coffee?" Leo asks Kade.

Kade is quiet. "You made it look so easy," he confesses begrudgingly. "I felt like an idiot for not liking it."

"And if I made jumping off a bridge look easy, would you try it?" Leo sounds just like Kade's mother. It's the same voice he uses on Nyla, his little sister.

I stifle a laugh.

"Look, this is coffee. Calm down," Kade grumbles. "No harm done." He takes another sip to finish the argument.

Leo turns to me, leaning forward on his knees. "What else don't I know about Kade?" There's mischief in his eyes, and we've got twelve hours to kill. I'll play this game.

"Well, back when you were in junior high, Kade actually thought you had a crush on this one girl and he tried to set you up..."

Realization sparks in Leo's eyes. "Not Nadia." He turns to Kade in accusation. "You're the one who told Nadia I had a crush on her? She didn't leave me alone for the next two years, Kade!"

Kade's cheeks are tight against the laughter he's failing at holding back. "Yeah, but she asked me about you, and I didn't want to hurt her feelings, man!"

"Kade, I swear, I'll kill you."

Kade throws his arms up in defense, cowering against the wall. "It was, like, a decade ago! Let it go!"

Leo lunges, trying to bat Kade's hands away so he can strangle him.

I know what you're thinking. Someone is trying to kill my Neshome and I'm just sitting here taking tiny, acclimating sips of coffee. Kade's fine. A few bruises won't hurt him. This, I should tell the flight attendant, is karma.

Leo settles down once the attendant returns with another tray. This time, we each get a small bowl of fruit and she leaves a small digital tablet on the table.

"In case you're looking for some entertainment." She winks at Kade, then flashes a cheesy smile at me.

I catch Kade's eyes scanning her, then his eyebrows go up. I kick his shin under the table. He mouths an "ow" and sends me an indignant look. I just give him a hard stare and a shake of my head. She is most certainly not part of the Plan. I want to tell him that, but I know I'd have a "Well, how would you know?" coming my way, and I don't want to hear it.

Kade pops a strawberry in his mouth and reaches for the tablet, still giving me a stink eye. He turns the screen on and swipes his finger a few times. He tries to look casual, but his face brightens like a child with a new toy. Kade and Leo have only seen this kind of technology on television. They can't even afford mobile phones, let alone extravagant technology. Leo reaches for the tablet, eager for a turn, and Kade yanks it away. "Wait for your turn," he mutters.

Leo laughs at him and leans back. "So," he ponders aloud with a mouthful of fruit, "if you've been trying to get through to Kade his whole life, and didn't have any luck, what did it feel like for you when he got hurt and stuff when he could've avoided it?"

Kade and I both freeze. I wasn't expecting a question like this, and it hits me in a sentimental place. I rub the back of my neck, looking anywhere but at them.

"I... you know, it... it wasn't the best feeling in the world... But I made do." From the corner of my eye, I watch for Kade's reaction. I don't want to lose all of my progress with him by making him feel ashamed.

"Did you have anyone else to talk to?" Leo presses. "Or were you on your own all the time?"

My eyebrow twitches. Is his Firn making him ask this? "I had the occasional visit from my superior, Mikael, and more visits than I'd have liked from Aropfain like Jordin."

Leo frowns. "Why so many issues with them?"

"They can smell failure," I explain with a humorless laugh. "They look for Firns who are having trouble with their Neshomes and they try to make the Neshome reject the Firn completely and follow them instead. That's what happened with Jett. Jordin beat his Firn somehow." I shudder to think about it.

"But they didn't beat you." It doesn't sound like a question, but it is.

I cross my legs and lean back into the cushion of my seat, pressing my clammy palms into the fabric. "No. No, they didn't."

"Wow," Leo breathes. "That sounds really lonely."

"Are you done?" Kade interrupts him, still swiping the screen, but not really seeing what's on it. Leo looks startled at the glare Kade gives him and Kade catches himself. He turns back to the tablet and Leo and I silently agree that this conversation is over.

"Boring apps," he mumbles. "It's pretty much all news stuff."

Leo swallows the fruit he'd been chewing. "Wonder if they've moved on from what happened at the train station yet..."

Kade looks at him. "Good point." He taps the news icon and props the screen up on the table against the wall.

The icon expands to fill the screen, and a frozen image of a cheery woman flicks into view. The triangular play button covers most of her face until Kade touches it and she comes to life.

"In greater news today, Jett Tyrrell has released his official engagement announcement to Nor'ilsk-born sweetheart, Danica Bree, and wedding planning has begun. While our sources could not reveal many details, they did promise that they intend to deliver the event of the century. Social figures from across the Beta Siberian Arrangement are flooding to Nor'ilsk for the engagement celebration where Jett and Danica will present themselves for the first time as an official couple, but for the rest of us, Jett Tyrrell has released this statement..."

The screen changes to previously recorded footage of Jett standing at a press podium, Danica behind his left shoulder, hands folded in front of her, staring at the crowd with a small, tight smile. I take what I want from that: She doesn't want to be there. This is just as annoying for her to endure as it is for me to watch. We still have a chance. Then I look at Kade. He balls up his hands and his knuckles are white. His eyes set angrily on Jett as he smoothly delivers his speech with no sign of prompt.

"And after the wedding, once my fiancé and I have time to adjust to our new roles, I will prepare to succeed my father, Donovan Tyrrell, as Chairman of the Association."

"Oh, how very medieval," I mutter as the room fills with murmurs of approval and applause and Jett smiles at the crowd with a thin, almost condescending smile. His eyes move across the crowd, a shining, piercing blue that would make anyone stop and stare in contrast to his dark hair.

Then I realize something. My eyes flick between Jett and Kade, who used to have dirty blond hair but now looks like a pathetic attempt at a Jett Tyrrell fanboy. I close my eyes and tilt my head back against the embarrassment. Hopefully, Danica doesn't see it that way too.

"I promise," Jett continues, "to serve as your Chairman with the knowledge and experience of my ancestors who came before me, but with fresh eyes on the future and the needs of the people."

The crowd erupts in applause, and something shimmers at Jett's right shoulder, pulling together to show the only other person I don't want to see.

Jordin smiles behind Jett like a proud general. He looks over the crowd of people like they're clapping for him, which is likely how he sees it. Jett's victory is Jordin's victory. Then his eyes find the exact camera that is filming for the channel we're watching. His smile spreads wider, like he knows he's looking me in the eye and he's rubbing his progress in my face. Well, I'm making progress too. Six hundred miles an hour of progress right to Danica's doorstep.

"I see we're moving along well enough," my favorite voice says as Mikael appears behind Kade's seat.

I completely forget myself. "Mikael!" Kade and Leo jump, and I hear a glass drop and shatter in the flight attendant's area behind me. Mikael looks toward the noise and waves a hand. The curtain between the attendant and the cabin closes. He glances over his shoulder. Canaan is awake and back on his phone, staring out the window. Not a threat.

"So, you've seen the news." Mikael nods toward the tablet where the video has ended.

"Yes." My voice is tight and hushed.

Kade and Leo follow my eyes and look up above Kade's seat, knowing we have a visitor but unable to see or feel him. Mikael notices this too and gives me a playful look as if to say, "Watch this!" He places his hand on Kade's shoulder, the same way Jordin had, and Kade bolts upright at the overwhelming presence of a Malekh. His eyes are round and terrified, and his first instinct is to look at me.

I don't know if Mikael meant to give me this moment, but I almost get misty knowing that Kade looks to me for comfort and assurance now. It's a dream come true after a life of being ignored, like Leo pointed out.

"Is..." Kade can hardly speak. "Is he back?"

"It's not Jordin," I assure Kade instead of what I'd like to say: "I just shouted the name Mikael. Why would it be Jordin?"

Kade only relaxes a little.

"I wanted to check on you," Mikael tells me, but Kade hears it too. "You've become a blind spot now and I don't like it. I've had others check on you from time to time, and I know it hasn't been a simple journey so far."

I flourish a hand in the air. "Oh, it's been fine. Flame-throwers and run-ins with the law are child's play." It's a joke. I was terrified the whole time. Mikael knows it.

He frowns. "I'm sorry, Anaya. I wish I could do more for

you." There's an underlying frustration in his voice that I appreciate. Malekh don't often show extreme emotion. They know too much to panic or get upset, but I'm a blind spot, like he said. That must frustrate someone as nearly all-seeing as he is.

"I'm fine." I wave him off. "We're moving along—look at us." I open my arms toward Kade and Leo. Leo looks nervous and Kade freezes under Mikael's hand. Not the triumphant heroes I'd like to present to my boss, but what can I do?

"You're doing exceptionally well," Mikael agrees. "Based on the reports I've been getting."

I frown. "You've really had people checking up on me?"

So, there was extra help when I thought there was. There was a Firn at work at the motorcade in Irkutsk. I should be happy about it, but I just feel useless. I wonder who it was. Maybe I know them. They might be friends of mine, and I can't see them to thank them or help them or anything. All I get to see is Jordin.

"Mostly Leo's Firn," Mikael explains. Kade's eyes slide to Leo, suddenly aware that we've never been alone. No one is. It's supposed to be comforting, but Kade finds it creepy. Of course he does.

"I wish I could see them," I admit without thinking.

I hear a cruel laugh. "Why? They're forbidden to speak to you, anyway. You're corrupted to them."

Well, I guess it was only a matter of time before Jordin came to gloat. He didn't seem to expect Mikael, though. They eye each other, electricity between them. Then Mikael turns away and ignores him. Jordin notices the hand on Kade's shoulder and looks impressed.

"I see we're using puppets now," he comments.

Mikael's hand tightens on Kade's shoulder and Kade jumps. I reach out to him and take his hand. "You have done nothing wrong. Jordin's here."

Kade and Leo turn a shade of green.

Jordin leans against Leo's chair. The back of the seat moves and Leo flails for a second, clinging to the arms.

"This is so pointless for you, Anaya." Jordin sounds frustrated. "They've abandoned you. Why would you continue to do their dirty work?" He leans toward me. I lean away. "Just finish the Shift. I think even Mikael would agree it's the only way to save you."

"I'm working on a better solution." Mikael keeps his eyes on me, masterfully ignoring the nuisance.

"How's that going?" Jordin wheels on him. "Because she still looks like she'll blow away with the next strong breeze."

"I'll have you know I handle breezes just fine." Not a convincing argument, but it's all I have.

Kade and Leo quirk eyebrows at me, but I ignore them. Managing multiple conversations and keeping it quiet is giving me a headache.

Jordin turns to Mikael. "You allowed this to happen." His tone is brazen. I can't believe he would talk to a Malekh this way, especially Mikael, who gave him so many second chances in the past. "You could've stepped in several times. I planned for it. I expected it, but you let me follow through without the slightest interference—again. And now you want her to keep fighting for you?" He turns on me. "Wonder what the Plan says about all that? Oh, right, you wouldn't know anymore."

I remember Jordin went through most of what I'm dealing with when he Shifted. We ignored him when he approached us afterward. We removed him from our lives because he'd done the same to us. He chose it. He knew what he'd lose, and he thought it was worth the cost. I don't.

"I'd sooner cooperate with Mikael and vanish than spend an eternity listening to your drivel, Plan or no Plan." My voice is stiff but sure. It hits Jordin like a dart. "You don't tell me what to do, Jordin. You don't get a say, no matter how much you try to force it. That's not how the world works. We deserve better. You think Narn's methods will make everyone happier? Well, I'm exhibit A of how it'll backfire. You tried to take my choices away from me and you failed. You won't convince me. I refuse to do what you want just because you say so."

I catch myself and see Kade's wide eyes on me, still scared, but also a bit of something else. I don't have the time or energy to think about it.

My breath comes in shorter puffs and my head spins. My elbow catches on the armrest as I slump toward the wall. I can almost picture the flight attendant pressed against the bulkhead behind me, trying to figure out what's going on, but I don't care. My arms feel like they're filled with air and might float away from me. Kade and Leo look concerned, but they're afraid to make a move while we still have visitors.

I feel a presence in the seat next to me and a warm pressure on my chest. In a swift moment, the pieces of me pull back together and I feel completely normal, not weak, not feeble, just normal. It comes with a flood of relief, and I look to find Mikael sitting with me. I smile at him and nod my thanks while Jordin stands useless. He doesn't seem to enjoy watching Mikael out-power him. He tenses up and inhales his rage, then vanishes.

Mikael doesn't have to look to know he's gone. He looks me over, taking stock of my condition. "I'll arrange something to help with that," he promises. He stands and the air shifts with the warnings of his departure.

"Wait!" My arm shoots out to him. He pauses, and the energy in the room seems to settle. "I've lost the Plan, Mikael." I shrink away at admitting it. "You know that."

He looks sad but doesn't deny it. "Help me out here. Are we on track? Give me something to work with. I know I'm not El Olam's favorite person right now." I still don't know why, because he should know the situation. "But I'm working for you guys. I can't go into this blind."

Mikael looks down at me with regret in his eyes. He pauses like he's checking his own Plan, which receives tiny updates almost constantly, almost like a direct email from El Olam himself. Mikael closes his eyes and wilts. He shakes his head. "I can't, Anaya. It's forbidden."

My mouth falls open and my vision blurs with tears. Why? I want to ask him, but my choked voice would embarrass me. He sees it in my face, and Kade and Leo do too. They heard my question and now they can assume the answer by my tragic expression.

"You're doing what you're supposed to be doing." Mikael doesn't even believe what he says, but he has to stick to the Plan. "Everything is still on track. You're doing a beautiful job, and you are not alone." He glances past Leo and nods to the Firn I know is there, but I can't see. I flush with anger and embarrassment. If I were in that position, I'd pity me, disgusted by the taint of Shifting and proud to be serving a larger role at Mikael's request.

I used to appreciate Leo's Firn's work. Now, whoever it is, I don't like them. I can picture the goody-two-shoes thumbs-up they're probably giving Mikael, the "You can count on me!" speech. I want to spit at their feet.

"You're taken care of." Mikael brings me back to focus on him. I hope for a second that he didn't notice my glare, but he's a Malekh. He notices everything. "You're still important to the Plan, Anaya. It won't happen without you. You're still written in as you were before. That hasn't changed. We fail without you."

I always appreciate compliments, but these don't inflate me quite as they should. It's all I can expect, though. I nod mutely.

"Don't worry," I tell him. "You won't lose me. I've got nothing better to do."

He takes comfort in that: that I still consider working for them more appealing than Shifting with Jordin. For me, it's just a case of whom I want to spite most at the moment. And Jordin still wins that race.

The air seems to lift around me. Mikael is taking his leave. He smiles at me, a grateful, guilty smile.

"Thank you, Anaya. We're still on your side, still working for you. I'll send help for your weakness. Don't lose faith."

He vanishes, leaving me a bit stunned at the pleading in his voice. How many people have had a Malekh beg them for anything? Will I ever understand why El Olam doesn't just rewrite the Plan and abandon me? That's what I would do in such a fragile time. What is going on that keeps me relevant to the Plan? I'm a skilled Firn, but I'm not that skilled. I'm replaceable. So why am I not being replaced? What is going on here?

The sound of metal on metal and the whoosh of the heavy curtain startles me. Kade, Leo, and I jump at the appearance of the flight attendant.

She looks confused at our frightened expressions.

She shrugs with the tray in her hands.

"Lunch?"

CHAPTER NINETEEN

For the rest of the flight, I'm exhausted. I don't want to move, don't really want to talk. I stare at the window, cheek mushed in my hand. Sometimes my eyes focus on clouds, sometimes the window. Neither really interests me.

Between phone calls, Canaan spends his time on his computer, occasionally pushing the flight attendant call button to refill his coffee or demand a bagel. Kade and Leo play various games with a deck of cards the attendant gave them, giving me space because what could they possibly say, anyway? I don't want to be cheered up, which I make clear with my reaction when the flight attendant tells me there is no bacon on board.

A short time before we land, Kade drops into the seat next to me and buckles in, signaling that he plans to stay until the end of the flight. He's quiet for a moment under my expectant stare. He twiddles his thumbs in his lap and finds them fascinating.

"So..." he breaks the silence. "How..." He closes his eyes, feeling stupid. "How are you holding up?"

I laugh to myself. "That was a good attempt. I don't think I could've done better."

He looks up at me with an amicable smile, scratching the back of his head. "Thanks. But, for real, we're worried about you." He gestures to include Leo because he doesn't want to admit that he, Kade Buxton, is worried about me. But I'm stunned. The hostility has left his energy completely. His defenses are down. He's not even thinking about the knife, wherever he's hiding it now.

"I don't blame you for worrying. I'm a walking mess."

He shakes his head. "That's not what I mean."

I look at him, my eyes open with curiosity.

He chews on his lip for a second. It's a tremendous effort for him to take things seriously. I give him time because I know how much growth this is for him.

"I mean, you seem to be stuck in the middle of something pretty crazy."

"We are," I correct him. "I'm your Firn, remember? I should probably ask how you're doing."

He lifts his head like he hasn't thought of it that way before. He doesn't seem to like the fit of me as his guardian angel. I don't blame him. It is stifling to acknowledge.

"Are you okay, though? I mean, no one would blame you for feeling stressed and..." He catches on the rest, bracing himself to say it. "And I haven't been too helpful. I'm..." Two whammies in one. Look at him go. "I'm sorry..." It comes out slowly, like he has to press certain buttons in his brain to get that word to come out.

I blink at him. "I'm sorry too," I say too quickly. "You weren't supposed to have to deal with me, but the rest was always in the cards for you."

"Am I..." His cheeks flush. "I don't want this to sound arrogant, so don't make fun of me, okay?"

I nod, too eager to hear what he has to say to risk ruining the moment with words.

"Am I really that important to whatever you're so focused on?" He chooses the word "focused," carefully. I think he wants to say "obsessed."

I laugh. "You're kind of a big deal where I come from,

Kade. Not as big as Danica—don't get a big head—but you're important."

"So, if I screw up, it's bad."

I give him an exaggerated nod. "Yes. Yes, that would be bad. Jett would win, which means Jordin would win, which means Narn would win, and goodbye free will for the rest of eternity." I nod. "So yeah. Bad news for everybody."

Kade processes the information, nodding and pursing his lips. "Okay, so then I should probably be nicer to you."

My breath catches and I don't have quite the air. I need to say, "Yeah, probably," which comes out too quickly, anyway.

"So..." He looks me in the eye. Something, I realize, hasn't really happened since I came to Velt. "I want to help you. If the people you're against are like that Jordin guy, I don't want them having any say over what people can or can't do. I don't want people to lose the freedom to choose for themselves."

I can almost see a glow around him, the bending of energy in the light from the window, a sign that his soul is shining through and taking charge. Kade's sense of purpose is finally clicking into place. The Kade I knew before he was born is finally showing up.

"So, you'll help me?" I ask hesitantly. "You'll talk to Danica? That's all I ask."

He shrugs one shoulder. "Doesn't sound that hard, does it? I don't see why not."

"Besides," I nudge him lightly, trying not to push my luck, "I'm sure you wouldn't mind getting to know her a bit."

He blushes and tries to man up. "She deserves better than a jerk like Jett," he decides. "If I can get her away from him, then that's great."

"There's the hero we need." My smile is so big it stretches my cheeks. Excitement floods my chest and I finally feel my fear and tension step aside, if only for a moment. My Kade is back. He knows what he needs to do. He's on board with the Plan.

Holy moly, maybe we can pull this off.

"Good evening, passengers," the flight attendant's voice rings out through the overhead speakers. Kade and I turn in our seats to watch her speak into the phone near the door. Leo lowers the newspaper he snatched from Canaan on his way to the bathroom—he set the tablet aside a while ago in favor of paper and crossed legs. I don't want to assume anything, but I get the idea that he feels closer to his father this way, emulating the way he used to read the paper when he was still in Leo's life. "To prepare for landing, please place your seats in their upright positions and stow away your tray tables. The flight attendant will be coming through the cabin to collect any discarded trash items shortly. Please power down all larger electronic items and stow them for landing." She looks nervously toward Canaan, who ignores her and continues the conversation on his cell phone, typing away at his laptop. She sighs. "Thank you." She hangs the phone back on the wall and grabs a trash bag.

We gather the trash on our table into a pile to make it easier for her.

"It was a pleasure serving you all today," she says directly to Kade, biting her lip in what society tells her is a sultry gesture.

Kade's face is blank as the moment stretches uncomfortably. He looks around, then gathers the trash and deposits it in her bag. "Thanks."

She frowns and glances my way. I just give an unsympathetic shrug. Better luck next time. She sighs and walks away.

"Better buckle up," I tell the boys. "We're about to see what the big deal is with Nor'ilsk."

We all look out the window. Nor'ilsk looks like someone

dumped a bucket of bricks on the landscape and called it a city. It's dark, but it is most of the time this time of year. We're in the arctic circle, the northernmost city in the world. Nor'ilsk used to be even more of a dump, but when its women caught the eye of BSA royalty, the Association pumped in money from their famous nickel mines to make it more glamorous. It was dirty business at first and led to a lot of pollution, but that's where Canaan stepped in with his clean energy ideas. This is the city that made Canaan who he is, according to Leo.

"It's going to be cold down there," Kade points out.

Leo nods. "One of the coldest cities on earth."

I groan, staring out the window and wondering how I'm going to survive that.

"Don't worry." Leo notices the dread on my face. "Almost everything is indoors, and buses can take you from one door to the next. People can't be outside for long most of the time, so we should be fine."

If we were people, we would be. We're not. We're intruders. Our best bet, according to Leo's information, is to be outside where we can move unnoticed.

"We're going to need heavier coats."

Kade and Leo look at me, piecing it all together. Suddenly, they don't look so keen on Nor'ilsk, either.

Customs in Nor'ilsk is intense. Kade and Leo are too aware of being on Security's watch list, despite their new looks. I'm actually the calmest of us, rattling off my name and birthday like they've always been mine—granted, I've had the same fake name from the start and Christmas is easy to remember, even though no one remembers why or what they're celebrating anymore.

I stumble on the birth year for a second, but Canaan sneezes and it sounds a lot like a year to me, so I use it. Sure enough, I pass once they root through my purse. I come away feeling dizzy from nerves, but no worse for wear.

Kade and Leo, however, mumble and stutter. Their customs agent shouts at them to spit out their details and something in their mind triggers. They shout at the same time. The agent squints at them, then Canaan steps in, assuring the agent that they are simpletons "hardly capable of walking a straight line, let alone committing an act of treason."

Canaan is like magic. When he speaks, people listen—and agree. He knows how to draw a laugh out of the most cynical people and lower their guard to his manipulation. I shudder to imagine what he would do under an Aropfain's influence. I send a quick, grateful prayer to El Olam, abandoned as I am, for Canaan's Firn. That's a soul I'd like to meet in person. It's a shame I never will.

Once we each get the customs seal of approval, Canaan herds us out of the airport through a private access and straight to a waiting limousine. He all but shoves us in and we're on our way, catching our breath and settling our nerves in relative silence for the entire drive.

The limo pulls up to an elegant hotel, but it's not a surprise this time. I've already stashed any spare snacks in my purse from the flight attendant and from the limo's snack bar like some kind of ravenous squirrel. My purse bulges with the pressure of so many snack bags, but I'm not playing games here. I need strength because this body isn't getting any stronger. Energy seeps from me now like it knows I'm not its true host and it wants to return to where it belongs. So, yeah, I'm always hungry.

"Get out," Canaan commands us. We're not affected by his rudeness anymore. We know what an imposition we've been, and he's a very busy man. That the frigid air around us, thick with the threat of ice, is breathable is a testament to his work, I suppose. It slams into me like a wall and breathing is the last thing on my mind. It's dark, the wind cuts like a knife as it blows by, seeming to push us away from the door that will give us shelter. I wish the north and south poles would actually shift. It's hard to imagine this place becoming a temperate paradise, but that would be nice right about now.

Kade, Leo, and I huddle together, amassing against the push of the wind and making our way to the door in defiance. When we break through the door behind an agitated Canaan, we all relax with heaving breaths.

"I'll dig a tunnel before I go back out there again," Kade says.

I nod numbly. That's a brilliant plan. "Best get started. I'm coming with you."

Canaan steps up to us, completely recovered, while I feel like I have icicles growing off me. He's displeased. We're making him look bad... again.

"Pull yourselves together. It's winter. What did you expect?"

He hands us two small key cards.

"You get one room. I get the bill. Room service is fine, but I don't want to hear about any damages or stolen property. You get me?"

We nod together. We deserve that. Kade accepts the keys and Canaan moves past us toward the door.

"You're not staying here?" Leo asks out of curiosity.

Canaan sneers over his shoulder. "Of course not. I have a private residence in Nor'ilsk. You won't catch me dead in a place this tacky. This is where our arrangement ends. It was a headache working with you." He dips his hat and strides through the automatic doors and out of our lives.

Time slows for a moment, and we realize we won't be seeing Canaan again. There's no one to speak for us or cover our mistakes. There's no time for mistakes. This is the end of the road. For Kade, at least, all roads were always going to lead to Nor'ilsk.

My stomach rumbles, shattering the surreal moment. "I'm hungry." I snatch a card away from Kade and check the number on my way to the elevator. Waving it in the air over my shoulder, I say, "Who wants room service?"

Kade and Leo trip into action, following me at the promise of a hot meal.

CHAPTER TWENTY

It's a good thing I'm going to vanish when I'm done in Velt, because I would miss food if I had to go back to Lemayle. From now on, I plan to treat every meal like it's my last, so I ordered one of everything on the menu.

"We need a plan," I announce once I've satisfied my more urgent need for food. Kade and Leo nod their agreement, mouths equally full. Whoever cooks for this place is good at his job, because I'm not afraid of Jordin or Narn or anything at this moment. I'm too blissed out from food to care. There's an overwhelming sense of comfort that comes with a hefty serving of potatoes and pasta that just can't be beat, except maybe by chocolate cake. I plan to find that out next.

Kade flips on the television while we eat. It defaults to a local news station and the dreamy anchor says, "Wedding plans are underway at the—"

Kade turns the television off, rolling his eyes.

"We could've used that," Leo scolds him. "We don't know where Danica is. They might have said something."

"I sure hope not," I cut in. "They're probably watching Danica like a hawk right now, thanks to whatever Jordin's gotten through to Jett. They wouldn't announce where she's staying on a public channel where people like us could find it. At least I wouldn't. That's bad battle strategy."

"Well, you would know, wouldn't you?"

My head falls back, and I can feel a headache threaten behind my eyes.

"Jordin's here," I announce dryly. Kade and Leo glance around like they'll be able to see him. It's almost embarrassing.

"For goodness' sake," Jordin complains. He closes his eyes for a moment and energy spreads from him like a blanket. My eyes pinch, while I wonder what he's trying to do, but then I notice Kade and Leo shiver.

"Testing, testing," Jordin drones. "Can you hear me?"

Two heads turn toward Jordin's voice. My jaw drops. He can do that? Since when can he do that?

Kade jumps up, ready for a fight with something he can't see. He doesn't want Jordin near him again after last time. I don't have time to tell him that Jordin isn't touching him this time before Jordin lifts a hand toward him.

"I wouldn't," Jordin says with distaste as an unseen pressure from his hand forces Kade back to his seat. My heart skips a beat I can't afford to lose. That's too much power, too much influence that a soul of Lemayle has no right to possess.

Jordin notices my face and wags his eyebrows to boast. I collect my reaction and scowl at him.

"Okay," he claps his hands together, "so we were about to form a plan?"

"We," I spin a finger to include all four of us, "weren't about to do anything. Get out."

His hand falls to his chest. "You wound me, Anaya. I'm trying to help you. Like you said, you don't know where Danica is. But I do. I just happen to have arranged it all for you."

I draw away from him. "And why would you do that?"

"Because if you get your Neshome to Danica, you'll fulfill your promise to El Olam. Then you can finish the Shift and everybody wins."

"Everybody wins, huh?" I fold my arms, hoping it looks defensive, but it feels more like I'm trying to comfort myself against the skill and power that Jordin's been hiding.

Jordin shrugs indifferently. "Everybody that matters."

"So, basically, just you."

He grins and doesn't deny it.

"Shall we begin?" He rubs his hands together like he's settling in for an enormous meal. That's one thing he can't do that I can, at least.

Somehow, that makes me feel worse.

I move to the hotel room couch and pull the desk chair out as I pass. Kade and Leo follow. Leo takes the desk chair and Kade sits on the couch with me. We will not let Jordin know we're uncomfortable. Jordin follows and positions himself on the bed to match our posture.

"So where is she, then?" I ask, crossing my legs and sinking into the couch like I couldn't be more at ease.

He smiles again, his classic gotcha smile. "The embassy."

I lean forward without thinking, rubbing circles on my temples. "Of course she is. You set that up for our convenience, huh?"

He nods. "Of course I did."

"Possibly the most secure place in the city," I emphasize, waiting for a helpful answer. "You set that up for us."

Another nod. "That I did."

My hands fly out from my sides. "How can you think that's convenient?" I shout at him. I shake my head. "This is like partnering with you all over again. You always messed everything up."

"I resent that," he says with a pitch in his tone. "I always did my best to help you, Anaya, but you were usually too headstrong to see any way but your own."

"How dare you?"

"I can actually see that," Kade says without thinking. He recoils when I glare at him, but Jordin sweeps an arm his way to illustrate his point.

I lean into Kade. "Whose side are you on again? He's the enemy. This is no time for jokes."

"Who's joking?" Jordin asks. "Sounded honest enough to me."

"You shut up." I point at him, my temper rising. "You're the reason he doesn't know me as well as he should."

I breathe as I feel my fingertips tingle with the threat of another episode. In, inhale, hold it, exhale.

"So, you say she's in the embassy?"

"She is," Jordin defends himself.

"She is," another voice chimes in. I look up to see Mikael. He doesn't look happy, and he doesn't look at Jordin.

Jordin twists himself to see Mikael. "Oh, hi," he says. "Nice of you to join us." He turns back to me. "You can tell things are getting serious when all the generals meet before the ultimate battle, eh?"

I steal a glance at my boys. They can still hear Jordin, but Mikael hasn't spread his influence to them. They only know someone else is here because of what Jordin said, and they look nervous, curling in on themselves and shrinking away from the voices in the room.

"Grow up," I chide Jordin. He may not respect Mikael, but I do. "What's going on, Mikael? Is everything okay?"

I feel stupid. Nothing is okay. We've hit crunch time. We're hours away from the moment we give one last shove, then have to stand back and watch what happens. Once Kade meets Danica, our work is done. He'll either convince her or he won't. She'll make a choice and it will shake the universe.

No pressure.

"I just wanted to tell you we have made the arrangements to combat your health complications, at least long enough to get you where you need to be." The words are for me, but Mikael's glare is for Jordin. I never want to be on the receiving end of that look. It's terrifying, especially from someone who normally looks so kind.

I guess no one is messing around anymore. No more Mr. Nice Malekh.

"What arrangements?" I ask. I see an intent look on Jordin's face as he listens, too.

"You'll see."

Ever cryptic. Of course.

"So, as I was saying," Jordin moves on. "She's in the embassy, and I can get you in."

I shift my eyes to Mikael, looking for any sign that Jordin might be lying. To be honest, I expect Jordin to be lying.

Mikael drags his eyes away from Jordin for a moment to give me the faintest nod. So, she really is at the embassy.

"Told you so," Jordin teases.

I pull my legs up onto the couch. Kade lifts an arm to the back of the couch behind me to give me more space. "And you say you can get us in? Why should we believe you?"

"Do you have another option?" He turns mockingly to Mikael, waiting for the answer. Mikael gives him nothing. He interprets it as a no. "I didn't think so."

"You're setting us up. Don't think I don't know that."

Jordin withdraws, feigning a gasp. "I would never!"

"What's your deal with Anaya?" Kade asks out of nowhere. "You're insanely creepy, you know that? That's no way to charm someone."

I hold up a hand, almost laughing. "It's not about charm, Kade. That means nothing to us. It's about power. It's always about power, and it's exhausting."

"Yeah," Jordin agrees flatly. "What she said." He sighs and shakes himself off. "So, shall we leave in the morning?"

"The morning." I raise my eyebrows. "Are you crazy? They'll catch us for sure. How do you expect us to sneak in there in broad daylight?"

"This is Nor'ilsk, Anaya," Jordin drags his voice out. "There's no such thing as broad daylight this time of year. We get a few hours of it, but you'll be in the building by then."

"Well, you've gone native," I comment.

He smiles despite my jab. "Oh, I like it here. You would too." He shoots me a suggestive look. "We should work together."

From the corner of my eye, I see Mikael bow his head. It's a graceful, sad movement. "Your help will arrive soon, Anaya. And I wish you the best for the rest of your journey."

Jordin and I turn to look at him. Leo and Kade notice and look at the blank space, too.

"You're leaving?" Suddenly, I'm afraid. I know what this means. This is the last time I'll see him unless he pays a visit while I fade. Somewhere below my rib cage, a strange heaviness sets in. This must be what true dread feels like. The knowledge that I'm going to die, really die, and I can't stop it.

"My work is complete." Mikael smiles. "I leave the rest in your capable hands."

"My hands are not capable!" I argue. That earns me weird looks from the boys and a chuckle from Jordin, but I'm devastated. I don't care how short a time we spend finding Danica, knowing that I won't be seeing Mikael again, that my purpose is so close to completion, is terrifying. What comes after? How will I handle fading away? What if I don't fade right away? Am I to just drift through Velt until one day the wind is strong enough to carry me with it? What better place for that than Nor'ilsk, but that's no life I want to live. Once my part of the Plan is complete, will I truly be off limits, even to Mikael? Will El Olam cut me off once I meet his purposes?

Will it tempt me to complete the Shift?

My heart skips a beat and anxiety fogs my mind. It isn't an episode like usual, it's just pure panic and fear.

"I can't do this alone." My voice cuts off and shakes like the cold from outside has seeped into me and won't leave.

Mikael's face falls with sympathy. Jordin laughs, ready to tell me to suck it up, but Kade's is the voice that breaks through my haze. His arm slips from the couch to my shoulders and squeezes.

"You're not doing anything alone." His words ring in my ears, and I see the soul I met with before he came here. I see the soul that was confident and ready to change the world, to be a hero, to make the necessary sacrifices, with a smile on his face. I look up and I see Kade, the very same soul.

Like someone pulled a sheet off my head, I find my grip on reality again. I breathe normally. I ignore the supernatural presences and smile at Kade. "Yeah, wow. Sorry about that. Big moment I guess."

Kade nods, almost laughing. "Big moment."

"Well, that was lovely," Jordin says tightly. "Do we have a plan then? I'll see you in the morning?"

I look to Mikael for his reaction. Any twitch of his face could tell me if it's in the Plan for us to do this. It's not unheard of to use an Aropfain's choices against them.

But Mikael is gone. I didn't even see him go. I almost question if he was ever actually here.

I sigh, defeated. "What's the plan?"

Jordin grins. "I thought you'd never ask." He reaches behind him and produces my purse, opening it to pull out our paperwork. It creeps me out to see Jordin so effortlessly strong. As a Firn, I barely had the strength to move a sheer curtain and here he is lifting a purse half-stuffed with snack foods. I glance at the boys because all they see is a floating purse right now and, sure enough, their faces are pale and slack.

"You're going to be applying for passports," Jordin explains. "You've made an appointment for travel visas. It's all in order."

Impressive. "But how did you get our new names?"

"I was at your interviews back in Ulan Ude. I saw your papers there."

It's my turn to be smug. "Such a shame you were so focused on my makeup in Irkutsk. You missed that Kade and Leo got new names."

Jordin's eyes flare in surprise for a second and he scans the papers. He looks up at Kade with disgust on his face. "Gerald Finley?"

Kade studies the space around his floating papers with a flat stare. "I don't want to talk about it."

Jordin laughs and the papers shake. "Oh, that Canaan guy must really hate you."

"He wasn't fond of us by the end." I snatch the papers from Jordin and he's left just holding my purse. "You'll have to adjust your appointments."

Hope flashes in his eyes. "So, you'll come?"

I eye him with suspicion. "Don't think I'm not onto you. I know this is a trap."

"Well, of course it is. But you never know, you might slip through my fingers. It'll be fun to see what happens, don't you think? I'm excited." He looks at Kade. "I haven't had this much fun since the gas station blew up."

I roll my eyes. "You're such a jerk."

He raises his hands in defense. "Hey, I'm just enjoying the ride. It's been a great one so far, and I'm looking forward to seeing where it ends." He moves around my shoulder and flips through our paperwork one last time, laughing again at Kade's name.

"Your appointment is for eleven in the morning," he says as he steps back. "See you tomorrow, Agnes."

He vanishes, and my purse falls to the floor. We all relax, exhausted. "Who gets the bed?" I ask, eyes already half shut.

"You do," the boys say together.

I give them a small salute for their wise decision and crawl onto the bed.

Then the doorbell rings and I groan, burying my face in the blankets.

"I'll get it," Leo volunteers.

He opens the door to see a bellhop with a small white box on a silver tray.

"Delivery for..." he reads the slip, "Agnes DiRoma?"

Leo keeps the door between him and the bellhop, just in case this is part of the trap we're willingly walking into. "Who's it from?"

"Ah, Mr. Canaan Sem, sir. He said it was important."

Leo moves around the door to accept the package. "Thank you."

"Have a wonderful evening." The bellhop smiles but doesn't leave. Leo realizes almost immediately that he's waiting for a tip.

"Oh... uh..." He pats his pockets for anything he can offer.

"We're poor," Kade shouts from across the room. He strides to Leo's side and grips the door. "We're a charity case. I'm sure Canaan's overpaid you already. Have a good night." He shuts the door on the bellhop, to Leo's shock, and goes back to the couch. "What's in the box?"

Leo shrugs, box in hand, and places it delicately on the bed in front of me. "It's for you. You should open it."

"How very brave of you," I tease him. He gives a weak smile and doesn't deny it.

I try to press my nails against the tape, but even they're not strong. "Hey Kade, can I see your knife for a second? I can't get this open."

"Sure," Kade says lightly. He reaches into his pocket and produces the knife without question.

I'd describe the sheer joy that blossoms in my chest, but I don't want to get sappy here. Instead, I run the knife along the tape, and it cuts so smoothly I get a chill, thinking of how Ramiro wanted Kade to use this on me.

Once the flaps pop free of the tape, I hand the knife back to Kade and he tucks it away again. "You're bringing that tomorrow, right? We'll need everything we can get."

"Duh," is Kade's sarcastic response. He nods toward the box. "What is it?"

I open the flaps to see a plastic black case with a white note on top. I pull the note out first.

"To keep you on your toes," it reads, and it's signed by Canaan.

I flip the latches on the case and toss the lid open.

"Oh, no."

"Seriously?" Kade leans in.

"It looks like… adrenalin shots?" Leo looks to each of us for our reaction, but I fix my eyes on the needles. Three rows of them and another set underneath.

Kade gingerly plucks one from the box and reads the instructions on the side. "One shot, twice daily as needed." He lowers the syringe and looks at me sympathetically. "Morning and night."

"This is the solution Mikael came up with?" My voice is nearly a shriek. "Shoot me up with drugs?"

"I hope they don't test us at the interview tomorrow," Leo thinks out loud.

"Idiot," Kade scolds him. "We're not really going to the interview. That's what Jordin wants us to do." He turns to me. "Right?"

My eyes sting. "I have no idea what's going to happen tomorrow. I'm cut off."

Their sympathetic silence stretches until I can't take it anymore. I look at the syringes. "I'll start them tomorrow. If I take them at night, I won't be able to sleep."

I don't actually know that, but I'm not in the mood to take the shot right now. I close the case and lay it on the side table, then I burrow under the blankets and keep them over my head to shut the world out long enough to fall asleep.

CHAPTER TWENTY-ONE

Have you ever anticipated something so much that you woke up way too early beforehand? I decide, as I stare at the ceiling, that winter is stupid. It's always dark, so I'm always tired. I can't tell what time it is, whether the middle of the night or the middle of the morning unless I check the clock.

It's five in the morning. I slept for about six hours. My head falls to the side to glare at the plastic box of syringes, knowing I couldn't prolong the shot for much longer and dreading every second that dragged me closer to when I'd have to deal with it. I'm not afraid of shots, per se, I just don't like that it's come to this. A Malekh has resorted to sending me drugs to keep me going. This is the least conventional job I've ever done.

I hear a rustling from the couch as Kade stands up, rubbing his eyes, and walks toward the bathroom. For some reason, I shut my eyes and pretend to be asleep. Kade does his thing and comes back out.

"I know you're awake," he drawls as he trudges back to the couch. I peek out from under the covers as he sits on the couch next to the bed, facing me with an expectant arch of his eyebrow. His black hair is a mess, sticking up all over, but he doesn't seem to notice. "Freaking out?"

I look away. "Maybe a bit."

"Because of Jordin?" His voice is more awake and a sliver of care wears away the roughness of it.

"Partly because of Jordin, but I'll spare you the list. We'll stick with 'because of Jordin.'" I sit up and wrap my arm around my knees, hugging a plush blanket like a teddy bear substitute to distract myself from the fear I'm trying to repress.

"Yeah, but we will not let him win," Kade says, as if it's a given. "He's pulling our strings right now, but we'll yank them back the minute we get what we need from him. We're playing him just as much as he's playing us, right?"

"That's true..."

"All we have to do is get to Danica, then it's out of his hands, right?"

"It's out of everyone's hands but yours and hers," I tell him, pinning him with my gaze so he understands the gravity of his position. "Are you ready for that?"

He scoffs. "No. Of course I'm not."

I bury my face in my hands.

"But you said I was born for this, so I'm sure it'll come to me. I'll do what it takes."

That was a shockingly confident statement. I peek at him through my fingers.

He notices my surprise. He exhales a long breath and drops his head. "Yeah, I know. I haven't exactly been on board with everything, but that Jordin guy ticks me off and..." He seems to think better of what he's about to say, squeezes his eyes shut, and says it anyway. "I respect you. I see how hard you're working for this stuff you believe in and I've seen enough to know something big is happening, and if it is, I want to be on your side."

"El Olam's side," I correct him automatically.

"Sure, yeah." He nods. "But I won't let them beat you. You've worked way too hard."

The stinging behind my nose warns me I'm about to get sappy, so I chew my cheek until it passes. Kade's sincere eyes move from my face to something over my shoulder and the moment shatters. My face falls.

"You're going to make me take the shot now, aren't you?"

He shrugs with a pained half-smile. "It's gotta happen eventually, and this way you'll be ready for a second dose before we go, and we'll know if there are any adverse effects."

"I'd rather not find that out in the middle of the embassy," comes Leo's gravelly agreement. I hear a sigh and the standing light near his spot on the floor flicks on. We all shrink away like nocturnal animals ready to scatter at the first sign of daylight.

"What time is it?" Leo rubs the sleep from his eyes.

I check the digital clock next to the bed. "Five thirty or so."

Leo groans. "And the appointment is at eleven?"

"That's what Jordin said."

"Could you imagine if he lied about it?" Kade asks, already offended.

I shake my head to calm him. "The appointment is his bait. Without it, we don't get through the door, and he can't catch us. He wouldn't lie about that bit."

We sit in silence for a while before Kade says, "You think we should come up with an escape plan? Since we know he's going to trap us there?"

"How do we do that?" Leo asks, frustration in his voice. "We know nothing about the embassy. We don't know the exits or what kind of security we'll find, and who else will be there, because Jordin arranged it."

"Is there an internet lab here?" Kade moves to sift through the pamphlets on the desk and Leo rises from the floor, reaching for the box of needles on the bedside table.

I shrink away from him as he sits next to me on the bed. He gives me a sympathetic look and places the case down, opening it delicately and turning to me.

"May I see your arm?"

I offer it slowly. Leo's touch is so light I almost don't feel it. His eyes focus and glaze like he's done this a million times. Then I remember.

"Your mother?"

He looks at me, lips tight against the memories and fears of his ailing family, and nods.

"Have I apologized for that yet?" I ask. "Because I'm really sorry. I didn't know it was in the Plan for you to come along with Kade, but..." I look down, catching Kade listening from the desk. "I was really glad it turned out that way, but not that you had to leave your family because of it."

Leo says nothing. He keeps working, expertly finds a vein with his fingers, picks up a syringe, tests it. I flinch as some of the serum squirts into the air. Leo meets my eyes for a second before pushing the needle into my arm. I tense against the pinch and screw my face up at the rush of cold fluid in my veins.

Leo gently removes the needle and grabs a tissue to press against the tiny bead of blood left behind.

"It's fine," he says stiffly. "I can see the purpose in it, I guess. I'd hate to imagine Kade helping with your injections."

Kade turns again like he's about to protest, but I look at him because we both know Leo's right. Leo was the scientist in training. Kade was to be the Security grunt. Kade turns back to the hotel directory.

"After today though..." Leo continues, missing our exchange. "Are we done?"

I wasn't ready for this question, but he's right. After today, we should be done. It's the only thing left in my head from

Lemayle: Get Kade to Danica. That's his endgame, which makes me a little nervous for reasons I can't recall. I look at Kade, but nothing jogs my memory enough to explain why my throat constricts and nerves stir in my stomach for him. If only I could remember what all the souls I've guided have in common. If I could even remember the name of one and what their life was like, maybe I'd realize why I feel so sorry about Kade's fate.

"There's so much I don't know anymore." I stare at the comforter, not ready to meet Leo's disappointment. "But, from what I do, I think so?" I look up, the weakest smile on my face. "I wish I could tell you more, Leo. Believe me, I do. I know you've sacrificed more than anyone to be here, and you've suffered the most for it." I remember the scream that tore from him when the moose broke his leg like it was yesterday.

Leo stares at the sheets like he could burn a hole in them. "I'm going home after today," he announces. Kade and I jolt at the news, but what did we expect?

I nod. "That makes sense. The point is for Kade to meet Danica and help her make her choice. Once they meet," I look over my shoulder at Kade, who's frozen at the desk, "everything should fall into place." Because that's where my instructions end. They meet, and that's that. No details about a relationship between them, no future that I can recall. They just meet and talk. Mikael didn't tell me any differently, so that must be right.

"If I'm still around," I tell Leo, "I'll help you get back home safely. I'm sure your Firn already has it all figured out, but it's the least I can do for all you've done for Kade and me."

Leo smiles. It's sad but genuine. He nods. "Thank you. But..." He turns to Kade. "Are you coming home too?"

Kade turns his head toward us but doesn't face us. "Depends, I guess."

"You don't want to." It's an accusation as much as an observation.

Kade spins the desk chair to face us but keeps his eyes on the floor. "I mean, there's got to be more to what I'm supposed to do with Danica beyond just introducing myself, right?" Now he looks at us, but we've got nothing for him. "I think we're going to have to get her out of there, and if we do, then I'm not leaving her."

There's my little hero. I'm surprised. I always thought he'd be loyal to Danica because of his infatuation with her, but it looks like a sense of purpose is motivation enough for him. This is the Kade I've been searching to find for two decades. Now, when everything has fallen apart, he shows up.

"So, it's decided then?" I ask them, rubbing the sore spot on my arm once Leo releases it. "After today, Kade will stay with Danica and Leo can go home. No hard feelings?"

"What about you?" Kade asks, eyes almost burning me with the pressure of the question. "Are you going to go back with Leo?" He looks down. "I guess that's the safest thing for you."

I'm touched by the sadness in his voice. I know what he's really asking: "What will I do without a Firn?" It's bittersweet. Kade has finally acknowledged our existence and I'm going to abandon him, anyway. I don't know if I'm strong enough to face him as I fade.

"I'll do whatever I have the energy left to do." The dread in my chest makes me clench my jaw. "I don't know how long I'll last after this. And I don't know how Jordin will react to failure. I'll just have to play it by ear."

Kade gives a solemn, disappointed nod. "I guess that settles everything then."

"Guess it does," I agree, but I'm not excited about it. I feel cheated, to be honest. This moment is what I've been working toward for over two thousand years, and we're all planning on going out with a whisper. No victory dance, no pats on the back, just a parting of ways into the end of the world. But that's how it would always have gone, I guess. I just would've been around to watch. Maybe it's good that I'm fading. I won't have to deal with the boredom or waiting for the Reyn Gayst to settle El Olam and Narn's dispute.

"I'm going to grab a shower," Leo announces. He stands and moves into the bathroom like he doesn't want to give us a chance to protest, but I know I wouldn't say anything against it.

"I found a computer lab," Kade tells me when the bathroom door closes. "We can at least figure out the layout of the embassy before we go in. The more you know, right?"

I smile at him, a tired, feeble smile. "Right."

We take turns showering and dressing ourselves to both impress and blend in, because everyone in Nor'ilsk is trying to impress everyone else. Kade does my makeup again, pulling the desk chair in front of me while I sit on the toilet. He works like a painter, trying to do everything the way Jordin showed him. His tongue occasionally pokes out when he concentrates on the finer details of my face, and I find my cheeks warming at the embarrassment of being so closely scrutinized.

"There." He leans back and sighs after what feels like an hour. He shakes his arm out and tries to rub circulation back into it. "Leo!" he calls into the bedroom. "Can you come check this out to make sure I did it right?"

Leo steps into the room. His eyes skim over my face and he turns back to where the TV is playing more reality shows. He looks back at me. "Looks good to me."

I curl my lip. "Not sure if that's a compliment, considering the standard."

"You look like a Nor'ilsk girl," Kade says. "Don't worry. You don't look as desperate, though. Your eyes are different." He rubs his chin. "You may want to work on that, actually."

I mock a laugh because that had better be a joke.

When we're all satisfied that we can pass as city people, we venture out of the hotel room in search of the computer lab. It isn't hard to find. It's on the first floor, just next to the hotel restaurant. Kade and I start on the research while Leo takes our key card to the restaurant to grab some breakfast for all of us.

"Plenty of exits," Kade says by the time Leo sets a plate full of bacon, toast, and eggs in front of me. I'll ruin my lipstick on this stuff, but I don't care. "Mostly front and side doors. Each one has a checkpoint. That's going to be tricky."

"Are you going to take the knife?" Leo eyes Kade like it would be a bad idea, and it would. We'd get arrested on the spot for bringing a weapon into the embassy where Jett Tyrrell and his future bride are staying, but Kade's fishing rod pen and the CO_2 knife are the only defense we have.

"Of course I'm going to bring it," Kade says without hesitation. "I'll hide it in my shoe or something."

I nod. Sounds good enough to me. Besides, who knows what Firns will be on site to help us? I can imagine it would be incredibly convenient for Jordin if we got arrested at Security.

"We just have to stay aware of where we are in the building." Leo points at the screenshot of a tourist map of the embassy. It's for public tours, so I'm sure there are several rooms left out, but there is a third floor, noted by an asterisk to be off limits because it serves as temporary housing for VIPs. Starry-eyed visitors can gasp and sigh at the thought of being in the same building as BSA royalty, but for us...

"Danica will be on this floor." I point to the third floor.

"But so will Jett," Kade points out.

"They might even share a room," Leo says, balking at the glares he gets from both of us. "What?"

"They're not married yet," Kade grumbles.

Leo scoffs. "This isn't a fairytale, Kade. That's archaic thinking."

Anger scatters my thoughts and burns my ears at the thought of Jett and Jordin having constant contact with Danica. Have they brainwashed her yet? Is the game already over? Why else would Jordin be so comfortable getting Kade close to Danica?

I press a hand to my heart. It beats fast, but I don't get the wash of weakness like I usually do. I guess the drugs are working.

"You okay?" Leo notices me.

I nod, smiling at him. "I'm good, actually. Just thinking."

They both nod. Who isn't thinking right now?

I change the subject. The only thing that relieves thinking is acting. "We'll need to escape from the third floor."

Kade's head perks up toward the screen. "Yeah, there are fire exits at each end of the hall, and two elevators in the middle."

"I wouldn't count on using the elevator," Leo says.

"It would drive me crazy if we did," I agree. "I can't move that slowly when I'm running for my life."

Kade makes an agreeable noise in his throat. "Me either."

"So, stairs," I decide, pointing to the stairs on the left of the image. "This will help us exit the building farthest from any crowds. It's the only side that isn't facing a street unless there are back exits."

I glance at Kade for an answer.

"There are, but we'll have a hard time getting to them from the fire exits. We're better off just coming out from the side."

I nod, processing. "Well, that's as good as we'll get, I guess." I grab the last piece of bacon before anyone can argue. Kade shoots me a withering look but says nothing and Leo hardly notices. He must not be a nervous eater. Good for him.

We return the dishes to the restaurant and make our way back upstairs in distracted silence. Kade slips the key card into the door handle and pushes it open with a little too much force. I reach out to say something to help calm his nerves, but I freeze.

Leo and Kade stare at the TV as channels flip by and I stare at Jordin lounging on the bed, a bored look on his face.

"Oh." He closes his eyes for a moment, sending a blanket of his energy over the room as we huddle inside and close the door. "There you are. I've been so bored waiting for you."

Kade and Leo glance around, hearing him but unable to see. I elbow Kade and lift my chin toward the bed. He can relay the information to Leo.

"Why didn't you just find us? It's not like you're incapable."

Jordin smiles, leaning into the pillows. He can't feel the bedding. He's just showing off. I almost feel bad for him. It's extremely comfortable.

"I got bored at the embassy this morning," he explains, still watching the television. "So, I did you a bit of a favor."

I cringe at the thought of what Jordin considers a favor. "What did you do?"

Now he meets my eyes. "I moved your appointment up."

All three of us jump. "To when?" My voice is nearly hysterical.

Jordin leans back on the pillows to glance at the clock on the side table. "Nine o'clock."

My eyes move toward the clock in slow motion because I know we will not have any time. Is this part of his trick? Is he going to make us miss the appointment? My heart freezes. Is Security on their way here?

"Oh, relax, would you?" He kicks his legs over the side of the bed and stands. He grabs the clock and spins it toward me. Seven thirty. "You have just enough time if we leave now. It's a bit of a walk and I'm told it's frigid out there." He imitates a shiver, a thin smile mocking me.

A hand clamps around my shoulder and Kade's voice is in

my ear. "We should grab another dose for you before we go. Just in case this one doesn't last long enough."

It pains me, but he's right. We can't fight Jordin on this. We have to go with him on his terms; he's our only in with the embassy, and we're short on time, if what Mikael said is true.

I scan the room but come up with a frown. "Where's the case?" I whisper over my shoulder.

"Do you have your papers?" Jordin moves toward the door. "We can't dawdle long. Make sure you have coats. You'll catch frostbite in seconds if we're not careful. Not very attractive to present an ice zombie to Danica." His eyes glitter with the games he plays, thrilled knowing we're fumbling and trying not to let it show.

We spread out to search. I move to the desk and grab my purse, checking that the papers are still inside. They are, but that's all. Where did that case go? I should've put a dose in my purse earlier, but how could I know Jordin would do this?

I mentally kick myself. Of course, Jordin would do this. I'm slipping. Is that part of the fade or am I just losing my touch? It doesn't matter now.

"Ticktock, you three. We have several blocks to go unless you've got a car."

We used to have a car. It would be amazing if we stepped outside to find Canaan's car waiting, but he made it clear that he was done with us. I doubt his Firn could convince him with how frustrated he is by the trouble we put him through. I don't hold it against him.

Kade, Leo, and I come together again of one mind. "We'll just have to go," I tell them. "We can't lose this chance to get in under the radar. Breaking in would be so much harder with Security on alert. And Jordin will see to it if we don't do things his way." I force air through my nose. "He's such a child."

"What are we talking about?" Jordin whispers as he appears in our circle. I fall back a step and the boys fall back three at the sound. It must be hard for them not knowing where Jordin might be.

"Why didn't you bring a car for us?" There's a deliberate air of accusation in my voice. He draws back, offended.

"I am helping you," he protests. "I'm not supposed to, you know. And now you want me to deliver the Reyn Gayst to my enemy on a silver platter? Such audacity."

I roll my eyes, slinging my purse over my shoulder and grabbing my coat. He is helping me. He's been helping me since the time came for Kade to leave Yuzhno-Shakalinsk and make his way toward Danica. This should be the point where Jordin begins working against me.

And that's probably what he's doing, drawing out his victory so Kade can face off with Jett Tyrrell while Jordin and I match them in spirit. If he can't win by Shifting me, he'll take me to my grave on his own schedule in the worst way he can imagine. He'll make me watch Kade fail before I fade.

He's a monster, but he still wears the face of my soul mate, my best friend, my partner, and even if I can't stop him in the end–even if I fade walking across a random street on the way to the embassy–I will fade fighting whatever this is that he's become.

"Let's just go." I trudge toward the door, and for once, everyone does as I say.

That would have made things so much easier a few months ago.

CHAPTER TWENTY-TWO

Jordin wasn't kidding about the cold. The moment we step outside, my teeth chatter. I had a sliver of hope that maybe Canaan's car would be here, by some miracle of Mikael's doing, but I'm disappointed. I'm on my own now, with only Jordin to help me.

I'm doomed.

"It's this way," Jordin walks in the open air, feeling nothing, cutting through the biting wind like a knife. My heart stops. The knife. I huddle toward Kade in a show to get warmth. "Did you bring the knife?" I say it so quietly I can barely hear myself, but he gives a slow, careful nod.

"Shoe."

I nod, my nose already stinging with cold, and flip my hood up before it gets to my ears too. That terrible burning and ache that shoots from my ears straight into my jaw is one of the worst parts of being alive again and I'll avoid it if I can help it.

The three of us huddle together and follow Jordin like he's our lantern in the eternal wintry darkness of Nor'ilsk. I focus on my feet, placing one in front of the other, eyes on Jordin. Ignore the cold, I tell myself. Just get where you need to go.

There will be warmth at the embassy and a whole new slew of problems. I try to keep my mind calm so it will be sharp for me later. My only goal now should be to make it to the embassy alive.

My whole body shivers against the cold. I haven't gained quite enough weight to keep myself warm. An arm drapes across my shoulders and I tense, peeking around my hood to find Kade with a concerned look on his face. I try to smile my thanks, but my cheeks are numb, and I don't know if it shows.

We take several turns that I can't keep track of. Maybe three of them? I hope someone is keeping count so we can escape later. Then I remember we don't have anywhere to go after we escape. The hotel is our only home.

I wish Enoch was here. I'm sure there's a hideout somewhere near Nor'ilsk. And maybe that's what we'll do. Just run until we're out of the city and hope to be taken in by the other outcasts. Then Kade can take Danica somewhere safe, Leo can go home, and I...

"Just around this corner," Jordin's muffled voice comes to me on the wind. He turns and frowns when he sees me. I probably should've brought extra makeup. I picture my face with streaks of eyeshadow and mascara racing toward my hairline thanks to the wind.

Jordin stops moving long enough for me to catch up to him, then moves at my side, opposite of Kade. "Will you make it, Anaya?" His energy swirls around just the two of us, and I realize this is a private conversation, at least for him.

I don't want to respond and deal with confused looks from Kade or Leo. I just want to get warm. So, I keep my eyes straight ahead, focused on the corner Jordin promised would be the last.

Jordin breathes a laugh. "I know that face. You'll make it. Come on then. Just around here and across the street. You can walk right through the front door."

He spreads his influence again so the boys can hear. "You'll need to pretend you're not as cold as you feel. They'll expect you to have taken the bus to get here."

"Why didn't we?" Kade asks, an edge to his voice.

"Because of your face," Jordin spits back. "I know you've changed your hair and that may fool an officer or two, but in a crowd, someone is bound to piece it together, especially for the reward."

I don't want to think about the reward, and I bump Kade with my shoulder when I feel him about to ask. It doesn't matter. We can't let anyone collect on that reward.

We round the corner and the embassy looms in front of us like a god. The light-colored brick is a beacon to the city. It's ornate, like every other show-off building in the BSA. It would fit right in with the architecture of Irkutsk. The front door is white and classically styled. It seems so far away. We're so close, but my legs don't seem to care. I have to focus on every step as we cross the street until we finally reach the pavement in front of the embassy. Kade helps me forward with his arm and Leo joins in when I miss a step in the middle of the street.

"All right, you all. Time to keep up appearances. Deep breath." Jordin mimics an inhale and an exhale sound so Kade and Leo can hear, but we all know he's patronizing us. He steps to the door and extends his arms to me with a small bow. "See you inside."

In a blink, he's on the other side of the door, smiling through a window.

Despite his mockery, I do take a deep breath. This is it. This is everything. Thank god Kade's arm is moving me forward because I have the distinct urge to pivot on my heel and run, even though my legs could never achieve it.

My knees buckle, but Kade holds me with both hands as Leo reaches for the door.

A welcome wave of heat washes over my face and lifts my

mood like a balloon. My limbs soak in all they can get, coming back to life, and soon the shivering stops. The fog in my mind clears and I dab the frigid windswept tears from my eyes.

"How's my makeup?" I hate that my life has come to this.

Kade carefully scans my face. He wipes a thumb at the corner of my eye until he's satisfied, then nods. "Perfect."

I'd crack a joke if a Security officer wouldn't have just cleared his throat for our attention. We straighten like soldiers and face the officer, Jordin grinning at his side. I swallow the lump in my throat, hoping Jordin will ease our entry rather than devastate it. He's carried us this far. To trap us now would be anticlimactic, and Jordin thirsts for drama. I pray that hasn't changed.

Moment of truth.

An officer with a clipboard approaches. "What are you doing here?"

"He means what appointment do you have," Jordin explains at my side. "They're a grumpy bunch, these guys."

I step forward, speaking for our little group, since my face is the least recognizable. "We have an interview for travel visas, sir."

The officer looks skeptical—or that might just be his natural expression. He makes a chore of putting his hand out, palm up.

Jordin leans in. "Papers."

"Oh, right!" I scramble to open my purse and produce the papers. I imagine myself pulling too hard and sending papers floating everywhere, but I keep a firm grip long enough for the officer to snatch them away from me. With Jordin at my side, I'm tempted to comment on the guard's manners, but I remind myself that I'm not in Lemayle with Jordin right now. They can hear me, so I can't insult the enemy.

The three of us, with air stiff in our lungs, find ourselves in the awkward position of waiting to see how sharp the officer is. Will he notice any flaws in our logistics? Will he see past the hair dye on Kade and Leo?

"When's the appointment?" he asks, not looking up.

"Ele-"

"Nine!" Jordin shouts in my ear.

"Nine!"

The guard looks at me, startled. Several others near the metal detector have noticed us too. I blush and fall back a step. "Sorry. Nerves." I hope my nervous laugh is enough to dispel any suspicions.

The guard nods slowly, not entirely convinced, but... "Paperwork checks out. Proceed to the checkpoint." He holds the papers out for me to take and sweeps his other arm in the direction of the metal detectors. Now I'm really nervous. I know Kade has a knife in his shoe. I know I don't want him to lose it and I don't want him to be detained. If he's found with a weapon, there won't be any saving him from prison this time and we'll miss our shot at seeing Danica. We can't afford mistakes anymore.

"What are we going to do about the metal detectors?" I say out of the side of my mouth.

Jordin leans away from me, feigning surprise. "You don't mean you have a weapon? Anaya, how violent and suspicious of you!"

"Shut up!" I can barely move my jaw now without drawing attention. Sweat beads along my hairline. Is he going to help us?

"I guess they'll put you in detention." Jordin shrugs. "Weapons aren't allowed in the embassy, and they'll pick it up on the scan from the detector."

I cast my eyes to the ceiling, restraining the long stream of air seeping through my lips. He could do something. It wouldn't be hard at all. He could protect us.

But why would he? Come on, Anaya, when are you going

to realize that he is not your friend anymore? He turned on you—he turned you!

A hand grips my arm and gently moves me forward. It's Kade putting himself last in line, and I can read the intention on his stony face. If he gets nabbed, at least we can find Danica. He's making sure I get to see the Reyn Gayst. He must think he's making good on his promise that he won't let us fail, but it doesn't matter if I see her! Kade needs to see her! I glance at Leo for a fleeting moment, considering using him instead, like I imagined doing so many times back in Yuzhno. I shake it off. No. It has to be Kade. The Plan always said Kade, and the Plan, according to Mikael, hasn't changed.

"Step through." A security officer waves me through the metal detector impatiently.

I glance at the detector, looming like a gateway to judgment. The x-ray scanner and the detector are one machine, so I clutch my purse strap for strength and step through, not breathing and waiting to hear the alarm reveal me for the fraud I am.

But I pass. I stumble to Leo's side, not even realizing he'd already gone, and he catches me. We watch Kade and time slows to a crawl. My stomach creeps up my throat like it might escape if this anticipation lasts much longer.

Kade stands before the gate, face blank, eyes resolved. Jordin stands just on the other side, next to the officer at the screen. My image is still on the screen. I can see my whole outline, head to toe.

We're busted. I know it. There's no way they won't see. This was the setup. I thought it would be inside, but it's now. I'm such an idiot.

Kade steps forward and the gate judges him, drawing an image line by line from top to bottom of what Kade is hiding beneath his coat. Nothing shows, just his pen-sized fishing rod, until the scan reaches his knees and moves lower.

A second guard stops Kade with his arm before he can join

us, waiting for the image to finish before he'll let Kade go.

I bite down on my cheek until I taste metal. A bead of sweat rolls down my temple. Leo's hands squeeze my arms.

"Oops."

Jordin kicks the machine, and the picture stops loading at the top of Kade's shoes. Leo notices too. Our eyes dart between the guards, wondering if they see it.

Green words flash at the top of the image: SCAN COMPLETE. The guards need no prompting.

"Okay, go ahead." The second guard lowers his arm and Kade's eyes flash to mine, awe and relief nearly bringing him to tears, like we've just come to bring him home from Pevek prison.

I'm smiling, wide and unabashed. I don't care who sees. Kade made it. We're in. This is where the Reyn Gayst is, and he just passed the test. Now we just have to move faster than Jordin before he puts his true plan into action.

Speaking of the Aropfain, Jordin strolls by me, waving a hand in the air. "No need to thank me," he lilts. "Just another day in Lemayle."

My shoulders tense and my hands ball into fists. "That's low," I mutter at him as we all collect ourselves and make to follow him toward the elevators at the back of the room.

Jordin spins on the spot in front of the doors. "Shall I give you an exclusive tour?"

I fold my arms. "Shall you stop showing off and get to the point?"

"To your right, you'll find the secretary's desk. To your left, detainment." He leans toward Kade, even though Kade can't see. "You almost got a tour of that yourself." He laughs. I reach around him and smash the elevator button. The doors open behind him and he steps backward inside, smiling. "Moving along."

The doors close, but none of us know which button to push. We think she's on the third and topmost floor, but we could be wrong and I'm not in the mood to have Jordin laughing at me that hard.

"On the first floor are the interview rooms," Jordin explains. "That's where Security thinks you're headed."

The boys shift on their feet sheepishly.

"Don't let him make you feel bad," I remind them.

They give weak nods, but they couldn't look more uncomfortable.

"On the second floor," Jordin continues, "offices. Nothing interesting at all." He holds up a finger, light catching in his eyes, even though he isn't real. "But the third floor..."

I cut off his whimsical description of the wonderland on the third floor and reach through him this time to press the button. "It's the only floor left. It's apartments, just like the website said."

Jordin looks smug when the elevator doesn't move.

"Private apartments and you think you can just go there, being the peasants you are?" He juts a thumb at a small metal keyhole on the panel next to the fire alarm and rescue buttons.

"Okay," I say, trying to sound unimpressed. "What are you going to do about it? That should be child's play for you, so what are you waiting for?"

His bottom lip pushes out for a second. "You could at least be grateful." He presses his hand over the keyhole and moves aside for me to press the button, which I gladly do.

I step back and bow my head as the elevator shudders into motion. "Thank you."

The air in the elevator car grows heavy, not just with the tension washing off Kade and Leo, but with a strange sense of remorse from Jordin.

Everything inside me feels hollow with dread. The moment has come. Time to put my guard up and sharpen my senses. This is when we trigger Jordin's trap. No one moves, no one breathes as the numbers across the top of the doors light up, first the number one, then two, and finally three.

The car settles into place and, before the doors open, I find Jordin's eyes. "This doesn't have to happen," I tell him. "You don't have to do this."

He looks grim. None of his usual playfulness remains. "That depends." He plants his feet and folds his arms across his chest. "Will you finally listen?"

I sigh, shaking my head, aware that Kade and Leo are watching for my response. "Jordin, I've heard everything you've been saying. I know what you think is right. I know what you believe." The hope in his eyes shatters me as I look up at him.

"But I simply don't agree. I won't turn my back on El Olam."

The doors should've opened by now. Jordin is keeping them shut, buying more time to persuade me.

He stomps his foot and the lights flicker. I keep my face blank. This is just another tantrum.

"You've heard everything I've told you?" he yells. He can afford to, after all. "You understand what I believe? Do you, though?"

I shrug. What does he want me to say?

"You don't know everything, Anaya. There's something I've been wanting to tell you, but it has to be at the right time, and you have to come back to us to do anything about it. Just finish the Shift!"

"I won't." My voice is steady and I'm pleased with it. Jordin isn't.

He stares at the floor, eyebrows knit together, shoulders tense. "I don't want to do this," he forces between his teeth. "I don't want it to come to this."

"Then don't let it." I make it sound so simple. If only it were. "Help us."

"Help yourself!" he explodes, eyes wide and wild. "You're going to fade, Anaya. How does that not bother you?"

I bite my tongue. My words are my advantage right now. I won't let anger take that away from me, and I won't let my body fall victim to the stress. Right now, I feel strong. I want that to last.

"It does bother me," I admit. For a second, I can feel Kade's fear that I might finally side with Jordin. I turn to Kade incredulously. "Really?"

He remembers that we're connected and his face falls in mild shame. "Sorry," he barely whispers. I point at him for emphasis, then turn back to Jordin.

"Let us go or come with us. That's all there is."

His face darkens with my ultimatum. "That's not all there is, but if that's the way you want it." He steps aside. The doors open. His face brightens like nothing happened and his voice takes on a teasing note. "To the left, second door from the end. Good luck!"

And then, as usual, he's gone.

"We don't have much time," I tell Kade and Leo. "Danica is just down this hall." I turn to Kade, joy filling me from the pit of my stomach to the top of my head. We did it. However convoluted the methods, we got here. Mission accomplished. Seconds from success, for me at least. I may fade today, but I'll go knowing that I never once failed in my work. People can tell stories about me: the Firn that sacrificed herself, never wavered once, and completed every mission above and beyond the call. I won't be around to revel in it, but I'll be a legend. That's the best I can hope for.

I take a deep breath. I don't want to get too excited. The game isn't over yet. I still need to get Kade to the end of this hall and into that room.

We step out and the elevator doors slide closed behind us. We look both ways as if a tractor-trailer could roll over us at any moment, but it's just an empty hallway for now. The back of my neck tingles, knowing that Jordin is already with Jett, trying to send him messages of our intrusion. I hope Jett is distracted today. I hope Jett isn't in the room with Danica. My heart freezes at that, but we can still work with it. As long as Danica sees Kade, as long as Kade opens his mouth, nothing will stop him from saying what he wants to say.

And I wonder what that will be. I don't remember much, but I don't think his exact words were ever in the Plan. I guess the words are his to choose. He's supposed to be so overcome that the words will just flow.

Walking down the hall is harder than I expected it would be. None of us seem capable of moving at a normal pace, each taking tentative and quiet steps, picking our way down the hall like it's covered in lasers. If it is, then it's only set off a silent alarm somewhere. We can still make it before we get ambushed by Security.

I scream at my legs to move faster, but it's like walking through waist-deep water. Something pushes back. I believe they're instincts. This body knows it's headed toward something threatening and it doesn't want to. How nonsensical is that? My head is all for it—eager even to reach that door—and my legs think they have a place to argue?

Then, after what feels like hours, we slowly turn to face the second door from the end. She'd better be in here. A fleeting fear that Jordin may have lied and abused my trust tightens my throat, but my options are limited. Why do I constantly forget to question him? Why can't I get it through my skull that he's not my friend anymore? I have to resign myself to the fact that I'll never know, and nothing interfered with this. No other Firn seemed to push against our actions, so at least there's that. This must be acceptable in the Plan. Not desirable, surely, but we work with what we're given.

"You ready?" I mean to sound confident and encouraging, but it comes out as a squeak.

Kade nods, flattening his palm against the door like it

might whisper something to him. Leo and I hold our breath as he knocks.

Three light knocks.

"I don't need anything right now, thank you," a soft but firm voice calls from inside. "Have a nice day."

CHAPTER TWENTY-THREE

Kade blinks in shock, fist hovering over the door. It was a female voice. That's a good sign. He looks at me.

"What do I do?"

I look at him with a flat glare. "What you always do when someone tells you no. Bug her until she opens the door!"

He straightens, suddenly remembering that it is in his character to do that. Nerves got the best of him there for a moment. He knocks again.

"I'm fine," the voice sounds annoyed. "Really. Please, just leave me alone. I don't need anything."

"Oh yes you do," I mutter. "Kade, fishhook."

He looks at me like I'm crazy, but I open and close my hand in a gimme gesture until he pulls the telescopic rod out of his pocket. I unclip the hook from the side and kneel in front of the door.

The lock clicks. I stand back and gesture for Kade to enter.

He gives me a disapproving look—the lawful goodness in him returning in the presence of BSA royalty as if he'd actually passed his Security exams—and knocks one more time. "Please, I'm not from the embassy." He leans away, eyes wide. "Should I have said that?" he whispers to us.

"Too late now," Leo hisses at him, slapping a palm to his forehead.

"Not from the embassy?" the voice rises in suspicion.

Kade's shoulders fall and he presses his forehead to the door.

"Go with your gut, Kade."

He looks at me. "I thought you were my gut."

I freeze. That's right. I was his conscience. But... "You've been doing fine enough without me," it pains me to admit. "You always have. You can do this."

He gives me a sympathetic smile and faces the door again. "No." It's firm and honest. "I'm not from the embassy. I just want to talk to you. It's important and I hope you'll give me a chance." There's a long pause. I guess she's considering it, which is fantastic, but precious seconds tick by, exposing us to whomever Jordin might send after us.

I bounce nervously on my heels while Leo picks at a thread on his coat, trying not to rush destiny. Kade drums his fingers on the door, sweat forming on his temple.

"I should also mention that we're not supposed to be here, and Security will probably be after us soon. So, if you could—"

The doorknob turns. The door moves away from Kade's hand, which falls to his side. We all stand limp and dumb as the door opens and reveals, to my great relief, Danica Bree, a skeptical eyebrow quirked as she takes us in, but we can work with it.

She steps aside and we forgo manners in favor of rushing into the room, Leo taking care to close and lock the door behind us. Danica spins on him when she hears the lock fall into place, and he immediately raises his hands for mercy.

"Come on, Leo!" Kade reprimands. "We're not trying to threaten anyone!"

"Sorry!" He moves to unlock it, but I slap his hand away.

"It'll give us a few extra seconds." I shove Kade farther into the room where Danica is all but tapping her foot in expectation. "Go!"

Wow. Here it is. This is the moment. I've officially succeeded. The world is safe. Kade will charm Danica. She'll learn from him about El Olam's method and free will, and she'll agree. She'll leave Jett, Narn will fail, and freedom will remain. I can finally relax as Kade opens his mouth to finish our business and save the cosmos.

"Wow," he scratches the back of his head. "You're shorter than I thought." He lets out a nervous laugh, but she doesn't take it as a compliment.

Honestly, why would she?

"Kade," I draw his name out through a forced smile and clenched teeth, "the course of history sits on this moment, and you basically insulted her. Try again."

"Right." Kade coughs. I catch a smile breaking out across Danica's face. That probably kills Kade's confidence, but it restores mine.

"I..." Kade's eyes drag across the room. It's a massive suite with a living room, kitchenette, and bedroom. It's glamorous. Vases of flowers cover every surface. Someone's been trying too hard to win Danica's affection. I can't help but think.

"Wait." Kade freezes. "Jett isn't here, is he?" He looks at Danica like she could pull a gun on him at any moment.

Danica's smile disappears. "He had business to attend to." Her voice is tight. I can't tell if it's sadness or something else. Does she wish Jett spent more time with her? Please, El Olam, don't let that be the case.

Kade rubs at the tension on his forehead. "Listen, I'm no good with fancy words and things, so I'll just tell you why we're here..."

My heart stops again. This is it!

"We want to get you out of here. Jett's a creep. You can do better."

Her eyebrow goes up again.

"And it doesn't have to be me!" Kade backpedals. "But you didn't get to choose this and that's..." Understanding dawns on Kade's face and he looks at me. The moment stretches as everything I've been telling him clicks. "That's not right."

Warmth fills the corners of my eyes as I smile at him, pride bursting in my chest, but I will not get sentimental here.

"You really think that?" Danica folds her arms. She wants to look skeptical, but she looks small and afraid instead.

Kade turns back to her. "Honestly, yeah."

Danica laughs, but there's now joy in it. "I appreciate your concern. It's a shame you didn't make it here a few days sooner."

I step forward. "Why?" I look at her, taking in every clue I can find, until my eyes fall on her left hand and my stomach falls with them. My knees buckle. I tilt to the side into Leo's shoulder for support. "Oh my gosh, you're married."

Without thinking, I point to the pair of sparkling rings loaded with excessively enormous diamonds on her ring finger.

"What?" Kade follows my finger and looks like he might faint.

My head fills with buzzing and nothing makes sense. This can't be it. This can't be the end. I won't go down like this! But then... she doesn't seem thrilled about it. I look at her with sad eyes. "Are you... are you okay?"

Danica knows what I mean. I don't have to say it, and that's good because I really don't want to. She hugs herself and looks away. "He's been very busy," she assures me. "It was just a short civil ceremony and I've been here on my own ever since. The public wedding is to be held in a few weeks. The committee hasn't finalized the date yet. We're scheduled to announce it at the engagement party."

Well, no wonder Jordin wasn't in a rush to stay at Jett's side. He thought he had Danica in the bag because some piece of paper somewhere says she belongs to Jett. That's just sick.

"That's so backward!" Kade protests. His face betrays his fear. If Danica and Jett are already—technically—married, does that mean it's over? Have we failed?

I set my jaw and look at them. I may not have the advantages I had before I was human, but I've kept my wisdom, my arrogance, my fierce belief that nothing can keep me from my goals. This is no different from anything else that has ever stood in my way. I won't let us just accept this injustice. That's ridiculous.

"Come anyway," I tell her. Everyone looks up at me in shock.

"What?" Danica asks. Her face tells me she didn't think that was an option, but her eyes hold something more that I can't place. They don't look as surprised as she lets on.

"Come anyway," I repeat. "Who cares if he gave you a ring and made you say some words? That's not real. It's just paperwork. It's stupid. You know what you want, and I don't think this is it."

"Yeah," Kade agrees, invigorated by my idea. "You're so much better than all of this." He gestures to the surrounding room, but then his eyes trace the elegantly papered walls, the expensive paintings, the plush leather couch, the excess of entertainment technology and finery, and his arms fall an inch. Who would want to leave all this?

Danica draws away from me. "What makes you say that? We only just met."

I roll my eyes. "You're all over TV and I'm an excellent judge of character. Besides, you've seen Kade before." I stick my thumb in Kade's direction so she knows which one he is. She looks at him and nods knowingly.

"The one from the gala." She stifles a laugh.

Kade blushes but smiles.

"Jett really doesn't like you, you know." She points to a poster on the wall: Kade's wanted poster. His hair is different, but it's easy to recognize him if you've stared at that poster day in and day out.

Leo's is conspicuously absent. Jett must not feel as threatened by him. Kade has made Jett feel unsettled. That seems to please Danica as much as it pleases me.

"Oh, I know." Kade wears a goofy grin. "He blew up our hideout to prove it."

Her smile vanishes. "He what?"

"He destroyed a hideout for outcast children," Leo says with a straight face. "Fortunately, we escaped with no casualties. At least that time." He frowns at his shoes. "We still don't know if everyone got out of Taltsy."

Danica presses the tips of her fingers to her forehead and shakes her head. "I'm so sorry. I didn't know he'd go to such measures. I asked him to leave you alone. I promise I did."

"It was meant to happen." I wave the sappy air away. "The point is, we can still make a change. But you have to come with us. Kade has so much to tell you, and we don't have the time while we're here."

"But what about her family?" Leo asks. He would bring that up.

"We'll make it look like a kidnapping," Kade says, like it's obvious. "They won't go after her family if they think she left against her will." He would know Security's thought process better than anyone.

Leo glares at him. It's not the heroic thing to do, but actually it is. "I agree." I flinch away from Leo's betrayed stare. "We don't have enough time right now to say everything that needs saying," I defend myself. I turn to Danica. "Of course, this all depends on what you want. Do you want to leave here, or..." I gag on what I'm about to say, "do you want to stay?"

"Well, of course I don't want to stay."

I punch the air. Okay, she's still my hero.

"But it isn't that simple," Danica explains.

"Of course it's not!" Leo's face is stern. He's taking this personally, empathizing with the hasty decision we're forcing Danica to make. But sometimes a hasty decision is what's needed. Less thinking, more doing. Just sometimes. Like right now.

"Why not?" Kade asks Danica, ignoring Leo's protest. "You could be done with this. We can spare your family, and forget the..." he gestures to her wedding rings like they're toxic, "wedding stuff. You'll be able to do whatever you want. We can find Canaan and get him to tell us where Ainsley might be. We'll go stay with them until we can regroup."

Danica smiles, a sad but kind of cheerful smile. She pulls it off well. "I appreciate that you came all this way and that you've done it before, just to help me secure the freedom to make my own decisions."

Oh, yes! She appreciates that Kade wants her to have free will! We did it! Surely this is the moment. She's on our side! Ha! Take that, Jordin. Where's your smug smile now?

"But the time just isn't right."

What?

Danica looks at me. Did I say that out loud? I'm on the receiving end of the weird smile now. She says nothing, just looks at me like she knows me more than just from these last two minutes. I frown in confusion because it's impossible to have met the Reyn Gayst. She's a brand-new soul. Straight from creation to Velt, this is her very first life. She never had a Firn assigned to her. How could she know me? I must be reading too much into that look.

Her eyes move away to a wooden coffee table behind her. She reaches for the small memo pad with the embassy's logo and information at the top. "Here." She scribbles something down. "This is how you can keep in contact with me. I'm not given much privacy, but if you follow these instructions, we should be safe.

They don't think me to be very clever." Her mouth forms a flat line after she says it. "It's for the best, it turns out."

"So, you're just going to become pen pals? That's how this goes?" I say it more to the air than to the people in the room. Though Mikael isn't here, I say it to him. I say it to any Firns who might listen and give me a sign, because what the heck is happening here?

I don't recall anything like this in the Plan. Just get the kid to the girl, they'll talk, and then something else before it's all over. What was that last thing? I highly doubt it was, "they'll become giddy pen pals and keep in touch."

But Kade looks giddy. The most admired girl in Beta Siberia just gave him her number. He must think he's a sly fox. I shake my head.

"I don't understand."

Danica steps forward and places a hand on my shoulder. "You will." She actually looks sorry. "You will, I promise."

I squint. There's something under there. I lift a finger at her. "You... know something..."

Red light flashes and an obnoxiously high-pitch whistle resonates through the room. Danica falls away from me and stares at the red light near the door.

"Security lockdown." Her eyes fall on me. "We're out of time. They know you're here and they'll come to protect me first on Jett's orders. He's only downstairs."

"He's only downstairs?" Kade echoes, but more angrily. "Jett Tyrrell is here now?"

"Well, Jordin was here," Leo says, giving Kade a look like he's the most idiotic man in the world.

Kade rolls his head back. "Jordin's been everywhere. How was that a clue?"

"We have to go. I won't let you die here. You've got..." I look at the piece of paper in his hand and back at Danica, "letters to write." She gives an embarrassed smile, shoulders coming to her ears.

I turn to face her. "It was lovely meeting you," I say over the noise. "We'll chat again soon. Now, how do we get out of here?"

CHAPTER TWENTY-FOUR

"Take the stairs at the end of the hall." Danica moves into action, crossing the room to grab a heavy coat. "I'll meet Jett to stall him before he finds you. The best I can give you is a few seconds, but you'll need them. Then he'll have me evacuated." She says the last bit with a weary tone.

"We will see you again." Kade's voice is more a question than an answer. Danica gives a small smile and nods to assure him. He smiles too. It's precious, but we have to move.

Leo and I each grab one of Kade's arms and head for the door.

"Down the stairs," I repeat before we open the door to an even louder whistling noise. Three sirens line the hall, all pulsing red light and screaming.

"Which stairs were the ones we decided on?" Kade asks, frantically checking for oncoming Security. "I can't remember."

Neither can I. The noise is too much for me to think, much less recall anything. I grab Leo. "You have to choose."

He pulls out of my grip. "Why me?"

"Because you're the only one here with a Firn!" Isn't it

obvious? "Stop questioning me and just pick one! Go with your gut! Your Firn will tell you which way."

Leo looks down both ends of the hall. The logical choice would be the stairs to our right. They're closer. But will they put us on the street where people will surely see us, or in a less secluded place like we planned for? He wrestles with himself, gritting his teeth and second-guessing his instincts.

I smack his shoulder. "Stop that. Now, which is it?"

He groans as he lifts his arm to point down the opposite end of the hall.

"Are you crazy?" Kade shouts over the alarms.

"Okay then." I grab them both and yank us in that direction before Kade can argue about it. I hope this is what Leo's Firn really told him.

As we pass the elevator, it stirs to life. Someone is coming. We run faster. Only four doors from the end. We can make it before they see us. We can do this.

Then, in the weirdest moment of my entire existence, a hand shoots out from the last door at the end of the hall and grips Kade's arm, yanking him into a custodial closet. Leo and I plant our heels and skid to a stop, spinning to go back for him. The door is still open and a serious-looking stranger in janitor's coveralls welcomes us, leaning on the handle of a push broom.

I squint at him. Something's fuzzy around his edges. Something more than just another random contact from Ainsley's underground network.

"Go down five flights." He shakes Kade by the shoulders. "Five."

"But there are only three floors and the main floor," Leo questions.

"Five," the man juts his face in Leo's direction. He roughly releases Kade. "And don't look back. They'll shoot you."

We exchange quick glances and nod, stepping backward

toward the door and he lets us. Then we run again, bursting through the door to the stairwell and catching on the rail to look down.

"Five floors," I gasp through ragged breaths.

"Was he one of yours?" Kade asks, already out of breath.

I shrug, not breathing so well myself. I don't know what that was, but I'll take it.

Shouts echo from the hall behind us. "Down!" I yell, like we need the encouragement.

We scale the stairs, skipping as many as we can. My heart beats like a hamster's and I occasionally trip on a step or two, but Kade always keeps me upright.

"Here?" I ask Leo at the first landing. He looks confused but catches on quickly. He closes his eyes, opens them. Firmly shakes his head. "Okay." We keep going to the next landing as the shouts of the Security officers enter the stairwell.

My breath comes in gasps, but I can keep going. "Here?" I wheeze.

Leo shuts his eyes, frowns. They burst back open. "Yes!" He grabs us with one hand and heaves the door open with another.

We run straight into a startled man. He catches himself on Leo and looks at our terrified faces.

This is it. We're done for. Leo chose wrong. But I can't blame him. That was a lot of pressure. It was unfair to expect it from him. I'll be sure to tell him that once the barred door closes when they toss us in prison.

"I've been looking for you!" the man says in a hushed voice. He holds his hands up. "Wait here."

He goes into the stairwell. "Guards!"

Kade and I make to run, but Leo stops us, a strange look somewhere between confusion and certainty on his furrowed brow. "No, wait."

I know this look. Leo's Firn is doing something. This isn't

Ainsley's network, it's Mikael's! And probably also Ainsley's.

"You're joking. He's turning us in!" Kade barks in Leo's face, but Leo ignores him.

"No..." He steps toward the door.

Mikael must have inspired Ainsley to make these connections from the start–decades before Kade was even born. A safety net, and it shames me that we needed it.

"I saw them go to floor one!" the man shouts. "Floor one! They're headed for Mr. Tyrrell's office!"

We freeze. Kade frowns. "Did he just... cover for us?"

After a few beats, the man opens the door again.

"Hello," he says, rushing introductions. "I'm the Trade Attaché for Yuzhno Sakhalinsk."

The boys melt a little at the sound of their home city, but we don't have time for nostalgia.

"I also work with Canaan Sem. Ainsley told him you'd be coming to see Danica. He expected there would be complications, so he sent me." That gets the reaction he wants from us. We move eagerly toward him, ready to follow whatever he says. People like this man and Canaan must be El Olam's response to the cheating ways of the Aropfain. He sends living souls to manipulate situations and set them back on course. Genius.

"I can get you out of here. There's a car waiting."

We don't need any more than that.

Kade gives an eager nod. "Let's go then."

We spill into the hall, now quiet save for the sounds of our shoes echoing. We have three more floors to go before we reach the level the weird custodian told us about, and Canaan's man seems to have the same idea.

On the next landing, I catch myself on the rail, but I can't catch my breath. My chest heaves, sweat soaks my hair, my arms and legs shake, and my head feels like it might just float away.

I'm not going to make it. My heart has circulated the

medicine out of my system. This is where I fade. It must be. I've accomplished my goal. My vision blurs with tears of panic. I used to face death like a champion, but that was when I believed in something that came after. Now I know that, for me, there is no after. This is the hard stop for my soul.

I stumble down the steps until I notice everyone stopped on the main floor.

The attaché turns to face us at the door. "I've got to be counted among the evacuees. Go down to the basement. There is a secret corridor there. You can follow the tunnel to the car. I'll join you once they have evacuated me, but you mustn't stop. Don't give them a chance to gain an inch on you. They will shoot you."

That seems to be the point of emphasis lately.

He says nothing more before slipping through the door.

"Down we go," Kade says, and we set off again, but I have a problem.

My knees buckle on the first step, and I know exactly what I have to do. No matter how much the fall hurts.

Swallowing the shout that rises in my throat, I reach out to grab a support bar on the rail to stop myself and I listen to the footsteps of Kade and Leo fade away from me. They don't look back and don't stop, just as they were told. Just as I want them to do.

My head drops to thud against the step and I try to breathe through the pain as another set of footsteps approaches.

CHAPTER TWENTY-FIVE

My chest heaves like a beached fish, and I close my eyes to find the stillness of acceptance. I'm about to be in trouble, but all I can think about is Kade. All I can think about is my Neshome. I know that if I focus enough, disassociate myself from reality, I can hear what he hears, feel what he feels, see what he sees. That's all I want right now as I prepare to slip away. I just want to watch over Kade like I always have, to go out on the job, still a vigilant Firn.

As thoughts scatter from my mind, I sweep into sharp focus on darkness with vague shapes rising before me. Kade has made it to the basement. He's nearly shaking with adrenalin, looking left and right for a sign of the promised tunnel. Leo makes for the walls to search for something beyond what he sees.

"It's got to be behind one of these shelves," he calls from the back. "They're all along the wall over here, nailed in." He shakes a shelf to prove it. It doesn't move. He pauses. "Kade, where's that knife you had?"

Oh, that's brilliant. There's something fulfilling in knowing that the cartridge of gas won't harm another person. I'm always willing to do what it takes to achieve the goals of the

Plan, but I prefer to spare people as much pain as possible, no matter whose side they're on.

Kade jumps into action, rushing toward Leo's voice. "How do we know which one?" he asks. "I only get one shot."

In the darkness, I hear knuckles on wood. Leo moves along each shelf and knocks on the backboard. The first three yield short, dense sounds. Not what Leo is looking for. The fourth produces an echoing, hollow sound. Bingo.

And just in time, too. Security appears to have made it to the basement from the other side of the building. I know because they'd have trampled me if they came from this side. I wonder why they avoided this side of the stairs. Did they think we crossed over to the other side somehow? Did they take the elevator? I didn't see a button for a basement level, but what do I know?

Kade and Leo hear the shouts and shuffling of Security approaching too.

"Hurry up!" Leo urges him.

Kade straightens and I feel a swell of confusion in his mind, so overwhelming that he forgets the danger. "Wait, where's Anaya?" He turns to either side, looking for me, listening for some kind of hasty insult from me to get him moving again, but I can't deliver. "Anaya?" he calls into the dark. His heart picks up, his stomach drops. "We lost her."

He turns to Leo. He can't see Leo's face in the dark, but he wants a reaction, anyway. "Leo, we have to go back to find her."

Silence fills the room, drawing out the moment as Security draws too close.

"We can't." Leo's voice is small. It's not what he wants, but it's what he knows they need to do. He's listening to his Firn. I can tell by the tightness in his tone. It comes out against his wishes.

"Are you insane?" Kade hisses in the dark. "We can't leave

her! You know she's probably passed out somewhere. They'll find her. Leo," he pauses, trying to catch his breath and calm himself, "Leo, they'll put her in a prison. She'll die there."

Leo doesn't respond, and I don't take it personally. I'm dying anyway. Does it matter where? I'm sure Leo would say the same if we weren't friendly. Instead, Leo's hand shoots out and snatches the knife from Kade. He ignores the protests from his best friend and rips the case away, shoving the blade between the shelf and the wall. A moment passes as he searches for the release switch, but he finds it and the high-pressure burst of gas loosens the shelf from the wall and knocks Kade and Leo to the floor at the same time. They scramble to their feet, moving of the same mind to shove their fingers in the new gap and force the shelf away from the wall.

"Tell me we got it," Kade says, out of breath.

The darkness deepens behind the shelf, the best sign they'll get that they've found what they're looking for. Leo runs a hand along the wall until it falls away from him.

"We got it," he confirms.

The beam of a flashlight shatters the darkness and puts stars in Kade's eyes. He flinches, but looks around, desperate to find a sign of me, hoping I collapsed down here with them, and that he wasn't so negligent as to leave me behind upstairs. I don't see it as negligence. It's smart. My role is done. I've served my purpose. As much as I wish I could keep working with Kade, help him get back in touch with Danica, help Leo get home, see the moment Danica stands firm in her ultimate choice, I don't have the strength to stay.

Kade's shoulders sink. Security is too close. He can't hang back any longer, and Leo's fingers clutching his sleeve and yanking decides for him as Security bursts into the room. It's time to go. A squeezing in Kade's heart puts an angry scowl on his face as he runs, sleeve still in Leo's fist, toward the end of the hidden passageway.

This is strangely like when he dragged Leo through the corridor away from Ainsley's shop back in Yuzhno, back at the beginning of this ridiculous journey. Leo was the reluctant one then. Now, Kade is accepting the same truth in a whole new way: He is not in control. He can't do as much as he wishes he could. The world is not his to wield.

It's damp in the dark passageway. Snow from the ground above has melted through, adding to the Nor'ilsk chill that seeps into Kade's skin, slowing his muscles and making the long retreat more difficult.

They hit an earthy wall. Leo feels around for the ladder that has to be there. He finds it and shoves Kade in front of him. Leo's Firn probably thrills at the action. I would.

A twinge of regret creases my forehead at the realization that those days are gone for me. I'll have to live these final moments through Leo's Firn, pretending I'm as useful as he is and not splayed and lifeless on the cold tile floor.

They climb the metal ladder and heave away a trap door as frozen earth rains on their heads. They emerge to the far side of the building, opposite of where the diplomats and important people of the embassy spill into the street in a panic. Kade insults them in his mind. They're stupid, useless. They know nothing. It's their fault.

"Hey!" a hushed shout draws their attention to the right, at the back of the building. A limo driver, hands cupped around his mouth, stands waiting for them. He gestures for them to hurry toward him and runs for the driver's door. Leo grabs Kade's arm and leads the way. Kade moves his feet, but his heart isn't in it. Blame settles heavily on his mind, and he doesn't process the events around him as Leo yanks the car door open and pushes him inside.

Leo slides in after him and I sigh in relief. Kade is safe. He can find sanctuary and take the information Danica gave him and keep the Plan alive. I can let him go now.

The corners of my eyes sting at the realization. I don't want
to let Kade go. We only just found our rhythm and now it's over.
Kade is driving away into the future, and I've fallen behind, quite
literally. As Kade drives further than I can reach him—apparently
my reach has limits—I feel his hand slide to his pocket as if it were
my own. Something solid makes the whole situation worse, but
leaves me feeling grateful to Kade. The shape of the syringe in his
pocket is undeniable. He must've pocketed it this morning. He
planned ahead for my sake. Kade really did care.

That's a thought I can go out on. I let my body relax and
slip away from Kade, feeling the solid floor beneath me, the
brightness just beyond my eyelids. I sigh and let it all go.

It's a funny thing when you finally welcome death and it
takes its time to come for you. Several minutes pass, long
enough for me to get bored waiting for the void of nothingness
to take me. Why haven't I faded yet?

I hear a set of feet coming my way. This'll be embarrassing. I keep my eyes shut to spare the both of us. But it's the
voice in my ears that makes me want to groan.

"I suppose all that's left now is the capture." Jordin sounds
amused. I try my best to play dead. Hopefully, he'll think I'm
already gone and leave me alone.

"Hmm. Is this her?" another voice asks. That would be the
owner of the footsteps. Jordin doesn't make sounds in Velt.
But who is this person talking to? I only heard one set of feet.

"Yep," Jordin says cheerfully. "That's her, just like I said."

The other person, not an Aropfain but a living soul, the foil
to people like Enoch, an Avoyde gone bad, heaves a bored sigh.
"All right then."

Arms slip under my shoulders and knees, and I'm hoisted
into the air. I crack an eye open and see a face I can only
recognize from television images and one other place.

I've seen this man before... at the gala standing next to Danica on the stage, then again at Phil's gas station during the raid.

Jett Tyrrell.

Wait, what? Jett's an Avoyde? Well, no wonder Jordin had so much time on his hands! He turned an Avoyde! Who put an Avoyde in the Tyrrell family, of all places? It's like they were setting Kade and me up for failure.

I squeeze my eyes shut again. My chest hurts and clenches, my throat closes, and I can't get any air. I feel hot and panicked. My body gives in. My hands are cold and clammy, but I don't feel any pain. In fact, I feel calm, like I'm floating in a peaceful pool, my ears covered with water, muffling the world around me.

Why? Why couldn't this have happened a few minutes ago when I could've died peacefully and happily? There's so much left undone. We didn't rescue Danica at all. She's still here. Kade needs to get back to her, and now he'll have to do it without me. What chance does Kade have against Jett now? Then again, was I that much good for him to begin with? I got him to believe. Maybe that was enough. I doubt it, but it's out of my hands now.

A pang of remorse spreads through me from my chest. I can't think anymore. It's too hard. It's too much. My body just wants to sleep, and, you know what? Fine. That's what I'll do. My work is finished here. I was never going to win, anyway. I take in a deep breath of cool air, appreciating it like I never have before. This is my last death, so I let myself feel it to the fullest. It's time to let go.

I hear a gasp. "Oh, no you don't, Anaya," Jordin threatens as I release my final breath. "I'm not done with you yet."

Unknowingly, Jordin has just given me a gift, because now my last thought before the darkness takes me isn't one of self-pity or loathing. It's triumphant.

Tough.

ABOUT ATMOSPHERE PRESS

Atmosphere Press is an independent, full-service publisher for excellent books in all genres and for all audiences. Learn more about what we do at atmospherepress.com.

We encourage you to check out some of Atmosphere's latest releases, which are available at Amazon.com and via order from your local bookstore:

Dancing with David, a novel by Siegfried Johnson
The Friendship Quilts, a novel by June Calender
My Significant Nobody, a novel by Stevie D. Parker
Nine Days, a novel by Judy Lannon
Shining New Testament: The Cloning of Jay Christ, a novel by
    Cliff Williamson
Shadows of Robyst, a novel by K. E. Maroudas
Home Within a Landscape, a novel by Alexey L. Kovalev
Motherhood, a novel by Siamak Vakili
Death, The Pharmacist, a novel by D. Ike Horst
Mystery of the Lost Years, a novel by Bobby J. Bixler
Bone Deep Bonds, a novel by B. G. Arnold
Terriers in the Jungle, a novel by Georja Umano
Into the Emerald Dream, a novel by Autumn Allen
His Name Was Ellis, a novel by Joseph Libonati
The Cup, a novel by D. P. Hardwick
The Empathy Academy, a novel by Dustin Grinnell
Tholocco's Wake, a novel by W. W. VanOverbeke
Dying to Live, a novel by Barbara Macpherson Reyelts
Looking for Lawson, a novel by Mark Kirby
Yosef's Path: Lessons from my Father, a novel by Jane Leclere
    Doyle
Surrogate Colony, a novel by Boshra Rasti

ABOUT THE AUTHOR

KristaLyn is an author, multi-certified metaphysical practitioner, and psychic mentor who specializes in Hellenistic astrology and Astrological Magic. They serve as a practicing astrologer, co-founder of The Forgotten Storytellers novel-writing mentorship, and co-host of The Alchemist's Inkwell podcast.

KristaLyn loves sharing about astrology, storytelling, and her corgis, Jack and Zelda, on social media @TheRealKristaLyn